The Lawmakers

Fay Carol Davies

Visit us online at www.authorsonline.co.uk

An Authors OnLine Book

ISBN 978-07552-0451-9

Authors OnLine Ltd
19 The Cinques
Gamlingay, Sandy
Bedfordshire SG19 3NU
England

This book is also available in e-book format, details of which are available at www.authorsonline.co.uk

About the Author

Fay. Davies was born in England and lived in London. She was evacuated to Surrey during World War 2. When her Father died she went to live with an aunt in Wales.

She went to St. Michael's School, Llanelli, Carmarthenshire.

After that she went to Salisbury College and trained as a teacher.

She taught in England and Wales and took early retirement to write and grow flowers.

Fay has written from an early age and has much of her work published in magazines and newspapers. Up until recently she ran a small press magazine from her home. Its name was Linkway and it went worldwide. She decided to give it up and concentrate on her own writing. more so as she is 77 years old.

She loves science fiction and this story of The Lawmakers just popped into her mind and she wrote it down. It has taken her 3 years to write and she has enjoyed every minute of it.

She lives by the sea in a quiet spot, which enables her to write, and has already started on a sequel entitled The Leader.

She also has 2 collections of poems published and is working on another one.

PART I

THE GAME

Chapter 1

Let me try," Cessie said.

"Certainly not; go away; stop bothering me," her brother replied. "Why do you keep on at me?"

"Because it isn't fair that we girls are not allowed to play and I can throw the ball over the wall as good as any boy." She grabbed the ball from him and bounced it all around him. He lunged at her and knocked her to the ground. She sat on the ground and glared at him.

"Jadex!" came a sharp voice, as Fador, the team coach arrived, "leave your sister alone."

"She's my stepsister and … " his voice faded as Fador frowned at him with annoyance.

Cessie got up, dusted her grazed knee, and looked at the team coach. "All I wanted was to throw the ball over the wall."

"I was trying to tell her that the game wasn't meant for girls."

"Let us see what she can do," Fador said with a smile.

Jadex looked at Fador with some surprise, but letting her try might be a good thing and once she knew how hard it was she would not bother them again.

They both stood on one side while she took the ball to the centre of the court.

"You can have three tries," Fador said gently, not to disappoint her.

Cessie stood on the shooting circle and focused on the higher part of the wall.

"Aim for the lowest first," Fador urged her.

She nodded thank you to him.

From somewhere in the building came the chanting of girls' voices, as they learnt the Laws.

She shook her head. "Bother, I'm already late for class." She dismissed the thought and stood quite still, her eyes trained on the wall. She drew in a deep breath, ran forward with the ball, bounced it high in the green circle, caught it and threw it high in the air; waited for it to drop and, catching it cleanly, took aim and flung the ball aloft and over the lowest part of the wall. She ran around to the back of the wall and caught the ball before it landed and went back to the starting section again. Then she repeated it all again and threw the ball over the next highest part and then, again following the same procedure, threw it over the highest part of the wall and returned to the centre, waiting to hear their reaction.

"Great," said Jadex grudgingly.

"I agree," said Fador.

"So can I train for the team?"

"It is not for girls," Jadex was quick to answer.

"There's no such law," she replied. "It says 'team member' not whether it is a boy or a girl." She looked at Fador, pleadingly.

"Certainly you can, providing your father gives permission," and as he walked away both she and he knew that permission would not be granted. "Pity though," he thought, because she was good.

Gina frowned at her as she slipped into her class quietly. Cessie opened her chant book and joined in the chanting.

The Lawmothers stood on stage. Each took it in turn to keep the class going. One raised her hand and motioned silence.

"You are late Celisia! Where have you been this time?" asked her Lawmother

"I am sorry, Mam; I was delayed."

 "What delayed you child?"

"I was trying out for the team."

"You are not a boy!" stated her Lawmother. "You just do not even think about the team …!"

Silence reigned in the room. The others stared at her in amazement. Then one bolder than the rest shouted out: "Did you get in?"

"Did *what*?" the Lawmother queried harshly.

"Yes, I got in!" Cessie said excitedly. "But Fador said I would have to get permission from my father first."

The girls began to talk aloud until the Lawmothers silenced them.

"This behaviour will be reported to the Council and you will be called before them this evening." The class was then dismissed early and the girls went out quickly to hear all about it from Cessie herself.

That evening she was called before the Elders.

"We have discussed your case," one said.

"I checked all the Laws first," she said quietly.

"We realise that, but you were late for class and rude to your Lawmother and upset the others in the class." They looked very serious and suddenly Cessie was very frightened, but she stood there in the middle of the room trying not to show it.

Fador arrived and, looking at her, said: "She asked if she could try out for the team. I made her late because I said that she could."

They looked at him now and said: "Did she make an appointment to see you, and did she get written permission from her Lawmother?"

"No," he said sadly. He looked at her. "I tried," he said softly, "they are not ready for a change yet."

The Elders stood up and chanted: "We The Elders of the City of Shadowex, do declare that this child is no longer fit to be one of us, and from this day on she shall be thrust out of the city to live as she thinks fit."

They stood up and left her feeling stunned.

Two guards took her to the city gates and pushed her outside.

She stood there in tears, alone and frightened. Somewhere a wolf howled. Darkness descended rapidly. She had never been outside the city before. What was she going to do?

Cessie stayed by the big doors all night, sitting as close to them as she could. She shivered with cold and several times, got up and stamped her feet to get her circulation going again.

At last morning arrived and she could hear signs of life from within. She stood by the small door in the main gate, waiting hopefully for someone to open it: after all, she had learnt her lesson and would do as she was told from now on – but the door remained closed. Sadly she left the safety of the city walls and followed a track that led away from the place where she had lived since she was five years old.

The track was rough, which was surprising considering that the inside of the city was kept so well, and on either side of it were tangled growths of small bushes which seemed to stretch as far as the eye could see.

She walked quickly, thinking that it must lead somewhere.

She stopped to empty a stone out of her shoe and then went on again.

Where was she going?

Where were the people?

Were there any people at all? Maybe the tales she had heard were true – that the only people who lived on this planet were the Lawmakers.

Did all the Lawmakers live in one city or were there other cities?

Would those other Lawmakers let her in their cities or was she to be alone in this wild place?

The sun came up and she felt warmer but now she realised that she was very hungry and thirsty. She must look for a stream. But she could not find one and, when she came to a crossroads, sat down on a fallen tree and wept bitterly.

Just what was she going to do?

One hour after Cessie had left the city gates a man slipped out and followed her down the track. He was very annoyed. The Grand Elder had recalled him for a special briefing. It was bad enough being assigned to this godforsaken hole without being told that he had to keep a fifteen-year-old girl in order. To think that he, Medrix, who had passed top of his training class on Estolan, had even been given this task on Chetner was ludicrous, for hadn't he been responsible for infiltrating two drug-running gangs and bringing them to justice? The more dangerous the jobs, the more he liked it. He was good and he knew it. He was an Elders' man through and through, feared by the very people who admired him. He was ruthless in getting all he wanted. He obeyed the rules to the letter and thought nothing of reporting those who did not, even if they were his friends. The Masters had taught him and taught him well how an Elders' man should behave. Strength was power and power was his to use how he liked, and he had used that power to get everything he wanted, including the beautiful Jessanda, a daughter of one of the city Elders. They had become betrothed only a few days before he had been sent here. He had thought he had everything. Happiness was his and then this had happened. He was assigned to spy on the exiles on the planet Chetner under the jurisdiction of the Grand Elder of City One.

It was bad enough that he had to mix with these exiles who had questioned the beliefs and rules of their Elders and so were beginning to undermine their authority to even rule them. He had to watch and report on all their movements and not let them know who he really was. It was easy. He did not like it easy.

They were a group of people who had had it easy in the city who had been thrust out of all the comfortable surroundings to rough it in a place where there were no such comforts. The youngest were in their twenties; others varied in age, to one woman who must have been there for years, for she was about sixty. They all called her the Mother and she ruled the whole place and kept a motherly eye on them all.

He had found nothing much to report; just little things such as the men saying that one day the Elders would get their just deserts and the women saying they were fed up with the men here, although they seemed to accept him: after all they thought he was Fador's twin brother and they all admired him, even though he lived within the city walls.

He had told them that he had never lived in the city but had been kept safely hidden away by his mother who had already lost one child to the Lawmakers. The Lawmakers evidently took young children and brought them up as their own and, though he did not agree with this, he supposed that those who had been taken would have been given the best of everything and would appreciate it in the long run – after all, they had been taken when they were very young and could not remember any other life.

So here he was and now he was to nursemaid this latest exile. She was trouble with a capital T he was told. Her stepfather said that she would come to a bad end and her teachers had said that she broke one rule after the other, was rude and disruptive in class and was a general nuisance to everybody and certainly not to be trusted, for she was as sly as they come and needed to be taught a lesson. He was to put her on the right track and, if she was taught to conform, then maybe she would be given a second chance within the city for they did not like to fail where a child was concerned. He thought she should have been given a good whipping and that would have been the end of it. Girls – women in fact – always obeyed after that punishment: a fact he knew was correct for that was how he treated any woman who annoyed *him*.

He sighed as Cessie came into view.

She was sitting on a fallen tree, crying. She was not wearing a bonnet and he saw that she had fair hair that shone like gold in the sunshine. He had this sudden feeling that he wanted to run his hands through that long golden hair and feel its silkiness. He shook his head. Those kinds of thoughts were not to be encouraged: he did not bed children.

He stopped beside her and said, gently: "Why are you crying?"

Cessie looked up, peering through her fingers at him. She had not realised anyone was there. He repeated the question.

She put her hands in her lap and said: "I thought I was out here on my own and I did not know what to do."

"I can assure you there are plenty of people around here if you know where to look."

She looked at him without saying anything, wondering if she could trust him. He wasn't a Lawmaker for he had long hair and every Lawmaker had the standard cut as dictated by the Elders. His long brown hair meant that he was an exile ... or ... what?

She jumped up and looked at him.

"Who are you?"

He smiled and she noticed that although he smiled, his eyes were ice cold. She shivered.

"Are you cold?" he asked.

"Yes. I have no cloak. I did not have time to get it before they put me outside the gates."

Medrix opened the large pack that he had on his back and brought out a small rug and put it round her shoulders. She thanked him, smiling up at him.

Her eyes were blue, his mind registered – as blue as the sky on a summer's day.

"Are you hungry?"

"Yes I am."

He gave her food and some water to drink.

Thanking him she asked who he was and then said: "You remind me of Fador, the Team Coach in the City."

"That's because I am his twin brother. My name is Medrix. I am a Chetnerite like him, the only difference being that he was kidnapped by the Lawmakers and I was not. Chetnerite twins are telepathic and can open a channel to talk to each other: that's how I knew who you were. Of course the Lawmakers do not know we keep in touch, because they would exile him, too."

"You must be careful, then," she said with concern.

"Now, have you got your bonnet?"

"Yes, it's in my pocket."

"Then put it on, for you are still a Lawmother and must wear one."

"I thought I'd be free of that!"

She pulled the bonnet from her pocket but did not put in on, whereupon he said roughly: "Put it on now. Hide your hair; you are too conspicuous like that."

She put it on and pushed her hair out of sight. Who was he to tell her what to do? She had hoped that she had left all those rules behind her.

"Now, we must get on," he said. "We have a long way to go and it does not do to be outside when darkness comes."

"Why? I am not afraid of the dark."

He sighed. Was she going to be one of those people who queried everything?

"There are wild things around us."

"Wild things? What kind of wild things?" She sounded interested but he was not going to tell her any more but hurried on down the track.

She was hard put to keep up with him and was soon some way behind him so he stopped for her to catch up.

"You must walk quicker; otherwise we will be out here in the dark."

She nodded and asked where they were going and he told her they were going to Middle City.

He walked more slowly so that she could keep up with him.

"Middle City – not that I have heard of the place – where is it?"

"Didn't they teach you anything in class or weren't you paying attention?"

She was indignant that he should think her ignorant and said that she was most attentive but she had never heard of it before.

He heard a different tone in her voice but all he said was: "Save your breath for walking and we will get there soon enough." And with that she had to be content.

They stopped once for refreshment. He did not seem keen on talking; in fact she got the idea that he disliked her. She wasn't far wrong!

It was getting dark when he stopped by an old barn filled with hay and told her they would stay the night there.

After they had had a meal, he settled down near the door to sleep and she went further in. She lay for ages listening to the strange sounds around her. She needed the lat so she crept past him to go outside and he grabbed her leg and told her to go back to her side of the barn.

"I need to go outside, unless you want me to wet myself."

He laughed and let her go.

She wasn't long but, as she was coming back, thought she saw someone in the bushes and was surprised to find Medrix where she had left him. She told him what she had seen and he got up and went outside to look. He came back in and said it must have been an animal.

She was still worried, but he did not seem at all upset so she settled back to sleep.

Medrix woke suddenly.

He could smell smoke and he realised the back of the barn where she slept was on fire. She was just lying there.

"Wake up, Celisia," he yelled.

She did not move.

He moved quickly, picked her up and ran towards the doors. They were locked. To his left was a high window used to bring bales of hay into the barn. It had a pulley which was fixed to the roof, both inside and out. He pulled at the rope and tied it around himself and, carrying her, hoisted himself up to the window. Already parts of the roof were on fire. He attached the rope around her inert body and lowered her down to the ground beneath, then swung himself over the ledge and climbed down the rope. He released her and carried her away from the fire.

She awoke coughing and spluttering and sat up seeming none the worse but, when she stood up, dizziness hit her and she collapsed in a heap.

Medrix knew without doubt that someone had tried to kill her or him or both of them.

Did someone know who he was?

Did someone have a reason to kill her?

Or, maybe there was another reason why the Grand Elder had asked him to see to her.

"We must get help, little one," he said gently. "You need to rest somewhere before we continue our journey, and I know a good place."

He left the track and did not stop walking until he came to some caves by a river. One of the caves had a sliding door at the back. He knocked and it slid open and he went in.

Cessie woke again to see a woman, a very small woman, sitting beside her who smiled at her and said: "Good. I can see you are much better."

Medrix came over to her and said that the people who lived here were huntersnouts. They usually lived in trees but their home had been destroyed by earthquakes.

They stayed in the cave for three days and, by that time she was better and again they set out for Middle City. Medrix was very gentle with her and seemed to have changed his attitude. In fact he was over-protective which she found a bit irksome but she made sure she stayed close to him all the way to Middle City, for he had saved her life and he would be her friend forever.

They arrived at Middle City as it was getting dark and suddenly she felt afraid and put her hand in his. He felt her stiffen and realised that she was afraid. His long fingers tightened round hers and he stood still.

"What's the matter?" he asked gently.

"They will be angry with me, won't they?"

"Why?"

"Because they are all Lawmakers – so they will be."

"Cessie, they are all exiles like you."

"But they will not like me."

"Why not?"

"Because Lawmakers go out of their way to be nasty to me."

He sighed. "We have to go in and you'll find that they will like you. Just be good and don't do anything silly, *that's* all." He let go of her hand and strode up to the city gates and rang the bell. She held back and he went back, grabbed her by the arm and pulled her with him.

The gates opened and swung back. They walked in and the gates closed behind them.

The place was a ruin. One side was just a pile of fallen stones but the other side had a roof on it. The whole city was a low scattered settlement that spread as far as the eye could see.

"It's big, Medrix."

"Yes, it's been used by many generations, and not only by Lawmakers."

Two women came towards them. They nodded to Medrix and told Ces to go with them. On the way to the part of the city where they lived, she saw a large game court but it had no wall and it was covered with rubble and leaves.

She thought Medrix was following but when she turned round he was not there and she knew she had to meet everyone on her own.

Two more women came out of a building and came over to her. One said that she was known as Mother Barta and was in charge of the whole place. She was elderly; the other was younger and her name was Nimma. They soon made Cessie welcome and took her into the building to meet the others.

The women were in one section of the building and the men in another. She was not allowed in the men's section but the men joined them in the communal dining centre although, otherwise, they were kept apart. She was to share her room with two other Lawmothers whom she would meet later.

It seemed that Mother Barta knew all about her but she did not tell Ces that she was wicked: she just welcomed her to the place, saying that providing she kept the rules, all would be well. Cessie asked about Medrix but they hushed her up and said she would see him at mealtime. She did, but not to speak to, for he was at the end of a very long table and he didn't even look in her direction.

It was all very strange at first but soon she got used to the place and the people in it.

She helped with the sewing and the preparing of food and sometimes she had to sweep the yard outside. She also took it in turns with her bed mates to keep their room clean and tidy. She only saw them at night for they were both in the laundry section.

She was given work to do in the morning but her afternoons were free. During the evenings they stayed in their rooms. She went to sleep early rather than stare at the ceiling. She was up early in the mornings and walked around the ruins, wondering who had lived there all those years ago. Once she came past the men's section and was shooed away by Medrix and told to keep to her side, but no one else bothered her.

The ruined game court troubled her. It had rubble on it and leaves but did not seem to be damaged in any way. She noticed that down one side of the court were steep steps and she went down them until she came to a door which she pushed open. As soon as she stepped in, a light came on and she saw that there was a long room with cupboards down one side. She looked in the nearest one and found a box of game balls. There was nothing wrong with them so she bounced one around the room. The other cupboards were empty but, on her right, was a sign which warned of danger from the machinery that raised the centre wall.

She was just turning to come away when someone said: "What the hell are *you* doing here?" It was Medrix and he was angry.

"Only looking. You know, I think the court is safe to play on: there are even balls here. The wall lifting gears probably need greasing before they will work but – here is a game court waiting to be used."

"By *you*, I suppose?" he said sarcastically.

"No – not by me: there are Lawmakers here ... why not them?"

"Because they are well past it," he laughed. "Would you cripple the workforce here? They have fields to plough and other work to do."

"Yes, but ..."

"But, nothing. Now, clear out of here. Out – now!"

She went and Medrix locked the door behind her.

"Where did you get the key, Medrix?"

"I found it in the door." But Ces knew he hadn't: therefore he must have had it in his pocket, but she said nothing: it was better that way.

Mother Barta called her to her room and was very cross with her for exploring the game court. So ... Evidently Medrix must had reported her.

She was told to stay in her room until further notice for venturing into places that were out of bounds. She stayed there for five days and was fed up by the end of it. When she joined the others she did not bother with them and refused to speak to Medrix.

Whereas she had been happy before, now she wasn't and wondered what life would be like outside the confines of the city.

She hardly spoke to people, and found places in the city where she could hide away. They were all Lawmakers under the thumb of the Elders still, and acted accordingly. She went off her food and was noticeably thinner.

She was sitting on a ruined tower one morning when a Lawmaker came.

"Mind if I join you?"

She shrugged her shoulders and he sat down beside her.

"My name is Sanor. I have been here six years. You get used to it after a while and it is a good thing to keep yourself to yourself as you are doing. Be careful to whom you speak; there are spies everywhere. Mother Barta reports to the Grand Elder in City One. She arranges through her what supplies are needed. If the report is good, we get big food parcels; if not, then we get very little."

"So – she knows about me and the game court?"

"Yes. We had a small amount of food then."

"Oh dear, I did not know ..." she put her hand over her face, "I am so sorry."

"Don't worry; you are not the only one to make a mistake. Now I must go and you must go for your meal. I'll see you around – and ... be careful."

Ces watched him go and made her way slowly back to her section.

So ... they knew. She would have to be careful ... be nice ... but careful.

Ces was kept busy every day and one day passed just like any other until she realised that she had been here for three moons. Medrix came and went and mostly avoided her. She kept herself to herself and that way avoided trouble. Nobody was unkind to her as they had been in City One, for which she was most thankful.

One lovely sunny morning whilst they were all eating breakfast. Mother Barta said that everyone was to go out for the day; to pick berries. There was a great cheer and they all went outside to where three wagons, each drawn by a horse, were waiting for them.

They all clambered up into the wagons and, amidst great cheering, set off.

The journey took over an hour and it was very warm. The berries grew wild and, when they had reached the spot, they all got out. Baskets were given to each man and he chose his picking partner. Ces had a Lawmaker named Thern, an elderly man, who smiled a welcome to her.

Mother Barta said: "Now, my dears, we have all these baskets to fill by the end of the day. As you know three quarters of them will go to City One as is our custom; the rest we can keep."

"Why do they have so much?" Ces asked.

"It is their right, my dear," she replied with a smile.

"But we will have picked them ... so we ought to tell them how much they can have ... if any at all," Ces said indignantly.

"Hush," Lawmaker Thern said.

"Now ..." Mother Barta got no further as some of the others agreed with Ces.

It was at this moment that Medrix intervened. "No one will pick anything if we go on like this," he said, "we should discuss it after we have filled our baskets and you, Celisia, are holding up everything so don't say another word."

"But Medrix, we should trade them for something and ..."

"That's it!" he said angrily. "You can spend your day in the wagons. We don't need you to tell us what we can and can't do!"

Mother Barta nodded to her and as the others spread out to pick the fruit, Medrix marched her back to a wagon and left her there.

She sat in it for hours. No one came back for her; she realised that she had forgotten Sanor's advice and had blindly rushed in. It seemed to her that although they were all exiles, they were still ruled from City One, yet Middle City was a city in its own right, so why did they not rule themselves? Next time she would shut up, she vowed to herself.

The hours passed slowly for her and, seeing an empty basket near at hand, decided she had had enough of sitting still and would go and pick berries by herself. If she went in the opposite direction to everyone else, no one would notice.

She had wandered quite a way and, being thirsty, decided she must go back to the wagons. Her basket was almost full and she needed to get back before the others but then she saw a small stream and made for it to quench her thirst.

The stream was in a paved area which seemed strange to her, but she knelt down and drank. The water was ice cold but very refreshing. The time was going on so she thought she must take her basket of berries back to the wagon before the others came back. She got up and stepped back from the stream, then slipped and rolled down the slope and landed heavily on a large paving stone which moved, tipping her into a deep hole. She landed on a hay-strewn floor which took the bite out of her fall. Shaken, she stood up gingerly and soon got used to the half light. There were steep steps leading out of the hole so she went to climb them only to find her knees were very bruised and she couldn't. She tried again but it was too painful. She would have to call for help. She shouted and shouted but no one heard, for they were still picking the berries.

It was getting dark and now she was frightened. What if the stone closed up again? No one would find her. She began to panic then calmed herself down. Passages went somewhere, so where did this one go?

She spread her hands across the wall and a door slid open. She could see a long passageway and it seemed to be lit up. Maybe it led to another entrance that she could manage, or someone could be there to get help for her. It was worth a chance, she thought as she limped along.

The passage went on and on. There were light vents in places and in one part it widened and there were wooden trucks in rows and, here and there, a rusty ladder led up to the roof above. Should she go on? She had come so far, she had better see where it led.

Medrix came back to the wagons, as did the others. He soon realised that she was not there. He was angry. Couldn't she do anything right? He looked across the slopes and saw her basket near the stream. He told the others he would go and get her but, when he got to the stream, there was no sign of her. He looked around and saw the hole in the ground and went to investigate.

Evidently she had gone down there and had gone exploring, otherwise, why hadn't she climbed back up? She couldn't be injured because there was no sign of her. He shouted to the others that he was going to look for her and that two of the wagons should go and the other one should remain. Sanor and two other Lawmakers brought him ropes and her pack of refreshments. Although they offered to go with him, he refused their help and went down the hole and along the passageway to find her.

By this time he was furious and decided that when he found her he was going to teach her a lesson she would not forget.

Cessie was almost giving up ever finding another way out when she saw a light in the distance which was evidently man-made. At last, she thought, people. She came to a large room and there were passages going in four different directions and all were well lit up. There was a table in the middle of it with a large map spread across it.

She was just about to try and work out which way she should go when she heard people coming along one of the passageways and she knew the person's voice quite well.

It was, without doubt, the voice of the Grand Elder of City One!

She couldn't be found here, not by the Elders. She had to hide. There was an arch leading to one of the other passages and she ran and hid there. Then she saw Medrix come into the room and then the Elders. There was no way she could have warned him. They would think he was Fador and then there would be trouble. She could do nothing but see what happened.

The Elders looked surprised and one of them said: "Fador, what are you doing here?"

"I came to look at the map."

The Grand Elder said: "I thought you had gone fishing. I gave you a pass, so why are you still here?"

"I wanted..." He got no further; Celisia knew she had to act to save him and Fador,

She stepped out from her hiding place and said: "I asked him to come."

"*You* ..." they chorused, "... what are *you* doing here?"

"I came to see Fador to ask him if ..."

"If what?" the Grand Elder said angrily.

"If he was interested in playing the game against another city."

"What city is that?" her Lawmother said.

"Middle City"

"Rubbish ... they haven't got a team."

"Of course they have."

"Just you, is it?"

"No ..."

"How did you get a message to him?" her Lawmother asked.

"I left a message in his room."

"How ...?"

"I know all the passageways in this city; I often used to hide from my stepfather. When Fador was coaching, I slipped in and left a note; and he was evidently interested because here he is, but of course he did not know it was from me."

The Grand Elder shook her head angrily. "Evidently you are not learning anything in exile. We will have to send you elsewhere."

She turned to go, but Celisia had not finished and stepped out into the middle of the room and said clearly: "*Wait!* I have something important to declare ..." and before anyone could say anything she said in a clear voice: "*I, Celisia Margaret Mantrex of Middle City, do challenge Fador and all the Lawmakers of City One to a match to be played in three moons' time on your court. This I declare and this I decree: a challenge I offer by the rules of our cities, one to another.*"

There was dead silence; then the Grand Elder said that she accepted the challenge according to the rule books. If Celisia's team lost the game, then she would be sent to the prison ship off Pertalinga. Of course, if the game was not played for some reason or other, then it would be as if no challenge had been given and nothing would happen to anyone. "You, Fador," she added, "must go to Middle City and check out the court there," – because it wouldn't do for people to know that she had let a child play ball on an unsafe court. She told him to go through the tunnels to the city and, without more ado he turned and did as she decreed. But she made Celisia stay behind after sending the others away.

Celisia smiled and thanked the Grand Elder and said: "There's one more thing, Grand Elder."

"What's that?"

"The elderly Lawmothers have no warm cloaks and shiver with cold at times."

"What do you want me to do about it?"

"Simply exchange the baskets of berries for fifteen warm cloaks. We should receive something for all the hard work that went into picking them."

The Grand Elder smiled and said: "How like your mother you are. Yes, we'll do that. Lawmakers will bring them over in the morning and exchange them for fifty-two baskets of berries."

"No. That's too many ... but ... thirty would be right."

"Very well ... I see you might be of some use to them after all. Go now," and she was dismissed.

Celisia went back the way she had come and Medrix met her and pulled her roughly to the waiting wagon. He was furious but could do nothing about it as the Lawmakers had accepted the story. Of course he knew that the Grand Elder knew who he was and he would have got out of it all easily but for Celisia's challenge, and he realised, too, that she had only done it to save him and, for that, must be admired.

Mother Barta took her to her room. She was very angry.

"I can see, girl that you are not to be trusted – you could have got Medrix into trouble."

"Ah, but I didn't, because ..."

"Medrix has told me how you saved him."

"And they believed me, too," Cessie said, with a laugh.

Medrix walked in and said angrily: "It is no laughing matter. It shouldn't have happened – you shouldn't have been there at all."

"I know ... but"

"You can't even keep the simplest of rules – I am not surprised you were exiled."

"Everyone, except you Medrix, is an exile, so I am no different to anyone else."

"No different – of course you are – you are as sly as they come – just waiting to cause trouble as the Grand Elder said you would."

"She told you?" Ces said quickly, "how could she do that?"

Medrix realised that he had said more than he should have done and quickly said: "Fador told me." Luckily for him, she did not query it.

Mother Barta said Ces was going to the punishment room for the next ten days and, without more ado, she was taken there.

Medrix inspected the court and wrote a report for the Grand Elder and gave it to Mother Barta to give to the Lawmakers who collected the berries.

Then, telling everyone he was going fishing, he left the city and made his way to see the Grand Elder.

Would she take him off this job, as he seemed to have failed where Cessie was concerned, or would he be allowed to stay? Although he didn't want to be here as nursemaid to a child, he didn't want to be sent home because he had failed. His fate was in the Grand Elder's hands – what would she say?

Chapter 2

Three days later, Medrix went into City One by a small side gate which led straight into the Grand Elder's private office. She kept him waiting and, when he had been there for over two hours, she came in looking grim.

"I was in two minds, Medrix, to send you home. You were highly recommended by the Masters on Estolan but even you are not able to cope with this situation, whereas a fifteen-years-old girl seems to have taken charge. She has run circles around you *LAWMAKER*."

"So I'm to go back to Estolan?" Medrix asked quietly.

"Certainly not: you got us into this situation so you can get us out. Try and prevent the game. She has never played in one, only watched. She hasn't a hope of winning and that means I will have to send a child to a prison ship."

"Can't you reinstate her here? Punish her another way...?

"Certainly not: the challenge has been issued and so has to be upheld, unless she can be persuaded not to play. She likes you, so that must be of some value. Make sure you use that. The trouble is that the others might back her up and then where will we be?"

"Others? What others?"

"The other exiles of course."

"You could take me off the case: someone else might be..." He got no further.

"She *likes* you, so you will do it. Anyway it is not a good idea for you to go home now – well, not until the gossip has died down."

"I don't follow you, Grand Elder. What gossip?"

"Rumour has it and I am sure it is true, that your betrothed has married her next-door neighbour."

"What! That can't be. She is promised to me."

"I have cousins on Estolan and they assure me it's true. She found herself to be pregnant; evidently you did not take any precautions when you slept with her. She did the only thing she could, for single mothers are usually sent to the House of Correction and their children are taken away from them, but her father acted quickly and so she married. Her husband is over seventy years

17

old but had agreed to bring up the child as his own. However, there were complications and she had a miscarriage, so now there is no child but she has decided to stay married."

Medrix shook his head in disbelief.

"But, Grand Elder – that child was not mine."

"What are you saying, Lawmaker?"

"I am saying that I kept all the rules where she was concerned and, if she was pregnant, then someone else is to blame."

"Be that as it may – people will talk – and better you find out now than once you are married."

"Yes, I suppose so," he sighed. He felt as if he had been punched in the gut but he half smiled. "I suppose ... I have to stay."

"Yes. Even the Masters think so. It'll take your mind off her."

"Yes – so I must return to Middle City."

"Not so fast – you must go fishing. We have a log cabin on the border river between our two countries, Chetner and Cordonia. Fador has just come back from there so you will have missed him. I am giving you a pass. You will travel as Lawmaker Edson. You are there on a fact-finding tour and are a keen fisherman. That wig comes off – and the mask. You will be clean-shaven but you won't shave. By the time you get back to Middle city you should have a beard so you will not look like Fador – but everyone will think you do."

"Why? Why change the disguise?"

"Because I think Celisia might realise that you are not related to Fador. Of course the wig will go back on when you do return. A Lawmaker will take you to the river now and – Medrix – the Masters assure me that you will stop the game going on. We are all counting on you."

As Medrix left the room, he saw a girl standing in the corridor. He asked her why she was standing there and she said that she was late for class and was waiting for the chanting to finish before she could go in.

"I see," he said. She could have heard him and the Grand Elder talking. "Have you been here long?"

"No – not long."

"I see – did you hear us talking?"

"I knew there was someone in there by the murmur of voices but I couldn't hear what they were saying."

"Are you sure?"

"Of course I am."

But, because the girl had flushed up as she spoke, Medrix did not believe her. He went back to the Grand Elder and told her about it and she came out to see the girl then said: "You can leave now, Medrix, I'll see to her."

It was only when he was in the shuttle that he realised that the Grand Elder had spoken his name in front of the girl. He hoped that she did not remember it for she would be telling all her friends and this place would no longer be safe for him.

The cabin was small and catered for four people but he was the only one there. He preferred it that way. He went out daily, spending more time staring into the water than actually fishing.

He was in a state of shock. How could Jessanda have treated him so? Cheated on him. He might never have found out if he had married her. He hoped the Masters didn't think he had broken the rules. Well, they were keeping him here weren't they? He was sure that they would have recalled him otherwise. He was a failure in his love life, and here. But he had another chance; stop the game and all would be fine. But, somehow, he thought it was going to be hard where Celisia was concerned.

Why had they sent him here? He should be in Middle City now. Of course, Celisia was confined to the punishment cell for ten days but, knowing her, she would have somehow talked herself out of there, he was sure of it.

He sighed. He should be there, not here, staring into the river.

Suddenly he heard shouting and, looking across the river, saw two men fighting. One hit the other so hard that he fell into the river and didn't come up. The other man disappeared into the trees and was gone.

Medrix slipped off his shoes and jacket and dived into the water. It was ice cold. He swam to the place where the man had gone in and dived. He saw him struggling to free his arm which was caught in a branch of an old tree.

He surfaced, then dived again and freed the man, who had a nasty cut on his head, brought him up to the surface and swam to the riverbank. He picked up the man and carried him to some flat ground and, bending over him, gave him the kiss of life (all Elders' men were trained in life-saving) the man coughed and opened his eyes. He seemed surprised to see Medrix.

There was a bridge further down the river and Medrix was able to carry him back to the cabin where he stripped the man and wrapped him in towels: that done, he dried himself and put on clean clothes and another pair of shoes. Later on he went and collected his things. No one had touched them.

The next day the man seemed better but, when he stood up, he felt dizzy and sat down again.

This was day four and Medrix knew that he should be leaving soon but he could not leave the man unless he was able to get help. Maybe the Lawmaker who brought him (he was to collect him on the fifth day and take him within walking distance of Middle City) would help. He would have to wait and see.

They had a long chat that evening. The man said that he was the Water Bailiff for Chetner and Cordonian border rivers and the man who'd hit him was a poacher. He thanked Medrix for helping him and said his name was Haldean and one day he would repay the debt but Medrix said there was no need. "After all, I just happened to be there at the right time."

That night there was a terrible storm and Medrix was unable to leave the cabin, even if he'd wanted to. There were trees down which blocked the path to the shuttle pad.

Help came five days later when the border guard came over to see if the cabin was still intact.

Haldean went with them and Medrix went to the shuttle pad and found there was no way a shuttle could land there so, heaving his pack onto his back, he started walking. Hours later he arrived at a mountain centre. He quickly put on his wig and went in. There he found someone who had a small shuttle and could take him to within walking distance of his destination, but not for two days. Realising that that was better than nothing, he accepted the offer. He was now overdue but what could he do? Celisia would definitely be out of the punishment cell and that meant trouble.

The shuttle set him down within two hours' walking distance of Middle City. The owner refused payment and wished Medrix well. Medrix watched as the shuttle flew off into the distance.

He had walked a short distance when the ground shook. He walked on: it would not be a good thing to be out here in an earthquake. He hurried on.

Another tremor shook the road. He quickened his pace but then it happened again and a small tree fell across the road. He walked round it and was glad when he saw the walls of Middle City showing in the distance. He arrived there without any mishap and was welcomed by Mother Barta.

He soon noticed a difference in the place.

The game court was clear; the central wall was up; wooden benches surrounded the court and a group of people were on the court. Lawmaker Thern was teaching the game to them. Celisia was not amongst them and he asked Mother Barta where she was.

"She's gone to the nearer settlements to tell them about the game."

"On her own?" He was shocked.

"Of course not, Sanor is with her."

"You sent her with a man? Is he trustworthy?"

"Of course he is, Medrix. Lawmaker Sanor thinks the world of her, as we all do."

"But why was he exiled?"

"Because he warned the Elders that some of the older tunnels weren't safe and would lead to earth falls. He said that they should be filled in or new roof supports put in. They wouldn't listen to him but they sent him here. Celisia will be safe with him. He knows where the unsafe tunnels are."

Medrix was still worried: after all, someone had tried to kill her and now they might try again.

"When did they go, Mother?"

"About ten days ago."

"But she was supposed to be in the punishment cell."

"I know – but she is so thoughtful – she asked for warm shawls for we older ones but the Grand Elder wouldn't give them, but she was willing to exchange them for our berries. I called a meeting and everyone agreed that Celisia's idea about exchanging goods was a good one so we let her off the punishment for, because of her, we are now a recognised city. Now we have our own council and we can exchange goods with Chetnerites and Lawmakers alike."

"When I was walking back here, there were earth tremors."

"Don't worry. She will be all right. I do believe you fancy her." Mother Barta laughed.

"Course I don't. She's a child!"

"I think you do. She likes you, but whether she'll like that beard is another thing." She laughed again.

Medrix left her to take his things to his room. Fancied her indeed ... and yet ... could he use that somehow to make her give up the game? He would have to think about it.

He sat on the bed and stared out of the window, remembering something Haldean had said. Haldean had asked him if he had a girl friend to which Medrix had replied 'No'. But Haldean had said that he must have seen someone he liked and he had said: "There's one: she's got golden hair and blue eyes which light up when she smiles – yes, I fancy her – but it's a no-go area: she's too young."

And Haldean had said: "Grab her while you have the chance. Marry her: she'll grow up to your ways."

Medrix had laughed at the suggestion and had said: "She's a Chetnerite and will stay here when I go back to Estolan."

They had laughed about it then talked of other things – so – all right, he was attracted to Celisia – so – should he play on it? It was an idea if everything else failed.

Sanor and Celisia had been to two fairly large settlements. The people there were very interested in the proposed challenge game and promised to tell everyone about it, even spreading the news further afield.

Ces said that anyone who stayed in Middle City for at least one moon would be counted as residents and would be taught the game and maybe would even be in the final team.

The two of them decided to return to Middle City as the time was passing quickly. Sanor said that he knew of a quicker way home and she agreed to take it. They crossed some hills and then came to a vast plain. This was a swamp and could be crossed following the marker posts. Sanor led the way and Ces had to hurry to keep up. He stopped for her to catch up and said that they had covered more than half of it. The posts seemed to go on forever but, suddenly, they came to a place where there were no posts at all, yet they could see across a large patch of ground so they continued without stopping.

"Where's the next post?" Ces asked nervously.

"Should be about here," said Sanor, stepping forward.

She watched him and he held out his hand to her. "Come, it's quite safe."

She had to trust him.

She reached out to him and came level with him. He went on slowly, tentatively trying the ground with one foot then, when he deemed it safe, nodded to her and she followed him.

They came to a stream that ran amid mud banks. Here grew a lot of purple flowers and they gave off a strange smell which made her feel quite sick.

"Take your shoes and socks off," Sanor said urgently.

She did so and he stepped into the stream. She followed. It was icy cold and her feet squelched in the mud as it seemed to want to suck her down. They came to a mud bank and he clambered up it and was gone.

Panic rose in her as she too scrambled up the bank to find he was sitting on a dry patch of ground, putting on his shoes. There was a post right beside him.

Ces sighed with relief.

"Someone," said Sanor, "must have moved the posts." She shivered – was someone out to kill her? Was it him? It couldn't be him for he had brought her safely through.

Beyond them the path climbed a steep slope and she saw a group of trees in the distance.

"We will pass City Four this way," he said gruffly. "We'll be home soon."

Just then the ground shook.

"Earth tremor," she said.

"We must keep moving."

They came to another stream with stepping stones. She was halfway across when another tremor came and she had great difficulty keeping her balance. Sanor helped her up the bank and as she scrabbled up she could feel the ground slipping away from her and it was with a great effort that she managed to reach the top and stay upright. Looking back, she saw that the stream had disappeared into a large crack in the ground.

Sanor was standing by a tree and she ran to him. He said: "We've made it and soon will be home."

"Next time, we'll go the long way round!"

He laughed. "You're safe – aren't you?"

She sighed. "Yes: but what is that?" She pointed.

Sanor looked and said it was a man sitting in a tree.

The man in question said: "I saw you coming. The view is good from here. You nearly lost her." He pointed to Celisia.

"But I didn't," Sanor said with a laugh.

"Who are you and why are you sitting in a tree?" asked Celisia.

"I am Tadrex the Magician."

"Magician?" said Celisia in surprise.

"Yes. In fact I am the greatest magician in the entire galaxy."

"Really?" queried Sanor. "Why are you sitting in a tree?"

"Why not? But I did have a purpose. I wanted to see you both and how you came across the swamp."

"Why?"

"Why not?"

"Do you always answer a question with a question?"

The magician laughed and stood up on the branch and they could see he wore a long robe which was covered with stars and moons. He put on a pointed black hat and bowed to them both and suddenly presented Ces with a bunch of flowers. She laughed with delight.

"Yes, you are a magician – but are you real or just pretending to be one?"

"Are you?" he asked her.

"Am I what?"

"Real, of course."

"Of course I am." She laughed again. "I see ... you are real. I do apologize for thinking you were not."

"Never mind, Celisia," he said.

"How do you know my name?"

"I am a magician – have you forgotten already?"

"Well, that explains it ... I think."

"Now ... Sanor there, he is very astute and polite; he did not doubt me."

Sanor seemed bemused, then said: "Then you know why we are here?"

"Of course: you are looking for people to play the game."

"Can you help?" asked Ces.

"Well, yes – my assistant, Thortrex, can play."

"Where is he?"

"I am here," said a small dwarf-like creature who had been sitting unnoticed on a lower branch.

"You are a huntersnout, aren't you?" said Ces.

He nodded.

The magician then said that he would give Thortrex a rhyme and he could teach it to the others and this would help them play the game and win."

"We cannot cheat," they said together.

"Ah, well – suit yourself. Just use the rhyme to practice, it will certainly help you and you can use it on the court if you need to. You could win, you know, and then you would be given the Champion's Cup and any favours you ask for."

"Oh, no!" said Sanor. "If Cessie's team win they have to play all the other cities.

"What other cities?" asked the magician.

"Well ... you know ... the other Lawmakers' cities."

"There aren't any."

"Of course there are – we learnt about them in school."

Oh! *those* cities. I know what you mean: there are no game courts there. In fact there are only about five people in each city."

"That doesn't make sense," said Cessie in amazement.

"They are mining centres. Each has a shaft and a tractor beam to bring in the mining freighters. The five men there just see that it all runs smoothly. Of course, there's the Old City, but that is a ruin."

"What about City Four, then?" queried Sanor.

"The same as the others – and that means that City One teams only play themselves – so you can't judge how good they are, can you?"

"So ... we could win," Cessie said with a smile.

"With my help you could. Anyway, take Thortrex with you and we shall see what we shall see." And with that, he waved his arms in the air and vanished.

Cessie and Sanor stared at the tree. The magician had indeed vanished, and so had Thortrex.

Neither of them believed in magicians but they had both seen him vanish.

"We won't see them again," she said, "but it was all very interesting ... but, we'd better get on."

They soon came to a sign which read: *City Four* and they had almost passed it when they heard someone screaming and ran to see who it was.

A girl of about Cessie's age was standing by a tunnel which was blocked by a roof fall.

"My Lawmother is down there. She was leading the way you see and there was a roof fall – she's trapped – I can't get to her. I have called and called but she does not answer me."

Sanor said gently: "Come away – there's nothing you can do."

"I can't leave her there."

"I'm afraid you'll have to."

"Why did you want to go into the tunnel, anyway?" he asked the girl.

"I was late for class one morning and I waited outside you see until the chanting had stopped and I overheard the Grand Elder talking to someone about a girl who had got herself pregnant and had married someone else rather than her betrothed. Then they came out of a room and were startled when they saw me. They asked me if I had overheard their conversation. I shook my head but I am sure they knew I had. They told me to tell no one and I would be given a special treat. Then, today, my Lawmother came to tell me that, as a special treat I was to go to some special caves where there were beautiful paintings on the walls. I was delighted but ... look what happened ... my lovely Lawmother is dead." She sat down and cried.

Sanor looked at Cessie but said nothing. They were both quite certain she was the one they were aiming to kill or leave down there in the dark. But then, maybe the girl had told the truth.

They persuaded her to come to Middle City with them. The girl, whose name was Santel, wanted to go back to City One to tell them what had happened and Sanor said that Mother Barta would arrange it for her.

As they walked on, they came to a crossroads.

"Look," said Santel, "that road goes to City One. I can go home that way," and she went down the road on her own.

Sanor was troubled. "I'll have to go with her as she is in such a shocked state. It will be better that way: she might see Medrix and may report the fact that she had seen Fador in two places at once and that would never do. You take the turning to the left and you should get to Middle City by nightfall."

"I could come with you," Cessie said, not wanting to go on alone.

"No – there's no need. If you hurry you will get there before dark." She watched him run after Santel and join her.

She sighed and walked quickly along the road. The sky darkened and it began to rain but still she walked, getting wetter by the minute.

The rain stopped and she was sure someone was following her but every time she stopped, so did the other person. She quickened her pace until she came to some bushes where she hid and waited. Soon she could hear noise but whoever it was stopped by the bushes. She peered through them and began to laugh, for standing there was a grey donkey and sitting on its back was Thortrex.

"Want a lift, girl?" he asked.

She climbed on the donkey's back and they all made their way to Middle City.

She wondered if Medrix had returned and hoped he was not still angry with her for she really liked him and she needed his support so she could organise the programme for the game.

Cessie was so tired when they finally arrived at Middle City that she went straight home, kicked off her shoes and lay on the bed. She fell asleep at once.

When the others came to bed they did not wake her but covered her with a blanket and then went to bed themselves.

Cessie woke up and looked at the timekeeper and saw that it was only the hour of two. She lay thinking of Medrix. What if he was still angry with her and was avoiding her. There was only one thing for it, she must go and see him now. Of course she knew that the men's section was out of bounds but she would risk it, so, slipping on her shoes, she quietly left the room. She was soon outside and as she could see no one around, got to the men's section without mishap. The door opened as she approached it and she went in. A light came on over a board which showed her where the various men slept. Medrix' room was number ten. It was upstairs and she hurried in that direction. No one stopped her.

She pressed down the handle on his door. It opened easily and she crept in.

He was fast asleep. She noticed with surprise that he had a beard and she wasn't sure at first if it was him but he turned over and now she knew it must be him for he mentioned her name.

The window was open and the curtains drawn back allowing moonlight to shine into the room.

She stood over him. He was talking in his sleep – something about the Masters not liking him. She smiled. She could get all his secrets if she stayed and she was sure he had some but that was not why she had come. She reached down and shook his arm.

He stirred but did not wake. She did it again and called his name.

He woke up with a grunt then, seeing her, sat up quickly.

"What the hell are you doing here?" he said angrily.

"I had to speak to you," she whispered.

"You are breaking rules even being here."

"I know, but it was important and I thought I might miss you in the morning and I couldn't sleep."

"Well, what is it? You could get me in trouble again."

"I wanted to say how sorry I am for getting you into trouble and jeopardising your way of life here. I really am sorry, Medrix."

"Right – now leave me and get some sleep. I have to go to the farm in the morning. I have to go early and I need some sleep."

"Yes ... yes ... of course. What are you doing at the farm? I thought you could help me with the game."

"I am building a loom with Lawmaker Jenkins. You are not going on with the game ...?"

"Yes, it will be fun."

"Fun! You could land up on a prison ship!"

"She won't send me there."

"Why not? I heard her myself."

"You don't know her like I do." She smiled.

He was about to argue the point when he stopped himself and sighed. "I think the world of you, Cessie, and I can't bear the thought of something bad happening to you. I really care for you."

She looked at him.

"I must do it," she said.

"But what will I do without you – please, love ... I ... hated it when I was away from you and I was very worried when you weren't here when I got back."

"Sanor looked after me." She told him then about the magician and about Santel. He was shocked – God, she could have recognised him!

"Medrix, you will help with the game?"

"If you insist – but you must go now – we'll talk about it after supper this evening."

"Thank you."

"Right – now go before someone thinks we are lovers."

"What? Don't be silly. No one would think that, Medrix."

"They would."

She went to the door and pressed the handle down only to find the door would not open. She turned to him: "I can't open it."

"Press harder then."

She did and the handle came off in her hand. She waved it at him.

"Damnation to hell, Cessie. Now what have you done?"

"I didn't do anything."

"Pass me my robe; it's on that chair."

She gave it to him.

"Look at the door and close your eyes. Don't ask why, just do it."

She did as he asked.

He jumped out of bed and put on his undershorts and then put on the robe and went to the door. He fiddled with the handle and shook his head and said that the other handle had fallen to the floor and he would have to go through the window to get down. He took off his robe, put on his shirt and trousers, climbed out of the window and was gone.

Ces did not know whether to laugh or cry at the situation she was in. She had better stand back from the window while she waited.

She did not have long to wait before she heard him at the door telling her to put her handle into the door whilst he did the same. The door opened and he came in quickly.

"Now go before anything else happens," and he pushed her none too gently out into the passageway.

She ran quickly out of the building and had just come to the game court when she saw him come out of the men's section and realised that he was going somewhere now. She waited for him but he turned left up an alleyway and she rushed after him.

The alley came out on to a track. She called him and he stopped. "What the hell do you want now?" he said angrily.

"Medrix, you are coming back, aren't you?"

"Of course I am."

"Are you going to the farm now?"

"Yes. I can't go back to sleep once I've been woken."

"Here," she said, "this is white heather. It was in my pocket. You have it for luck. My father came from planet Earth and he said it was called heather – I don't know what they call it here – but you have it for luck," and she reached and put it in his buttonhole.

He looked at her but said nothing.

"You really are not like Fador. His eyes are lighter than yours and his hair has grey streaks in it. It must have been the dim light down in the tunnel or their eyesight was poor." She laughed and then reached up, put her arms around his neck and kissed him.

Startled, he said: "Don't do that. You are far too free with your favours ..."

"I know what you mean, but you are my friend and I trust you with my life. Now, I won't keep you," and she turned and ran back the way she had come.

Medrix felt awful. She trusted him and he wasn't trustworthy. Well, that's how it goes in my game. But he hoped nobody else had noticed the differences. She was very astute and might notice other things, too and then where would he be? He hoped she had not seen the mark of the Elders' man on his back but, as she hadn't mentioned it, he had to hope for the best. All Elders' men had the mark, a tiny dragon, imprinted in their skin.

He hurried on his way. He looked back, thinking she might be following him but there was no one there and he breathed a sigh of relief.

He would send a message to the Grand Elder. He looked back again to make sure Ces really had gone then left the track and walked until he came to some caves. He went in one and touched part of the wall. A door slid open and lights came on. He sat down by a computer and sent a message to the Grand Elder.

Later he went to the farm.

Chapter 3

Medrix knew he had to stop the game being played. He had a few ideas but decided against each of them for one reason or another.

A stream of would-be players kept arriving and members of Middle City were kept busy signing them in and finding them somewhere to sleep and eat. Some of the older buildings were opened up for them.

Some of the newcomers were completely hopeless but Cessie made sure they all had a chance to play on the court.

The Lawmakers who had once played the game in City One took over the teaching and, when they weren't able to, for they still had their jobs to do, then she took over so that the practice went on non-stop.

Medrix watched her as she shouted out orders whilst playing herself, and he realised that she was very good indeed. He had played in his college team at one time and therefore knew the meaning of 'good'.

They played on the court every day and it was that which gave him the idea that, if they did not have a court, they could not practice. That night he went to the room under the court. The wall was always lowered at night and he knew his plan would work. He worked on the links of the hauling chain and, by the early morning, had cut through a few of them. Then, satisfied with his work, he crept out of the room and went to bed.

In the morning he saw that the wall was only halfway up and was wobbling. A group of players were standing near it and he ran to them to move them out of the way, then he went to see what was wrong. A Lawmaker had got there before him and shook his head when he saw the broken links.

"Evidently these links must have worn out with age," he said and Medrix agreed with him.

"It will be too dangerous to play on the court now," he said.

"But we can make new ones in our workshop."

Medrix knew that he had only held up the game for a few days but then Mother Barta said they could all go to the field outside the city and she would take food for them all.

"But," said Thortrex the huntersnout, "we can't bounce the ball on the grass."

Cessie said that they could practice throwing and tackling, so everyone agreed it was a good idea.

The field was not far from the city and they were soon there. Almost everyone who could be spared was there.

The field was fairly flat but, at one end, it sloped down to the river. The people who were not playing sat by the river and the players went to the flat area. All players were divided into groups of ten with the exception of one group who only had eight. Rather than let them sit out for a while, Cessie decided that she would play and coach at the same time. The other groups had a Lawmaker teaching them. She looked around for someone to make up the number for her group and saw Medrix standing and watching them.

"Medrix," she shouted, "come on, you must join us."

He shook his head and smiled ruefully. "I am no good at ball games," he said.

"Well, now's your time to learn," she said with a laugh.

"No ... really ... I am hopeless at that type of thing."

"Come on. You have only got to throw a ball; you can do that, surely."

Well, he knew he could but that wasn't on, was it, where he was concerned? He shook his head again.

"Well, you are spoiling it for everyone," she said peevishly.

Thortrex spoke up: "Medrix, I think you should try and help out. If I can have a go, and I assure you ball games are something I never play, I am sure you can!"

The others agreed with him and one of the girls, a pretty thing with dark hair, took hold of his arm and tried to bring him to where the others stood. She whispered something to him and he laughed but he joined her in the line up.

Cessie nodded to him and explained that five of them, including herself, were to stand in a line and the other five were to stop them getting the ball to a marker.

She threw the ball to player number two, who threw it to number three. Number three threw it to player number four, Medrix. He dropped it and looked to see where it had gone and waited for someone to bring it to him.

"Medrix!" shouted Cessie, "get the ball yourself."

But by this time the girl who had got him to play, whose name was Myra, had picked it up and said something to him at which they both laughed.

Cessie ignored them and the play went on.

The huntersnout who was in the other team tackled Medrix as he threw the ball and Medrix tripped over him and fell.

All the girls except Cessie helped him up. The huntersnout was already up and ready to play.

Cessie realised that the practice was turning into a shambles and wished now she had not asked him to play but she said nothing. Play started again and, when the ball came to Medrix, he dropped it again.

She shouted at him: "Keep your eye on the ball and not on the girls and maybe you will be able to catch it."

Everyone laughed except Medrix. He picked up the ball and threw it to Myra who caught it, winked at him and said: "Never mind, man, I bet you are better in bed."

Medrix laughed and said: "Want to try me?"

Cessie was furious now but tried not to show it and went on playing.

The next time the ball was passed without mishap.

She stopped the players and sat them down for a rest.

"What about the rhyme?" Thortrex asked.

"The rhyme can be used on the court only and we will do that when we play there."

"What is the rhyme?" asked Medrix.

"I'll go over it when we are on court," she answered.

"Let's hear it now," he smiled charmingly at the players and winked at Myra.

"Yes, I'd like to hear it, too," she said and the others agreed.

Cessie looked at Thortrex, who stood up and smiled.

"This is the rhyme the magician gave me:

> Bounce ball, bounce ball
> All around me
> Throw it to your partner
> And then set it free
>
> Kick the ball, kick the ball
> Now you set it free,
> Who throws it to a player
> And circles round me.
>
> Throw the ball, throw the ball
> Don't let it free
> Try and stop the player
> Who throws it to me.

"I don't think much of that," said Medrix, and the others agreed.

Thortrex smiled. "You need only say the first verse. It will help you get the rhythm of the play."

Everyone repeated the first verse and clapped the rhythm out. Then Cessie got them back to the practice again.

Now she played all kinds of team ball games with them so that they could get used to handling the ball. Medrix was hopeless at these until, in the end, she shouted at him: "You are not trying, Medrix. A child of six could do better than you. I do believe you are doing it purposely. A grown man of your age should be able to do it easily, but you are not trying."

There was dead silence.

Of course, she was right, he knew that. He had been one of the top players in his time and ... but things were different now. He turned on her angrily.

"I think you *forget*, Celisia that I am your *senior* and *you*, in the Lawmakers' scheme of things, are a *child*. I am *not to be spoken to* like that. Fador is *right* when he says that you do not know your place in society. *No wonder* you were exiled from City One."

He was about to walk off when Myra intervened. "I am sure she meant no harm. She is just worried that the court is out of use, but I suggest we carry on playing. I am sure, Medrix, you will have improved from when you started, only she has got it all on her shoulders and it is a big burden for her to carry. I think we should listen ... and you, Medrix ... and we should try again."

They all nodded.

He looked at Celisia as she stood there ashen-faced and felt sorry for what he had done. She said not a word but picked up the ball and threw it to a player.

The play went on.

Myra laughed with Medrix over some private joke as he caught the ball easily and he said out aloud: "And I could teach you a thing or two, Myra, but not on the court!"

She laughed and said: "We'll meet in those bushes later on."

Celisia made a mental note to check which settlement Myra came from and, when the players were picked, she would definitely not be one of them.

It grew hot.

The game went on until Medrix threw the ball high in the air and declared that it was too hot to go on and the players disbanded, leaving Cessie to go and collect the ball. As she picked it up, Medrix came over to her.

"You will never control players until you learn to control your temper. I think you were dreadful and if you decide to cut Myra out of the team, then I shall know that you are a really spiteful bitch," and with that he walked off leaving her almost in tears.

It was Sanor who came to get her to join the picnic. He said that Thortrex had told him that Medrix had been nasty to her. She half smiled and said that she had probably provoked him, whereupon Sanor said that Medrix was moody but expected it was because he was getting over a relationship that had gone wrong. Medrix evidently was betrothed to someone and she had married someone else.

Cessie looked surprised and asked him how he knew that but Sanor couldn't remember. They joined the others for the picnic but did not sit near Medrix who, together with other members of her group, was sitting beside the Mother.

In spite of everything, Cessie enjoyed the picnic for Sanor was a good friend and could make her laugh. Medrix saw them together and scowled; he knew in his heart of hearts that he was jealous. He left the picnic early, telling the Mother that he wanted to see how they were getting on in the workshop. Cessie never even saw him go.

It was getting dark when they arrived back at Middle City. Mother Barta called Ces to her rooms as soon as she arrived and she went in wondering why she was wanted.

"Close the door," said Mother Barta sternly and Celisia did so.

"I have heard how rude you have been to Medrix. He tried to help you out and you treated him like a six-year-old child, scorning him in front of other members of the team. I am thoroughly disgusted with your behaviour. You have been brought up to know better than that. In City One your stepfather would have whipped you for such a thing but I do not use whips here. You will hold out your hands, palms upwards."

Ces put her hands behind her back. "You can't do this to me, Mother. I can't play with sore hands."

"You should have thought of that before. Do as you are told or I will fetch some helpers."

Reluctantly she held out her hands. Evidently the Mother was not on her side but was trying to stop the game for some reason or other.

She was struck three times with a cane. The third stroke cut her hand and blood trickled down her arm and she tried not to cry.

"You will also sleep in the stables for three days. You can collect your meals from the kitchen. You may go."

Cessie almost ran from there, still trying not to cry. She rushed past Medrix without seeing him and ran over to the stables.

A light was on but there was no one there and she went up the ladder to the hayloft and sat down and cried.

It was obvious that the game was not to be played. There were people against it. There were Lawmakers here and others who thought she was trying to be clever. No one, except Sanor, liked her. She was a naughty child, that's all and was treated accordingly. Others could treat her like dirt and not be punished. What was the point of it all?

She had given them a new freedom and they had spurned it. Adults could speak crudely in front of her and not be reprimanded. There was not much point in going on.

The game was her dream, not theirs. She would live out her life here, doing mundane things, letting her dreams fly away with the wind.

Her hands were so sore and she had nothing to ease the pain.

She heard someone moving in the stable and remembered how someone had set light to the other hay barn and now she was petrified. She crept quietly to the top of the ladder and peered down. She could see a shadow of a man and then he spoke: "Whoever you are, I'm armed, so come down slowly."

She knew that voice. It was Medrix.

She smiled with relief and started down the ladder.

Medrix put down the pitchfork when he saw who it was.

"What the hell are you doing here?"

"Mother Barta sent me here for a punishment," she said.

"Punishment? Why, what have you done?"

"Argued with you."

"She knows about it?"

"You must have told her."

"I did not but I can make a few guesses who did."

He grabbed her hands as she wobbled on the ladder and she yelled with pain.

"What's the matter with your hands?" He looked at them. "She hit you?"

"That's the Lawmaker way."

She could see he was amazed by what had happened. If he had known her thoughts now regarding the game he would have been pleased and the game would have stopped right there, but he didn't know and he put his arms around her and gently wiped her tears away.

"I'm sorry, Medrix, if I treated you badly. I really am."

"It's no matter, love. I was wrong, too." He kissed her gently on her eyes and cheeks and whispered that he was a beast and should have had the punishment. He lifted her up in his arms and took her to one of the empty stables and laid her down in the sweet-smelling hay and kissed her gently on her mouth. She sighed and was comforted. She and Medrix were not angry with each other. Later she would tell him that she was giving up the idea of the game. He stroked her sleepy body and all the time he was scheming, thinking how he could use this situation to his advantage. She was like putty in his hands and he said: "Celisia, I am very fond of you. More than fond ... in fact ... I love you and I want to marry you when you are older. I know you have to be eighteen to marry but I am prepared to wait."

She stared at him in amazement and sat up quickly. "I ... "

"Sh. Listen to me ... we can elope."

"No."

"Let me go on."

She waited.

"If you play this game I will never see you again. Fador is putting his best team in so that means your team will lose and you will go to a prison ship. No one will ever see you again."

"The Grand Elder won't do that!"

"She will. Fador says she will."

"She won't, Medrix. I know her very well."

"You cannot risk it. But if you don't play we will be safe and I will take you far away from here."

"I cannot marry you, Medrix."

34

"Why not?"

"Because I don't love you enough ... in the same way; I don't want to marry because ..."

"Because you intend, *in spite of everything*, to play the game."

He stood up. "Well, that's it. Sleep now and may you dream of winning," and he laughed. "You are selfish. Fador is right. All the Lawmakers are right, too, you think of no one but yourself. Fador says that your stepfather knows exactly what you are like and that is why you are here."

He left her then and went to see to the horses, for that was why he had come, but he slept in the hayloft for he too remembered the fire in the other barn.

Celisia dreamed that she was holding a star in her hands; a shining star that glided up in the sky. When her mother died, her father said that she became a star in the sky. She knew then that, despite everything, she would play – win or lose – she would play the game.

Three days later she was out on the repaired court, practising; chanting the rhyme with the others. She was the only one with bandaged hands.

Mother Barta shook her head. "She has courage, that one," was all she said.

Everyone chanted the little verse and the more they sang it, the better they were. Thortrex winked at her with his middle eye.

That evening Medrix told Ces that a messenger had arrived from the city. When she went to the hall, she saw that it was Jadex, her stepbrother. She was so pleased to see him and he smiled back at her.

"Sister," he said seriously, "I bring a message from the Elders. They offer you a second chance. They did not know how keen you were to play in the team – but are ready to grant you that chance now and you will be welcomed back into the fold of the Lawmakers." She looked at him.

"Will you come back with me now?" he asked.

"What do you think, Jadex?"

"Knowing you as I do – I don't think you will. I can see the Elders would never know what you would do next."

She laughed "You know me well, Jadex. But I have learnt a lot more as an exile than I ever did before. Now I have a sense of purpose – yes – win or lose, there's a lot at stake."

"You have to win, Cessie. The game will be in twenty-eight days time. The Elders say you must bring a referee and a timekeeper. I'm sorry I can't help, as I am the messenger."

"Tell the Elders I am turning down their offer and the game is still on."

With that, Jadex kissed her and left her standing there, a lonely figure with a great burden on her shoulders.

She turned away, her heart heavy with misgiving. Had she done the right thing?

She told Medrix about the offer.

"Have you accepted it?" he asked.

"No – we have to play," was all she said.

Thortrex came up just then and she asked him if he knew of anyone who could be a referee and he said that Jator, a very tall exile, would do it. He had already offered his services and his brother could be the timekeeper.

Later Cessie had another visitor. It was her Lawmother.

She smiled at Cessie. "I have brought you these," and she put a great pile of uniforms on the floor. "We have three teams – as only one team is playing, I thought you could use these."

Cessie thanked her and her Lawmother kissed her and wished her well. "I have always had a soft spot for you, my dear," she said. "I'll see you on the day of the match."

As she was leaving, she saw Medrix and said to him: "Please tell Celisia that she has to have an observer for the match." Then she walked out of the ruined city into the darkness.

Medrix, of course, never even mentioned what he'd been told to Celisia. No observer meant no game.

A few days later, a runner arrived with a message for Celisia. He gave her the letter and stood waiting for a reply.

She opened the message quickly and read:

The game will be played in fourteen days time. Transport will be provided. The match starts at the hour of fifteen.

The man turned to go, then stopped. "Here is a picture of our team, may I have yours?" She ran to her room and picked up the sketch she had drawn and came back and gave it to him.

When the runner had gone, Ces knew for certain that now there was no turning back.

The great day arrived and people made their way to the City where the game was to be played. The Elders had sent transport for the team, so they arrived in style but, deep down, she felt sick with apprehension, though she smiled at the others for she knew that showing her fear would upset them.

The magician met them at the gates. It was with mixed feelings that she again entered the place that had once been her home.

Someone led them to the changing rooms. The women had been working hard altering the uniforms and her team looked smart in them.

Then they left the safety of the changing rooms and walked down the long enclosed corridor to the court. The noise of the crowd was tremendous but when she led the team on to the court, she felt very proud of them; all dressed in green with red sashes that had 'Middle City' embroidered on them. The City team then came on to the court, all dressed in white with green sashes. They were all very tall and looked so very strong that her heart sank when she saw them.

On a raised stage at one end sat the Grand Elder, two Lawmothers on each side of her: the trophy was on a low table in front of them.

The spectators were mostly Lawmakers but a few exiles had braved the stares to sit among them.

Some laughed when they saw Thortrex, the little huntersnout, as he played the clown and turned cartwheels for them. They laughed and clapped and cried out for him to do some more.

Cessie stopped him. "You are one of us, now. If they laugh at you, they laugh at us," she said gravely. He bowed to her wisdom and stood still.

The Grand Elder stood up and all went quiet.

"Who challenges our City to a game?" she said in a clear voice.

"I, Celisia Margaret Mantrex: an exile now, living in Middle City. I make the challenge."

"Who is the observer for your team?" demanded the Grand Elder.

Cessie stood still. What was an 'observer'? She had not heard of this person. Was it some new rule?

There was a hushed silence around the court.

The Grand Elder was about to speak again, when a man stood up and said: "I am the observer for the challenging team. My name is Haldean, I am a Cordonian. Who is your observer?"

Medrix was sitting at the back and smiled wryly when he realised why Haldean was helping Cessie's team.

There was a deep sigh from around the court, and a spectator stood up and said: "I am. My name is Stepton. I am a Lawmaker."

A murmur of approval ran round the court and the Grand Elder said the game could begin after the rules were read out.

Cessie felt this was done purposely so that the tension would build up, and her team was nervous already.

A Lawmaker stood up and spoke in a clear voice:

     1.The aim of the game is to throw the ball from the green circle up and over the wall.

     2.The shooter or any member of that team has to run to the other side of the wall and catch the ball before it touches the ground or is caught by the opposing team.

     3.The lowest part of the wall scores 2.

     4.The middle scores 3.

     5.The highest scores 5.

     6.The ball is thrown from one player to another.

     7.The play starts from the right-hand side of the court (marked S on the court).

     8.The ball may be bounced or kicked.

     9.The opposing team has to stop them.

     10.Each team plays for thirty minutes.

11. After each session the teams change places.

12. There will be a short rest time after two sessions.

13. The opposing team may get the ball away from the players in any way they like – but they cannot go in the green circle.

14. The team with the most points will win.

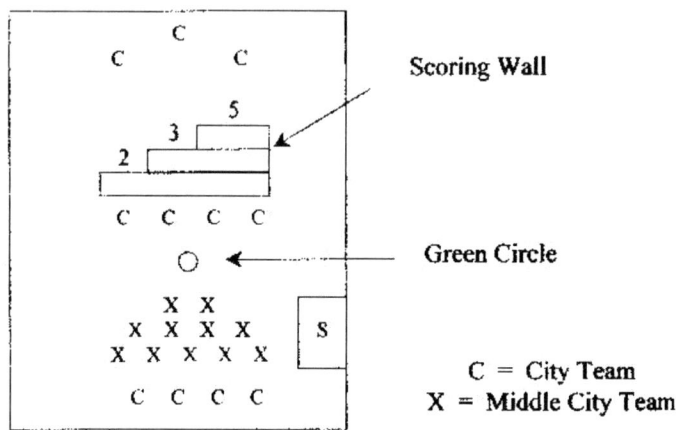

The Lawmaker sat down and the game began.

After the first two sessions, Cessie's team was way behind the other, the score being 9 points to 50. Her team was tired and disheartened: they were bruised and battered and one member had been carried off injured. What chance had they to win? she thought to herself. She should never have brought them into this. Medrix had tried to tell her how good the City One team was but she hadn't listened to him. What a fool she was to think a mixed team of players could ever play well enough against this well-trained team. At the end of it all she would lose her freedom and be worse off than she was now. Her team would not be punished – but she would be, and she would never see any of her friends again.

Then the magician came on to the court. "*Now,*" he said, "*now* is the time to play them at their own game," and he laughed. They looked at him in amazement – couldn't he see they were exhausted?

But he went on: "Remember the rhyme – this is not the time to hold back as we planned in the first half."

"But we haven't held back," said one. "We are so nervous, we haven't – it is all hopeless – we might as well give up now."

"You have to chant the rhyme – out loud – and don't stop – just concentrate on the rhyme and the game. Then you will see what happens."

The whistle went for the second half and the teams spread out to play again and Cessie's team began to chant the rhyme and the more they chanted it, the better they felt and soon they were only 20 points behind City One. Then the City team objected to the rhyme and the referee told the Middle City team to stop saying it so Cessie told them to chant it to themselves, and the game went on.

Their score reached 75 points, and their players seemed to be everywhere. They ran faster, jumped higher and the City One team began to tire.

Then the sun came out dazzling the City players so much that they missed the catches and scored even less.

When the game ended, the Middle City team had 105 points to the City's 79 points. Cessie's team had won.

The applause was tremendous but it died down when the Elder stood up.

"Congratulations – you have brought us a very good team, but before I can award the trophy, you have to play against City Number Four and if you beat them, then the trophy and the favours are yours."

Everyone cheered and stamped their feet because there would be another good game to watch.

Cessie stood still. She knew the Elders were not accepting defeat so easily, for there was no City Number Four, and they knew it.

She said in a loud voice:

"City Number Four does not exist. The buildings were destroyed by an earthquake. One person was killed. No other people lived there. It was a decoy city just like the other nineteen.

"Each hides a mineshaft leading to tunnels. The earthquakes are caused by these.

"Soon all the planet will fall into itself and the Elders will leave and you, ..." she pointed to the spectators and went on in an even louder voice, "... all of you will be left to die!"

There was a murmur around the court and then they all looked towards the Grand Elder. "Partly true," she said, taking command of the situation again. "We have had reports of earthquakes. All planets have them you know, but City Number Four is ..."

"Destroyed!" pronounced Fador, "so Cessie's team wins the trophy."

The audience roared appreciation and stood up to clap as the trophy was presented to Cessie.

She stood on the stage and held it up for everyone to see. The noise subsided and someone shouted: "Speech! Speech!"

She said in a clear voice: "Today I claim my right to ask for favours for so the Elders have decreed:

1.Everyone is free to leave the City if they wish.
2.All mining must stop for at least 500 deceans (years).
3.All Elders must return to their own planet – never to return here.
4.All land must revert to its rightful owners."

The Grand Elder stood up and smiled at Cessie.

"It shall be so – as our Laws decree." Then, turning, she left the stage.

Medrix jumped up onto the stage. She expected him to congratulate her, but he walked past and followed the Lawmakers.

"Medrix!" she said in surprise, "where are you going?"

"With them," he replied. "With them – I am one of them."

"But I thought you were Fador's twin brother?"

"No," and he peeled off his wig.

"You were a *spy*! – and to think I even *liked* you," she said incredulously.

"I liked you as well, Cessie. And what is more I admired your courage. It was a pity you were on the wrong side."

"*You*, it was *you* who told the Elders," shouted Santel, "*you* killed my Lawmother."

He stared at her then. "No. It was *you* who was to be left in the tunnels. You knew too much. The earthquake saved you – just chance, my dear."

"Then Fador does not have a twin brother?" queried Cessie.

"Yes – but he died at birth."

"No – you are wrong," Santel said. "I am Fador's twin sister."

"No – *you* are wrong. The Elders would never have allowed that," Medrix said with a scornful laugh.

"I was hidden by my true mother because she knew I was in real danger from the Elders because Chetner twins are telepathic. My Lawmother had overheard her telling someone about me and when my real mother was dying, my Lawmother came and took me."

"I don't believe it," Medrix said with scorn. "A Lawmother would never do that."

"This one did. She told me to keep the secret then all would be safe. But now it won't matter, will it?"

"You had better go now," Cessie said, "before anyone else realises you are a spy."

Medrix turned then to leave but turned back and said to her: "I *will* come back one day, and *on* that day I will have my *revenge*." And he kissed her on the forehead and left her staring after him.

She shrugged her shoulders. They had won. What harm could he do? Now was the time to celebrate and save their precious planet.

As soon as Medrix left the shuttle on reaching Estolan he was arrested by Law Officers and taken to the Masters' residence.

Even though it was late at night they were there to meet him.

He had failed his mission – and Elders' men don't fail, he knew that.

He was questioned over and over again, then they gave him a choice: either resign himself to be a failure and join all the other ordinary men at their labours or be retrained as an Elders' man. The choice was his.

He chose to be retrained.

They seemed pleased.

He was taken to be whipped for his failure but, as the lash hit his back, all he could see in his mind's eye was Celisia, the cause of his downfall, smiling up at him so trustingly. Then, as the whipping went on, her face became Jessanda's until the two faces were muddled in his head. He felt as if he was on fire and pain ripped through him with such ferocity that he collapsed at the feet of the Masters.

"Ah," said one of them, "first the punishment and now the training. We have an excellent candidate here." And they all smiled with satisfaction.

* * * * *

PART II

THE WEB OF MAGIC

Chapter 1

Eight years had gone by since the Lawmakers had left Chetner. Life had not been easy for Cessie or any of her friends. Many people still lived in the City, but others lived in small settlements around the countryside. The Lawmakers had destroyed many of the main things that made life easier. Luckily there was one computer base left in operation, but not much else. Little work had been done on the tunnels - they did not have the money to do much.

After that she busied herself with promoting the game and teaching at the Community School. She went to other planets and got them interested in the game.

She often thought of Medrix and his threat to return, but as the years went on and nothing happened, she began to think it was an idle threat and put it from her mind.

But she never forgot his friendship to her when she was first exiled or how he had betrayed them all by telling her that he was, in fact, a spy for the Lawmakers' regime.

Then came an invitation to go to far-off Temra, a large planet on the edge of their galaxy. She said that she would go and they sent a special shuttle just for her.

She was welcomed aboard and given a seat at the back of the shuttle.

Once they had started, they brought round drinks and small biscuits. How nice, she thought, to be away from Chetner for a few days.

She sipped her drink. It tasted bitter and she left most of it.

After a while she felt very drowsy and drank some more to wake herself up. Then, too late, she realised she had been drugged.

She just passed out and knew no more until she heard a voice saying: "Welcome to Estolan, the Lawmakers' planet."

She was taken to a small well-lit room. Standing by a table were two Elders. One said: "Welcome, Cessie. So glad you could come. I think we have a little matter to settle before you can return home."

The other Elder nodded to a man standing by the door who came over to her and said that she was being held here because she had tricked the

Lawmakers into losing a vital game that upset all their lives. The matter had been looked into and they knew that she was indeed guilty. Therefore she was to be imprisoned on Jailfa Island for as long as they deemed necessary.

He began to put chains on her wrists. She was horrified. What was she to do?

"Wait!" she said, jerking her wrists away from him, "I claim Lawmakers' rights. I claim a trial."

The man hesitated and looked at the Elders. "Release her." He did so and stood back waiting for new orders.

"In two days you shall have your trial and a lot of good it will do you," said one of the Elders.

Cessie knew that nothing much had changed. Still it was something.

She looked at them defiantly. "I claim my right to have a Counsellor."

They smiled and one said: "Who do you want? Tell us and we will see if it can be arranged."

"Medrix. I choose him. Is that possible?"

"Of course, my dear. He will be just the one for you." the older one said as they both laughed at some private joke. "He will come to you tomorrow morning."

"But what about today? If he comes tomorrow, I will only have one day."

"Well now, isn't that a pity, my dear," said one scornfully. "Medrix is very busy today. He is teaching self-defence classes. But he is free tomorrow, so he will see you then."

They turned to leave the room. But Cessie said: "Before you go, please tell me how I have tricked you for I have to know in order to work on my defence."

They looked at her in triumph and the older one said. "You used magic. You had the help of a magician and so won the game."

She knew that this was some kind of revenge on their part, and how she could prove otherwise she did not know. They knew she was trapped and this was one exile they would happily hold for ever, for she had to learn that no one made fools of them and got away with it.

They laughed at her. She had no chance of winning this time and she stood there in total despair as they left the room.

She was taken to a large room that was a Holding Centre for four people. She was the only one there at this time.

There were four beds down one side of the room, each with a table, a chair and a cupboard.

A large table with four chairs stood near the window, and scattered around the room were armchairs, each with a footstool. Brightly-coloured rugs covered the wooden floor. Through a further door was a wash area and kitchen.

"You can come and go as you like," the jailer told her. "Food can be got from us or from the dining centre. If you leave the centre you must be back before dark. Let us know if you want anything else. We are always around the place somewhere." He left her then.

She stood by the window and stared out. Outside, in a small yard three runabouts were parked. No one was anywhere near them, so why couldn't she take one and explore the area? After all, Medrix was not coming until tomorrow – she had all the day to herself.

The track she followed led straight up a hill and then veered to the left, following the coastline as it went.

On one side of her, the cliff side was a sheer drop to the sea below. The other side was flat and covered with pretty flowers.

The track petered out into another parking space, at the end of which was a look-out tower of some sort.

She parked the runabout and went to investigate.

Steep steps led up to a door, which was open. She peered inside. No one was there so she went in.

There were all kinds of computers, screens and buttons with printed instructions under them.

She went to the window and looked out. A man was at the bottom of a steep path, kissing a girl.

"Ah," she said to herself. "You stay there, my friend, while I see what I can do here."

One button said 'Self-destruct' – she laughed. She wouldn't be pressing that one; too dangerous.

But another one caught her eye – it said 'Warning of Planet Invasion'.

Now that would be a good one to press as a protest. After all, an enemy of one could create a lot of trouble if left on her own.

Medrix and the Elders would be really sorry that they had given her only one day.

She pressed the button, then ran down the steps and quickly got into the runabout and made her way back down the track.

As she entered the Holding Centre a siren went off and the lights went off and then came on again.

She sat in a chair and waited to see what would happen next.

A jug of hot chen had been left for her on the table so she poured herself a mugful and started to drink it.

"So you are back," said a voice. Medrix was sitting on her bed.

"How long have you been there?"

"Long enough." He stood up. He was dressed in dark-green but over his shirt was a thin, brown leather jacket.

He wore long brown gloves that reached to his elbows and his feet and legs were encased in long laced boots. In his hand he held a long whip. She shivered at the sight of it, but went on drinking her chen.

"What the hell have you been doing?" He walked across the room slowly.

"I thought you were too busy to come to me today," she said sarcastically.

"I was. Then I had this message to say you were in a forbidden area and that you had pressed a certain button, and the rest you already know, don't you?"

"Yes." She looked away from him and went on drinking.

The next thing the mug was knocked out of her hands as the whip curled around it. Startled, she stood up quickly and faced him.

"The Elders are furious and I can't say I blame them. What right have you to do such a thing?"

"It was a protest. They have declared war on Chetner and this is the reply. At least I have replied for them. I have attacked the enemy where it hurts."

"Do you realise there are women and children here, and you have made them afraid for their lives. Was that fair?"

"FAIR! ... is it fair that I am to be given no time to prepare my case?

"Is it fair that I am to be considered guilty even though I am innocent?

"Is it fair that Lawmakers are bad losers?

"Is it fair that they kidnapped me and brought me here to put me in prison without a trial because they felt they could never be wrong about anything?

"Yes. I attacked them. I am only *one* person against all of them. Why should they complain?"

"You have gone too far this time."

"Gone too far; what about them? They don't like a taste of their own medicine."

"What do you mean by that, Cessie?"

"These high and mighty Lawmakers took over our planet and made our lives hell. But you should know, because you are one of them!"

"It is not your place to interfere with the running of our planet. If there had been a real emergency, think of the harm you could have caused," he shouted at her.

"In one way they should have thanked me for showing up the weakness in their defence system."

"Oh, they will thank you all right. They will make sure you are sent to a place where even you will be hard put to get into trouble. And as for me, I shall be glad when you go there so I can get on with my life here in peace."

She moved nearer to him. "Medrix, I didn't mean to hurt you, but I am hurt too."

"Hurt ... You hurt? ... Never." There was a coldness in his voice that she had never heard before. "You have hurt everyone since you were a child. You have hurt your Lawmother, your stepfather, your school friends and the people who have fed you, educated and clothed you. You have never even thought about all they did for you. Don't tell me you feel hurt: you do not know the meaning of the word."

"You Lawmakers," she said angrily, "took me away from a loving home and expected me to live like you lot. But I remember my father and he wasn't at all like them and somehow I just did not seem to fit in. They treated me differently to the other children. I did try."

"You deliberately went out of your way to defy them. Of course they treated you differently, but only because you would not keep the rules. If the others could, why not you?"

"I did not know the rules: I did not know them: how could I keep them?" she felt the tears come to her eyes.

"Don't expect to get sympathy by crying. That old trick won't work with me. You are the most ungrateful person I have ever known."

"Just because you are a Lawmaker and a man, does not make you a better person than me. You call me ungrateful. What about you? You expect all we women to keep your silly rules and your cruel outlook on all we do."

"We care for our women folk. The rules are there to keep them from harm, but you would not realise that because you have not even thought of what we men do for you."

"What you do for us – now I've heard everything. Why are you dressed in that fancy get-up. Is that supposed to be for us, too?"

"Yes – I was instructing a class in self-defence if you must know. Your stupid action interrupted that class."

"Good – I am glad it did."

"You are glad. You are always thinking of yourself. I had to leave a class of youngsters to come to see to you."

"So, I am not important enough to warrant any help, but this way tells you I mean to get some, even if your stupid class is brought to an end."

"Well, I have come. Here I am – and I mean to see that you never do anything like that again."

She backed away from him, not sure what he was going to do. "How?"

"By making you promise to behave yourself."

"Oh – and if I won't?"

"There are ways and means of making you obey," he retorted grimly.

"I bet there are – you are just like the rest of the – a bully and coward."

He slapped her hard across the face. "Nobody calls me that and gets away with it – let alone you!"

She lurched backwards in surprise, fell over a stool and landed on the floor. She sat there looking at him.

"Get up, get up. Do not pretend that you are even hurt. I know the tricks you play, the Elders have told me all about you." He bent down and grabbed her by her arm and pulled her to her feet.

"Let go. Let go, Medrix, you are hurting me."

"Good. I am glad it hurts," and he tightened his hold.

She kicked out at him hard and he released her.

"You little devil. That's the sort of thing I would expect from you. Well, we don't allow such behaviour from our women," and he hit her again. Luckily he missed her face but got her shoulder.

The pain shot up into her head and down her arm and, losing her balance, she fell against the table.

The jug of chen slithered across the table and on to the floor, spilling its contents everywhere.

The tray hovered on the brink. She picked it up and sent it spinning in his direction. It caught him in the chest.

For a moment he was knocked off balance but, grabbing his whip, he came for her.

He slashed it down hard across her back and legs. She let out a cry of agony.

He raised the whip again and brought it down again.

She fell forward but somehow managed to crawl out of the way as it came down again.

She made a great effort, got to her feet and, as he again raised the whip, turned towards him grabbed the whip as it came down yet again, and held on for dear life, the leather cutting her hands and sending blood trickling down her arms.

"Let go," he commanded. "Let go now."

She held on, her whole weight stopping him from raising it again.

He let go and she spun across the room with the force of it and landed by the wall.

"You have to learn that we Lawmaker men are in charge here, not the likes of you. What we say and do counts. You have to learn that you are nothing – you are nothing compared with us. Do you hear me?" he bellowed: "YOU ARE NOTHING. Now I hope you have learnt this lesson; that people like you have to give in to us before you will ever get any help from us. We cannot put up with your defiance any more. Do you hear me? Do you? You have to give in to me and then, only then, will we get along. Do you understand me? Do you?"

"I don't want any help from you. I don't want you as my Counsellor – go and tell your Elders that. You are not in charge – they are. You are only their puppet," she yelled at him.

"Then you are only asking for more punishment until you learn," he said slowly, almost sadly.

She picked up the whip and started to flick it backwards and forwards. He watched her warily.

She stared at him, almost daring him to attack her again. Defiance shone in those blue eyes. She said nothing.

He had never encountered any woman who would retaliate in the way she had. He knew that he had strength on his side, but he had expected her to plead for mercy before this.

He saw her swollen face, blood-marked arms and fair hair turning blood-red in parts. He remembered how she had challenged those Lawmakers long ago and how nothing they did had made her give up, and he felt a wave of guilt coming over him for the brutality of his actions.

Yet the Elders had warned him about her. About all the trouble she had given them and he knew he was justified and maybe if she had been taken in hand all those years ago, he would not be in this situation now.

Still she stared at him like some cornered animal, and he knew how dangerous that could be.

His anger lessened a little and he tried another tack. "Stop now, Cessie, there's no need to go on like this."

She listened but she did not utter a word.

"It's all over now. I know you were never a real Lawmaker and do not act like one," he softened his voice, almost pleading with her.

She half-smiled at him then looked at the whip in her hands.

"Put the whip down, Cess. Put it down now."

But she still held on to it. It was almost as if she was in some kind of trance. Perhaps she was long past the stage when she knew what was happening.

He stepped to one side and it was then that she acted.

She ran forward with the whip held in both hands, then raising it high, she brought it down hard on his legs.

He stepped out of its way, but not before it caught him on his ankle; only the protection of his boot saved him from any damage. Yet pain shot up his leg.

She turned and went for him again, but he managed to get around the back of her and grabbed both her hands. She tried to get free, but couldn't. She suddenly relaxed back against him and let go of the whip, kicking backwards as she did so. Her breath came in great gasps. He held her firmly and she did not struggle.

"It's over now," he said softly.

Tiredness and pain throbbed through her whole being. She knew that without his support she would fall.

"I'll have to give in, I suppose," she thought. "I cannot fight them all. I will have to give in and never fight anyone again, for what is the use if I cannot win – I cannot fight them all. I am only one against them all." She put her hands over his and tried to get him to release her.

"Let go," she said in a dull voice.

"Is this some new plan of yours?"

"No," she whispered.

"If I do are you going to fight me again?"

"NO – I can see it is no use – nothing is any more. There's nothing for me any more. Please … let me go. I promise I will be no trouble any more to anyone here. I promise to do what you want."

"Are you saying that you give in to us ... to me?"

"Yes, Medrix," tiredness echoed in her voice, but she thought to herself, "I must find a way of escape from this awful place."

"Do you promise to keep our Laws?"

"Yes, I will try. I promise I will try."

He let her go. She swayed without his support and she found herself falling.

He picked her up bodily and carried her to her bed. She lay there in a kind of stupor.

"Cessie," he said softly.

But she was too far gone to hear him and just lay there.

He looked at her. He should feel good now that he had won. He always had before. Brute force always gave him a feeling of power, but not this time. For some strange reason he felt he had lost out: something had changed in his life and he was not sure that he liked it.

He sat on a chair and looked at her. She never moved or tried to speak. Her face was white but was turning purple where he had hit her. He bent over her and whispered her name, but she did not answer him.

He realised that he could not just leave her there like that. He bent down and picked her up and carried her over to the Medical Centre.

The doctor came to meet him in the hallway. "This is the one that pressed the button and caused all that trouble. I can see she has been punished for her stupid act. Leave her with me now. She will have every care, in spite of what she has done. I will send a report into the Elders and I expect they will contact you about it all. Make sure you put in a report as well. I will contact her Lawmother for you."

Medrix went back to his quarters, satisfied that he had done the right thing by not leaving her in the Holding Centre.

Much later Cessie woke up to find her Lawmother sitting beside her. She felt terrible – but more so because now she hadn't got a Counsellor. She decided to write a note to Medrix begging him to forgive her – that would make him think he had in fact won a victory over her; after all she had promised to obey him. Then she could see if she could escape from here somehow.

She wrote:

Medrix,

I am really sorry I argued with you yesterday and as I have promised to obey you and the rules, wonder if you could still be my Counsellor, in spite of everything.

I am your obedient servant.

Celisia M Mantrex

Her Lawmother took the note for her.

The next morning, she awoke to see him standing beside the bed.

"Thank you," he said stiffly, "for your note. I will stay as your Counsellor. At least we have more time now. But don't do it again."

He did not tell her that the Elders were furious with him for delaying the trial and had decreed he should still be her Counsellor.

Cessie smiled as he walked away. She was back on course again. Let him think of her as the one who had given in – he had a lot to learn had that one.

Chapter 2

Medrix came to get her on the day of her release from the Medical Centre. He told her that a house had been lent to them for the duration of the trial. She had a sitting room, bedroom and washroom for herself, on the ground floor. Lawmother Kella (her Lawmother) and Lawmother Grey had rooms on the next floor and he had the whole of the top floor. They were to share the kitchen/sitting room which was on the ground floor. They could sit in the garden. She was not to wear Chetner clothes – but new Lawmother outfits were to be found in her clothes cupboard. She was to do all the household jobs for all of them and to cook an evening meal. An extra Lawmaker had been assigned to her case. His name was Eldon and he usually worked in the maintenance office. She was not on any account to go out on her own – but she could go out with the Lawmothers, or Eldon or himself – in the evenings only. All of them went out to work during the day. That meant she would be on her own most of the day – but the house being big would keep her busy. The date of her trial would be fixed at the next Elders' meeting which would take place as soon as the Grand Elder returned. She was away attending meetings elsewhere and could not be reached.

Cessie liked her rooms and settled in easily. She did all the work and cooked them a meal. Some evenings she went out on short trips. Medrix never took her, nor did he discuss her case – and so she just had to wait for him to tell her what he was doing: she thought he was avoiding her purposely.

One morning as she was cleaning a window, she saw a group of women, all carrying baskets and talking together. They walked down the road and disappeared from view. The next morning she saw them again and then she had a great idea. Tomorrow she would join them. She had seen a basket on a high shelf in the kitchen. She would need money. She had only Chetner notes, but in the kitchen cupboard was a cashbox. She took out two notes; when she could change her notes she would put them back.

The next morning she was waiting for them. They nodded and smiled at her and she joined them – wherever they went she would also go. She felt excited at the prospect.

They went to a closed market and queued up at a baker's stall. He filled their baskets and hers. She handed him a note and he gave her some change. When she turned round all the others had gone. She went out of the market and began to walk back. How was she going to explain all this extra bread? A man came up to her and said, "I'll have a small loaf please." She gave it to him and he gave her ten creds for it and walked away. Then an old woman stopped her and bought two loaves and gave her twenty creds. She soon realised that the women were no ordinary Lawmothers – in fact they were bread sellers.

When she arrived back – she discovered that she had made a profit.

The next morning she was again ready and waiting for them and again she made a profit. On the third day she took her bread basket to the shuttle bay and sold no end of small loaves. She also picked up free timetables, maps and photographs. When she got back she hid them under her mattress. The next day they did not come – but on the next, there they were again and she joined them once more. She had decided to go to the money office to change her notes – she would pretend that she cleaned the house for the Chetner woman and had agreed to get the money for her. All went well and as she came out of the office people crowded around her to buy bread. She could see a Law Enforcement Officer coming her way. She turned away – (now her basket was almost empty) and bumped into a man who had come up behind her.

"Sorry," she said, "I didn't see you," and then she realised it was Medrix.

He said grimly, "Smile at me while I am talking – I'll have that loaf now." He took the loaf and put ten creds into her basket. "Come this way quickly, no questions – just follow me." The Law Enforcement Officer was almost up to them as she followed him into a nearby house. He shut the door with a slam. He led her through the house and out the back. "Leave the basket here," – she did so. They came out onto another road and he took her arm and walked swiftly up the road. "Smile while I am talking to you – you have had a lucky escape." She smiled, nodding her head, "just wait though until we get back. I suppose you didn't know you have to have a permit to sell bread?"

"No … you see I thought they were Lawmothers who were just going shopping and …"

"You soon discovered they were not, but decided to use them as cover. Am I right? Smile when you answer me." He kept his voice low.

"Yes," she smiled. "Will this smile do?" She felt like kicking him.

"Very good – quite the little actress aren't you. Now here we are." He opened the door and she went in. He slammed the door and pushed her so roughly into the sitting room that she almost fell.

"You … are – a … devious, … sly – little vixen. So nice to me when I am here, but as soon as I go out – you are slipping out somewhere on – your – own." He emphasised the words angrily. "Stand over there – with your back to the wall." He pointed to the wall near the window.

She did so.

"I thought you promised to obey me?"

"Yes," she whispered fearfully.

"I told you not to go out alone."

"I wasn't alone – I was with all those people."

"You know what I mean – you twist things to suit yourself. Where did you get the money to shop?"

"I borrowed it …"

"From where?"

"From the cashbox in the kitchen. I will put it back. I have at last been able to change my Chetner money to …"

"If you took money without permission – that – is – stealing."

"No – I have the money here," she held up a couple of notes.

"Give it to me."

She counted out the money owing and gave it to him.

"All your money – give me all your money – now … please."

"But it is mine! No Medrix – that's not fair – this is mine!"

"You won't be needing it," he snatched her purse from her and put it in his pocket.

"Now who is stealing?" she said angrily. He ignored the question.

"The Elders told me you were sly. I can see it for myself now. In this house we are all people who do not mix with bread sellers … and you – Celisia – bring shame to this house."

"Arrogant pig," she thought – but she never said a word.

"Lawmaker Eldon told me this morning that he thought he saw you in the shuttle bay yesterday. But as you were selling bread he thought he was mistaken. How wrong he was – wasn't he? You thought you could stow away – escape our clutches – is that what you thought?"

"Yes – maybe … and you would have done the same in my situation."

"Yes … I would *BUT* the difference is; I wouldn't get caught."

She just looked at him. Someone should give him hell – and why not her? But she never said a word.

"What you really need is a good whipping," he touched the top of the whip in his belt.

"But you won't do that," she said quickly, "because that would delay the trial again and nobody wants that – do they? Not even you?"

"Quite right – the sooner you are out of my life – the better – but in the meantime, you will be locked in your rooms when no one is in the house. When someone is here you can do all your usual jobs. There will be no evening trips out for fourteen days, and as soon as there is an Elders' meeting I will ask them to transfer you to the Holding Centre – where you will be guarded night and day."

"When is the next meeting?"

"When the Grand Elder returns – she cannot be reached at the moment."

He ran upstairs to his rooms. She sighed – it could have been worse, she supposed – at least she still had the timetable and the photographs. Something would turn up in her favour she was sure.

In the evening – she was sitting down for a meal which she had cooked, when he said.

"Don't sit with us. We don't want a bread seller here. Go in the kitchen until we finish."

She picked up her plate. "Leave it there – until we've finished."

Lawmother Grey intervened, "The dinner will be cold then."

"So what? Leave it, Celisia. Go in the kitchen now."

She went – and waited in the kitchen. She had promised to obey him – she could do it, if she tried.

Much later on she went to clear up. She looked at her dinner – and scraped it into the other leftover scraps – she wasn't hungry any more.

Then getting a tray – she piled it high with everything and made her way into the kitchen. She never saw the book someone had left on the floor, by the long seat, and she caught her foot on it and fell headlong. The sound of the crashing tray and china echoed through the house.

Gingerly she sat up – she began to cry – the shock of the suddenness of it all made her heart race, and she began to tremble. She comforted herself – as if speaking to a child.

"No bones broken – only the cups – bruises yes – but they will go – now sit on the long seat – there's no rush – sit – just sit a while – no need to cry …"

"Are you all right?" Medrix was standing beside her.

"Yes … I tripped over something. She reached down and picked up a large book – the title of which was *Trials on Sport* – it was a law book. She shook her head. He sighed.

"You should look where you are going – you should put less on the tray."

"Yes," …

"Stay there I'll get you a coffee."

He brought her a coffee and she drank it. He began to pick up the things and take them to the kitchen, until everything was cleared. He even washed the floor where the coffee had spilled. He brought her some bread and cheese and an apple. "Eat this later. Now stand up," she did so – "go to bed now – can you manage?"

"Yes – thank you". She went into her rooms. She could hear him going upstairs.

The next days were different for all of them. Cessie did no work at all. On the first day, apart from getting food and drink for herself, she stayed in bed all day. She was very sore and had a headache. The next day she got up but only saw to herself. He came to her in the evening to enquire when she was going to do the work. She told him she was not interested in the house or the work that went with it. When he insisted – all she said was – "What are you going to do? Hit me? The Lawmaker's way of solving problems? The only thing I am interested in is my case – perhaps as my Counsellor you will tell me about that."

But all he did was walk away in disgust, saying: "The Elders told me you could be difficult – I can see they are right

So the days went on. The home looked uncared for – he slept in an unmade bed. The Lawmothers did not do it for him. Soon he ran out of clean clothes and had to wear them twice over. He asked his mother to help out – but surprisingly she refused.

The door was locked every time she was left in the house alone – and she seemed happy enough. He made it worse one day by telling her that her punishment would go on for another six days as she was not obeying the rules. All she said was "If you like," and walked away from him.

Then one evening he called her into his study. He was furious about something. He accused her of using his computer. But she told him that she hadn't touched it. Then suddenly she started to laugh. "You've got odd socks on."

"Better that than no socks," he said grimly, "that's all I can find. Don't laugh woman. What have you done with them then?"

She laughed again. "I haven't seen them. Where did you put them?"

"I didn't put them anywhere, damn you Cessie."

"Well if you didn't put them anywhere, you won't find them will you. Don't you ever laugh Medrix?" She grinned.

"Damn you to hell, Cessie – I am trying to work on your case. You are no help at all. You disobey me. You do not do the household jobs. People will think I cannot control what goes on here. I have to go on living here after this trial. My life has been turned upside down by you. You are a devious, sly, thieving little pest and I shall be glad when you have gone from here. Go on laugh then – but if you lose your case – it is because you do not care for anyone but yourself."

She was serious at once, then said: "Is my Lawmaker losing control of the situation here? I thought you were trained to deal with every situation. But I can see you are not. Go downstairs, Medrix, and make us some coffee and I will see what I can do here to help."

"Are you giving me orders now? Have you forgotten where you are? Or why you are here? You are not here to give ME orders" he said sarcastically.

"I know why I am here Medrix," she took a clean pair of socks out of her pocket. "I'll give you these in exchange." She held them up high. He made a grab for them; she dodged out of the way.

"Hell cat. Where did you get those?"

"Coffee – Medrix," she laughed.

"Oh all right." He went downstairs grumbling and swearing and a few minutes later returned with the coffee. She gave him the socks.

"I have a clean shirt in my room."

"What have I got to do to get that?" he said sulkily.

"Help me make your bed – go on the other side of the bed, Lawmaker and…"

He went and, listening to her instructions, they made the bed together.

"The shirt – now please."

"Later – I haven't finished sewing the buttons," she smiled up at him and reaching up to him she kissed him. "Oh Lawmaker mine – I love you." Then laughing – she went downstairs taking the dirty cups with her.

He stood there. What did she say? Oh no – not another complication! The damn girl is running circles round me – what did she mean love me – she can't love me – she hates Lawmakers – or does she? He switched on the computer and began working, muttering to himself. "Damn the little pest – what will she say or do next? Why is the Grand Elder delaying this trial? I thought they were in a hurry for it. Once she goes – what a relief – life can return to normal … just get her out of my life once and for all."

Suddenly he realised that she was standing behind him, she must have heard everything.

"There's a note here saying you have to attend an Elders' meeting tomorrow."

He turned round – now she wasn't laughing. "I'll sew these buttons on for you now," she said softly, "and pack my things up ready to move to the Holding Centre."

As she left the room he suddenly felt he wanted to hold her in his arms and tell her everything was going to be all right. He shook his head – what was the matter with him? This is what he wanted, to be rid of her once and for all. Tomorrow he would know the date. "Oh Hell and damn, I am going to miss the little pest."

At the Elders' meeting he learned that the trial was in five days time. His job, they told him, was to see that she lost. They had blocked all pictures going out to various planets which described the magician. Witnesses from Chetner had not been granted safe passage and they themselves were to be the judges. All he had to do was to make it look as if he was defending her. He argued with them about the judges – but they said it was quite legal. The town Elders had every right to try criminals. He was well paid by them – so he would not suffer in any way.

Walking back to the house, he felt sick at the thought of telling her the trial date. He felt sorry for her. She hadn't a chance in hell of being found innocent. Even if she was a pest – she did not deserve this treatment. She was one person against them all.

He told her as soon as he got back.

"At last I know. I have been so afraid – and now I am petrified. I may have acted as if I don't care – but deep down I do." Tears flowed down her face.

"Hey" – he said gently, "we are in this together." He put his arms round her and drew her close. "You are not alone – you have me." He bent down and kissed her on the forehead. "Why don't you and Lawmother Grey go shopping tomorrow. I'll give you your money – and maybe Lawmaker Eldon can take you to see a game."

She pulled away from him. She was not sure if she trusted him. "When am I to go to the Holding Centre?"

"I never asked for the transfer. I can't be running over there all day. I am needed here now and you know where my socks are." He laughed softly – "and your door will be unlocked from now on."

She thanked him and went to unpack her things.

Did she know how mean he felt? Did she know he was in the Elders' pay? Did she know she couldn't win?

Cessie stood in her sitting room – looking out of the window – they would both need a miracle to win this case – she had to trust him. Who else was there? Over the days of the trial maybe new witnesses could be found. Just maybe someone would recognise those pictures of the magician that Medrix had sent everywhere. She shivered – only time would tell.

Chapter 3

The next day Medrix heard that the Grand Elder had died in the night. She had taken an overdose of sleeping tablets. It was suicide. The trial was again postponed until a new Grand Elder was appointed.

When he told Cessie, she was shocked and stared at him white faced.

"My grandmother is dead!"

"No, Ces – the Grand Elder not your grandmother."

"My grandmother was the Grand Elder! When my mother died she had me brought to the city."

"What about your father?"

"She said that he was dead – but I knew he would come for me one day – because he said so – and he gave me a locket! She gave me a new father but my father was still alive!"

"Who was your new father then?"

"Lawmaker Vendon – he is – was a vile man. I lived in hell from that day on."

"I suppose you wouldn't keep the rules and he punished you," he said grimly.

"I didn't know the rules – I was brought up to behave well. My father – real father saw to that – but stepfather ... he was ... " Tears ran down her cheeks.

"Was what?"

"Cruel, vicious – always punishing me. I hated him."

"But the Elders say you were rude, sly and lazy since day one."

"I tried hard – I tried hard. At last she has done something good for me – at last."

"She gave you food, an education, clothed you."

"Yes – but she didn't give me the thing that all children, all people need ..."

"What's that Ces?"

"Love – she didn't give me love. Exiling me from the city was a good thing for me – and then she brought me here for a trial."

"I expect she was outvoted."

"We will never know – Medrix," she bent her head and cried.

"Sit down," he said quietly – "sit there while I get you a coffee." She sat on the long seat and he went to make her a drink. He brought it back and sat beside her.

"You were the victim here, Cessie, don't upset yourself." He put his arm around her and kissed her wet face. "I think she took all those tablets for a reason."

"What reason? What reason?" she sobbed.

"So that you would have more time – she knew, Ces, that to appoint a new Grand Elder would take time – she knew that."

"Yes – I hope it works for me ... for us ... "

"So do I, love, so do I."

From that day on Medrix spent every day with her, asking her questions, questions, questions. Sometimes she cried and cried but he was there comforting her; other times she laughed and was happy.

Lawmaker Eldon wrote copious notes and discussed her case with them. Some days Medrix took her out on picnics, or walks to the beach, or to visit friends but all the time the questions went on. But now she began to relax with him and they were often seen together laughing at some private joke. She knew that now he was just like the friend she knew all that time ago, yet she knew she felt more than that. Did he feel it too? But she must remember how cruel he could be and that he was a Lawmaker. But even so – she enjoyed being with him. One day he took her to see his grandfather, who made a great fuss of her and made her laugh and on another occasion she met his parents and they all had coffee together.

"If only!" she thought, "if only she wasn't here for a trial and this was a holiday – then something else might happen ... oh God was she falling for this man? But there was no future there for her – so why didn't her mind accept this fact. Did he feel the way she did? You couldn't tell with him. This Lawmaker was a great mixture and she knew it – but still – enjoy it while you can," she said to herself, for one day, she would only have memories left. "Yes," she said to herself, "enjoy what little time you have left."

A few days later the news spread that a Grand Elder had been appointed. He was coming from their sister plant Jadeston. He would take up his appointment in three days' time. A great picnic was to be held in one of the fields and every adult was welcome. Medrix offered to take her and she accepted his invitation on condition that he asked Eldon to invite her Lawmother, as she was sure she liked him. Medrix called her "little nosey match-maker", but he was laughing when he said it!

During the days leading up to the picnic the women worked on their clothes; long pretty skirts, white embroidered tops, bonnets with pretty ribbons were all prepared. Cessie adapted one of her skirts and she embroidered flowers on to her white top. She decided to wear a bonnet, making it out of cotton material, embroidered it with flowers and sequins. Her Lawmother was amazed to see such beautiful work. "On Chetner everything has to be done by hand, no one is going to do it for us."

The evening arrived and the women were all dressed up in their finery. The men joined them; both were dressed in a dark-violet colour, over which were embroidered short-sleeved jackets. They wore sandal-type shoes, which had silver buckles. They looked very fine in their outfits.

Everyone walked to the field as it wasn't far.

The field was very large. It had a campfire in one part, around which were benches. People were gathered in groups, some singing, some reciting. The men drank a kind of beer out of big glasses and the women had wine from small ones. They stayed a little while there. Medrix sang a song that she thought she had heard before. He had a lovely tenor voice. Then they went round the decorated stalls and bought a few things. Medrix won a large bear and gave it to Cessie. Then they went to the refreshment tent. They ate great moon-shaped biscuits and drank warm soup out of wooden bowls. Cessie saw three Elders in the tent and they stared at her. She looked away. A tall grim-looking man joined them and she asked Medrix who he was, and was told that that was the Prosecutor. She shivered and Medrix hurried her away from there to the dance area.

She liked dancing with him. He was very good at it.

She told him that he should dance with someone else because people were staring at them. So he did for a while then he came back to her. Suddenly a messenger stopped them. They were wanted in the Elders' tent at once.

Both Eldon and Kella were already there. Three of the Elders were there also. One of the Elders spoke out. "I cannot think, Medrix, why you have brought her here. This is our celebration, for our people, not for the likes of her. She is a disgrace to her sex and is not welcome here."

Another Elder went on, "I think, Medrix, you cannot be in your right mind to bring her here, where all decent people gather."

Cessie turned pale and said, "Don't worry I will go for I do not like all the company here either. I will certainly go. I do not want to upset anybody else. Medrix, will you bring my bear home?"

"I have every right to bring her," Medrix said quietly.

"She is to go now," the Elder went on. "You, Medrix will stay here. If you do not you will no longer be her Counsellor."

"Stay, Medrix, stay. All of you stay and enjoy your celebration. I am a little tired so will go now." She moved away from them.

"She must not go back on her own," Eldon said kindly.

"Yes she can. She will come to no harm. Let the little witch go back on her own, then she will know who rules here."

Cessie was furious. She turned and walked back to them and said in a loud voice to the three of them. "This witch curses the ground you stand upon. May it open up and swallow you. May the wind blow and the rain pour down so that you are flooded out." She pointed at each of them in turn. "As I have decreed so let it be."

She ran across the field and out on to the track. She knew she should not have cursed them but at least it got rid of her anger. One look at their faces was enough.

The three Elders looked aghast. "See what we mean," said one, "best leave the little devil alone. Don't be tempted to go after her. It will do her good to go back alone."

After a while Cessie knew she had come the wrong way. In her anger she had gone through the wrong gate. It was very dark; trees stood thickly in her way. The ground began to shake beneath her feet, and opened up in front of her. She ran back towards the field, but cracks seemed to be opening up everywhere. She jumped over them, willing herself to get over and past them. The track led to a lake. Water swirled and spurted high into the air.

"It's an earthquake. They will think I did it."

She ran along the path around the lake. The track led up a hill. She followed it, up, up, up she went. Here the ground was still. She looked back towards the field and saw great flames shooting up into the sky. She prayed that everyone was all right. They would now see her as someone who could work magic; lay curses that came true. It couldn't be true; she could not do things like that, but everyone who heard her curse would believe it. It was best for them all if she did not get back at all and best for her too. She would find a way off this planet if it killed her.

Down in the field panic spread. The ground under the fire cracked open and it quickly spread across the whole area. The refreshment tent fell with a crash to the ground and the Elders had to be rescued as the ground cracked open at their feet. The sky went black, a wind whipped up and as they all rushed for the specially-built shelters, it began to rain. It was so heavy that it flooded the roads around the city.

When it was deemed safe they all went home. But Lawmother Kella was in tears. "I cannot find her. She's not here. I have looked everywhere. We will have to send a search party out for her, Medrix."

Medrix stood there. He was angry. "No. It happened as she said. She is a conniving little witch. She cursed them and it happened. My God, she *can* do magic, the Elders are right; she will find her own way back, or perhaps not, maybe she will stay away from us. We do not want her back. She has turned my life upside down. Now perhaps life can go back to normal."

"Medrix, you can't believe that," Eldon interrupted. "It's just a coincidence that it happened. We do have earthquakes; you only have to read about the history of our planet."

"No search party, Eldon. Leave it. It is better this way."

"You can't leave her out there on her own. That girl thinks the world of you. You cannot do this. Please send out a search party to find her."

"No. I have said 'No'. I will report her missing and that is all I will do."

The Elders did nothing. "The little witch will find her own way back. Let the new Grand Elder decide what to do," was all they said.

At night Medrix could not sleep. The house seemed empty without her. Her things lay everywhere; her sketches, her embroidery all waited for her. When he did sleep he saw her laughing and happy. One time he had a nightmare that she was falling down a crack and shouting for help. He woke up in a sweat.

After that he left the house and moved in with his grandfather. He could not settle to anything. His grandfather said: "How could you do that to her? She loves you or didn't you know that. You have only got to look at her when your name is mentioned. God, man, how can you leave her out there?"

"She has fooled you as well. The Elders have told me she will pretend to love in order to get her own way. I nearly fell for that, but I am a Lawmaker and can get over it."

"Once you were different, Medrix, but after you were trained by those Elders you became a different person. A person I do not like very much and I hope and pray that one day the Medrix I knew will come back before it is too late. Anyway, when she does come back you will still have to defend her, or are you going to rig the trial so that she loses. That is what the Elders want you to do, isn't it? That is why you are in their pay. Don't look at me like that. You know I know that you work for them. But I thought her love for you would change all that. But I can see I was wrong. You are the mean, stern Lawmaker that accepts bribes in order to make money. If you rig that trial, you will never be welcome here again for she is the one bright spark in all our lives, only you cannot see it. By all means stay here but stay out of my way."

Medrix sighed and went back to the single men's quarters. His life was a muddle and he grieved for her in his own way.

Ces carried on up the hill. The track seemed to go on and on. "It must lead somewhere," she said out aloud. The ground shuddered under her feet and she quickened her pace. It began to rain. Great drops, falling faster and faster and a wind whipped up. The noise was deafening but she still went on. In no time at all she was soaked. She came to a shepherd's hut. It was empty but she did not stop for the whole place shook. She felt safer outside. Sheer terror kept her going.

Then the rain stopped, the wind died and the shuddering stopped. The moon stood out clearly. Everywhere was still; dampness rose causing a shroud-like mist everywhere.

She slowed her pace, her wet skirt weighing her down. Tiredness seeped into her body. She rounded the next bend and found that the track led on to a narrow, wooden bridge. It was held up on both sides by thick ropes attached to metal posts. Rope-woven walls ran the whole length of it. She looked at it and then looked back. There really was not much choice for her. She stepped on to the bridge and, holding onto the rope walls, started to walk across it. The boards were slippery under her feet. Halfway across she looked down. The space below her fell away into a very deep gorge. Suddenly fear caught at her and she stood there too afraid to move. The wind whipped up again, swinging the bridge to and fro. The movement jolted her out of the panic she had felt and she hurried across. The bridge creaked and groaned as the wind attacked it with such force, that every moment felt like her last. Then the whole bridge began to shake so she ran across the last bit and jumped on to the bank, grabbing the metal post for dear life.

A steep path wound up the hill in front of her and she left the safety of the post and started up the hill.

Then she was on a flat piece of land. She turned to see the way she had come. She saw the bridge break away from the other bank and swing back and forth with such force that it broke away from the post and disappeared from view. She shivered, staring at where the bridge had been.

Now she had to go on – there was no other choice. The path must lead somewhere. The path twisted and turned through giant rocks until it came out on to a flat piece of land on which was built a large grey stone building, standing like some fortress guarding the planet.

She walked up to the two heavy doors and pulled the bell rope. The clanging noise echoed back at her. A small panel was slid open. "Who is there?" said a gruff voice.

"I am seeking shelter from an earthquake," she shouted back and the wind seemed to whip her voice away so that she wondered if he had heard.

The big door opened and someone pulled her in. She heard it close behind her.

She stood in a darkened courtyard. A man, roughly clad, held up a lantern to look at her.

"Come this way," he said, not unkindly, and led her into a warm and well-lighted room. Standing by an enormous fireplace was a man and two Lawmothers. The servant left her there.

"Well, who have we got here?" the man spoke softly.

"I … there was an earthquake … I got lost … parted from my … the others … and I followed a path that led me here."

"You will have come over the swinging bridge … so tomorrow, after you have rested, you can go back that way."

"No … no, there is no bridge. It broke away, just after I crossed it."

"Well then you are stuck here, until our lift is repaired, aren't you?"

"We don't often get visitors here," one of the women said.

"No," said the other one with a laugh, "well not the type you are anyway."

"Why?"

"No one wants to come here." He laughed and the women joined in with him. "Welcome, my dear young woman, to Jailfa Island Prison."

"What?" she stared at him in horror. "I thought it was an island in the sea."

He roared with laughter. "No … here we are perched high on Jailfa Rock

… deep gorges all round … we are in fact a kind of island. We get cut off from time to time but otherwise earthquakes don't seem to affect us."

"Now," said one of the women. "She is proper worn out, better she go and bathe, have some food and go to bed." She led Cessie out of the room and took her to a tower bedroom and left her to herself. Cessie had a shower. Food was brought up on a tray and after she had eaten, she went to bed and fell asleep at once.

Late the next morning she woke to find the sun streaming through the window. A servant had left her a tray of food. One of the women came in and asked how she was and brought a clean Lawmother's outfit in for her.

"Now, my dear, my name is Seena. My sister, whom you saw yesterday, is Lynna. What is your name?"

"Margaret … my name is Margaret," she said quickly, hoping the woman did not know already.

"Are you married, dear?"

"No – I am staying at a Lawmaker's house."

"If you tell me his name, we will notify him as soon as the lines are repaired. He must be very worried."

"His name is Lawmaker Medrix."

"Oh, someone important. Do not worry, we will let him know as soon as possible. Have a good rest now. Get up when you like."

Later that day she went downstairs. They were all in the sitting room.

The man was there, talking to one of the guards but as soon as she came into the room he went out.

The jailer smiled at her and said "We are honoured to have the friend of such an important Lawmaker with us. Every comfort will be given to you as befits you. Are you a relation or his betrothed?" She shook her head and laughed at the thought.

"Ah, you don't know much about him then, my dear. I don't like to say it but that man is a very devious person. Likes his own way. We have many prisoners here who have fallen foul of him. But that, of course, won't affect you, my dear, unless you cross him. Just a friendly warning, that is all."

"Thank you for telling me."

"Good. I do not want to cause trouble, but I know a thing or two about that Lawmaker. Ah, but there I go again. I must not run him down to you. I thought you would like to look around my prison … my work place … as I say, we don't get many visitors here. When you go back mention my two precious daughters, Seena and Lynna, for they are of marriageable age and who can they meet up here?"

She nodded and he seemed pleased that she wanted to see his prison, although she had not said so.

He led her into the main section. There were lines and lines of small cells, each with two women in them. They were chained to the walls and looked

66

underfed and hollow-eyed. Then he took her down some steps. Here the cells were bigger and housed up to six prisoners, all chained like the others. Then he took her down to the dungeons. The people who have offended the Elders were kept here. There were six to a cell. She felt the coldness of the place seep into her. This is where she would live out her life. The prisoners sat on the floor, mumbling to themselves.

"We lost a lot of prisoners owing to the fever. My dear wife nursed them but without necessary supplies it was hopeless. She caught the fever and died and I am lost without her. But these things happen and you have to get over it as well as you can." He sighed. "And here, my dear, is a new cell. Just for one this time. The Elders had it cut out of the rock about five moons ago. It is for a prisoner from another planet. She cheated them using magic, or so they say, but I know better. They are out for revenge. It will go through the courts, all right and proper, and she will land up here, poor thing. The Elders will have their way; they always do."

"But Medrix is defending her in court, he will get her off."

"Oh, my dear, you have a lot to learn about him. He is in the pay of the Elders. Whatever they want he gets for them and they want her."

She shivered. But he went on. "He's clever that one, he will seem to be doing the right thing for her, but that is his way. He will even pretend to be in love with her so that she is lulled into the trap. No, she has no chance. She will have two prosecutors at her trial. I wouldn't let my daughters near him."

She felt faint and held on to his arm. He saw how pale she was and took her back to the others.

The days went on and she rested. Played cards in the evenings and got to know his two daughters.

Two weeks later Medrix learned where she was and he went to get her and bring her back. She would hardly look at him, even when he spoke to her she turned away. She was very subdued with everyone and sat for long hours staring into space. The doctor said she was suffering from shock.

Medrix and Cessie were called to a meeting for the next morning. When he told her, she just sighed and said: "At last, I have waited long enough." Then she went into her room and cried. He left her, did not try to comfort her, but he was very troubled at her condition. She would not really be fit enough for the days ahead but there was nothing he could do.

Chapter 4

The morning arrived and they both went to the meeting of which the new Grand Elder was in charge. All the other Elders were there also. The Grand Elder thanked them for coming and was pleased that she had come back to face her trial. Ces stared at her feet and took no notice of him or the others.

"Now then," said the Grand Elder, "we must get on with the business in hand. What is your full name?"

She did not look up or say anything.

"Cessie, he is talking to you," Medrix whispered.

"Oh. My name is Celisia Margaret … Mantrex."

"What is your address?" She looked at Medrix then looked away.

"City One, Chetner."

"Name of next of kin?"

"Father: Andrew Mantrex. My mother is dead."

"How do you plead?" She did not answer. He repeated the question. She stared at each member of the Council sitting there; they shifted in their seats uneasily. "How do you plead?" She did not reply. "If you say you are guilty then we will not go on with the trial and you will go to the House of Correction until your sentence is fixed by this Council. But if you choose to plead Not Guilty then of course the trial will go ahead. Do you understand everything now?"

"Yes, thank you."

"So how do you plead?"

She said not a word. Medrix interrupted them, "Grand Elder, I wish to speak to her alone."

"Agreed, take her into my office."

She got up and followed him into the office.

"Why aren't you answering, love?"

She stared at the floor.

"Come on, you have to answer."

The door opened and the Grand Elder called out: "We will see you both tomorrow as we have other business to get on with." Medrix thanked him and looked at Cessie.

"Come on, love, let's go back to my office."

Once at home she made coffee and sat down by the table to drink it.

"Now then, Ces, you have to answer, so what is it?"

"I am pleading Guilty, Medrix."

"You are what? You can't. Must not. Have we come all this way for this?"

"Guilty to all the charges." She looked into her cup.

"But why?" he shook his head, "why?"

"No one will be hurt and I do not care what they do with me. The Chetnerites will not give the trophy back anyway, they would rather die than do so. It will mean war but they will cope with it. And I will cope with prison life. I won't give my answer yet. I will have a few more days freedom then, won't I?"

"Ces – you have to give them an answer straight away; if you do not you will be taken to the market square for a public whipping for insulting the Grand Elder. Do you want that?"

She shook her head – and leaving him she ran to her own sitting room.

He was at a loss what to do. Should he let her do what she wanted? Or try again?

Later Eldon came in and he told him all that had happened.

"You can't let her plead Guilty, Medrix."

"I cannot make her plead otherwise."

"Have you considered why she is pleading Guilty?"

"No."

"Could it be that she does not want anything bad to happen to you?"

Medrix stared at him. "Perhaps she is guilty."

"*You* know she is not. *I* know she is not."

"How do you know Eldon? Do you love her?"

Eldon stared at him. "In a way, yes. She is just like my eldest daughter who died of the fever at Cessie's age. She is young and full of dreams, like my daughter was. She is in shock. First of all she is insulted at the picnic by three Elders who should have known better. In anger she curses them and runs off, only to be caught in an earthquake. How frightened she must have been all on her own. But she survives and her shelter of all places is the very prison where the Elders want to send her. She realises that no search party was sent out and she deduced from that everyone thinks her curse came true and that she caused it and maybe she thinks that too."

"Eldon, you are so wise. What should I have done?"

"You should have at least shown some relief at finding her. You should have held her in your arms, kissed her, told her everything was all right. You should have made love to her; anything to show her that you were on her side. She has a right to have a good defence whatever you think of her. What about Chetner, don't they count for anything? You lived with those people; you know how much help they need. For goodness sake try again, and tell her that you are for her, for her people and, if you love her, tell her that too. She has to plead Not Guilty. Why let those Chetner Elders win?"

But how could he persuade her – now that she had really given up?

After Eldon had gone Medrix sat for ages on the settee. His life was a mess. True he had been trained as an undercover agent by the Elders of Estolan but when the Chetner Elders had asked for a spy he had been sent there. He had found the work easy, the people friendly and he had no trouble at all in fitting in with them. Granted things changed when she came on the scene. He liked her, admired her and despised himself for cheating her, but that was his job. When he came back, the Chetner Elders gradually took over his city and of course he was still employed by them. When he found out about the trial he had been glad it was only to be for a short while. The less he had to do with the business the better. But he had dealt with everything the wrong way, treating her with such harshness that he knocked the fight out of her. His grandfather was right. He was a mean bastard. He was supposed to rig the trial. They expected him to do it. But he knew also that, anyway she really had no chance of being found Not Guilty. Without the magician there was no answer. Maybe it was better her way. But before the picnic they had been so happy, laughing and joking together. He had felt more like the person he had been all those years ago. Then the curse and what happened afterwards had made him believe the Elders. Yet he had grieved for her. It was as if two parts of him were in a fight. She had done that. She had turned his life inside out. The mean, stern Lawmaker who seemingly had it all, hadn't really got anything.

Kella came in. "What's wrong, Medrix?"

"Everything. She wants to plead Guilty."

"You can't let her."

"I know."

"Where is she now?"

"I am here, Lawmother. I was upstairs but I thought I had better get us some food, that's my job isn't it?"

"Cessie, Medrix has told me what you want to do. It isn't right. You are innocent, my dear."

"I know."

"So why?"

"Yes, Cessie, your Lawmother and I want to know the real reason."

"Well, yes I can see that. But I will only tell him, if you don't mind."

"No, my dear, I don't mind. I have some sewing to do. Call me when you have finished." Kella left them.

She sat on a chair by the table. "I will plead Guilty … it is easier this way … you will not have to go through a mock trial for me …"

"A mock trial! What do you mean?"

He stood up and came over to the table.

"You are a man who is in the pay of the Elders … What they want you get for them. To you it does not matter how … it does not matter who gets hurt in the process as long as you get what they want. Those Elders are out for revenge and your job is to get it for them."

"No. No … it is not true."

"You'd even pretend that you are in love with someone if that is the only way you can lull her into the trap."

"No, Cessie, you are wrong. It isn't true."

"Isn't it? It all started when I asked for you. I could tell by your manner that you did not want to help. I was not important enough. Then I protested. And you let me know in no uncertain manner what you really thought of me. But then I asked that you should be my Counsellor. I asked the very one in the matter who could rig the trial. They pointed out that you were on a par with the Prosecutor except that you would not go by the Court rules as he would … I, poor fool believed your loving words, your clever explanations why I should not do this, that and the other. I believed that you would get blamed for the things I did wrong. Again and again I was taken in …"

"Please Cessie … I am not that person now … You have to believe me."

"Believe you, why should I? I saw for myself …"

"Saw? … Saw what, Cessie? Saw what?"

"I saw the inside of the prison. The jailer showed me around. I must say he does quite well considering he has not got enough food to feed all those prisoners properly, nor has he enough guards, so that means the inmates have to stay in their cells always. He has not enough medical supplies. If you catch the fever there, you die, as his wife died there the last time as she tried to nurse them all.

"Then he showed me a new cell … carved out of the rock, just six moons ago. It has a tiny slit window to remind the prisoner of the outside world. This he said was for the prisoner of the next trial. It was such a sure result that the cell had been got ready for her. That prisoner, of course, was to be me. It is waiting for me. The only thing it hasn't got is my name on the door. I am not meant to go free. They know it … you know it … and I know it … and you are the one who is going to put me there and take my life away for ever just because I won a game and they are bad losers. A return match I could understand, but this I cannot."

"I do not know anything about a special cell. I am working hard on your case. If you win, I will be sent for retraining or to work in the mines on our sister planet. Yes I will lose my status as a Lawmaker, but I don't care as long as you get a fair trial. You have to believe me."

"You did not send out a search party for me. You believe I am guilty of causing the earthquake and if you do, so will everyone else. I almost believe it myself."

"I thought you were dead."

"You hoped I was dead then you would not need to conduct my trial."

"No … no …"

"Staying there has made me realise what my life is going to be like. I will be chained to the wall with a metal collar around my neck and chains on my feet to stop me walking far. I shall never see the sun rise over the bay at Chetner or see the wonderful sunsets over the sea. I will be incarcerated in a stone place dripping with damp. The food will be bread and a thin kind of soup. My hair will become infested with lice and my skin encrusted with dirt."

"Oh my God, Cessie, I wouldn't do that to you."

"But I will always remember your kindness, your laughter and the man I might have loved if things had been different."

"But I am working on your case …"

"I know, but without the magician, I cannot prove anything. I am innocent and when I am in that prison I will scratch it on those walls so that everyone will know. If you come there with the Elders to gloat, then you will see it too."

"Don't, Cessie, don't. You make me out as some devil and I am not you know."

"Maybe the Powers-that-be need me to go there to show the others that someone does care for their plight and maybe bring some hope in that dark dank place."

"You are in shock. You cannot believe me to be so merciless."

"To show mercy is something a powerful Lawmaker like you and all the others are not allowed to do. Am I right?"

"Yes."

"I will always find a little room in my heart for you. I will never forget you, for some things will always be with me. But make sure you marry an Estolan girl and have many children; and be sure to call one of your little girls Celisia Margaret and may she be a radiant gem in your life. I do not want to see you degrade yourself by rigging my trial. Once you were my friend, that memory I want to keep. I cannot fight any more and I do not ask for your help for I know you have to obey the Elders."

Medrix got up and walked into the hall. His face was wet with tears. After a while he went back to her. "Ces, you have to fight. We have to fight."

She shook her head.

"The only way I can prove you are innocent is for you to plead Not Guilty. Why give those Chetner Elders what they want. Don't you realise that if you do this thing all Estolan will suffer. All those others who have offended the Elders will suffer the same fate and you cannot do this to all those in the future. I want you to be the one who fights back. The one who challenged a whole nation to a game because a whole planet was in danger of dying. The person who brought all the exiles together in one cause. I want the one who pressed the warning button as a protest. The one who fought me with a tin tray because she believed she was right. I want the one who cursed the Elders and made them fear for their lives. I want the one who acted as a matchmaker when she realised someone was so lonely. I want the one any man would want for a daughter or a wife. I want the one who treats all people alike and in so doing breaks down the barriers of hate that have been there for decades. I want the one who can save a dying planet and only she can do it."

"I am not that person any more."

Medrix shook his head. He did not know what to do. He heard the doorbell ring and Lawmaker Eldon talking to Lawmother Grey and he went to talk it over with him.

They both came into the room together. Eldon smiled at her. "You know, my dear, there is something very odd about this. It does not make sense because no person in charge of a prison would tell you such things, even if they were true. He would lose his job for letting out confidential information. So I think he was told what to say by the Elders themselves. This would make sense. They want you to plead Guilty. Now why do you think this is?"

"Could it be that they thought Medrix had more information that would incriminate them in some way?"

"Yes, to be sure, my dear, that must be it."

"They saw us together every day and ..."

"I think, Medrix, that they thought you two were getting too close to each other, so much so that you could be thought by onlookers to be in love. I know you were only together working on the trial, but people were beginning to notice a change in both of you. I know I did. Now if they think you have some damning information, even if it is not so, they would have to do something to discredit you and what better way than to show her the actual cell that they had prepared for her. The jailer must have reported her as soon as she got there and of course there was only one person missing and that was you, Cessie. It was rubbish to say that he waited until you could tell him who you were. He already knew and he played you along so that you would think your case was hopeless."

"It makes sense, Ces."

She looked at them both and smiled. "Yes. You are right ... I am sure of it now ... and you, Medrix, can dig a little deeper to find out why they do not want to go on with the case ..."

"Does that mean ..."

"It means I am going to plead Not Guilty. Let us make them sweat for a change."

The next morning when they went to the meeting she pleaded Not Guilty to the charges. She seemed to have a new light in her eyes, so much so that they remembered that game challenge all those years ago when a fifteen-year-old girl stood fearlessly before them. Would she win this time as she had then?

Medrix went out early the next morning. Cessie was still in bed and he hadn't woken her.

The Elders had called him to a meeting, one he could not and did not want to avoid. Only the Chetner ones were waiting for him.

"Now, Medrix," said one. "We are speaking for the City Elders and so we need some information from you. We also need to remind you of your responsibility to us as your paymasters."

"I know what you mean, but why call me to this meeting when I am so busy?"

"Yes, but you do not seem to be doing anything that we want."

"Nobody must realise what I am doing otherwise it will be no secret. Do you want everyone to know that the trial is rigged?"

"No, of course not. But you have been seen everywhere with that woman. I expect you have been sleeping with her as well."

"Would you have me break my cover by behaving differently?"

"No … if this is what it really is. But is it?"

"Do you mean that I am so good at my job that you cannot even tell what is really what?"

"So it is some kind of plan on your part?"

"Of course. You know how devious I can be. She is clever but I am watching her like a hawk. I won't let the little bird fly free. She will be all yours when this trial is over."

"Good, but remember who pays you and pays you well for your services."

"How can I forget? Do you know how hard it is to rig a trial? Yesterday I was almost on my knees pleading with her to change her plea. I know that you want her to be found guilty so that she can slowly rot in that prison. I am so good at my job, that the stupid bitch thinks she is in love with me and strangely enough I believe it. Now you see the trap closing around her. So help me, do not hinder me. I have had enough trouble as it is, what with your interfering and the stupid bitch annoying the Grand Elder and almost blowing my cover. We have imbeciles all around us, haven't we?"

"So, you're doing what we want? But you got her to change her plea?"

"Of course, if she pleads Guilty, the Chetner Council will want an inquiry into why she wasn't given appropriate counselling – the case will go on non-stop for years. Do you want that?"

"We found it confusing."

"Good. If you did, so will everyone else won't they? But when it is all over give me my money and the honours that go with it for Estolan will be revenged. Find me a nice Estolan girl who will give in to my every whim and give me many children and also send me somewhere on another job because I like my job. But there is one thing I need you to do for me."

"Of course we will help you. What is it you want us to do?"

"I want to know why the Prosecutor has not called you as witnesses. You were there. You saw it all. You saw how clever it was. You can tell the Court all about it – and how they won the game seemingly without any effort. You can say what you saw, what is hard about that? Nobody will think that there is anything wrong because there will be nothing wrong with your answers. You do want her to be found guilty, don't you?"

"Yes, of course. Right, we will do as you ask."

"Good ... then I will expect to see you there. Then watch her pale and realise how cruel I can be to her. What a triumph that will be for me. What fun we will have at her expense, as her devil lover moves in for the kill."

They looked at him in awe. This monster that they had created and they shivered at the thought ... but then were glad that he was on their side. They would pay him well this time. They would honour him for all time.

He left there humming a little tune. He said to himself: "I must go back to the love of my life and take her in my arms and kiss her and tell her I love her and hope that she will believe me for the days ahead are going to be sheer hell, but of course my darling does not know that."

The day before the trial, Medrix wanted Cessie to go on a picnic with him. She was delighted to be away from the place for a while. His mother packed them a hamper and, taking a runabout, they drove a long way into the countryside, until they came to a lake. It was very remote, being situated on a high mountain. He put the hamper down under a group of trees and spread a rug and some pillows over the ground.

Firstly, they left everything and walked by the lake and then came back and opened the hamper. The food and drink were delicious – afterwards they relaxed back on the pillows, just talking about the beauty of the place.

"My sister and I used to come here as children."

"Sister – Medrix – I know you have a brother – but you've never mentioned her before."

"My sister Stella died when she was nine. She was eight years younger than me. She always said that she would be safe because she had me to look after her. Everyone adored her – she was very sweet-natured. Anyway, we went for a picnic by the river. I had seen a strange bird in a tree – I climbed the tree to find its nest. When I came down – my sister had gone. We searched everywhere. We found her in the river – she had drowned. I blamed myself – I hadn't been there for her. The family moved into the city – and instead of joining the family business of land reclamation – I joined the Lawmaker's training scheme. I learned to be tough, to show no weakness such as pity, gentleness, tears and love and caring. I learnt that strength was power – the hard, mean, tough men ruled and that way the Lawmakers would be a great power. After three years training, my grandfather said I was a mean bastard. The Elders sent me out as a spy – hence I came to Chetner. But other times I worked as an undercover man to bring criminals to justice. The harder the job the better I liked it. I was punishing myself for my sister's death. But now I know better – since you came here. I tried the Lawmaker's way and somehow it did not feel good after all. But I carried on in that manner when you first came to the house. I didn't understand what it felt like to be in your position until the time you teased me about my socks. Here was someone who did not treat me like everyone else – yes, I thought you were a pest – yet somehow you were getting through to me that I was too serious, too stern – and some rules were really stupid.

"Then the Grand Elder died and I heard for the first time about all the suffering you had been through and marvelled how you could have come through it and be laughing and joking and still caring for everyone, even the likes of me. Whatever happens, Cessie, I want you to know that I will do my very best to defend you and hopefully get you acquitted, but whatever happens at the trial – you must trust me to be doing the right thing for you, however hard it seems. You just have to trust me."

She looked at him and said very quietly: "Yes – I will trust you."

Then he took her in his arms and kissed her.

Much later they returned to the house. That night she slept with him in his big four-poster bed.

In the early hours of the morning he woke up and looked at her. Her fair hair spread over the pillow, her face soft with sleep and he said to himself. "Sleep well my fair one – for tomorrow you travel to hell itself and you will find out what a mean bastard I really am."

Chapter 5

Ces awoke early and could hear thunder rolling in the distance. Quietly she slipped out of bed leaving Medrix still sleeping. She went downstairs and made two cups of coffee – bringing them up just as he woke up. He took the cup from her and sipped the hot coffee.

"How are you feeling love?"

"All right – I suppose."

"I have to go early to the court as the Grand Elder has to give us a little talk before the trial begins. So you come later, with your Lawmother. Walk if it is fine but not otherwise."

He finished his coffee, got out of bed and went to the washroom.

When Ces walked into the courtroom with her Lawmother, the black-robed judges were already in their seats facing the main court area. The Grand Elder was sitting behind them on a raised dais. The Prosecutor, dressed in severe black, looked like some bird of prey ready to pounce.

Medrix' dark-green outfit gave colour to the sombre room. Her grey outfit suited the whole mood of the room. To her the spectators were a blur of dark colours. She shivered even though the room was warm.

The Grand Elder called the Court to order.

"The judges have been sworn in. They are not from this city but from cities scattered across our planet. The witnesses have been brought here at great expense from our planet, Chetner, and Tendra. All those from Chetner have been granted safe passage for I wouldn't have it said that the Lawmaking Nation was biased in favour of the accusers in this case."

Ces smiled with relief when she heard this statement and looked at Medrix, who smiled back at her.

The Grand Elder read out the charges and Medrix declared that she was 'Not Guilty'.

The Prosecutor rose from his seat and began to speak: "She sits there before you, knowing that she cheated you all. She ensnared people into her life to make it so. She enlisted the help of a magician and had the cheek to let him be at the game, for she knew the day was hers. She had always been a troublemaker when she lived in their city and that is why she was exiled from it. She hated those Lawmakers so much that this was her revenge and before their very eyes, she did them out of everything they held dear. Afterwards things happened so fast that no one realised they had been tricked. But later when those Chetner Elders made inquiries they discovered that it was all a plot and by using magic, weaving a web of lies, she did them out of their rightful heritage. I will prove it to you and when I have, I want her to be severely punished so that she will never be let loose to do it again. All Estolan and the entire galaxy we live in, will know of her treachery. Don't smile at her – don't talk to her – keep your little ones away from her – she is dangerous to know – she uses magic – she cheats – lies and traps people – and I can prove it." He sat down and drank from a glass of water.

Some people began to hiss at her. The Grand Elder stopped them. Medrix stood up; he was obviously nervous.

"I am going to show you how this citizen of Chetner has been brought here to stand trial for a trumped-up charge by the Chetner Elders because they wanted revenge. They did not believe that they could be defeated in the game, so they had to find an excuse for their failure. All they could think of was that she had somehow cheated. The magician they saw on the field was an old man. 'Good,' they thought, 'he is probably dead now so she can never prove otherwise. What a perfect chance they would have in getting their revenge and prove to all Lawmakers that they had not lost the game but had been cheated out of everything.' No one was allowed to cross them and get away with it. No woman was to make a fool of them and not be punished for it. But you will see how wrong they are. You will know how cruel they are – you will realise that the accused is in fact not guilty of any crime at all and I will prove it." He sat down. Ces looked at him, but he just looked down at his notes.

The Prosecutor called one witness after the other. Each had seen the game in question and each said that the exile's team were very poor in the first half and only improved after the magician came on the court.

Medrix objected twice and questioned some of them – asking them if they thought the exiles could have been nervous – the witnesses agreed to this but said that their game was so brilliant afterwards, it was almost unbelievable.

The Prosecutor asked Fador why he had even considered her to be good enough for a trial game and he said that she pleaded with him so much that he gave in. Whereupon the Prosecutor said that she could manipulate people to suit herself.

The Prosecutor then called Lawmaker Vendon, her stepfather.

He walked slowly up the courtroom, leaning heavily on a stick. He needed help up the steps of the witness stand. The Prosecutor waited patiently for him to sit down.

"How did you know the accused?"

"She was put in my care when she came to live in the city."

"Was she a good child?"

"No – a little devil in fact."

"Why?"

"She would not learn the rules; she stole, lied and cheated."

"Was she punished for this?"

"Yes – but it didn't seem to work – she'd disappear for ages and no one knew where she was – up to some mischief I don't doubt."

"Why was she given to you?"

"She was a problem child – that type of child was sent to me. She was always up to some devilment. Even used magic spells."

"Magic spells! Are you sure?"

"She used them on me twice and they worked. Of course when I found out I punished her: a lot of good it did her for she was exiled and left my care for good."

"Thank you. The Counsellor may have some questions for you."

Medrix nodded: "How many children were in your care?"

"Five girls."

"No boys?"

"No – only girls. I had a son of my own."

"Thank you, that will be all."

Lawmaker Vendon stared at Cessie when he left the room and she looked away.

The Prosecutor then called five Chetner Elders in quick succession to the stand. They were all asked the same kind of questions about whether or not they saw the game – and what was odd about it. They said exactly the same as the first lot of witnesses. Medrix had no questions for them.

Then a man named Fairson was called. The Prosecutor looked at him keenly.

"You are and were a resident of Chetner?"

"Yes."

"Did you know the accused?"

"No. I knew her father. A very weird man."

"Weird? In what way?

"He would stand on a flat rock and vanish – people said he was a wizard."

"Objection: that is rumour only."

"Objection overruled," pronounced the Grand Elder.

"Thank you, that's all from me. Your turn, Medrix."

"No questions, thank you."

Members of the City team were then all questioned. All were surprised that the exile's team won and thought that the exiles cheated in some way. They saw the magician come on the court at half-time and heard the rhyme the exiles chanted and from then on their City team lost the game. They had no chance because she evidently was using magic.

Medrix asked no questions.

The Prosecutor then questioned the referees, observers, scorers, some more spectators and all said the same as the others, and again Medrix said – "No questions."

Then there was a break for lunch.

Medrix took her to the dining centre for a meal. Then at the hour of fifteen they were back in their places. The day had turned very humid and there was thunder in the air.

Medrix then called Thortrex the huntersnout. The little fellow had difficulty in climbing up on the chair in the stand but was helped by the Clerk of the Court.

Medrix wanted to know why the huntersnout was with the magician. Thortrex said that he was his assistant. Had been for six moons. Ever since, in fact, he had lost his home in an earthquake. Medrix then asked him if he himself could do magic. Whereupon the huntersnout laughed and said that there was a logical explanation for the tricks but he had never learnt how they were done, it was a secret.

Medrix nodded and then asked him if Cessie had arranged to meet the magician – but the huntersnout shook his head and said that it was just by chance.

Medrix went on: "But it is true that the magician gave them a special rhyme to use when they played; that's true isn't it?"

The huntersnout smiled. "Yes it is true. I learnt it, then taught the Middle City team. The more they chanted it, the quicker they moved. They forgot to be nervous and so got on with the game."

"Why didn't the team chant the rhyme in the first half?"

"We were so nervous seeing all those people looking at us. We did not go into the city unless we had to. The team looked so big and strong. We had been told to hold back our best play until the second half. But we were so nervous that that happened anyway."

"Why were you told to hold back?"

"To tire the City team. If they thought it was easy they would make mistakes, and they did."

"Who told you that?"

"The magician."

"What did he tell you at half-time?"

"He said we should now chant the rhyme."

"And did you?"

"Yes, and we got better and better."

"Why was that?"

"We were concentrating more – we forgot to be nervous – and we won."

"Thank you. That will be all."

The Prosecutor stood up."Wait, I have some questions for you. So you had a plan for this game?"

"Yes."

"And what was that?"

"Well, the magician knew the City had three teams, but they never went outside the city to play a game. So they did not really know how good they were. Their three teams played each other only."

"And that was important?"

"The magician told Cessie that this game was different. It was a battle and as such should be well planned."

"How do you mean?"

"If you go to war, you don't just rush in blindly. You make your plans."

"And the magician knew about such things?"

"Yes."

"At half-time he told you to chant the rhyme?"

"Yes and it startled the other team and they complained, so we then kept saying it to ourselves."

"It worked for you?"

"Yes, even the sun came out for us. So when the ball went high, the City team could not see it. It was fun."

"Thortrex, you are a huntersnout aren't you?"

"Yes."

"Why were you in the team at all? You weren't an exile, were you?"

"No, but I lived in Middle City."

"Don't you think it was cheating to trick the opposing team?"

"No, not really."

"Why?"

"In every game you have to work out a strategy. When I go out hunting, I have to be cunning."

"Cunning – sly – deceitful, would also describe how your team played the game, wouldn't it, Thortrex?"

"No – it was just a game. You have to outwit the enemy. There were no rules to say otherwise."

"Huntersnouts live in trees – am I right?"

"Yes."

"How do you get to your house?"

"I can jump high."

"None of the opposing team could jump that high, could they?"

"No. But I was not as big as they were. They had longer legs."

"Without the magician's help you would have lost. Am I right?"

"There is no telling. Once we were less nervous we could have had a good chance."

"No, my friend, no chance at all. And that woman sitting there knew that and that is why she employed a magician so that her team would win. That was the plot. That was the plan. She used magic to break all the rules to get what she wanted. Thank you, Thortrex, you were a great help to me."

Thortrex went out slowly, his figure one of complete dejection.

Medrix stood up. He called the defendant. He smiled at her as she walked to the witness box.

"Why were you living in the city?"

"I was brought there by the Grand Elder when my mother died. The Grand Elder was my grandmother."

"Why didn't your father come with you?"

"He was living as an exile – I was kidnapped – my father had no choice."

"How old were you?"

"Five years old. My mother died when I was four."

"Have you a picture of your parents?"

"Yes – in my locket – I've kept it safe all these years."

"What was your life like in the city?"

"All right."

"Only all right?"

"They said my father was dead and gave me a new father."

"Was he any relation?"

"No."

"Was your new father kind to you?"

"No," she whispered.

"Why?"

"He got very angry when I said my father would come for me."

"What did he do?"

"He beat me and shut me in a cupboard."

"Your grandmother was the Grand Elder. Surely that made a difference?"

"No one knew."

"What happened one time when you climbed a tree?"

"I was whipped and tied to the tree during a thunderstorm. He said that lightning sometimes struck trees – I have been afraid of storms since then."

"How would you spend your free time?"

"I would get a book from the library and find a place where I could read it."

"Any book?"

"Yes, any one that was on a shelf by the door."

"You could read that well?"

"Yes. My father taught me."

"Why did you want to play for the team?"

"I thought I was good enough. I used to watch the boys play and I would write down everything the coach told the team. At night I would go down and practise."

"No one saw you?"

"No."

"When Fador let you play, where were you supposed to be?"

"In class."

"You were breaking the rules by being there with Fador?"

"Yes."

"But Fador said you were good enough to join, but you had to ask the Elders. Why were you exiled?"

"Because I broke the rules and got Fador into trouble."

"How did you feel standing outside the city gates?"

"Terrified."

"But you met with me and I took you to Middle City."

"Yes."

"When you made the challenge, whose life did you think you were saving?"

"Yours."

"You did not know I was a spy trying to make contact with them?"

"No."

"Why choose a game?"

"That's all I could think of at such short notice."

"You need not have gone on with it though."

"No. But I liked the idea."

"What if the Lawmakers had not accepted the challenge? What would have happened then?"

"I would have been punished for my insolence and you would have been found out."

"Thank you. You may step down now."

"Not so fast, young woman. I have some questions for you." The Prosecutor stared at her and she looked away.

"You practised the game at night, and no one heard you – if you did it once I could believe you – but not several times. And no one saw you taking the books – not once. Oh, come now – this one could use magic – that's how she did these things. You might call it luck, but I would say it is magic!"

"Objection. He cannot prove that."

"Overruled."

"You meant to issue the challenge and you entrapped Lawmaker Medrix in your plans – didn't you?"

"No, I did not."

"You knew you could win because you knew how to use magic."

"No, it is not true."

"You cheated in the game because you pretended to be weak – but you knew otherwise. You knew you could win – that is why you made the challenge and for this you should be punished."

"No – no – no."

"You entrapped Lawmaker Medrix into your schemes and he, poor fellow, did not realise what you were doing. You made him forget how to behave like a Lawmaker and in so doing he did not realise what you were plotting. You knew he was not Fador's twin brother; you were clever enough to work that out for yourself. You could have blown his cover, but you did not. You did not because you needed him there in your scheme of things. Didn't you?"

"No – you are making it all up."

"The people of Estolan are shamed by his weakness. He was and is besotted with you. You who work with magic can manipulate whoever you want in order to make your schemes work. Am I right?"

"No – no – no. I am on trial here, not him."

"I am just showing the Court how you work on people. They should know and as this trial progresses they will see how you do it."

"Objection. This is purely conjecture and has no basis on the trial in question."

"Objection overruled."

"What did your father do?"

"I don't know."

"He worked away?"

"Yes."

"I have evidence that he came and went easily. He stood on a rock each time. The same one each time and just vanished into thin air. People thought that he was a wizard. He always wore a locket just like the one you wear. A thing that protects witches like yourself. Am I right?"

"Objection. What is this rubbish that the Prosecutor is talking about. She is not a witch, has not been accused of witchcraft. It is all a story that he is making up. Absolutely no proof of it is evident."

"Let him go on. I want to see where all this is leading." The Grand Elder nodded to the Prosecutor.

"Did you see him vanish?"

"No. Never."

"Well, she would say that. A wizard's daughter would not let on about what her father could do. She would be sworn to secrecy from an early age.

"When you mother died, you were taken in by the Lawmakers?"

"Yes."

"You were given a new family – a new stepfather?"

"Yes."

"Did you like him?"

"No."

"No. She hated him. She hated him so much that she tried to kill him and nearly succeeded. Isn't that so?"

"No – no."

"I have witnesses to prove that you did."

"No – you can't have."

"Wait and see. Wait and see. This Court will see your wickedness for themselves. Now you stole books from the library, didn't you?"

"I borrowed them. I put them all back."

"Yet no one ever saw you do that, did they?"

"I just took the ones that were nearest the door."

"You broke the rules then?"

"Yes."

"Name me some of the books then."

"I can't remember. It was a long time ago."

"Let me jog your memory. 1. *Medicines*; 2. *The Magic of the Planet*; 3. *Lawmakers' Rules*; 4. *Making the Rules for the Game*: 5. *Moon Magic*; 6. *Magic and Witchcraft*; 7. *Midnight Magic*; 8. *Magical Methods*; 9. *Magic Ways with Animals*; 10. *Moving through Space*. Now do you remember?"

"You could be right."

"And you tried some of the magic that you read about?"

"Yes," she said softly.

"What did you say? Speak up so everyone can hear your words."

"Yes – I did." She spoke louder.

"Tell me one of them."

"You had to peel an apple and throw the peel over your left shoulder."

"What was that meant to do?"

"It should land on the floor in the shape of a letter."

"What did that do?"

"The letter would give you the initial of the man you would marry."

"Did you do this?"

"Yes. We all did."

"All!" he shouted. "What do you mean, all?"

"The other girls in my class. It was only a bit of fun."

"You led those others into breaking the rules?"

"The choice was theirs."

"What letter did you get?"

"I got a W every time."

"Fun – you call it – but think of that letter. If it is viewed upside down, what letter do you get?"

She hesitated, realising how clever he was.

"Answer me," he shouted. "Answer me Celisia Margaret."

"M …"

"Yes. And we all know who that is, don't we?"

She looked away from him.

"Anyway, there was another spell you did – wasn't there?"

"Yes."

"Tell us about that one."

"I filled a bowl with dirty water and floated the name of the one I did not like on it. Then I spat in it."

"Then you wrote a spell: 'I cast a spell upon this date and write the name of one I hate, in five days' time he will see, he cannot mess around with me'. That's what she wrote, this devious little devil that she is. Whose name did you put?"

"My stepfather."

"Yes, this is what she did. Five days later her stepfather fell down the stairs and broke both legs. It could have killed him."

The spectators began to hiss and some were chanting: "Witch, witch, witch …"

The Grand Elder quietened them with a warning to those taking part that they were breaking the rules and could be punished for it. They stopped at once. Cessie bent her head. She looked at no one.

"Who else did you make a spell for?"

"No one."

"Why not?"

"It frightened me."

"See her standing there – this is the person who dealt in magic at an early age – this same person challenged the Lawmakers to a game that she knew she could win. She would only have to use one of those spells and the day was hers."

"It's not fair. It's not fair. He is using a childish prank to malign me."

"Be quiet woman," the Grand Elder said angrily.

"But it is nothing to do with the case."

"Be – quiet – now," he repeated, glaring at her.

"Cessie, Sh," Medrix warned her.

"Listen to your Counsellor now."

She looked down at her hands. She must remember not to interrupt. She felt hemmed in on all sides. She knew a childish prank did not prove anything. But Medrix had not objected so was he really on her side?

The Grand Elder called a halt to the day's proceedings and told them all to meet at the hour of ten on the morrow.

Chapter 6

The trial started again and Cessie returned to the witness box to face the Prosecutor once more.

"This person – this evil person – while waiting for her trial upset the whole planet by pressing the warning button. She did this as a protest. She was of course duly punished for her insolence but she is and always has been out to cause trouble for other people, and she does this to attract attention. For what good is a worker of magic unless people know about it. She is dangerous. Not even a beating from her Counsellor stopped her, although she promised him that she would keep the rules but, as soon as his back was turned, she was off doing something else. The Elders had a day and night watch put on her, yet, my friends, she slipped away. How could she do this? Well, witches can make themselves invisible. She has kept up this pretence of keeping the rules to keep Lawmaker Medrix happy. Rules that she herself despised. She is, in fact, a witch – aren't you?"

"No. I am not a witch."

"How many of you were at the picnic? I was there. I saw her there. I saw how she reacted to three Elders who spoke to her. I heard her lay a curse on them. You did, didn't you?"

"Yes," she whispered.

"What did you say? Everyone wants to hear your answer."

"Yes, I did." She spoke louder.

"Why did you?"

"Because they said I was not wanted there."

"And what were the words you used?"

"I – I said – I said it in anger. I did not really mean it."

"She told them that the earth should open up and swallow them and that it would rain and the sky turn black and it did. You did that, didn't you?"

"I ... I ..."

"She did that to all her new-found friends. She did that to you, people of this city. She had no thought of the danger she was putting us all in and she vanished. Vanished from our sight."

"I … took the wrong path out of the field … I got lost … I was in the earthquake too … I nearly died too."

"But you did not come back to us, did you? So where were you?"

"I told you. I got lost. I did not mean any harm to anyone. I was just so angry." Everyone could hear a thunderstorm gradually getting nearer. She shivered.

"Then, wonder of wonders, she returns unharmed. But she never asks how everyone else is because she does not care about them at all. It is all put on for she knows that the locket she wears protects her. That locket kept you safe, didn't it?"

"No. What do you mean?"

"Your father wears one and he vanishes just like you. Am I right?"

"No. No – no."

"It is a special charm to protect you, isn't it?"

"No – no."

"Take it off."

"No. No I won't."

"Give him the locket please," the Grand Elder demanded.

She fumbled with the catch. Medrix went to her and undid it and gave it to the Prosecutor.

"Right. Now watch this." He opened the locket and dipped it in a glass of water. It lit up. She stared at it. People everywhere shifted uneasily in their seats. Her Lawmother left her place. "It is sending out a signal. See. So her life has been protected by this magical charm. No wonder she won the game. No wonder she couldn't fail."

The storm was almost overhead now.

He closed up the locket and put in on his table. "Now we see what was protecting her. You knew all the time that it was not an ordinary locket, didn't you?"

"No. Oh – no."

Suddenly there was a flash of lightning in front of them all and the locket fell off the table on to the floor. She went to pick it up. But before she could do so a flash of lightning homed in on it and it disappeared completely. She stood there too petrified to move. Medrix ran to her and gently took her back to his seat. "It's all right love, sit there a minute. It's only a storm."

There was screaming from everywhere. "It could have killed me. It could have killed me," she said in a shocked voice.

"Quiet please. All of you. No one has been hurt and we will stay as we are."

The room became quiet and the Prosecutor went on. "She must go back to the witness box first."

She walked slowly back to it and stood waiting.

"Now we all saw what happened. That proves it's devil's work …"

"Objection. It doesn't prove anything. Lightning does strike at times anyway."

"Overruled. Go on."

"We take the locket off her and it almost killed us."

"Objection. The lightning struck the locket. There is no proof that it meant to kill any of us."

"Overruled."

"You – woman – " he pointed at her – "you were saved. You took it off and your contact went from all your wicked friends. Your magic talisman tried to kill us but luckily for us it failed. You knew that would happen, didn't you?"

"No," she said softly. "No. No. No."

"Speak up, witch. Let everyone in this courtroom hear you."

"No," she shouted. "No. No. No!"

She covered her face with both hands and sat down, rocking herself back and forth.

"No. No. No. It's just a locket that my father gave me when I was little. Now it has gone. You, evil, evil man. You are a devil. Nothing happened until you touched it. Nothing."

"Now you shout and cry without your talisman. See how the witch behaves now. See for yourselves – all of you."

"This court is a farce," she sobbed, "when there are people like you in it."

"Objection. Objection," shouted Medrix. "He is harassing the accused. She has just had a terrible fright and he is goading her. Making her retaliate without thinking what she is saying."

"Objection sustained."

Cessie looked at Medrix thankfully. She had provoked the wrath of the Court and he had saved her.

"No more questions for now," the Prosecutor announced.

Cessie sighed and went back to her seat.

Medrix called Sanor to the stand.

"Sanor. You were with the accused when you met the magician. Was it an arranged meeting?"

"No. We had just escaped being killed in an earthquake and we came to a wood and there he was sitting in a tree."

"What was he doing in the tree?"

"He seemed to be looking at the surrounding countryside."

"How did you know he was a magician?"

"He was dressed in a long robe. It had stars and moons all over it. It also seemed to have a lot of pockets and he said he was a magician."

"I see. Did he do any tricks?"

"Yes. He brought flowers out of nowhere and gave them to Cessie."

"How did he know about the game?"

"She told him."

"What did he say to that?"

"He said that she would only need to play one city as all the others were decoy ones."

"How many were decoy cities?"

"Nineteen."

"Were you surprised at this?"

"We both were. We thought there were only five and three of those had already been destroyed."

"Did he offer to help?"

"Yes. He said that he would help. He taught Thortrex a little rhyme and Thortrex taught it to the team."

"Did you believe that he could really do magic?"

"Only as an entertainer. Not as someone who could really do it. There would be a logical explanation for each trick – I am sure of that. It really did not matter in this case because we needed everyone to know about the game and support it."

"So he left you?"

"Yes, in true magical style he vanished from our sight."

"He vanished, did you say? How did he do that?"

"I have no idea. They both did. We hurried on our way. We did not wait to see if he reappeared."

Did Cessie think he could do magic?"

"We laughed about it and wondered how he did it. But we had to get on our way and had no time to work it out. Though I did say we should ask others if they had seen him anywhere else."

"And did you?"

"Yes – he went around the planet entertaining and asking questions."

"What kind of questions?"

"About the earthquakes and what damage they had done. He kept a notebook – wrote down the answers he got."

"Had he been to the City?"

"I found out afterwards that he had been invited into the City more than once to entertain the Elders."

"But wasn't he an exile?"

"Oh, no, he came from another planet. He wasn't an exile."

"Could he have been a spy?"

"Yes, I think he could have been."

"Thank you. I may re-call you later."

"Wait! I have questions for you, Sanor. Medrix cannot have you all to himself." The Prosecutor laughed.

"Why did you play in the team? ?"

"I lived in Middle City. I had to learn how to play."

"And you were good enough to play in a team in that short time? Oh, come now, you would only be good enough if something very strange happened. Shall we say that a magician came on to the field at half-time and cast a magic spell which made you all play so well that you won the game. She arranged with him just how and when to do this. No more questions for now."

"We will have a break here for a meal," the Grand Elder said. "We will meet here at the hour of fifteen."

The court cleared. Medrix took Ces to the dining area for a meal. He said she was doing very well but must learn to count to ten before answering the Prosecutor because he could not always save her from the wrath of the Court.

They enjoyed their meal. Medrix was making her laugh by imitating the Prosecutor. He was very good and she relaxed. Lawmaker Eldon came and sat with them and gave Medrix some messages. Then it was time to go back into court.

Medrix called an Elder to the stand. Cessie was surprised at this.

An old man walked to the stand and waited for the questions.

"Your name is Elder Stains?"

"Yes."

"You were an Elder on Chetner?"

"Yes."

"Are you an Elder of this City?"

"No. There can only be so many Elders at one time and I decided against it."

"Were you at the meeting when the accused was exiled?"

"Yes."

"Did you agree with it?"

"No. I thought she was too young to be exiled. She should have just been warned about her wayward behaviour. Then she could have gone up to the Senior Girls' class with Lawmother Grey and learnt housewifery in order to get ready for married life. She would have been kept so busy there that the silly notion would have just disappeared."

"But they did not agree with you?"

"No. And look what happened."

"Quite. Were you there when she made the challenge?"

"Yes. She was very good."

"What do you mean – good?"

"She knew she was on safe ground because she knew the rules concerning a challenge. We had to accept it, but we thought she would back out at the last moment – but she didn't."

"Where did you sit at the game?"

"Near the front."

"Did they look nervous?"

"Very. The huntersnout did some tricks but she stopped him. All of them stood there looking apprehensive. When the game started the City team just rushed round them and took over much of the play. The ball seemed to slip through her fingers. I was sorry for them; the City team thought it was all going to be easy. In fact I heard them say that it was an insult to bring such a poor team to play them. But, after half-time, after the team coach came on the field, they improved and ran circles round the City team. I thought they were excellent. The City team forgot that the game was not over until the whistle blows."

"Thank you Elder. But what about the favours she asked for?"

"This is how I view it: we were due to come back here anyway once the mining was over. It was long overdue because of storms that held up everything. We just went home a bit earlier, that's all."

"Did you agree to her trial?"

"I was asked to join them, but I refused. It was only a game after all. She was safe in Chetner. What harm could she do? Best to leave it alone, I said, if that was a real magician on the field – that is if you believe in things like that – then we could really be in trouble."

"But they went ahead anyway? Was she happier away from the City?"

"Yes."

"Why?"

"Her stepfather was awful to her and the others."

"What others?"

"The other children in his care. Poor little thing, she was always being whipped for something or other. One of the girls died. He said it was the fever, but I do not think it was. She could say what it was. She shared a bed with her and she never caught the fever herself, which was very strange – and I know he drank. I saw him once weaving from one side of the road to the other. How he got away with it I do not know. But the Grand Elder thought he was good."

"Thank you, Elder. The Prosecutor wants a word with you now."

"Yes I do," said the Prosecutor. Am I to believe that as an Elder you condone her bad behaviour; her magic spells?"

"She was only a child, but a very bright child. She was five years old when she came here. She did not know all the rules. Other children learnt them from babyhood but not her. She should have been put in a higher class. Her reading was very advanced and she could do number work quicker than I could. Once she stayed with Lawmaker Steffan when her stepfather was ill. He did the Elders' accounts. She would sit by him when he was doing them and tell him the answer long before he could. She was always right. She was kept back by her stepfather and the Grand Elder."

The Prosecutor smiled, and said: "She was too advanced for her age. That is why she read the books on magic and tried them out, and when they worked she realised how she could get her own back on the Lawmakers. No more questions."

After the session was over, Medrix told Ces to wait for him as he had to attend a meeting and no one else was available to take her back.

She waited and waited. The cleaners came into the court room, so she waited in the corridor. She walked up and down for ages and still he did not come. She could hear music and she went to the main doors to see what was happening.

A little way down the road, by the turning to the shuttle bay, was a group of people. They seemed to be singing and dancing. She was so intrigued that she went to see what was going on. I will keep a watch for Medrix from here, she said to herself and she joined the group. A woman told her it was a wedding – they were bringing the bride to the groom who lived on Temra. He was the Ambassador's son.

A woman with two small children came and stood beside her. The children could not see what was happening. The mother lifted one up and asked her to lift the other one. She did so. She did not notice that a crowd had built up behind her. Suddenly, the whole group moved forward into the shuttle bay, taking her with it. Then the crowd behind her kept pushing her until she found herself getting into a space traveller. She looked round for the mother of the child and saw her sitting in the front of the traveller. Cessie still had the child in her arms. She managed to get to the mother and give her the child, then made her way to the exit, only to be pushed into a seat by a man who told her to "belt up, unless she wanted to be crushed, as they went into warp drive."

"I have to get out," she said, struggling to get up.

"If you do, you'll step into space," he said with a chuckle. "It seems you are going to a wedding. Let me introduce myself. I am Lawmaker Sketson, brother-in-law to Lawmaker Eldon."

"Oh dear," she said. "How far away is Temra?"

"Six-hour journey, my dear, so sit back and relax – we have one pass for all of us – and nobody has bothered to count us – you can come back with us – go to the wedding – enjoy yourself."

"When do we return?"

"In four days time. So have yourself a nice time."

There was nothing for it but to sit back and relax. But she could not be away for four days – but what else could she do? Medrix would be furious – if she had just gone on waiting for him she would be back in the house now, having a nice meal.

She relaxed back in the seat and fell asleep.

Much later, when she woke, the man passed her a tray of food. "You know," he said, "you can get a shuttle from Temra to Chetner – it goes through Listra – Chetner is your home planet isn't it?"

She nodded. He went on.

"Not everyone wants your trial you know. You haven't got a chance of winning. I was talking to Lawmaker Eldon and he told me so. And of course your Counsellor works for the Elders – he always gets what they want – much better for you to go home to Chetner. Once there you could get a new Counsellor; also look for the magician – give yourself time. The Grand Elder would have to get an extradition order from the Interplanetary Council to bring you back and that would take ages – but it would give you more time."

"That's all very well, but I have no money and no papers – as you well know."

"I could get them for you. I could say you are my niece going to Chetner to visit friends."

"Why would you do that?"

"Because, my dear, I know you are innocent and I want to help you. Lawmaker Eldon has told me how badly you've been treated and I don't believe in witchcraft – not in this day and age. So do let me help you."

She knew he was right – it would give her more time – so, she agreed.

When they arrived on Temra the man bought Ces a ticket and took her to the dining area for coffee. Then he said. "There's a shuttle in now – it goes out in fifteen minutes, so we've just timed it right. We'll go now."

She followed him to the waiting shuttle and he saw her inside, finding a seat in the centre of it.

A voice came over the tannoy that the Chetner shuttle was due out in ten minutes.

"I'll leave you now, my dear," he said. "I must hurry. I am due at the wedding and I am late already." He handed her a large box covered in gold paper. "Here," he said, "some chocolates for your journey, and may the powers that be take care of you."

She thanked him and watched him walk away until he was out of sight.

The voice came again. "This shuttle goes out in five minutes." Ces sat back in the seat. It would be lovely to see Chetner again – then she thought of Medrix and her heart missed a beat. She had promised to trust him. All these witnesses would be stranded on Estolan. The Lawmakers might hold them hostage in exchange for her. She stood up. She couldn't do it – not to Medrix – not to all her friends on Estolan. She ran to the door and jumped out then ran to the washroom and was sick. She felt cold and she trembled. She stood by the door and watched as the shuttle pulled away and was gone. Then she remembered that she had forgotten the chocolates and her cloak. They were still on the seat.

She sat for ages. She had no money – no cloak – no way of getting back to Estolan. But she did have a pass and ticket to Chetner.

A voice announced that the shuttle for Jadeston was due out in four minutes. Jadeston was the sister planet – it was a Lawmakers' planet – and it was not very far from Estolan. If she ran she could make it. As she got to the gates she held up her Chetner pass – the man waved her through – he had no time to look at it, but told her to run. And run she did and jumped on to it just as the doors were closing.

She sat down. She was on her way back and prayed that no one would ask to see her pass.

The steward brought her food and coffee, after which she relaxed back in the comfortable seat and dozed.

Much later, they arrived at Jadeston. The town of Kepla turned out to be a grey place with a low mist hanging over it. It was a mining town, with rows of small box-like houses everywhere.

She walked a little way then went to the shuttle office and inquired how she could get to Estolan from there.

The man in the office said that mining shuttles went every twenty minutes at peak times; other times, once every two hours but if she hurried she could get on one now.

She did exactly as she had done on Temra and again no one looked at her pass and she got on the shuttle which was full of miners going home. There were also a couple of women and she recognised them as bread sellers.

When she arrived on Estolan it was quite dark, but she walked back with the bread sellers. They parted company at the house and she went to ring the bell, but suddenly stopped – what was she going to say? Would Medrix be furious with her? Would she be at all welcome? She had to face them – she could not stand here all night worrying. She rang the bell and turned away, looking down the road. The door opened and she heard Lawmother Grey say, "Yes, what is it?"

Cessie turned and said: "It's me, Cessie. I have come back."

"Oh my dear, we have been so worried about you. Come in. Come in."

She went in just as Medrix was coming down the stairs.

"Ha!" he said scornfully, "our wanderer has returned. Come in, come in – let's have a look at you. Let's all look at the sly little vixen who can't keep rules." He called her Lawmother in.

Ces stood still, not looking at any of them. They were not pleased to see her – that much she knew – she was in dire trouble.

Medrix went on: "When you went missing, we searched your rooms and found the timetables, maps and photographs under your mattress. We found how you planned to travel on the shuttle to Temra, then on to Chetner, so, when I was asking you to trust me, you were busy planning your escape. You don't know the meaning of trust. But what surprises me is why you came back. Well, why did you?"

"I … didn't plan it … it just happened … I got caught up in a wedding party and was pushed on to the shuttle."

"Do you think I can believe that? Do you? I have your plans here." He slapped them on the table in front of her.

"Those plans are old. I got them before my grandmother died. I forgot about them, that's all"

"We have an undercover agent working in Temra. He saw you with a man, a contact, who seemed to be looking after you. You got off the shuttle with him. You went for coffee. He even bought your ticket and gave you chocolates when you got on the Chetner shuttle. So don't tell me your lies."

"I … I … he did persuade me. Yes, I did get on it, but after he left I knew I couldn't do it. I had promised to trust you and I knew I couldn't leave you all.

So after he went I got off and in my hurry left my cloak and the chocolates behind. But I still had the ticket and I used that to get through the gates as I ran past the men, in a hurry to catch the shuttles. Each time no one bothered to look at my ticket. I walked back from the bay with some bread sellers that I knew. I couldn't leave. I had promised, you see. I had disobeyed you – I did not wait and I went out alone. I can see the trouble I've caused. I am sorry I have brought shame to you and this house and to myself – but I got tired of waiting," she began to cry "and I know I must be punished – I know – but I just had to come back you see." She bowed her head.

"It took great courage to come back," said Lawmother Grey.

"Have a shower, then something to eat, then write out a statement – include everything Ces – even the name of your contact," said Medrix. "Tomorrow you will see the Grand Elder. You will probably be whipped for your rank disobedience but you must have known that. I am going out now. When I come in I don't want to see your sly face." He strode out through the door angrily.

"He was very worried about you," her Lawmother said. "You had better do as he says."

Cessie sighed. Why, oh why had she come back?

She wrote out a full statement but did not name the man. He had been so kind to her – she just could not do that.

The next morning Medrix took Ces to see the Grand Elder. He read her statement and said gently.

"What a good thing you decided to come back. Medrix, she is to be praised for doing that – it takes a lot of courage to do that and I know the judges will see it favourably. But there is something else – in your statement you didn't name the contact. Do you know his name?"

"Yes – but I cannot tell you."

"I think you will tell me when I tell you the news." He hesitated, and then went on: "News has just come through that the shuttle travelling to Chetner blew up in mid-space on its way to Listra. There were no survivors. The salvage crews are already there for an investigation."

"What? What did you say?" She sat down.

He repeated his news.

"No – no," she said, the tears pouring down her face. "No, it can't be true – there were people and children – oh no."

"It is true," he said quietly. "It is quite evident that you were not meant to get to Chetner my dear. I have had letters threatening your life if the trial went on. That is why I did not want you to go out alone at any time."

She looked up at him. "You should have told me the reason. I am not a child. I am not a child," she sobbed.

"Yes, I can see that now, but I did what I thought was best. Now tell us the name."

She told him, but Medrix said that Eldon did not have a brother-in-law, so it was a false name. But he asked her for a description.

"From now on, my dear, you will have a law enforcement officer with you night and day."

"And my punishment – what's that?"

"You came back, so why should I do that. Medrix, take her back to the house. Look after her, she's one very special person – keep her safe."

Much later it was established that the explosive device must have been in the centre somewhere – perhaps in the guise of a chocolate box covered in gold paper!! The man who had led her into the trap had disappeared.

Medrix took her into his arms and kissed her and said, "Celisia Margaret, never go off like that again please – I couldn't bear it if I lost you again – not now you have been returned to me – please take care."

And somehow, in spite of everything she had heard about him, she believed him.

"I will be careful – I promise," she said as she clung to him and kissed him back. "I am glad I am back here with you all." And as she stayed in his arms she felt so safe. So why was a warning voice echoing in her mind with, "What the Elders want they get."

Chapter 7

Medrix and Cessie were in their places long before the Grand Elder arrived at the court: two Law Officers sat beside her. Gradually the court filled up.

Everyone waited for the Grand Elder. He was late coming in. As soon as he arrived, he nodded to Medrix to begin.

"I call Janeen." A pretty woman took her place on the stand. She was nervous and kept looking around the courtroom.

"You are Vendon's wife?"

"Yes ... I was."

"What do you mean … was?"

"I left him years ago."

"Why?"

"He was violent."

"To you?"

"To me and the girls in our care."

"You left the children to him?"

"There was nothing I could do. I did tell the Grand Elder that he was sadistic but she did nothing and she told him. I made it worse for everyone. He threatened to kill me so I left him."

"But you came to the game?"

"Yes. I hoped they would win."

"You did not want your own people to win?"

"No. I prayed that she would win this time."

"Why did you think they played so well after the magician came on the field?"

"I did not know who he was. I just thought he was the team coach."

"But after he came on the court, they won. Didn't you think that a bit odd?"

"No. I just thought they were very nervous in the first half and the coach gave them some encouraging words."

"Thank you, Janeen."

"Wait! I want to ask you some questions now." The Prosecutor smiled at her. "I think a woman who leaves her husband and children is now trying to have her own back on him by telling tales about him, to hurt him. Would I be right?"

"No."

"Is Jadex your son?"

"Yes."

"And you never worried about him?"

"He never hurt the boys."

"Boys? There was more than one son?"

"Yes, I had another son. He died of the fever."

"I suggest that you are taking revenge on your husband because you blamed him for your son's death.

"No. Certainly not."

"I do not think your evidence is reliable. What mother would leave her children to face such a man? No more questions."

At that moment a messenger came in and went to the Grand Elder. The Grand Elder stood up and said that the Chief Elder had just arrived and wished to interview people regarding the earthquake. He smiled and said: "For the benefit of those who do not know what a Chief Elder is, I will explain: He oversees all planets where Lawmakers live; he negotiates mining rights and deals with land reclamation; he makes sure that all cities are run according to our Laws. The first person he wishes to see is the Accused - so she will go there now and the Court will meet tomorrow."

Medrix nodded and took Cessie to see him.

An elderly man sat at a big desk. He smiled at her and told her to sit down. As she did so, she saw a young man at another desk who was taking notes.

She explained her part in the earthquake.

Afterwards he thanked her for being so helpful. Before she went she asked him if he had ever been to Chetner and he said that he had met the Elders once and only once.

She then told him that Chetner was a dying planet and needed his help. He said he would look into the matter. Then she was dismissed and left the office to find two Law Officers waiting for her.

She found Medrix in the courtroom. He was collecting his papers together. She touched him on the arm.

"Don't do that," he said, "can't you see I am busy. Go back to the house and get yourself some food."

"But," she said, "I have been thinking ..."

"I *told* you to go back to the house – so do that *now* and let *me* do the thinking."

She left him then and walked back to the house with her two guards. She spent the rest of the day by herself as the two Lawmothers were out somewhere. When Medrix did come in, he hardly spoke to her and went upstairs to his rooms.

She followed him but, before she could speak to him, he rushed past her, saying: "Not now, not now." He ran downstairs and out through the main door and was gone.

She saw him the next day, in court. He nodded to her as she sat down.

The Prosecutor looked at her and smiled. Someone is pleased to see me and she laughed to herself at the thought.

Medrix re-called one of the prosecution witnesses.

Elder Stonic came up to the witness stand and waited for the questions. He smiled at Medrix and he smiled back at him.

"You are an Elder of this city?"

"Yes."

"And you were on Chetner?"

"Yes."

"What was odd about the game?"

"The good play did not come until the end."

"Why did you think that was?"

"Because the magician gave them a magic spell."

"Did the referees complain?"

"One told them to stop the chant."

"And did they?"

"Yes."

"Why did you have her kidnapped to bring her for trial instead of applying to the Interplanetary Council to get her extradited to this planet?"

"It would take too long."

"You wanted everything over quickly so you could send her to prison without a trial?"

"Yes … it is quite legal if she is a threat to our nation. But she claimed Lawmakers' rights so we had to have a trial. We chose her Counsellor in advance should this happen and the funny thing is she chose the one we picked. We laughed about that. But then the little devil went and protested, by putting our whole planet in jeopardy, for which she was severely punished. She is a troublemaker; always has been. Of course it delayed the trial, but it won't do her any good. It just shows the Judges her wicked ways."

"Do you have a cell all ready for her?"

"Objection! It won't affect this trial how or where she is to be punished. New cells are added every so often."

"Sustained."

"Is it true that you wanted revenge because you lost the game?"

"No. Certainly not!"

"Now I have looked into the past life of a little girl on Chetner. A little girl who lived in terror of her life; who knew no comfort; no love, and was most cruelly treated. Surely someone like that would want revenge. But you and the other Elders lived in comfort while she starved. You had servants and power while she had nothing. *Her* revenge I could understand – but *yours* I cannot. Surely if you wanted her imprisoned you could think of something less of an ordeal for this prisoner, and I plead with the Judges of this Court, if they find her guilty, not to punish her in such a way. Show her some mercy in exchange for all the cruelty she has suffered. Now, Elder: why would the Elders seek revenge?"

"We don't. We just want our just rights. We want our Trophy back. We want to show all Estolan how we were treated by an ungrateful person who was out to ruin us."

"So why did you employ someone who could trick his way into her life in order to make sure she could not get any evidence at all to support her innocence?"

"We ... we didn't."

"Didn't you? Remember, as an Elder you are duty-bound to keep all the rules and speak the truth."

"Objection! He is hounding the witness."

"Overruled. Go on, Counsellor."

"I have evidence that you did."

"You can't have ..."

"I have ..."

"I ...!

"Yes? What were you going to say?"

"Yes – we employed someone to advance our interests in this case. It is a natural thing to do. After all, we want to win."

"Of course you did," he almost purred, "of course you did. But why did you offer her a place in the City team before the big game?"

"Because we realised how keen she was and we decided to accept her request."

"A bit late weren't you? After all she had trained a team of her own."

"Yes: but she was a Lawmaker and we reconsidered her request."

"So, you did not think it was some kind of revenge on her part or some kind of plot to overthrow the regime then?"

"No. But she refused and the game went on and we lost."

"What was so important about winning this game? It's only a game."

"The team that won had to play other cities and if they won those, they would win the Trophy and be able to ask for favours on that day."

"Who made those rules?"

"We did."

"Weren't you asking for trouble?"

"No ... because ... we never lost any games."

"You never lost because there were no other cities, were there?"

"After the earthquakes there were none."

"So why didn't you change the rules?"

"Rules can only be changed ..."

"... When enough people vote against them and you did not even think there was any danger because all the other cities were decoy cities only, and when the Accused challenged you, you had to accept. For one who was so bad at keeping all the rules, she seemed to know more about them than you. She beat you at your own game, if you see what I mean. Do you really believe in magic?"

"Yes ... yes, of course."

"So why weren't you frightened when she cursed you at the picnic?"

"I had to show the other people that I was not afraid because I did not want to start a panic. But I also thought that without the magician's help her magic would not be so strong. But I was very wrong."

"So, you really believe in magic?"

"Yes … yes, I do."

"If the Accused can work magic, why can't she do it now?"

"What do you mean?"

"Why, she could point to the lights, like so, and make them go out." He pointed to them and the lights went out and then came on again. He laughed. "Magic is all around. Cessie, my love, turn the Elder into a toad, please. Stand up; look in your bag for a spell that will turn him into a toad. I am waiting."

"I cannot do it today, Medrix," she laughed.

"Sorry, she won't do it today, Elder. I must say you must have nerves of steel for you did not show a sign of fear, did you? The reason being, you know she could not do it."

"Objection! The Counsellor is wasting Court time by playing party games."

"Overruled. Go on, Counsellor."

"I put it to you, Elder, that you knew she did not use magic. You might have decided that they cheated in some way – but you bring no evidence of that, do you?"

"No ... but ..."

"No. You do not. Thank you, Elder – you have been so helpful. Now it is the Prosecutor's turn – go ahead."

"Elder, Medrix has been very rough with you., but of course you have left out a very important point."

"What is that?"

"That they had a plan. They had worked out a way to defeat the team. They need not have used magic to carry it out – with this plan they could fool your team into thinking that they were weaker than they actually were."

"Yes. But we did not know that until the case came to trial. But we knew they had cheated in some way though."

"There you are, Elder, fielding a city team: a team that gets regular training, a team that has the best of everything, a team who love the game and know the rules, and yet they are beaten by a team of exiles, some of whom have played the game before, some who have never played or seen the game played, some who do not even live in Middle City, and this team, because of cunning and set plans, win. They win because her life depends on it – their lives depend on it. This game was a plot to rid the planet of the Lawmakers who had made it their home for years and had every right to be there. This was a plot, Elder. This was a plot against all of the Lawmakers in the galaxy. Of course she must be punished. She deserves to be punished in such a way that she will know that Lawmakers do not allow such treatment from people, whether they be Lawmakers or not."

"What you say is true."

"Yes. They planned it and she ensnared Medrix eight years ago and so completely fooled was he that he did not see what was happening in front of his very eyes. And still he does not, for the poor fool thinks that he is in love with her and he thinks she is in love with him. Think again, Medrix. You have been brought into this, for this is her cunning plan.

"He has been trapped in this web of magic that she has spun around him and spun around everyone around her. The sooner she is sent to prison, the sooner he will be released from her spell and can be sent for retraining as the man has forgotten how to be a Lawmaker. All Estolan must be ashamed of him. She is an excellent actress – makes everyone sorry for her. Do not be sorry for her, people of Estolan, otherwise she will draw you into her web. Beware! But the Judges can see to that."

"Yes – they can, and the sooner the better."

"I think that Medrix has forgotten his place in our society."

Cessie took off her bonnet and began to comb her hair.

"Objection! They are making it up. *I* am not on trial here."

"Overruled. Carry on Prosecutor."

"She is pretending to love him."

"I think so."

The Prosecutor turned and stared at Cessie. "Grand Elder, that woman has taken off her bonnet. Does she not break a rule?"

"Yes, she does. Why have you taken it off?"

"Oh … I … I … was too hot."

"Put it back on, *now*."

"But it is too hot in here."

Medrix glared at her: "Stop arguing and do what he says, *now*."

"As I said before – it is too hot in here."

"I am telling you to *put it back on*, woman," the Grand Elder demanded.

She just sat there, fanning herself with the bonnet.

"You, woman, you go too far – you will be punished for your insolence."

"But I will still be too hot," she said quietly.

Suddenly there was a murmuring in the women's section of the court, as one by one they took off their bonnets. The Grand Elder stared at them all. He knew he had to back down. He could not punish them all. The men looked shocked, but said nothing.

Lawmaker Eldon stood up. "It is very hot in here. Do you think we might have some windows open, please?"

The Grand Elder nodded. "Yes, Lawmaker, I think that might be a good idea. You and Lawmaker Hewer may open some windows."

They did so and Cessie put her bonnet back on, and so did the other women.

"The Accused will write out the Court Rules and give them to me tomorrow."

"Oh … but that's not …"

Medrix interrupted her and said: "Of course, Grand Elder. She will do as you ask. I shall see to it personally."

The Grand Elder nodded. "See that she does."

Cessie stuck her tongue out at Medrix and said: "Crawler."

He shook his head, hoping that the Grand Elder had not heard. He seemed to be talking to one of the Judges, and he never even showed that he had heard anything, which was just as well for her.

The Prosecutor looked at her and said: "No more questions, Elder. Thank you. I think her insubordination speaks for itself."

Medrix said: "I call the Accused." He looked at her, grimly.

"Janital was your friend, wasn't she?"

"Yes."

"Was she older than you?"

"Yes – she was one year older."

"Did your stepfather beat her?"

"Yes – he hit all the girls."

"Why?"

"He hit them when he felt like it – more so when he was drunk."

"Did she die of the fever?"

"He said so."

"That was not my question – I am asking you. Did she die of the fever?"

"I cannot answer that question." She lowered her voice and looked at her hands.

"You can be punished if you refuse to answer the question."

She just sat there. He tried again.

"What caused her death?"

"I can't answer that question." She began to cry.

"Tears won't help you. You have to answer or you will be punished. She shared your bed on that night so you must know the answer to that question."

"She shared my bed because she felt poorly. I wanted to tell someone but she would not let me. She said it was for the best; that she could not go on living here in this … in this evil place … she made me promise to stay with her until the end … so I did …" Tears ran unchecked down her cheeks.

"Who should you have told?"

"My stepfather: she was afraid of him."

"Why?"

104

"I cannot answer that question." Still the tears rolled down her cheeks and she twisted stiff fingers in her lap.

"Celisia, you are duty-bound to answer my questions."

She shook her head and refused to answer.

The Grand Elder interrupted. "As you will not answer the questions, you are sentenced to five strokes of the whip for your insolence to the Court – the punishment to be carried out after this session."

She stood there, shaking and crying and then said in a small voice: "I accept the punishment you have decreed, but I still cannot answer the question." She sat down.

"*Stand up*. Stand up *now*!" roared the Grand Elder.

She stood up, but looked down at her feet.

"Are you afraid of your stepfather?"

"Yes," she said softly.

"Why?"

"Because he said that if I did not do what he told me to do, he would kill me." She sat down again, and drank some water. Someone shouted: "Liar!"

"Stand up *now* – I will not tell you again," demanded the Grand Elder.

She stood up. She held the bar in front of her, looking frantically around the court as if looking for a way to escape.

Medrix went on. "Why would he kill you?"

"Because I was a wicked person who would not conform to city life."

"But Celisia, one of the rules is that no Lawmaker may kill another one … so it was just a threat and no more."

"He meant it all right. He said my mother did not obey her mother by marrying my father. Her marriage was not recognised as a true marriage and therefore I was a child of a whore and as such did not come under Lawmaker Rules. My mother was a beautiful person and my father loved her very much."

"You must answer my questions. No one is going to harm you."

"Aren't they? Someone blew up the Chetner shuttle I was supposed to be on. It was only because I decided to return here that I escaped, so I cannot be sure of anything, can I?"

"We have no proof that anyone was trying to kill you. It could have been some malfunction of the shuttle itself."

"Yes, I suppose it could."

"So answer the questions then."

"If it was you – would you answer the questions?"

He hesitated, and then said: "Yes – of course I would."

She took a drink of water and said: "She was pregnant. He gave her something to drink to get rid of the baby. It killed her – she bled to death."

There was a murmur round the court and someone shouted: "Remove the filthy bitch from the court before she maligns him further."

Law Officers tried to see who it was, but failed to find him. The Grand Elder ordered everyone to be quiet.

"Why did you say she died of the fever?"

"Because he told me to."

"You should have told the Grand Elder."

"She wouldn't have believed me. He was cunning – sly – all the things he said I was … he … he …" she stopped and sat down.

"Stand up, please," Medrix said quietly.

She did so. "I did what he said because I did not want to die too. My father said he would come for me one day. I wanted to stay alive for him." Tears flowed down her face and she buried her head in her hands.

"Objection! Objection! What has this to do with the charge in question?"

Well, Counsellor?" the Grand Elder asked. "How do you answer the Prosecutor?"

"The Prosecutor went into a background to build his case. I am just doing the same."

The Grand Elder nodded. "I see. Objection overruled. Go on please."

"So you did what he said?"

"Yes – but Janital told me to keep away from him, so I did. I was lucky because my Lawmother said that I had done some beautiful sewing and she took me to see the Grand Elder, who was very pleased with me about my stitching, but she was also displeased with the report on my behaviour that she had from him. She gave me extra work as punishment but, luckily for me, it was with the Lawmothers so I saw less of him. I think my sewing saved my life."

Medrix went on: "Who was the father of the baby?"

"My stepfather."

"She was raped?"

"Yes."

Someone shouted: "Liar, liar, liar!"

The guards went into the men's section and removed a Lawmaker from the court.

Medrix went on: "And you – did he rape you?"

"Oh no. I kept away from him. I would hide away in a cupboard or under the stairs. He turned his attention on to the other girls. I was sorry, but what could I do – no one would have believed me. I wonder what happened to them. Maybe they have a story to tell."

The Grand Elder was writing something and two Law Officers were sent somewhere.

Medrix went on: "Now we have looked into her life as a child. What do you think a person growing up in such a situation would do as the years went on? Surely as she got older she would plan some sort of revenge. She would plot and scheme to find a way to pay them back. She would have to do something that would take them right away from Chetner."

She looked at him in amazement. What was he doing?

"Now, Celisia Margaret – you plotted and planned to make those Elders pay – didn't you?"

106

"No ... no ... no ... I did *not*," she shouted.

"Of course you did," he said scornfully.

"No ... NO ... NO ..." she yelled at him.

"You set up the whole thing in those caves. You knew how to get in them. You knew where the tunnels led. You knew the Lawmakers would come there. You already knew I was a spy but you pretended that you did not. You pretended that you issued the challenge to rescue me. You had it all planned from the very day you left the City – is that not so?" he sneered.

There was complete silence in the courtroom. The Prosecutor looked at him as if he had gone mad. She just stood there, too shocked to say or do anything.

"*Answer me*! The Elders of Chetner said that you were a liar – a sly little bitch only out for what you could get. But remember you are on oath and are duty-bound to tell the truth – that is if you know the meaning of the word – answer me *now*!"

"I ... did ... not ... plan ... anything ... it ... just ... happened" she said slowly and clearly. If he was trying to trap her she was not going to let him off so easily.

"You met a magician and got him to help you?"

"He offered to help."

"He gave you a magic spell?"

"No ... only some tips to help us ... the rhyme helped us to concentrate on what we were doing."

"You intended to win at all costs?"

"No ... we hoped to win ... that's all."

"Hoped to win! Of course you wanted to win. Why do it otherwise?"

She hesitated, trying to gather her thoughts together.

"Well, bitch – tell us," he sneered.

"Counsellor," interrupted the Grand Elder, "mind your language. It is not fitting to use such words in this Court. For this you are fined six hundred credos."

Medrix bowed to him and apologised to the Court and then went on: "I need an answer, please."

"It gave us all something to do. It brought us all together in a common enterprise."

"Of course it did! You challenged those Lawmakers on Chetner because you knew you could win. You held back in the first half in a cunning game that you knew they could not win. This was your revenge wasn't it?" he shouted at her. "It was a plot to overthrow the City and the Lawmakers you hated so much. Using magic you could not fail to win and you knew it ... didn't you?"

"I ... I ... I am not guilty ... I ... am ... innocent of the charge," she sobbed.

"Come on. Are we to believe that you did not hate those Lawmakers? In fact you hate all Lawmakers, don't you?"

"No … I do not … they are just people of another race – just people."

"You hated those people living in the City on Chetner. You hated living there, didn't you?"

"No … no …"

"Of course you did."

"When … I came … to … live in the City … I … was … five years old. I thought everyone would love me as I was a child …" the tears ran down her cheeks. "But I was wrong … no one loved me … even my grandmother who was the Grand Elder … looked at me with scorn … I had … come from a loving … home … so … why … was I brought here … if no one wanted me … I looked like my mother … every time my grandmother looked at me … she thought of her daughter … she had not forgiven her … she blamed me … she took out her spite on me … they all did … I was not to be loved … I was to learn how to bow to their every whim … but even though I tried … no one … even thought … I was worth loving. But ... I do not hate them … or their city … it was just that love and caring … had been buried … it was there somewhere … but the Elders made sure that everyone kept in line … they exiled me …" She took a drink of water, then went on: "When I lived in Middle City … I … discovered that love had not died … it was there all the time … they might have been poor … but they cared for each other … and unless the Lawmakers … learnt to care … then their people would find that a mightier power than they would one day take them over … I did not know I could win … I just thought to rescue you … you were my friend … one of those people who cared … or so I thought then. Then the idea seemed to take off … I could at last show them that I could do something well … If we lost … only I was to be punished … All I wanted was to play the game … could I help it if they were such bad losers …?" She sat down and drank some water. There was absolute silence in the courtroom. She stood up again and said: "If you are trying to trap me into saying that I am guilty then I will know for sure that you are not working for me, but for my accusers … but if you are … remember that revenge always falls back on to the avenger. So be warned Lawmaker!"

The Grand Elder said: "I hope Lawmaker, you are not trying to rig this trial, for I have heard that you are an Elders' man. The Judges will not tolerate such behaviour. I hope you are being true to the Court – are you?"

Medrix flushed red and bent his head, then looked up and said: "I want to get at the truth … for who would blame her if she was guilty of this terrible thing."

"I will see how you go on … but be warned … you might land up at Jailfa Island prison yourself if you defy our Rules."

Medrix bowed to the Court and went on – perspiration ran down his forehead and he dried his face with his kerchief: "Now, Celisia, let us get back to the game. The actual day: how did you get to the City?"

"The Elders sent transport."

"How did you feel?"

"I was petrified."

"Were the crowd happy to see you?"

"They seemed to be in a happy mood."

"Did you feel happy on the court?"

"No … I felt so nervous."

"Tell us the rules of the game, please."

"The aim of the game is to throw the ball from the green circle, up and over the wall. Then the shooter or any team member has to run to the other side of the wall and catch the ball before it touches the ground or is caught by the opposing team. If they can do this, the players score points. The lowest part of the wall scores two points, the second scores 3 points and the highest scores five points. The ball is thrown from one player to the other; a player may bounce or kick the ball also. The opposing team has to stop them in any way they like but they cannot go into the green circle. Each team plays for thirty minutes per session. After two sessions there is a twenty-minute break. The team with the most points wins."

"Thank you. Did the sun come out only when the City team were trying to score?"

"I don't know."

"You do know? You were there."

"I cannot remember."

"Why were you so poor in the first half?"

"We were nervous of the crowds; of the whole thing."

"But you planned to hold back?"

"Yes – but we didn't because we were so tensed up anyway we could not seem to do anything right."

"But after the magician came on the field you improved. Why was that?"

"He told us to chant the rhyme and when we did, we concentrated on the game, blanked out the crowds and began to play for the fun of it instead. When saying the rhyme it took our minds off everything else."

"Did you intend to send all the Lawmakers away?"

"No. Only the Elders."

"Your revenge on them?"

"No … they were the troublemakers.

"Did any Lawmakers stay?"

"Yes."

"And they were accepted by the Chetnerites?"

"Yes … yes, they were."

"Why?"

"They wanted to build a new life for themselves without the restrictive rules."

"So you saved your planet?"

"No ... we have not got the equipment to do this yet."

"What will you do when your planet is no more?"

"Travel everywhere and teach the game and give lectures on the danger of over-mining, of pollution, of destroying the natural environment of a planet as the Lawmakers, well, the Elders of Chetner, have done."

"What is your dearest wish?"

"I would like the Lawmakers to restore our planet to its former glory."

"No more questions, thank you. You have answered very well. It is now your turn, Prosecutor."

The Prosecutor stood up.

"They exiled you for being a troublemaker … they gave you your freedom … yet you took their freedom away from them by making them leave their homes, didn't you?"

"Put like that – yes – I suppose I did."

"But … surely – that is revenge?"

"No. I was entitled to ask for anything, so I did."

"Yes. You mean if you had not sent them away, they might have re-claimed your planet as is usual in these cases."

"I did not know that."

"Did you ask?"

"No."

"So, you had your revenge on them – but like you said, revenge has a way of falling back on the avenger – your words not mine – that's true isn't it?"

She did not answer. He went on.

"Because of you, your planet is doomed. Can you honestly say that your planet will be there for very much longer because of your actions against the Elders?"

"Maybe not … I don't know."

"There! Shall I say more? She admits it. She admits her treachery. Her guilt is there for all to see. I am right … am I not?"

"You twist my words."

"Do I?" he shouted scornfully at her. "Do I indeed? See how she replies … this person who dared to drive the Elders away from their homes. This person who cheated in order to win a game. You shame the Lawmakers' Nation … but your days are numbered. No more questions."

The Grand Elder said: "Now this has been a very long session. We will meet again in four days time. I have other meetings to attend and I am sure we could all do with a break. The Accused will report to the punishment centre for her punishment. The Law Officers will take you there," and with that pronouncement, he left the court.

As Ces was taken to the punishment centre, she passed all the Elders in the corridor. They laughed at her and rubbed their hands together with glee. She had admitted her treachery. She would soon be sentenced by them for it.

Later that evening she returned to the house, went to her rooms and shut and locked the doors. She wanted nothing to do with any of them. No one was on her side. Even Medrix had betrayed her. She lay on her bed wondering what action to take next.

The bottle of painkillers was on her bedside table. She looked at it. That was one sure way to get her out of an impossible situation – she would make some coffee and then take the tablets. She was willing herself to get up and go to the kitchen but her back was too painful and she felt so tired as she lay there that she fell asleep, at last knowing what she would do when she woke up. It was the only and final answer to her problem.

Chapter 8

Ces woke up suddenly. Someone was banging on her door. She went to see who it was. It was Medrix. He was shouting through the door: "Open this door. I am going to count to five and if you have not done so by then I will break this door down."

She got up, went slowly to the door and opened it.

"What took you so long?" he said angrily.

"I was asleep."

"It is the hour of eleven. Where are the painkillers?"

"On my bedside table: why?"

"Lawmother Grey has a headache and cannot find any in the medicine chest. You should have put them back."

"These are mine," she said picking up the bottle. "I bought them the other day. But she can borrow them of course." She handed him the bottle.

He thanked her rather gruffly and took the bottle. "Don't lock your doors in future."

She went back to bed. But he came in a few minutes later and said: "Get up. Don't laze in bed. Your Lawmother has scrambled you some eggs and made some toast and coffee, so come and eat it now."

"I don't want anything to eat. All I want to do ..."

"I don't care what you want to do ... your Lawmother has cooked it for you, so come and eat it. Then you can take a couple of those painkillers afterwards and your Lawmother has some cream to rub on your back – and don't go back to bed. You will be better walking around or you will stiffen up and won't be well enough for court."

"It's all right for you to talk – you haven't been ..."

"I know what happened to you and I am not surprised after all that trouble you caused arguing with the Grand Elder of all people. Because of your stupidity you made him back down. Any sympathy he might have had for you went out of the window with the hot air."

"Oh, you would rather that I had fainted because of the heat ... is that it?"

"Yes, that would have been better."

She sat down at the table and said: "Oh God, I don't think I can sit down."

"Well, stand up then, but eat now!"

She did so and felt better for it. She took two tablets. He put her bottle of tablets in the medicine chest and locked it. He looked at her and said: "They will be safer there."

It was almost as if he had read her thoughts. If he had, he never said anything, which was just well, as the suicide idea did not seem right now. Her Lawmother rubbed the cream on her back and said she would put some more on before she went to bed.

Three days passed and she had one more day of freedom before going into court again. Medrix had said he wanted to talk to her about her case, which surprised her, as he did not usually do this, but any talk was better than none, so she agreed.

"Have you written those rules out?" Medrix asked her. "You have to give them in tomorrow."

She looked at him in horror. She had forgotten all about them.

"You haven't, have you?"

She shook her head. "I'll start them today … I will tell him I haven't finished them because of my back."

"He won't accept that. I promised you would do them. You are going to let me down again."

"Again … what is that supposed to mean?"

"If you are going to argue with me, I will go."

She sighed. "Don't worry Medrix. I will get them to him in time."

"Good. Now tomorrow the Prosecutor may call on Rule 226 which states that the Prosecution can call the Defence Counsellor if he deems it necessary for his case."

She opened her Rule Book and read the rule over again and then she went on to the next rule and said: "It says here in Rule 227 that I may cross-question the witness."

"Yes it does. But in your case you must not."

"What?" She laughed. "Are you afraid that I will ask something you cannot answer or would prefer not to answer?"

"Do as you are told, Cessie – ask no questions," he said angrily.

"But the rule says I may."

"And I am telling you not to do so."

"I cannot do what you want. Something important may arise and I might have to ask a question."

"If you do that you could upset the whole case … now promise me."

"Sorry … really I am … but I cannot make that promise."

"Sorry!" he shouted at her. "You'll be sorry … you stupid, selfish little bitch!"

She stepped back as his tone became savage.

"You won't be helped, will you ... you must go your own way."

"I must if I have to ... after all the questions in court sounded as if you were working for the Elders, not me."

"Are you insinuating that I am rigging the trial?" He was furious now.

"The Grand Elder thought so ... he warned you about it ..."

"And you?"

"It looked like it ... " she hesitated, then went on " ... perhaps they were right after all ... I can see you would not want me to ask you that question ..." Her voice faded. She looked at him. His eyes were as cold as ice.

"Who was right, Celisia?"

"The jailer ... and the man from Temra. They said there would be two Prosecutors at my trial and it certainly sounded like that."

He moved over to her. "I told you to trust me ... but you could not keep that promise ... could you ... you selfish little whelp ..." He pushed her away from him and she stumbled over the mat and fell against the long seat, bruising her ankle.

The shock made her cry out and she put her hand out to save herself from falling. Tears ran down her face. Her Lawmother came to see what was going on. Medrix shut the door in her face and locked it. He turned back to Cessie. She moved away from him and stood by her sleep room door.

"You would believe them before me ... is that what you are saying ... is it?" His body was stiff with rage.

"Who?" she asked, now somewhat confused by the question having lost the thread of the conversation: "Who?"

"The man you met on the shuttle to Temra. Your pal, your contact, your lover perhaps ... yes, the man you were seeing when you were pretending to love me. Well, answer me bitch!"

"I told you I did not know him," she sobbed.

"Of course you knew him. What woman would go off with someone she didn't know? You little slut."

"The trouble with you, Lawmaker, is that you are just plain jealous," she said, and laughed.

"Don't you dare laugh at me, or I will give ..."

"You will hit me ... I am used to being hit by Lawmakers ... you revert to type easily don't you, Lawmaker ... you are the mean, stern Lawmaker who likes to have his own way. I was a fool to think you were working for me." She went into the washroom to bathe her ankle. It had gone purple. He followed her.

"I don't care what you say about me; just promise me not to ask questions tomorrow, that's all ... that is all I want you to do."

She shook her head. "You are asking me to break a rule. I get punishment if I break rules and now I am to be punished if I don't do what you say and now I am trying to keep the rule ..."

"Well, that's it. From this moment on I am no longer your Counsellor. Get someone else." He put a key on the table. "That's for the cupboard where all my files are kept, plus the password for the computer."

"But Medrix, I don't know anyone else ..."

"That is your problem, not mine ... I want nothing more to do with you ... nothing ... you and I are finished ... do you understand?"

"Yes ... I understand. So the trap is set and I have fallen in."

"If you say so," he said grimly. "There is no need for tears. They do not affect me any more."

He unlocked the door but she called him back and he turned towards her. "Well, what is it?"

"If you do this it will look as if you are rigging the trial: more so if I lose but not otherwise."

"If you lose the Elders will reinstate me. If you win I shall be praised for all my work. But I expect to see you in Jailfa Island prison because I am the only one who can get you off." He left her then and she heard him go out of the main door, slamming it behind him.

She looked at the key on the table and said to herself: "Well, Cessie, there is only one thing for it – you will have to defend yourself. If you can train a team and win, you can certainly beat a whole lot of Lawmakers at their own game. But maybe I won't have to. Maybe he can be coaxed back in some way. Think, Cessie, think. In the meantime I had better write these rules out as I promised." She sighed. "It is too late to contact the Grand Elder now. I will have to speak to him tomorrow."

Medrix sat in his quarters and groaned. What had he done? His foul temper had trapped him again ... he was better out of it ... but in his mind he saw her shocked face and somehow he felt so guilty ... the Elders would be very pleased though. He knew that for sure.

He awoke at the hour of three. The bleeper on his contact bracelet was flashing. He sat up and picked it up. "Yes? Who is it?"

"It's me, Medrix ... Cessie."

"What do you want? It is three in the morning. You should be in bed."

"I know ... but I am writing these rules out. You said the Grand Elder will want to see them."

"Yes ... but that is up to you now, nothing to do with me, so why are ...?"

She interrupted him. "There's a rule here that says: 'A Counsellor may resign from a case if he gives the Grand Elder six days' notice before doing so. So that means you have to go to court tomorrow, or rather today, whether you like it or not ... Medrix, are you listening?"

"Yes ... I'm listening ... you have just made that up. Goodnight, Cessie."

"No, Medrix, I have not. It is here in the book. It is rule 409 ... look at your book and see for yourself."

"But you have my book. You lost yours, so you said."

"Well, I'll come round now and show it to you."

"No, you won't … Lawmothers are not allowed in the men's quarters, and certainly not at this hour of the night."

"I wouldn't lie to you, Medrix – and another thing … I have come across another rule."

"And what is it?"

"It says that a Counsellor for the Defence can only give the Accused advice on how to proceed in the case in question. He or she can follow it, if it is to their liking, but if not, they may tell the Counsellor what they would like him to do and it is his job to do it to the best of his ability."

"And what number is that?"

"… 216 … are you still there … did you hear me?"

"Right, Ces … I see I am stuck with you whether I like it or not … so you win."

"Ah, but Medrix … it works both ways … I am stuck with you … and I fancied that good-looking Lawmaker who came in with the Grand Elder last time … he had a lovely voice … he would, I am sure, have been a good Counsellor. He smiled at me."

"Ces, I am tired and I am sure you must be as well. I will come over for breakfast at the hour of eight. Perhaps then you can tell me what you want me to do about your case – until then, goodnight!"

Cessie put the bracelet back on Lawmother Grey's bedside table. As she came downstairs she laughed and said: "Got you Lawmaker mine." So saying, she hid the Rule Book under her pillow and went to bed.

He arrived at eight and sat down to breakfast with her and the two Lawmothers. She said that the only thing she wanted was that she be allowed to keep Rule 227. He said that he would do what she wanted … but he shook his head at the thought and told her that he could not be held responsible for the result of her action … and she smiled at him and said: "Of course I know that Lawmaker."

Lawmother Grey said that they were like a couple of children arguing all the time and if it was up to her she would put them over her knee and give them a good hiding, whereupon Cessie roared with laughter at Medrix' red face and she said; "Lawmother Grey, I think he is a bit too old for that treatment … but we will try to behave better in the future."

Medrix got up, saying he had work to do and he mumbled something as he left. It sounded like "Women … I … have had enough of them … I really don't understand them at all."

But from then on he went out in the evenings. It seemed he was going everywhere with a woman called Jessanda – an old flame by what Lawmother Grey told her. She was betrothed to him years ago – but now she was interested in him again – and Medrix seemed interested too. "Good thing" thought Cessie, "an Estolan woman would know all the rules and that should keep him happy.

The next morning they both arrived at the court earlier than usual. Cessie sat down at her place and went on writing out the rules and then handed them into the Grand Elder. The Prosecutor claimed the use of the Rule 226 as Medrix had predicted. The Grand Elder explained the meaning of it and Medrix went to the witness stand. He looked tense and anxious.

The Prosecutor smiled. Cessie felt sick with apprehension. The Prosecutor hesitated, looked at Cessie and began: "Lawmaker, who sent you to Chetner?"

"The Elders of our City."

"Why?"

"The Chetner Elders wanted someone to spy on the exiles."

"Were you accepted by them?"

"Yes ... I was supposed to be Fador's twin. Fador was brought up by the Lawmakers, but he was a Chetnerite."

"Why was he brought up by the Lawmakers then?"

"The Elders took babies. Fador was taken, but his twin was not."

"He had a twin?"

"Yes ... he had died at birth, or so they thought ... he did indeed have a twin, but it was a girl, not a boy ... but they did not know that."

"Aren't Chetnerite twins telepathic?"

"Yes ..."

"So Fador would have known you were not his twin?"

"Yes ... he may have done ... but unless he opened a channel to his twin he would not know. After all he was the team coach ... a good position, a respected position in the Lawmakers' eyes. Why would he even think of jeopardising such a position?"

"The Grand Elder asked you to keep an eye on the Accused. Why would she do that?"

"At the time she said that she was younger than most exiles. But of course I know now, that she was her grandmother."

"How old was the Accused then?"

"Fifteen years old."

"Fifteen! And just getting to an age ... when men ... perhaps would be attracted to her ... and along you came ... with your good looks ... and fall in love with her. Am I right?"

"No ... she was one among many exiles that is all."

"So why did you become her friend?"

"I ... I became a friend to them all, not only her ... I was a spy. That was my job, to seem to be friendly with them all."

"But did you like her?"

"Yes ... I admired her."

"Why?"

"She seemed different from the others. She did not seem to mind that we all lived in such poor conditions and that sometimes there was little food to be had. Sometimes baskets of food were left in certain places for them, for the

Elders did not want dead exiles everywhere ... but, otherwise, there was not much to be had, apart from what they could grow."

"Now we know that Santel was Fador's twin – so wouldn't she have told the Accused?"

"No. She did not know until after the game, when Santel realised who I was ... she couldn't have told Cessie."

"Did it ever occur to you that the Accused knew you were a spy?"

"No ... I never thought anyone knew who I really was."

"Oh ... come now ... she used you to make her challenge ... why make the challenge then?"

"To save me ... she thought they had mistaken me for Fador and was in dire trouble."

"But you see, the clever little witch knew and used you to further her cause ... you can see that, surely?"

"No ... because if the Elders thought that, I would have been taken off the case."

"We know she is clever; if she can outwit you, she can outwit them. Why didn't you stop the game?"

"It just took off ..."

"Did you try?"

"Yes ... but I failed ... I did not tell her that she had to have an observer ... the game would have been stopped there and then ... but luck was on her side and someone stood up and claimed that position."

"Luck you call it ... she was dealing in magic ... she had powerful allies on her side."

"She seemed to ... nothing was able to stop her ... her enthusiasm seemed to carry her through."

"Were the Elders pleased with you when you got home?"

"No ... they sent me for retraining."

"Why?"

"Because I did not stop the game."

"But you have worked for them since?"

"Yes."

"Doing what?"

"Objection! Objection!" said Cessie. "What he worked at since is nothing to do with the trial."

"Objection sustained." The Grand Elder nodded and smiled at her.

The Prosecutor went on. "So, eight years pass and she asks for you as her Counsellor. Don't you think that is odd – after all you betrayed her to the enemy?"

"Objection ... this has nothing to do with the charge."

"Objection sustained."

The Prosecutor bit his lip but went on: "Are you in love with her?"

"Objection! Whether he is in love with me or not has absolutely nothing to do with the charge."

"Objection sustained. Go on please, Prosecutor."

"After the earthquake … did you refuse to send out a search party?"

"It was not my place to do so. But I thought she was better off dead."

"Why?"

"Because … I …"

"Because you thought she was guilty of …"

"Objection! Objection! Whether he believed me to be guilty or not should not interfere with him defending me at my trial."

"Objection sustained. You should change your questioning, Prosecutor."

"You thought she was guilty of causing an earthquake …"

"Objection … Objection … What is the matter with you? I am not on trial for causing an earthquake."

"Objection sustained. Change your line of questioning, Prosecutor. Listen to my warning."

"Yes, Grand Elder," the Prosecutor said, making a small bow to him.

"Lawmaker, have you been asking the same questions that I have?"

"Yes."

"Why?"

"To get at the truth."

"And have you reached a conclusion?"

"Yes."

"What is it?"

"Objection! Objection! Rule 228 states that the Prosecutor may not ask the said Counsellor anything that gives any hint of his tactics in dealing with the Accused's case."

"Objection sustained … I think you should look up the Court Rules again as the Accused seems to know them better than you, Prosecutor."

The Prosecutor sighed and looked at her and said: "No more questions, thank you."

Cessie smiled. Medrix went to go back to his seat but the Grand Elder stopped him.

"Now you may ask questions." He smiled at her, as did the Prosecutor. Medrix was biting his lip and glaring at her.

"Well," she said … "I do have a few questions to ask," she hesitated and looked around the court. Medrix was looking at the floor. Someone coughed.

"Please … do go on …" said the Prosecutor. She would fall into his trap, just as he had planned.

"As I was saying … I have a few questions to ask … to ask … the Prosecutor … but of course I am not allowed to do that. But for Lawmaker Medrix I have none … none at all."

People began to laugh. The Prosecutor flushed red and glared at her … she smiled at him. He looked away, and she knew she had won the day. Medrix walked stiffly to his seat.

The Grand Elder announced that there would be a short break for coffee and the court cleared.

Medrix came over and held her arm very tightly and steered her out of the courtroom and into a small room nearby. He slammed the door behind him.

"Very clever Celisia … very clever … at least you went by my rules, which is just as well for you because the Prosecutor was just about to pounce…"

"I knew what he was up to … I am not dull you know … but you are quite wrong about the questions … if there had been some to ask, I would have seriously considered asking them."

"Oh, would you? You deliberately kept the Court waiting … didn't you?"

She smiled, her eyes lighting up with laughter. "Did I?" she said, looking straight at him. "I went by the rules of the book … I did nothing wrong. The Grand elder did not think so, and he smiled at me."

Just then the door opened and his grandfather came in.

"Excuse me, you two … but I had to congratulate you both. What a good team you make together. You tricked the Prosecutor well and truly. I bet he is now sorry that he claimed that rule. Well done, both of you! Must go now, your brother is waiting to take me for a coffee." He left the room, laughing.

"Hmmm …" Medrix said. "I think one little monster enjoyed a battle at my expense. Team indeed! He does not know you as I do."

Then his sister-in-law came in and she too congratulated them both.

"Don't congratulate her, Lawmother. She has a big enough head as it is."

"She is a tease, Medrix. You should laugh more."

"Laugh more! How can I do that when this one goes her own way anyway? Don't praise her, she will be even worse and I have to put up with her for the rest of the trial!"

"Oh, Medrix, don't be like that … she's won a lot of people over to her side: maybe some of the judges, too."

"Yes, I am sure … it will be the men she has won over with her wide blue eyes and her flirting ways," he said scornfully.

"Don't listen to him, Cessie. He's jealous because you were so good. He does not like to be crossed, but I think he has met his match in you. It will do him good, my dear."

"Don't be too cross with him, Lawmother. He is working very hard on my case … and for that I can never repay him," she said seriously.

"You owe me nothing, Ces. I am just doing a job that I cannot get out of … that is all."

His sister-in-law left them and he was just about to say something when in walked a tall woman carrying a tray with two cups on it. She said: "Medrix, I have brought you in some coffee. I know how you like it … see, I have remembered." She put the tray down and handed Medrix a cup. "I thought you did very well today, but why the Accused had to keep butting in like that, I cannot imagine … because everyone knows you could have handled everything yourself without any trouble … but at least she did not ask any questions at the end, so she got something right." She sat down by him and drank from the other cup.

Cessie expected him to tell her off for her downright rudeness, but he didn't. He just laughed and said: "Just as outspoken as ever, my dear." They then went on talking together as if she wasn't there.

She walked out of the room and found her Law Officers waiting for her. "Shall we go and get some coffee now?" she asked them and they said that they would go with her as Lawmaker Medrix was otherwise engaged. She did not think that Medrix was even aware of her leaving the room. He was too busy looking at that dark-haired beauty with green eyes to even think of her. Well, she was welcome to him, as far as she was concerned, for they were both as rude as each other.

She enjoyed her coffee and sat with the two officers. She laughed to herself – she had enjoyed most of it – but what were the next few hours going to be like?

Cessie was still drinking her coffee when Medrix appeared and seemed to be annoyed with her again. "Where did you go? I needed to talk to you before we go into the court again."

"Oh, I thought you were otherwise engaged, so I left you both."

He handed her a bunch of clothes and some shoes and socks. "Put these on. They are your Chetner clothes."

"But Medrix, I cannot wear those. I will be breaking the rule."

"Do it. I have not got time to argue."

"But …"

"Do it now."

"Yes … Bossy Boots," she said, as she went into the washroom to change. He is supposed to tell me what is going on but it is the same as usual. She sighed, "Blast the man. He is more interested in Jessanda than my case."

She was late coming into court but no one said anything. The Prosecutor looked daggers at her.

The witness stand had been moved away and in its place on the floor was a green circle. Were they going to play the game? Surely not … She sat in her place. Medrix told her to go and stand in the circle. She did so.

"Now then, the Accused is going to give a little demonstration. She is dressed in her Chetner clothes so that she can move more easily. Cessie, please say the rhyme, the chant you used on the day of the game."

She looked at him in amazement and said nothing.

"Come on, we want to hear the rhyme, say it now."

"I … I … can't remember it."

"Of course you can … you used it when practising for the game and you used it in the game. So come now, let us hear it again."

She shook her head. "No … I cannot remember it … Maybe Thortrex or one of the others can remember, but I cannot."

"Then say another rhyme … any rhyme you like … make it up."

"Umm … 'Bounce ball, bounce ball … umm … on the floor … throw it up ever so high … and catch it once more'. Will that do?"

"Yes, that will do nicely. Now say it while you are moving around, bouncing the ball and throwing the ball up in the air."

She started slowly at first, but the quicker she said the rhyme the quicker she moved, until she was moving rapidly and in complete charge of the ball. Then she stood still in the green circle and looking up high, she saw a beam going across the ceiling and without more ado, she threw the ball high and it sailed over the beam and she caught it coming down. "Will that do Counsellor?"

Everybody stood up and clapped her performance, well everybody except the judges and a few other people.

She stood waiting for Medrix' praise but he only told her not to show off. She began to bounce the ball around her again. But he told her to stop and stand still.

"Now you see why the rhyme was used. It was not a magic rhyme, only something to make them concentrate more and to speed up their movements. Now if the Prosecutor wants to ask her questions, now is the time."

"Well, well, my dear, what a good idea of yours to give us this little demonstration of your skills. Of course she could not use the original rhyme, because it was a magic chant and what would have happened here if she had chanted it I hate to think. So she cleverly pretends not to know it and then thinks up another one to take its place, not telling her Counsellor when they were talking it through last night what she was going to do. She is a clever one, manipulating everyone to suit herself and, look at her dressed like a boy, except no one would say she looked like one in that get up. She goes dancing around the courtroom flaunting her body and flashing those witch eyes at any man that looks at her. Trying to get them on her side. She is a disgrace to her sex, a disgrace to our Lawmakers' society. See, she covers her face with her hand. She knows we have found her out, the little schemer, the little witch charmer. Well, we do not encourage such behaviour here. Your plans have been upset. See, we're too clever for you. You expected this demonstration to work, didn't you?"

"I had no plan."

"Did you think to entice us by wearing such clothes in our court?"

"I'll have you know, Prosecutor, that on Chetner we wear clothes like this all the time. You insult a whole nation when you insult me. Wars have been started for less than those remarks and I think you need to watch your words. People are more important than the clothes they wear. You do not know the meaning of …"

Medrix interrupted her, "No, Ces … no …"

"I have to tell him he has insulted our ..."

The Grand Elder shouted at her: "You have said enough. When are you going to learn how to behave in court?"

"But ..."

"You will not argue with me. You are to stay in the women's prison ... The House of Correction, when this session is over. You will stay there for the rest of the trial."

"Yes ... I understand perfectly ..." she bowed her head and went back to her seat. The session ended and the court cleared. She went after Medrix. "I have to see you now."

He led her into a large office and closed the door. She was seething. "*You,* Lawmaker did not discuss this idea with me, otherwise I would have pointed out the drawbacks and you let me take the blame for it, as if it was my idea and you know full well it wasn't."

"We thought it was a good idea."

"We? Who do you mean by we?"

"I had the idea of you demonstrating the game and she said to make it authentic, why didn't you dress in Chetner clothes."

"Who exactly is 'she'? Could it be Jessanda? You've discussed my case with her? You go too far – I could report you for this." She shook with anger.

"Well, go ahead – then I will be taken off your case – and that would be a good thing – for you do nothing but criticise and argue with me and try and score off me, as you did in court today."

"But you should have talked it over with me. I could have told you the drawbacks."

"I did not decide to use the idea until the early hours of this morning – it was actually Jessanda who gave me the idea."

"How – when?"

"Yesterday evening. She said that wouldn't it be a good idea for you to demonstrate the game and let you wear Chetner clothes – and the more I thought about it – the more I liked it."

"So why didn't you tell me?"

"I needed to get to court early and then, at break time, you went off somewhere."

"But you were talking together – you forgot I was there – so I left you together."

"You should have waited. Anyway, if you want to report me – go ahead, that will release me from the trial – so go ahead – I don't want to go on working with you anyway."

"Are you sure of that?"

"Of course I am sure – you do nothing but upset the Grand Elder – who seems to dislike you – how am I supposed to find you innocent when you behave so badly? Yes I want to opt out – the sooner the better."

"Then I release you, Medrix," she said in a tight voice.

"It is not as easy as that, as you well know."

"I can release you – and I say you can."

"Rule 409 says that …"

"Medrix, Rule 409 is not in the book. It only goes up to 350. Why do you think I did not give you back your book? Rule 109 says that you can give six hours notice – not six days ..." she flung the Rule Book down on the table.

He opened it at the page and saw for himself. Now he was furious – "You little, devious bitch … you – well, that's it. I'll take these folders back to the house – Lawmother Grey will give the key and my notes to the new Counsellor for the Defence and then I will write my resignation letter."

She turned away from him and stared out of the window – trying desperately not to cry.

She heard the door slam as he went out. She felt weak and sick.

She had to think. She locked the door and went into the washroom and washed her face. It was cool in here, she thought, and looking around she saw that there was a window open. She pushed it further open and looked out. It wasn't far to the ground and without more ado, she went back and locked the washroom door and then pulled herself up to the window – she would make a run for it – hide up somewhere until it was safe to smuggle herself onto an outgoing shuttle. She would go somewhere where no one would ever find her.

Chapter 9

Medrix strode out of the room angrily. He had had enough of her once and for all. He would go back and write that letter now. He had only walked so far when someone called to him to wait. He turned round and saw Jessanda. "Lawmaker," she said, "I've been waiting ages for you. You remember, don't you, you promised to take me to the dining centre for coffee after the trial."

"So I did. But I can't stop now as I have to write a letter to the Grand Elder as Ces has released me from the case. Later on, when my resignation has been accepted, I will have plenty of time to take you out." So saying, he left her and hurried along the road. If he had turned back he would have seen her smile of satisfaction at his news as she went on her way.

When he got back to the house, he looked at the Rule Book again, and discovered that Ces also had to write a letter to the Grand Elder. "Oh, damn," he said out loud, "I'll have to go back now and get her to write one as well, as I am sure she does not know." He took paper and pens and went back to the court buildings.

Cessie got down from the window. She could not just run away, hadn't she already been tempted to do that and look what happened then? She had had a lucky escape not getting on that shuttle. She had to face the situation squarely. She could defend herself but first she must read the Rule Book to find out if this was possible. She unlocked the washroom door and went into the main room. She picked up her Lawmother outfit and fetched out the Rule Book from her pocket. As she did so, someone tried the door, then knocked on it. She went over to unlock it and was surprised to see Medrix standing there.

"Oh! Did you forget something?"

"No. But I have to talk to you." He came in and locked the door behind him. "Why was the door locked?"

"I was going to change into my Lawmother outfit," she said hurriedly, "I am not supposed to be in my Chetner clothes am I?"

"I see."

"Well, what did you want?"

"I was reading the Rule Book again."

125

"Oh. So what?"

"It says that you can't just release me by word of mouth, you have to write a letter to the Grand Elder explaining why you are releasing me and then I write my letter of resignation and we send both letters to him. So you will have to write that letter now." He put pen and paper on the table.

"Oh … I see …" she slipped her skirt over her trousers and did it up.

"You can dress later." He was annoyed, she could see that. "I have brought more paper in case you make mistakes and have to write it again."

"Oh … well, I can see you have thought of everything." She smiled; an idea was forming in her mind. Just how long could she stretch this time out before she actually wrote the letter? She began to shake herself as if doing a dance.

"What are you doing now?" he said angrily.

"Taking my trousers off," she said as she bent down to remove them completely.

"Well, sit down now and start this letter." She sat down and then dived down under the table.

"What are you doing now?"

"I've dropped my pen … ah, here it is." She put it on the table and then bent down again. "I am now changing my socks and shoes … and now I must change my top."

"No … no … no … sit down," he emphasised by banging his hand on the table. "Write the letter now."

"But I break a rule if I am not dressed properly."

"Shut up. Sit down. Now write." He sat beside her.

She picked up the pen and began to write. "What address shall I put at the top?"

"The house address." She wrote slowly.

"Mmmm … Dear Grand Elder …"

"Don't put 'dear' … you must leave it out."

"Well, yes, he is certainly not a dear of any sort, well not to me … of course he must be a dear to his wife, unless he is not married. Is he married, Medrix?"

"Shut up and write."

"How do you spell 'release'? Is it one L or two?"

"One."

"Grand Elder, I am writing this letter to say that I am releasing my Counsellor from the case because … Medrix, what do I put next?"

"Say why you are releasing me." He tapped his pen on her letter. "You have put his title on the same line as the letter. Start again and put the date." He gave her another piece of paper.

She tore the letter up in little bits, then went and put them in the waste box. Then looked out of the window and waved at someone, then came and sat down.

"What's the date, Medrix?"

***"The twelfth day of the 7th Moon 4017 ..."

She started again, then looked up and smiled very sweetly at him. "What reason shall I give for releasing you?"

"Well, you released me, so why did you?"

"Because you wanted to be released, Medrix ... so I will put that." She bent her head as if writing.

"No, no, you can't put that."

"Why not? It's the truth, isn't it?"

"Because it is not a valid reason."

She picked up the Rule Book and looked in the back. "Ah ... there's a list of valid reasons here," she began to read them out: "1. If the Counsellor has illness in the family and is unable to give enough time to the case: 2. If the Counsellor is thought to be rigging the trial: 3. If the Counsellor is some relation to the Accused or the Accusers: 4. If the Counsellor ..."

"Stop it now Celisia ... put your reason." He snatched the Rule Book from her hand.

She sat there writing and then pushed the finished letter towards him. He read it and threw it back at her. "You cannot put that I am not listening to what you say ... it's not true."

She crossed it out and wrote something else. He crossed it out. "Do it again."

She wrote again. "Listen, Medrix, this is what I have written ... mmm ... 'because he does not like me any more, he spends more time with his girlfriend than me, he discusses my case with other people rather than me, and he expects me to flaunt my body in front of the whole court so that everybody thinks I am guilty' ... will that do?"

He was furious. He stood up and, catching her by the shoulders, he turned her chair round so that she half fell off it and had to grab his arm in order to stay upright. He pulled her from the seat. "Very funny!" he growled, "wasting my time are you? I will tell you what to write and you will write it and write it now." He pushed her on to the seat, turning it back to the table. "Now, write this: ... 'because I am unable to do what my Counsellor advises and do not think his line of questioning will bring a good outcome to the case' ... now you copy out the whole letter again and if you make one mistake in it I will take my whip to you ... do you understand?"

She said not a word but began to write ... and tears ran down her face as she did so. He wrote his letter and when he reached 'because' he wrote in words similar to what he had written for her. She laid the pen down and ran into the washroom. He picked up her letter and read it ... parts of it were wet and she had not signed it.

"Come here, Celisia. You have to sign it and then we are finished and I can get out of here."

She did not come. He went into the washroom after her. She was sitting on the window ledge. "Come down from there now." She did not move. He reached up and pulled her down. "Stop being silly," he dragged her into the other room and pushed her on to the chair. "Sign it now." She never moved.

"I am not signing it."

"Sign now or I will ..."

"I am not signing it because it is not true. I tricked you because I know you might very well get me off. Perhaps I should not have done it but I thought that in years to come you would thank me for doing it, for I would not have you take the coward's way out ... if I had known you were going to let me down, I would have got on that Chetner shuttle, but I came back because I knew that of all the people that I know, you would try the hardest to bring me through this trial. You asked me to trust you and I did. I still do. So I cannot sign that letter. I cannot free you any more than you can free me. And if you think about it, all this started with this stupid rule and I think the Prosecutor did it purposely to split us up, just like the jailer on Jailfa Island. The Prosecutor knows you are brilliant as a Counsellor and he is going to try anything to split us up. How he must be laughing now, for if I have to defend myself, the judges will see me as a troublemaker and I won't get a fair hearing. So, Medrix, I cannot – will not – release you. Use the whip on me, if you must ... but I will not change my mind." She bent her head and cried.

He stood up. "You think your pleading will bother me. I do not want to defend you any more – have you got that into your thick head? Tears do not have any affect on me because you are a conniving little pest ... just like the Elders said you were, and you have proved them right. Now – sign the letter! ... Well – I am waiting ... sign it!"

Someone knocked on the door. He walked over and answered it. It was a Law Officer with a tray on which were two cups of coffee. "I thought you must be tired, working so late, so I got you some coffee to help you along. The one with the spoon is for her as she likes it sweet and you do not."

Medrix thanked him and brought the coffees to the table. He went back to the door and locked it. "Now then, drink this coffee and then sign the letter."

"So – you think I am guilty?" She took the coffee cup in her hands and warmed them.

"I never said that ... Look – I will stay on your case on one condition."

"What's that then?" she drank some coffee and screwed up her face. "It's too sweet ... ugh."

"Drink it up – they were very kind to think of bringing it to us."

"Yes ... I suppose so ... I did not know the dining centre was still open ... What's the condition?"

"Do you remember how you promised to obey me after that quarrel we had? The one where you landed up in the Medical Centre."

"Yes, but that was different." she drank a little more of the coffee: "I can't drink it – it's horrible ..."

"No difference. Now I know you have not kept that promise but I am giving you a second chance. If you do everything I tell you to, then I will stay on your case."

"You will?"

"Yes … Well, what do you say?"

She looked at him and smiled. She had won – well almost – he was staying on. She nodded … would she be able to do that … "Yes, I agree Medrix – thank you."

"Stand up."

She stood up.

"Sit on the floor." She did so. "Good, now sit at the table and sign the letter."

"What?"

"Sign it, or the deal is off."

She sat there, staring at the letter. He had tricked her. She put her hand over her mouth. He waited to see what she would do. She bowed her head – she knew when she had lost – signed the letter and stood up and pushed it towards him then reached across the table to get her bag for her kerchief was in it. As she did so, her elbow caught the coffee cup and sent it hurtling to the floor, spilling its contents as it went.

"Another of your little tricks …" the coffee had stained the letter.

"I couldn't help it … it was an accident … I'll get a cloth to wipe it up. I'll write it again."

He grabbed her, pulled her over his knees and slapped her hard several times. "This is your last chance. Wipe this mess up, then you can go back to the prison and write this letter again and sign it. I will come over to the prison later on and collect it. It will be held as your promise to me … to obey me … is that understood?"

She stood up … walked a few paces away from him. "I hate you, Lawmaker … I..." she seemed to stumble … "Medrix, I cannot see you … where are you? … My throat's on fire … I don't hate you … I will …" her knees buckled and she fell headlong, hitting the chair as she did so.

Medrix looked at her. "There's no need to act stupid … the Elders told me you were a good little actress … so get up … you won't get my sympathy that way."

She didn't move. He bent over and turned her over. Her face was green, her eyes dull and she was foaming at the mouth. "God …" he gasped … "she's not acting … Ces … Ces … Oh, God, Ces, I'll get help now …" he contacted the Medical Centre and the Law Officers. Only one officer came. He said that it must be a bug for his partner had been rushed to the Medical Centre earlier with the same symptoms. "The funny thing was how quickly he became unwell. He had a cup of coffee … and the next thing he was ill."

She was rushed to the Medical Centre. The doctor questioned him asking how much coffee she had drunk … she had evidently been poisoned as the other man had … but he was taking a blood sample to find out for sure.

"She'll be all right, won't she?" Medrix asked anxiously.

"We'll see," was all the doctor said.

Her Lawmother arrived and sat with him. She went to ask the doctor how the Law Officer was and came back in tears. The Officer had just died. Medrix put his arm round her. "If it's the coffee ... she did not drink very much of it; she said it was too sweet." He remembered he had told her to drink it. "Oh God, Lawmother ... what have I done? I thought she spilled the coffee purposely to spoil the letter ... I gave her a hiding because of it. I ... I ... had got her to agree to obey me in all things ... but I did not mean to give up the case ... Oh God ... if she dies ... it's my fault." He put his head in his hands. "What can I do?"

"Pray, Medrix, pray – you were not to know the coffee was poisoned."

The blood sample verified her condition. Luckily there was an antidote and she was given it. The doctor told them that she would be better by the morning, as she had not drunk as much of the coffee as the Law Officer had – and she had come in sooner than he had.

They sat beside her bedside all night, but by the morning she had not improved. The doctor could not understand it. "It's as if she has given up – she's not fighting the poison," he said sadly.

Sometimes she spoke softly: "Tell Poppa I waited and waited for him ... I could not wait any more ..." At other times she screamed in terror: "No, no, Cessie's been good, why are you hitting her? No one likes me here ... I want to go home ... go home with Momma ..."

The next night she slipped into a coma and lay there, staring into space.

Chapter 10

Everyone was devastated at the news but Medrix more than the others. He and her Lawmother stayed by her bedside so that she was never without anyone she knew.

The days passed slowly. Three moons later, Medrix was called to a meeting. The City Elders were there and the Chetner Elders, plus the Prosecutor and one judge and the Chief Elder.

It seemed that the Accusers wanted the life-support machine to be turned off as Cessie could be in a coma for any length of time. This, they said, proved that she was guilty of the crime and this was her way of escaping punishment. They were willing for the Chetner people to keep the trophy as a compromise, for what had happened was not their fault.

The Grand Elder thought the offer made good sense, because the judges would not want to be here indefinitely. The judge agreed.

Medrix did not agree. He said that someone had set out to kill her and that person must be found. They had promised her protection and they had failed to give it to her. But the Grand Elder said that he could not afford to keep all the witnesses and judges here for much longer.

The Chief Elder thought it was a good idea too, and as Chief Elder he would grant it that she should be left to die in peace instead of hooked to a machine for maybe the rest of her life. He said he had the last say in the matter as her father was not here and she had no husband who could say otherwise.

The Grand Elder then said that a meeting would be called in ten days time to make arrangements accordingly.

Medrix told her Lawmother what had been said and that if Cessie did not wake up in ten days' time then that was the end for her.

Her Lawmother smiled at him. "Medrix, the answer is clear. She must marry someone as soon as possible; then she will be safe."

"Yes ... who have you got in mind, Kella?"

"You, Lawmaker: why, you of course."

"Me? Me marry that little wild cat ... I would never have a moment's peace and she hates me."

"She doesn't hate you … she dislikes what you have to do. Cessie does not hate anybody … she saved your life once … granted she thought you were Fador's brother at the time, but she did it for you … you owe her one, Medrix. Anyway, once the trial is over you can part company if there are no children; that's our rule …"

"What about if she stays on that machine for ever, then?"

"But you will have the power to turn it off – do what is best for her – do something for someone else rather than yourself, Medrix … and you can do this … I will stand in for her … what do you say?"

"Yes. It's the least I can do, I suppose. I'll arrange it at once – she won't like it," he laughed, "she will be furious." He smiled at the thought and the promise she had made to obey him always – life could become very interesting.

A few hours later Cessie had married her Lawmaker. She wore his ring on her finger and Kella had promised that she would keep all the rules of marriage as befits a Lawmaker's wife.

Kella drank a toast to the couple. The bride lay staring into space. Medrix bent down and kissed her cold lips. He shivered and wondered what his life was going to be like and whether he had done the right thing.

At the next meeting he said, that as her husband he did not give permission for her life-support machine to be turned off. So everything was left as it was for the time being.

He had a bed put in her room so that he would be near her at night. During the day her Lawmothers were with her.

The Grand Elder said that he had to go back to teaching the defence class, for if she did not recover, he would have something to fall back on. He agreed and went back to teaching, but he still worked on her case.

His grandfather told him to talk to her, tell her everything about his day. Read stories and poetry to her, even sing to her. He did just that and encouraged her friends to come and talk to her. The bread sellers came with their baskets and told her about their days. Schoolchildren brought drawings to pin on her wall and to sing to her. His family were always visiting. His life circled around her and he gave up other interests to be with her.

Lawmother Grey said that he should have a change at times and do something that he enjoyed for once. But he said that he wanted to be with her and get her well if it were possible.

So the days went on and she just lay there, staring into space. He felt it was his fault, he had only cared for himself and he could see what she had become because of it.

Jessanda had come to see him to try and get him to go out with her family, but he sent her away telling her she was breaking the rules by trying to tempt him away from his wife.

One evening he was late back from class, and it was getting dark by the time he got to the Medical Centre. Law Officers stood talking in the corridor, but there was no Lawmother with Ces. He sat on the chair by her bed and relaxed back and fell asleep because he was so tired.

He woke up suddenly. Someone was standing by her bed. At first he thought it was a doctor but then he realised it wasn't, as the man was tugging at the tubes of the life-support machine.

Medrix fetched out his whip and, with a flick of his wrist the whip snaked out towards the intruder, encircling him, trapping his arms in its embrace. The man fell backwards as Medrix jerked the whip tighter.

"Ah ... Lawmaker ... you startled me ... think man, think ... we are in this together ... she dies, you will be free to marry your first love ... the case will be over ... I will get paid ... the whole matter will be solved and I won't bother you again, it will be our secret ... what do you say?"

"Who are you?"

"I cannot tell you that, Lawmaker. Now release me and I will do the job as I promised and then collect my money. It was a pity she did not go on the shuttle – but there it is – I have nothing against her, of course, but I will be paid good money for doing a good job."

Medrix pressed the alarm bell and the Law Officers came at once and took the man away. The man fitted the description Cessie had given the officers of the killer she had met on the shuttle to Temra.

From then on he did not leave her side, and although the Grand Elder told him to go back to work, he refused; saying that he still had to work on her case.

Three moons later he was standing by her bedside talking about huntersnouts, when he asked her how many of them were in the team. He was holding her hand, intertwining his fingers with hers, and he felt a slight movement against his finger. He asked the question again, and she moved her finger again. He smiled. "Come on, Ces ... tap once for yes and twice for no. Are you ready, love?"

She tapped once.

"Good girl. Do you like eating soap?"

She tapped twice. He went on with the questions and she answered them all. He bent down and kissed her, then called the doctor who also ran some tests.

Five days later he awoke in the night and heard her asking him for water. He gave it to her and then she lay back and went to sleep. From that day on she improved.

Three moons later she was told she could go back to the house.

She had been informed by Medrix that she was now his wife and had to live according to the rules of marriage as befitted a Lawmaker's wife. He also told her that she was not to do the housework because she had been so ill. Her Lawmother told her why he had married her and that, after the trial, the marriage could be annulled if she was not pregnant.

She had been shocked at first, but then she realised he had saved her life and she promised herself she would keep every rule there was.

When she returned to the house, she had her own rooms and life went on as before. Medrix was kindness itself, praising her when she did anything well and bringing her little gifts to amuse her. At times he took her visiting his family and friends.

Medrix noticed how quiet she was and he had the idea that she was frightened of him. The only one she smiled at was Lawmaker Eldon and at times he saw the old Cessie come to the fore when she was with his assistant. But he did not say anything – after all, Eldon had not been unkind to her as he had.

Five days later he was told the Court would meet again. He told her and she just nodded and thanked him for telling her.

On the night before the trial he took her out for a meal. She looked beautiful in the dress Lawmother Grey had bought her. They danced together all the evening and she was so relaxed in his arms that she smiled up at him.

When they got back to the house the Lawmothers had already gone back to bed and he took her in his arms and kissed her and she did not pull away because she felt so safe in the tight band of his arms. He pushed her hair out of her eyes and kissed her again. Then letting her go he said: "Go to bed – I'll see you in court tomorrow."

She turned away from him and then turned back and said: "Whatever happens, Medrix, I know you will always do your best for me," and she reached up and kissed him, then said: "Thank you for a lovely evening." Then she ran into her rooms and closed the door.

He went up to his rooms and knew without a doubt that he loved her but he also knew that after the trial he would let her go back to Chetner where she belonged. If they lost, well that was another matter. Hopefully she would not lose for he only wanted the best for her, and if it meant she went away, then so be it.

Chapter 11

The court was packed on the day when the trial restarted.

Medrix and Cessie walked in together.

The Grand Elder started the proceedings by telling Medrix to call his next witness. He called the Chief Elder. There was a murmur around the court, which stopped as soon as the questions started.

"What exactly does your job entail?"

"I negotiate mining rights on different planets. I also see that the place is left in good condition once the miners have left. I also bring criminals to justice if they have abused the system in any way which is not in keeping with our Lawmaker rules.

"Did you go to Chetner?"

"Yes."

"To negotiate mining rights?"

"No … that was before my time. I went to see them, for according to my records they should have left there many moons ago."

"Were you welcome?"

"Yes. The whole Council met me plus two representatives from the Chetner Council."

"Representatives of the Chetner Council you say? I know for a fact that there was no such Council."

"But they were there and they asked sensible questions, too. Such as, would their land be put back as it was? Would it be safe to farm it? Would the Lawmakers be able to claim money to do that? There were other questions. They seemed to know what they were talking about."

"Had they over-mined?"

"Yes, but the Chetner Council had agreed on the understanding that they would be paid and all agreements made for the other areas would cover the new areas also."

"I see. But why had they done that?"

"They had been cut off by interplanetary storms and had been unable to return when planned. So they had to work with the Chetnerites who, in fact,

135

were nomads who tended goats and chersers (a kind of cow) and seemed only too glad to have their help. So they had shown them how to build cities and houses so that they gave up being nomads. Unluckily for them, many of the cities were destroyed by earthquakes. The Lawmakers then helped by taking in a number of children and bringing them up as their own rather than let them be neglected by their parents."

"What was the outcome of the meeting?"

"They agreed to stop mining; to get their finance officer to work out the financial cost of putting the land back as it was. They agreed to have the work done and to pay for it out of their profits and then return to Estolan."

"Did you go back to check that they had done the work?"

"No."

"Why not?"

"I then heard that, because of circumstances beyond their control, they had to leave without doing the required work."

"Thank you. No more questions. Prosecutor: your turn."

"If the Lawmakers had to return before they had finished all they had to do for some reason beyond their control, would they still be responsible for the work?"

"No."

"Thank you, that's all I need to know." The Chief Elder left the stand.

Medrix called Lawmaker Steffan.

"You knew the Accused as a child?"

"Yes … she stayed with me when her stepfather was ill."

"What was she like then?"

"A lovely little girl but very timid. She was covered in bruises when she came to me. She said she had been very naughty and had been punished for it. I reported her condition to the Grand Elder but she said that the child was lying and she had fallen downstairs."

"Was she naughty?"

"No. She was very anxious to please. She was very bright, for a girl. She could read well and add up numbers quicker than I could and I was the official Council finance officer. She was a very gifted child but, being a girl, she was held back of course."

"If you were the finance officer, then you were the one that worked out the cost of the land reclamation on Chetner. Did you do the work?"

"Yes."

"How did you do that?"

"I looked at all the maps and worked out the cost. It was a vast job because so much mining had been done, but then she decreed that we should all leave. It was just a good thing that we were already packed and ready to go, and had been for many a moon. I had arranged with haulage companies to collect all things from the city and our mining equipment, as well as our people. All we needed was a date … she gave us that, and so we went as our rules decreed."

"No more questions." He nodded to the opposition.

"So it proves without doubt," said the Prosecutor with a smile, "she sent them away before time and left her planet to die?"

"It could do, but … no you are wrong. They had planned to go anyway. They had over-mined the land so much that their profits would not cover the work, so it was decreed that it was beyond their capabilities to repair it and it was best left as it was, and maybe they could put in a claim to the Mining Society of Lawmakers to bear half the costs. But when they got back, they did nothing … and no one knew how badly they had treated everybody back there on a dying planet."

"But she had doomed the planet, hadn't she, by her request?"

"Yes, I suppose she had, but they should have honoured their promises to the Chetner people; she gave them a way out."

"Thank you. No more questions."

Medrix pointed to a screen that had been put in place earlier. "I want to show you some sketches, all of which have been taken from the Defendant's sketch book. Now, look please as I point them out to you.

"The first one is of a group of Chetner Elders, all talking together. The next one is the late Grand Elder. The next is the Prosecutor. Then it's one of me as I looked on Chetner. This one is of me, as I am now. It's good isn't it?" There was a murmur around the court. "Here is Fador and Jadex. This is the magician … have a good look at him. Does he remind you of anyone you know? Here are some Lawmothers – this one Lawmother Grey, this one is Kella, and here, we have Jessanda. Next, here is Eldon – and his children. This is Thortrex and, here is a group of the City Team that were scheduled for the day or so she thought … but two of this team were not in the team on the day because they were taken ill and could not play … so weren't on the list that Fador gave her beforehand … Remember, the rules state you have to declare your team before the game, and they both did this.

"Here are some more of me …" Everyone clapped and smiled as they recognised each person.

"Objection! He's wasting Court time playing games."

"Sustained. I enjoyed the show … but that is all it was, Counsellor."

"Oh, no. You will see how it fits into my case, Grand Elder, as I go along."

"Very well I will allow it. Carry on for now."

"She has an excellent memory for faces. There were thirteen Elders on Chetner but there are only eight of them on this City's Council. The other five were not required, as there were five of ours still here and, anyway, they did not want to be on the Council. We know by the sketch which ones stood down. No. 1 died. No. 2 did not want to stand for office again and is travelling around the galaxy. No. 3 went to live with his son on Jadeston. No. 4 is housebound with crippling rheumatic pains and No. 5 has gone back to teaching. None of these agreed with the trial.

Let us look at the picture of the magician again. Now, look at his face again. Does he remind you of anyone? Look at the Elders. One of them has short grey hair and green eyes, but what would he be like if we added long hair and a long beard and the magician's costume?" He pressed a button and there they saw him as the magician.

"Objection! It could be any man with green eyes. That Law Officer has green eyes … is he also a magician or an Elder?" There was laughter around the court as the Law Officer began shaking his head.

"Objection sustained."

Medrix smiled, and went on. He re-called Thortrex and waited while the little man climbed up on to a chair.

"When did you meet the magician?"

"After an earthquake … he offered me the job of helper … for six moons … we went everywhere."

"How did he vanish from the tree?"

"He had a magic device that transferred us from one place to another."

"Were you with him all the time?"

"I never went to entertain the Elders when he went there, or to the wild country beyond the mountains; then I stayed in Middle City."

"Thank you … that's all." The Prosecutor shook his head.

Medrix re-called Fador and asked him to point out and name the team shown on the screen. Fador also said that the last two did not play on the day because they were ill, and the Accused must have done the team from memory before the match. He also said the players were in their quarters. Medrix also wanted to know if the referees would have stopped her team chanting if no one had complained. Fador said that he would not as no one could possibly chant all through the game and keep up the pace. It is physically impossible to do so … and even if they said it to themselves, they would stop as soon as they had settled down to play … the chant would hinder them more than help them.

The Prosecutor asked him no questions. The Grand Elder said that they would have two hours off before continuing the next part, so the court cleared and Medrix took Cessie out for a meal.

Two hours later they were back in court and Medrix called Lawmaker Tennix to the stand.

An elderly man walked in – he was the one with green eyes.

Medrix asked him if he was a teacher, and Lawmaker Tennix said that he taught history and art – including the history of the game and therefore he knew all about it. Medrix then asked him if he had ever taught magic. He said that he hadn't. He was then asked if he could do card tricks, whereupon he laughed and said that he could and therefore he was very popular at parties. He was then asked if he had watched the game and he said that he had. Medrix wanted to know where he sat and he said that he sat in the back row near the exit door – it was his job, he said to go and check on the players who were ill and, yes, he had gone to their quarters to see them.

"Ah," Medrix said, "and you came back then?"

"Yes."

"But you came back as the magician, didn't you?"

"No – certainly not."

"I have witnesses that say you did."

"Then they are lying."

"No – they are not lying – you did not go to the players' quarters – you went straight to your room to change your clothes, didn't you?"

"No – no, certainly not."

"You lie, Lawmaker – you see … the two sick players left their quarters and came to your corridor to watch the game through the big end window. They hid behind cupboards when they heard someone coming, and they saw you go into your room and come out dressed as a magician. They were surprised and after you had gone, they looked in your room – there wasn't anyone else in there. If you had gone to their quarters you would have found their rooms empty also!"

"They are lying," he said angrily.

"No – they are not – you were placed in the enemy camp as a spy. Oh, yes, you told her things to make her think you were on her side – things like how many decoy cities there were, tips on playing the game and a special chant that would help them concentrate on their play – you nearly gave yourself away when you seemed to know such a lot about the two of them – the rhyme was to slow them up – for if they concentrated on that all through the match, they wouldn't be able to concentrate on the game.

"It was easy enough to appear at the gates. You went to the small gate tower and changed into your clothes there and just stepped out of the door to appear as a magician.

"When you went to entertain the Elders you were, in fact, reporting her plans to them. When you went to the wild country, you were checking the new shuttle bays that were being built for all the crafts that were to come in. That's right – isn't it?"

"No. Certainly not."

"I have witnesses to prove it. Cessie did not plan to meet you – you planned to meet her!"

"No – you are wrong."

"My witnesses will prove it and you did not want to join in and bring her here for trial because she might remember you."

"No – no – no – you are wrong. I am innocent."

"Innocent is the last word I would call you – *Deceitful – yes! Cunning – yes!* But *innocent? No!*" Medrix shouted at him.

"You are wrong, Counsellor."

"Am I? In your house the Law Officers have found the magician's outfit."

"No – no – no – they couldn't have done. I threw …" he stopped and put his hand over his mouth.

"You were going to say you'd thrown it away – weren't you?"

"No – no – no." He shook his head. "You are bluffing, Counsellor – trying to catch me out to prove something that has no truth in it whatsoever."

"Oh – am I? Your wife, who like every Lawmother on Estolan is very thrifty – goes through the rubbish bags to check that nothing has been thrown away which could be used in some other way – she found the outfit – washed and pressed it and put it away in a chest in the attic – all ready for when you would need it again. She had no idea it was evidence, for even she did not know the role you played in this affair – and … here it is …"

He held up the outfit for all to see.

He stood there – all colour drained from his face, and he answered in a muffled voice.

"Yes – I played that part. All you say is true. The others you see – seemingly had thought of everything – so that she couldn't win – or even play the game. But in spite of everything, she won – I think her grandmother was very proud of her then and easily granted her the favours she required because we were all ready to go anyway. I was against the trial. I said that their revenge could fall back on them. But they said that you, Lawmaker, would see she would lose. How mistaken they were – and how right I was.

"They thought they had taken care of everything – a magician that had disappeared – she could never prove anything at all."

"Thank you: at last you tell the truth and show up the Elders for what they really are – at last you tell the truth. No more questions – Prosecutor: your turn."

"Yes … Well I am very interested in why you did this. Tell me."

"Quite simple really: we Elders thought it was all a plot on her part to overthrow us. Not only us but all the Law-making nation, for once the news spread, other dissidents would take up the challenge and our whole nation could be plunged into a civil war."

"I see. Why was she offered a place back in the City?"

"We could keep a strict eye on her there, and her grandmother would see to it that she was brought under control. She gave her another chance but she refused. When she refused we knew for certain that this was a plot, otherwise, why make the challenge? She knew who Medrix was; in fact we were thinking of withdrawing him altogether as we had the magician in place, but we let him stay in. He was very close to her and if we let him disappear just like that, she might have got wise to the fact that we knew what she was doing.

"When she won the game, then we knew she had cheated in some way. At half-time, they all sucked some kind of sweet. We thought that this could have been some kind of energy sweet which, of course was against the rules of the game.

"The Grand Elder praised her for winning, but was quite unprepared for the favours she asked for, and being who she was, had to bide by the rules, and leave."

"Thank you. By asking for those favours she sent them home and because of this they were unable to do any reclamation work at all. She has killed her own planet. No more questions."

Medrix called Cessie once more.

"Did you cheat in the game?"

"No."

"Did you eat some kind of energy sweet at half-time?"

"No. But we did suck sweets – they were thirst-quenchers, not energy sweets."

"Did you play the game out of revenge for all the unhappiness you had experienced in the City?"

"No … it was just a game. I just wanted to play the game. I wanted my grandmother to see that I could do something well."

"Did you think you could win?"

"No … and in a way, because we thought winning was out of the running, we just enjoyed playing and, in so doing, we relaxed – and imagine our jubilation when we played so well that we won. The sun was very helpful too because it shone in the other team's eyes, but things like that are allowed in the rules of the game. We could have experienced the same thing as well."

"Thank you. No more questions."

"Wait, please. I have questions for you." The Prosecutor nodded to her and she stood looking at him. "If you had your time over again, would you ask the same favours again?"

"Yes."

"Why?"

"If they went on mining, the land could not be reclaimed."

"The sweets you ate were energy sweets, weren't they?"

"No – just thirst-quenchers. We always eat them at all our games."

"I have proof that the sweets you ate were energy sweets, and so you cheated to win."

"No – you are wrong."

"But I am right. Your Lawmaker should take his whip to you for you have not even told him about eating sweets at the game, have you? Did you tell him about the sweets? Answer me."

"No," she said, "I did not."

"There …" he paused, "you didn't tell him because they were energy sweets. The Observer saw the bag you held – the bag of sweets. You threw the empty bag on the ground and he picked it up and gave it to an Elder. I have the bag here." He held it up. "It reads: 'High Energy sweets – to give you a lift'. Those are the sweets you ate – you cheated to win the game and I can prove it."

"No. You are wrong. That is a white bag – mine was yellow – they have lemons in – no sweetener – they just quench your thirst, that's all."

"So you say. There she stands, the little cheat – sly as they come – as I have proved today."

"Why didn't he report it then?" she asked.

"Because in all the fuss of rushing back, the Elder never looked at it until he got back to Estolan. No more questions."

Cessie stood up and claimed Rule 39 – which was time to discuss new evidence with her Counsellor. It was granted. The session was brought to an end until the following morning.

Chapter 12

When they got back to the house, Medrix was furious with her because she had not told him about the sweets. He said: "You have had all this time to tell me and now I have to hear it from the Prosecutor. Why didn't you tell me?"

"I forgot all about them. I didn't think they were important. They were thirst-quenchers – no sweeteners in them at all – we always eat them at games."

"I believe you deliberately didn't tell me because they *were* energy sweets and because of them my case is in ruins … and you are, without doubt, guilty of cheating in order to win the game." He shook his head.

"No, no! You can't believe that. You can't! I'm innocent. *We* are innocent. They were lemon sweets. Thortrex didn't eat one; he is allergic to lemons … Medrix, *please* …"

"I should take the whip to you for deceiving me."

"But I haven't, Medrix. I did not think it was important …"

"Get out of my way before I … Oh God … what am I going to do now?" he went to the main door and opened it.

"Where are you going now, Medrix? We have to talk this over … we …"

"There's nothing to talk about … I am going out … out of your way …"

"You are going to her, aren't you? You are going to Jessanda … going to discuss this with her instead of me …"

"If I am, what is it to you?"

"It's everything to do with me! I am your wife – or have you forgotten that?"

"If you are inferring that I have been unfaithful in my marriage to you … you must know I keep the rules and would never do that. But when I go out it is my business whom I see and it is certainly not for you to question it. Number 118 of Marriage Rules – and if you question me further I shall have to take steps to punish you." He pulled the door open and was gone before she could answer him.

It was all over. Fancy it ending like this. She couldn't bear to see his face contorted with rage or everyone to think she was guilty: yet there was nothing she could do. She had about three days of freedom left. She sat down: it was no good running away. She went to the window and looked out. The sun was out and it was still warm. She needed to go for a long walk; the fresh air would do her good. It could be the last walk she would ever take before she was incarcerated in that jail. She didn't blame him; he had done his best for her, she knew that.

She changed into her Chetner clothes and looked in the drawer for a cap and, finding one, put it on her head, hiding her hair under it. She did not need her cloak. She went out the back way, walked down the garden and into the bushes by the wall. Here an old shed leaned against the wall and where it did, there was a gap. She squeezed through. It led into some trees then into the park. There were a few runabouts parked. She took one and drove out of the park and onto the track that led to the lookout point. She parked it there but walked along the cliffs away from the lookout tower.

She noticed how green the grass was and the colours of flowers that grew to perfection on the rough cliffs. It was as if she could sense the very essence of what she saw. It calmed her. She stood still, arms outspread as she looked at the blue sky and the whirling seagulls, and she felt that she was a small child again who found everything enchanting. She put her arms down and carried on walking. She could smell the sea and hear it crashing against the cliffs. She was alone with nature and it was all hers for the taking. She turned to look back at the way she had come and saw a man with a dog, not far behind her.

The dog suddenly saw her and raced towards her with a ball in its mouth. She laughed and threw the ball for him. The dog raced away but was back with it before she had gone very far. She threw it again and the man caught up with her as her cap blew away in the wind, revealing her golden hair. She ran after it but he picked it up before she got to it and, as he gave it to her, she realised it was Medrix. He laughed at her surprise. "Where are your Law Officers, Ces?"

"Watching the front of the house," she laughed.

"You shouldn't be here on your own. You break a rule."

"I know, but I just had to get some fresh air." The dog dropped the ball at her feet. She threw it for him and he raced away.

"Well, you have me now. If you look along the cliffs you won't see Jessanda anywhere." The dog put the ball at her feet again and she stepped away from Medrix to throw it, and then walked on quickly so that he had to hurry to catch up. "What's the hurry?" he asked.

"I want to enjoy this last walk, so I do not want to hear your snide remarks regarding anything to do with the trial or anything else," she said firmly.

"I'm sorry," he said, as he caught up with her. "Don't let me be the one to spoil it for you. Enjoy while you can … I mean it, Ces …"

They walked together but neither of them spoke until the dog went through the usual routine and she had to throw the ball. "I never knew you had a dog, Medrix."

"It belongs to my grandfather. I borrowed it for this walk. I had to get away from everything to do with the trial."

"Oh," she said quickly. "Does that mean me as well?" She walked away from him towards a paved area with seats. He followed her and sat on one.

She walked nearer the edge of the cliff and looked over. The sea was up to the foot of the cliffs. He shouted, as he got up from the seat: "Ces, come away from the edge. It's dangerous." She came back a little way.

"What a good idea, Medrix, the Elders don't want me dead do they? I could defeat them yet by diving off the top of these cliffs." She laughed and waved her arms about.

"Stop being silly … haven't you seen the notices all along the cliffs, saying 'danger cliff falls – keep to the paths'? Come back on the path now."

"Always giving orders aren't you, Lawmaker – what if I don't obey you? Will you take the whip to me? But you won't because you would have to come over here." She felt reckless. He had spoilt her walk by being there. She sighed; she shouldn't tease him. The sweets weren't his fault … no, they weren't. One enormous wave hit the cliffs, sending spray high up into the air, soaking her and, for a moment her vision was blurred. Another wave hit with a crash and the ground under her feet began to shake. She screamed and, turning, tried to come back to the path but her foot slipped as she tried to regain her footing. Then Medrix grabbed her and pulled her to safety. She leaned against him, sobbing, her arms tightly around him and her heart thumping. She was aware of his heart beating fast, too.

He put her down on the seat. "You stupid, stupid woman. I told you. Would you listen? No, no – you would not. You nearly got us both killed. Get up from there." He pulled her by the arm. "We are going back now." She got up slowly and tried to pull herself away from him. He still held her arm, pulling her roughly and she went with him. Her legs trembled with shock and she felt sick. The dog came and put the ball at her feet. She looked at it and kicked it a little way.

She stood by the runabout and said, "Thank you. You saved me from falling. Thank you."

"Get in. I'm driving," he said angrily. "I don't want your thanks. You are thoughtless. You don't care for anyone but yourself. I came up here to get away from it all only to find you here by yourself and trying to throw yourself off the cliff. I shall be glad when you have gone from here and left me for good."

She turned and shouted at him then. "That's right! Blame me for everything: the trial – the Chetner shuttle explosion – the poison I took – go on: blame me, I can take it. I was raised the hard way. I am used to it." She raised her fists and punched him in the chest again and again, shouting at him. "I am to blame for everything." And tears of fright and frustration rolled down her face.

The dog stood up and growled at them.

Medrix grabbed her wrists and held her at arm's length. "Stop it – stop it, now!" he commanded.

She kicked out at him but she was held too far away to hurt him. She stood still, her head bowed, making little whimpering sounds.

"Don't think," she whispered, "that I don't appreciate what you've done for me, because I do."

"There's no need for all this raging," Medrix said quietly.

"I know. But, Medrix, I've tried so hard – I've tried to keep all the rules in the marriage book. I've kept to the washing timetable, made sure there was a different colour cloth on the table each day as the book says. Made sure your boots were lined up in the order they should be …"

"What are you talking about now?" He shook his head impatiently but she went on, as if she hadn't heard him.

"I've turned out cupboards, polished furniture, cooked the meals it gave; and, in court, I have tried so hard to follow those rules, too – and all for nothing – for you have been to see the Grand Elder, haven't you?"

"Not yet – but what has that got to do with the house?"

"You told me that if I made another mistake, you would take our release letters to the Grand Elder … and I have tried … so hard … and …"

"Ces – you remembered that?"

"Yes – but no – I knew I had to do it – but I have only just remembered why – and when I was cleaning your office I found the letters we had written and I wondered why we wrote them and when – but now I remember all – and I know now that I am on my own – all because I didn't tell you about the sweets. I'm so sorry Medrix – you can let me go now – I won't do anything silly."

He let her go and she just stood there with her head bowed. He put his arm around her shoulders.

"Ces – I am glad you remembered – I was a mean pig to you – I was so angry that I couldn't have my own way in everything that I bullied you into writing that letter – if I had really thought about it I could have seen the funny side of you trying to hold up the letter writing – but I was a mean bastard of a man then – a typical Elders' man! I have learnt a lot since then – my God – I told you to drink that coffee – if you had, you would not be here now – and I would have never forgiven myself for what I had done. When you spilled the coffee I thought you had done it purposely to annoy me – and I lost control of my temper and hit you. Only when you collapsed did I really realise something was wrong. During your illness I stayed with you. And when you went into a coma I wouldn't let them turn your life-support machine off so I married you to keep you safe. And as I looked after you, I learned to care for someone other than myself. And bit by bit I fell in love with you. But I was a mean, vicious bastard – and I don't know how I will ever forgive myself for my disgusting behaviour to you.

"Eldon and my parents said that you must have believed in me to get me to keep on with your case. They thought it was very funny, the way you had teased and tricked me. I can see that now – and although I love you as you are now, the person I love even more is the person I used to know – the wild, outspoken person who cared for us all in the house. Now you are afraid of me, afraid of the court, afraid of making a mistake, almost afraid to breathe. And I have done that. But even with the court situation as it is now, I will find a way out if it's at all possible. I am not taking those letters to the Grand Elder – I am going to see him to ask him for more time that is all – I promise you. You do believe me, don't you?"

She smiled and nodded 'yes' to him.

He bent down and kissed her wet face, and she clung to him.

"I'll try to be the person you want me to be."

"No, Ces! Just be yourself." He kissed her again, then gently released her. "I want you to go back to the house. On no account go out anywhere on your own. But, firstly, we must take the dog back."

They had stayed a little time with his grandfather, drank some chen and then started on their journey back, when his contact bracelet flashed. The Grand Elder wanted to see them at once.

The Grand Elder held up two letters. "I received your release letters this morning and I accept you resignation, Lawmaker. But you have left me with a problem as to who will take on your position at such a late stage."

Cessie looked at them both with horror. White-faced she asked to see them for herself. He handed them to her.

"These weren't written today – the date is right, if somewhat smudged – mine has a coffee stain on it – but this is not my signature." She laid them down on the desk in front of her.

Medrix picked them up. "I did not send these in," he announced firmly. "They were in my office drawer. I meant to throw them away ..." and he proceeded to tell the Grand Elder how they came to be written. "... And yes, this is not her signature. It was then, of course, but being my wife now, she would sign her name Celisia Margaret Rees-Jones or Celisia Margaret, wife of Lawmaker Medrix."

"Then it seems," said the Grand Elder, "that someone is trying to split you up. I'll send them to have the fingerprints checked. You had better make a list of all the people who come to the house. Be sure to lock important documents away." He dismissed them then.

Now they suspected everyone – the Lawmothers, Eldon, his parents, even – but then they dismissed that as crazy – anyone who knew about the letters could have got in when they were in the garden.

"The Grand Elder could just have accepted it without contacting us," said Celisia. "We'll have to be careful, Medrix."

He agreed with her.

When they got back to the house, Medrix suddenly remembered that he had to go back to the control base to see if there were any messages. He left her, saying that he would see her later. She waited all evening but he did not come back and she gave up and went to bed.

At breakfast she learned that he had gone out early and would see her in court, so she had no time to discuss her situation with him and she felt very apprehensive when she went back to court.

The Prosecutor re-called her.

"Did your husband take the whip to you?"

"No."

"Then he's getting soft in the head. Who's idea was it to eat energy sweets at the game?"

"No ones."

"Do you like them?"

"No – too sweet."

"Crafty plan of yours wasn't it?"

"No."

"You know your fingerprints are all over the bag?"

"Yes," she said firmly. Medrix looked at her in astonishment.

"So, you admit it?"

"Yes," she said again.

"Listen, Counsellor. The sly creature admits it. Now that you have admitted it, everyone can see your guilt, can't they?"

"They might think so, but they can't."

"Why is that then? I expected you to come up with something – let's hear it now."

"The bags were recycled. Even in City One they did this – the sweets were used for medical purposes only. They were stored in jars at one time because the sweets deteriorated faster in the bags. Lawmaker Steffan told me this when I stayed with him. He also gave me some when I was feeling poorly. They were very sweet. But the bags were not thrown away. The Lawmakers would leave the exiles food parcels every moon or so. They didn't want us dead. Our food was put in them. One might have cheese or butter, nuts or just about anything in them. Of course we then used the bags for other things. There was always a residue of powder – it didn't matter how often we cleaned them out. So my sweets, you see, were in one of those bags and, as I had put them in there, my fingerprints were on them. My sweets were very hard and didn't deteriorate like the others: they were made from herbs and fruits. Thortrex couldn't eat them as the fruits brought him out in a rash. If someone picked it up from the ground, then it wasn't mine. I was always most careful – because we needed the bags."

"Well, I got an answer, didn't I? So, you want me to believe you?"

"Of course. You are a reasonable man and know fact from fiction, don't you?" There was laughter around the court. "Or maybe not – for you think my spell worked on my stepfather – and you believe in magic and witchcraft – or maybe fairies," she said with a laugh.

The Grand Elder jumped up. "How dare you speak like that to one of our Lawmakers! You will apologise at once to him and to the Court."

She bowed to him and did what he asked. "Good," he said. "Remember, I won't tell you again."

"Where did you put your sweets when you were playing?"

"On our team bench with our two reserve players."

"You say your bag was yellow. The one you dropped was white."

"I didn't drop it. I put it back on the bench; someone else put that bag on the ground."

"Ah – but you forget, my dear – this white bag had your prints on it."

"Then it is one of our recycled bags and it could mean that someone – another exile – put it there, but why I don't know, unless they were in the pay of the Elders."

"Very good answer. I expect your Counsellor put it there?"

"No," she said firmly. "He couldn't have – because he was nowhere near there – but there were plenty of others and, once a Lawmaker, you are always one – hence the rules that helped me claim a trial."

"Our witness proves our point. What witnesses have you?"

"Our two reserves."

"Well of course – it goes without saying that they will support you. No more questions; Counsellor, your turn."

"Celisia, do you think the other team ate the sweets before the game? Their play was brilliant in the first half but poor in the second, as it would be if they had no more sweets?"

"Objection! How dare he malign our team."

"Objection overruled. He has quite a good point in that assumption."

Cessie smiled – at last – someone seeing their side of the picture.

"Celisia. I am waiting for an answer."

"Could have – except, Fador was not a cheat."

Medrix frowned. "Perhaps Fador did not know."

"Well, yes, that could have happened."

"Good."

"And Thortrex did not eat a sweet – and he jumped higher than ever."

"Quite right – he did – so he did. No more questions. I wish to call another witness. I'm sorry, Grand Elder but I was not able to tell the Prosecutor about this witness as I was not able to contact him until the hour of two this morning."

"Apologies accepted, Counsellor," the Grand Elder replied. Medrix went on.

"I call Andrew Mantrex."

Cessie jumped up in surprise – but sat down quickly, when the Prosecutor glared at her.

"Are you any relation to the Accused?"

"Yes. I am her father."

"You lived on Chetner?"

"Yes – until my daughter was kidnapped. I thought she would have been well treated by her grandmother – I tried a couple of times to visit her but I was turned away – 'she was well', I was told – so I left her there. If I had known I would have transferred her out of there."

"How? How could you do that?"

"With this." He held up a locket just like the one she had lost. "I gave her one of these with the instructions on how to use it if she needed me. But in the rush of being taken away, she did not understand what I said. But then I got a signal from here – in a thunderstorm. I tried to transfer her to my shuttle – but all I got was the device itself and, here it is!"

"Is it a magic talisman?"

"No," he laughed. "It was invented by the people on Earth many years ago. I suppose it's like magic to people who do not understand such things."

"Why were you in our space?"

"I came to ask the Grand Elder for supplies we needed for our spacecraft. He very kindly helped us."

"What craft is that?"

"The *Red Dragon* spacecraft from planet Earth. My brother Robert is the commander – we are here in this galaxy on a mission to save various planets from extinction as ours nearly was."

"When you lived on Chetner – did you use the same device to come and go?"

"Yes, I did. I worked then for the Intergalactic Committee which encouraged people to live within their environmental boundaries."

"Meaning?"

"To work with the nature of the planet rather than against it. On Earth we cut down rain forests, over-mined, polluted our rivers and seas – poured fumes into the atmosphere – only by some radical thinking did we turn it around – but even so, we lost a great deal of land and animals that were driven away for ever."

"Thank you – no more questions. Prosecutor – your turn."

The Prosecutor just shook his head.

Medrix then said all he wished to do was to give his final address. The Prosecutor wanted to do so, too, whereupon the Grand Elder said that they would all meet the next day at ten.

Celisia was overjoyed to see her father again and he went to the house with the others. They talked for ages together – and Medrix left them – feeling very pleased with today's work – but still wondering who had tried to split them up.

Chapter 13

The next day in court the Prosecutor gave his summing-up of the case:

"I have shown you all that this woman has always wanted her own way. As a small child, coming into our society, she did everything to upset her superiors. She dabbled in magic, stole books, irritated her teachers and asked for favours no other girl was allowed to have. Was she thankful that she had a roof over her head? No! Was she thankful for her clothes, food and education? No! She was an *ungrateful* child! An ungrateful child who began planning a revenge on the Lawmakers she hated so much.

"She knew about the tunnels leading to City One. As a child she disappeared for ages – no one knew where. Well *we* knew. She was exploring and found those tunnels.

"When she was exiled she met up with a spy – and she soon sussed him out and used him in her plan – in her plot.

"The challenge was made to the Lawmakers and, because of the Rules, they had to accept.

"Then she trained a team. She used everyone – the magician, the spy Medrix and anyone else who could further her plans. She knew a magician only did magic by sleight of hand – so she knew who he was – she recognised him – of course she did. She had sketched them all – hadn't she?

"She pretended to follow his advice, letting him think that they were going to slow up their play in the first half. Good wasn't it? She knew then that the City Team would play their hardest in the first half and slow up in the second half. Her Counsellor deigns to say that the City Team ate those energy sweets in the first half – when in fact it was *her* team that ate them in the second half. It was true they were nervous in the first half – but they did score and they were brilliant in the second half.

"The Grand Elder had to grant the favours and because she did, the Lawmakers had to return before time – before they could do any reclamation work at all. She doomed her own planet to a slow death by her actions. She is guilty of using trickery, i.e. taking energy sweets and pretending to slow up in the first half and planning a game she knew she could win in order to get her revenge on them – or maybe it was just revenge on her grandmother, who had taken her away from her father. Her grandmother, who had done so much for her was tricked into giving in to her.

"This woman is sly – she's like a killer spider who weaves its web of viperous magic over everyone she meets – more so those people she can manipulate for her own cause.

"Judges. Please do not let her go free. She is guilty. Please make your verdict show that. Thank you."

He sat down and drank some water.

Medrix went to the centre of the Court and waited until the murmuring stopped.

"I've shown you the life of a little girl who was cruelly treated. No one cared enough for her to do anything about it. She grew up in fear of her life.

"It wasn't until she was exiled that her life changed drastically. She discovered that people still cared for others outside the City.

"While wandering around some tunnels, she is surprised by a group of Lawmakers: she uses the challenge as a ploy to get out of there. Only when it works does she go on with the idea. Everyone is enthusiastic – why not try? It gives everyone a new purpose in their dull lives.

"She tells everyone and help is offered – even a magician who seems to know a lot about playing the game. She must have thought he was an exile to know so much. I could have told her too, as I used to play the game. But I didn't because that would have given away my cover.

"So they play. I've already told you the magician's part and why he was there. The Elders knew he did not use magic. They knew already, as I have shown you.

"The Lawmakers of Chetner had already planned to leave – they chose the date of the game – they built extra shuttle bays – they packed up everything – cut off the power and broke the water pipes – they would have gone anyway, whether her team played the remaining City or not. If she did not know about that City, she would have waited in vain for the game because they would have gone anyway.

"The Elders of Chetner are guilty of decimating the Chetner population; over-mining, and they tried to stop the game – or to prove they were cheated in some way – because they wanted revenge. No one could get the better of them, for they thought themselves invincible.

"But they reckoned without me. She was to be brought here and sent to Jailfa Island prison without a trial. I say to my shame that I was annoyed that she claimed a trial and that she protested. I punished her – as only an Elders' man would do – except she fought back and the trial was delayed.

"Her grandmother committed suicide because she knew Cessie was innocent. Before that time there were no witnesses and no open channels to get them. *Ces was one against them all.* So I changed sides and fought for her instead of them.

"I have shown you how evil they are – how devious, how sly – and I hope you realise that if they are allowed to get away with this, then this City will be doomed also, for they think they are invincible. They think no one can upset them – and that means you" (and he pointed around the Court) "are doomed also to live a life watching them to see how their power will affect you.

"Please bring in a Verdict of 'Innocent' – 'Not Guilty' – and turn the tide for ever."

He sat down. No one spoke, and he closed his notes. Then the Grand Elder said that the Judges would now withdraw to consider their verdict.

Two hours later they were called back to the Court and a Judge stood up and said: "Grand Elder, we have discussed the trial and now know the Verdict.

The Grand Elder said: "What is your Verdict?"

Cessie felt sick and looked at Medrix. He half-smiled, then looked at the Judge.

"The Verdict is agreed by all of us. The Defendant, Celisia Margaret, wife of Medrix Rees Jones, is NOT GUILTY of any of the charges brought against her."

Cessie burst into tears – but she was smiling.

There was a loud roar from the spectators as they cheered in jubilation.

"Wait," said the Judge. "The Elders of Chetner will pay for all reclamation work. Any extra money needed will be paid by our society. A Liaison Officer will be appointed to work with the Lawmakers' reclamation team and the Chetnerite Council.

"The sum of 12,000 credo will be given to the Accused – it won't make up for the awful things that happened to her – but it will help her in the future.

"Her Accusers will be arrested and charged with Treason.

"The Defendant is free to go, but she can't leave Estolan without her husband's permission. He may do this by annulling their marriage – in two moon's time.

"Thank you everybody for attending this trial and may everyone go in peace." He sat down.

Cessie flung her arms around Medrix and kissed him.

"Thank you – thank you," she said.

"He pushed her away gently."Go and thank the Judges."

She went – but when she came back he had gone, and someone said that he had gone out arm-in-arm with Jessanda.

Her father joined her as she walked back to the house. Law Officers were everywhere, keeping the crowds back.

That evening was spent in celebration. Medrix came back with bottles of wine and they all drank to their success.

Cessie awoke early and found herself in his bed. He was fast asleep. She went to the washroom and then was halfway across the room when he said: "Ces – get into bed – you'll freeze like that."

He opened the bedclothes and she got back in beside him. "Go to sleep," he mumbled. She stared at the ceiling. She hadn't remembered coming to bed – not after finishing her wine. In fact she didn't remember anything at all.

"Oh well," she thought as she snuggled closer to him, "best enjoy while I can, for in two moon's time I'll be leaving here, leaving him – unless, of course …" She shook her head. Surely he wouldn't want to go back to Chetner with her? Then she remembered the promise he had made her all those years ago – that he would go back to Chetner in order to get his revenge. She shivered.

"Still cold?" he mumbled, as his arms came round her. "I'll keep you warm love – I'll keep you warm."

She sighed as he kissed her. Promise or no promise – she did not want to lose him!

Chapter 14

The first moon passed very quickly. There seemed to be people in the house all the time. Ces worked with the Lawmothers making sure everyone was given refreshments.

At the beginning of the next moon her father went back to work and the Lawmothers went back to their quarters. Medrix then said that he had to write a report on the trial and he went back to the men's quarters to do this. He also told her he would sleep there.

Strangely enough, no more visitors came to the house and she began to hate being there alone so she went out as much as possible.

One afternoon she went over to see how Medrix was getting on – but there was no one there so she started back to the house. If he was supposed to be working why wasn't he there? She decided that he must have gone out to get food.

When she got back to the house he was there waiting for her. He seemed very annoyed.

"I've waited ages for you," he grumbled.

She laughed when she told him where she had been but he went on:

"I do not want you coming to my quarters while I am working. Is that clear?"

"Very clear ... so why are you here then?" She said with annoyance.

"You thought you were going to get away with it, didn't you?"

"Medrix – I don't know what you are talking about."

"The release letters. You sent in those release letters. I can understand why you did it but what I can't understand is why you blamed other people instead of owning up."

"But I didn't," she said, shaking her head.

"You didn't own up – you even blamed my mother!"

"No, I didn't – I didn't send them in and I only wrote a list of people who had been to the house – I accused no one."

"I'm disgusted with you – the Grand Elder has proved that you did it. The messenger described you and a strand of your hair was found trapped in the glued part of the envelope."

"No, Medrix. I didn't do it – I didn't," she protested.

"The Grand Elder says you must be punished for wasting his time – and I agree with him."

"Medrix, you must believe me – somebody is lying and it isn't me," she said emphatically.

He turned away from her. "Well, damn you Ces – they have proof; I have proof. Anyway – the Grand Elder says that you must be in by the hour of eighteen every day until you go home to Chetner. Is that understood?"

"Yes – quite clear – is that all?"

"Yes."

"Then you had better go hadn't you?" she said as she realised he was not going to listen. "Believe it if you want to. See if I care."

He hesitated and was about to say something but thinking better of it, he left, banging the door behind him.

She was angry and annoyed and if they thought that she was not going out in the evenings, then they were sadly mistaken – and she would make some inquiries of her own. She'd start with that messenger – find out who he is and deal with him. She was not going to take this accusation lying down.

Medrix strode out angrily – and then slowed his pace – what if she didn't do it? He'd make some more inquiries – after all anyone could put a strand of her hair in that place – well anyone who had access to their house – and he'd question that messenger again. He'd not tell her until he proved it either way – after all, he'd proved her innocent all through the trial, why not now?

Cessie decided not to break the Grand Elder's decree – unless it was something very special. But she found the evenings very long so she went to bed earlier than usual and got up earlier in the mornings.

One morning she'd done a lot of baking and she decided to take a basket of home-cooked products to Medrix – for he loved his food and she wanted to know how he was, even if they had quarrelled.

She arrived at his quarters and knocked on the door. He shouted: "Come in, Jessanda, the door's open for you." She was shocked. He had told her not to come and yet he was expecting Jessanda? She turned and ran down the corridor – then she could hear Jessanda talking to someone at the foot of the stairs. She turned and went up the stairs waiting for Jessanda to go to Medrix' quarters. When she heard the door close she came down the stairs, only to see three of his friends coming up. She went back up the stairs again. So, she wasn't good enough for his friends – these friends used to come to the house – and that's why no one came any more. She ran along the corridor until she came to another staircase and went down that one. It came out in a lane which led to the park.

She carried the basket of food, wondering who she could give it to. She came to a large fountain and sitting beside it was a man. He had an easel and was busy sketching the view in front of him. She sat on a seat near him and then moved nearer to see his work, leaving the basket on the seat.

He smiled at her and discussed his sketch with her. She was so interested that she told him she also liked to sketch and paint. She stayed a long time with him. He said he was a Temran, studying art at the art studio here in this city. His name was Ledra. He was twenty-three years old and was hoping to have an exhibition of his work at a later date. He asked her to sit by the fountain so that he could sketch her. She did so and stayed for ages, offering him food from the basket and they ate it together sitting on the seat in the sun. She forgot her troubles. He invited her to join him at the different venues as set down by his tutor and she was thrilled at the idea.

Every day she went sketching and on the last occasion he made several sketches of her and she of him. Then, one day, he wasn't in the appointed place and she never saw him again – but in the long evenings she worked on the sketches.

A few days later Medrix came to the house again. This time it was to tell her that the Chetner Inquiry was on the following day and they were both to travel to Temra on the night shuttle so she could attend. It was a rush but they made it. He settled her in one of the seats and then went off somewhere – she wondered where he was – and waited for him until sleep caught up with her. He returned when they arrived in the City of Jedran on the planet Temra.

He took her out for a meal but she wasn't very hungry. She was dreading the Inquiry but she did not say anything.

He left her in the waiting room and said that he would call back for her at the hour of fourteen. She asked him to stay but he said he had business to see to for the Grand Elder.

They called her into the courtroom. It was a big room.

The judges sat in a circle and she was told to stand in the centre of the circle. All the judges were men – old men with long white hair and beards. They were all dressed in dark-brown. They asked questions and she answered them. Then, when every judge had asked a question, one stood up, started walking round the circle and shouted the questions at her. She had to turn round to answer him so that she soon felt dizzy.

"You knew this man?" he shouted at her.

"No."

"So you travelled with him?"

"Yes."

"But you didn't know him …?"

"No."

"Where was he going?"

"To a wedding."

"Where were you going?"

"Nowhere. I wasn't supposed to be there."

"You knew him before?"

"No."

"You must have done."

"No – I did not."

"You went off with a man you didn't know?"

"No – well, yes."

"Which is it? Yes or no."

"I …"

"Right – you got to know him on the shuttle …?"

"Yes."

On and on went the questioning until she realised that they did not believe her story.

"You were in this with him?" he pronounced emphatically.

"No! No! No!" she shouted.

On and on went the questioning. Then there was a short break and she was taken to a small room and left there.

Food was brought and a drink they called tea. Then she was called in again and all the questioning went on again.

She was taken back to the small room – where there was now a bed – and left there overnight. She was tired, confused and very frightened.

The next morning, after a very restless night, she was fed and then questioned again and again.

She was kept another night but in the morning she was released – and they did not want to see her again.

Medrix met her in the hallway – she was in tears and felt so weak.

"Medrix – hold me," she said. "Just hold me – just this once – please – I know you hate me – but do this for me, please."

He put his arms around her and held her close. "I don't hate you. It's all right, Ces – it's all right," he said and she felt so right in his arms. Then he let her go and said that there was no shuttle back on this day. They were to go and stay with a cousin who lived near the city.

It was midday when they got there. It was a long, low, sprawling house, set in fields and fields of vines. His cousin exported fine wines to Estolan and other planets.

His wife, Leah, was a Temran with dark eyes and long flowing black hair that was bound into several plaits around her head. She was a big woman with a ready smile. It had been her father's business until he died and her husband, Lawmaker Tenson, had taken it over. They had three small children.

She welcomed Cessie and took her into a long, cool room and gave her a cooling drink – for Temra got very hot during the day and very cold at night.

Medrix went off to see the state of the vines. He was wearing a big straw hat and Cessie laughed to see him in it. He was gone for ages.

She told Leah all about the Inquiry and she cried as she went over it. Leah comforted her and then left her to rest in the cool while she prepared the main meal.

Medrix came in to find her relaxing in a big armchair. "Ces, I need to ask you something."

"What is it?"

"I have been told on more than one occasion that you have been seeing a man – and you are in fact, lovers – I want to know if this is true."

"You think I have broken my vows?"

"It looks like it. Your Lawmother and Jessanda think you have."

"I see – I may not – but you can?" she said sarcastically.

"What do you mean? I am faithful to you, Ces."

"Really? Still it doesn't matter does it? Our marriage will be annulled and I can go home."

"I want to know the answer Ces – because it matters a great deal to me. Is there a man in your life that you love?"

She looked at him. Why did he want to know? He had Jessanda – then she said sweetly: "Yes – there is such a man," she half-smiled and fiddled with her socks.

"Who is he?"

"I am not telling you that."

"Is he a Temran?"

"No, he is a Lawmaker."

"Oh! A Lawmaker, not Temran," he looked puzzled. She realised then that people had seen her with the artist and had jumped to the wrong conclusion.

"Where does he live?"

"In our city," she looked at her nails.

"Where?"

"In our road."

"What colour is his hair?"

"Dark brown," she looked at her skirt and brushed a mark off it.

"What colour eyes? Is he good looking?"

"Dark-brown eyes." She scratched her head. "And he is very good looking."

"How tall is he?"

"As tall as you." She looked at her nails again.

"I'll kill him when I find out who he is."

"That, Lawmaker, would be suicidal. Lawmakers don't kill."

"I'll report him and you – you'll both be punished."

"You'll have to find him first, Medrix," she said with a laugh.

"Don't laugh at me. Where does he work?"

"In the court and other places." She stretched her arms above her head and yawned.

"Have you ever made love with him or kissed him?"

"Yes."

"The devil! When? *Not* in the house?"

"Mm – yes," she again looked at her nails.

"Oh no! Not in my bed?"

"Yes," she said softly.

"I see. After your annulment are you going to marry him?"

"No."

"Why not?"

159

"He doesn't love me," she sighed.

"Doesn't love you – yet you love him?"

"Yes – I do – very much."

"Is he married?"

"Yes." She bit her top lip, tentatively looking at him.

"So he can't marry you?"

"He could – if he wanted to – his marriage is over."

"Why?"

"He prefers an older person – one who keeps the rules."

"Mm – tell him he's right there – he needs someone like that – he's been playing games with you hasn't he?"

"Maybe – maybe he has. Yes I think you could be right," she said sadly.

He sighed. "When we get back I'll report your lover and your behaviour to the Grand Elder."

"Medrix, like I said, you have to find him first – otherwise no one will believe you – will they?

"Don't worry – devil – I'll find him."

He left her then and went to find his cousin who wanted to know why he was so miserable when he had such a beautiful wife.

"She's been cheating," he said, "seeing someone else while I was working."

"Who is it?" his cousin asked.

"I don't know. He's a Lawmaker – that puzzled me because everyone said that he was a Temran. But she says he's a Lawmaker."

"And you believe her?"

"Well, yes … she described him to me. Brown eyes and hair, about as tall as me, is very good looking, lives in our road, works at times in the court. I can't think who it can be."

"Can't you?" His cousin laughed. "Sounds like a good description of my cousin Medrix."

"Me! Of course it's not me. I don't want to marry an older woman – I …"

"She thinks you do."

"Oh God – it is me. She loves me. The little devil – the little tease – I'm jealous of me! I said I would kill him and she said that would be suicidal." He laughed. "Don't let on that I know, will you?"

"No. I should ask her about the Temran."

"Yes I will – but don't tell her I know."

The two men came in laughing. Cessie looked startled but they just sat down and talked about the vineyard.

It seemed to her that Medrix was much happier. Was it because he now thought the end of their marriage was in view? That must be it – if she had told him the truth he wouldn't have believed her anyway. She might have guessed someone would have informed him about the Temran she had met in the park. Could that have been the reason why he did not turn up at the last venue? Maybe he had been told to leave. She would have to find out and put things right for him.

Chapter 15

Celisia was still sitting in the cool when Medrix came back to sit beside her.

"I've been to see the winery – my cousin's offered me a partnership in the business."

"Are you going to take up his offer?"

"No … well not at the moment. The Grand Elder has other ideas for me, after you've gone back to Chetner."

"Medrix, do you think I have time to have a shower before the evening meal?"

"Yes – if you don't take too long. I'll show you our sleeproom."

He took her hand and led her along a dark passageway which eventually opened out into a hall. Here there were several doors, one of which he opened and they went in.

It was a very large room, the centre of which was dominated by an enormous bed. To the right of it was a door leading into a cupboard; to the left was a washroom. The large windows looked over the shadowed garden. Medrix pulled the curtains across and switched on a bedside lamp.

Cessie went over to the bed and tugged at the long pillows until she had pulled one clear.

"What are you doing, Ces?"

"This pillow I'll put down the middle of the bed." She did so.

"Why? It's a big enough bed for both of us. It could sleep six."

"To keep you over your side of course."

"Why? Do you think I'll attack you in the night?" He laughed.

"No – but whenever I have slept with anyone else they said I kicked them in my sleep."

"Oh, I see – do you mean you have shared your bed with other men apart from your lover?"

"No, of course not, Medrix. Don't be so stupid. It was when I was little – my mother put a long pillow between us – she called it Fat Amma."

"We don't need her. Do you think I am even going to touch you after you have slept with that other man?"

161

"Fat Amma stays or you can sleep in the cupboard!"

"If anyone sleeps in the cupboard it will be you, Ces."

"Don't be silly – there's plenty of room for a Fat Amma and you."

He sat on the bed. "Have it your own way. I am sure I am not going to quarrel with you over a pillow – Fat Amma can stay – but not now."

"Why not now?"

"Because Leah might see it."

"Does it matter?"

"Yes – because she thinks we are happily married – she's thrilled for us – at long last I am married to a beautiful woman who is a credit to any household."

"But didn't you tell her about the annulment?"

"No – she's happy for us – so I want you to behave as befits a Lawmaker's wife while we are here." He pulled out the pillow and put it back with the others. "Do you think you can do that?"

"Yes, Medrix. I'll try – I'll try – but only when I am with them."

"Good – now go and have your shower."

After her shower, Ces was surprised to see him sitting sprawled out on the bed. She pulled the large towel around her more closely and went into the cupboard to dress. She came out to brush her hair.

"Finished? Come and sit beside me."

"Well, I am not sure if I should …"

"Don't be silly – I want to talk to you. No silly nonsense, I promise."

She climbed on to the bed and sat beside him.

"Now then – I have more questions to ask you."

"About what?"

"You were seen, while I was busy working in my quarters. You were seen with a Temran man."

"Oh, him."

"Yes – and it seems you were breaking your marriage vows."

"I was not! I certainly was not."

"You were seen hugging and kissing him – it was reported to me on more than one occasion – who is he?"

"Whoever told you that is lying."

"No; they are honest people just reporting what they saw. Now – who is he?"

"Don't talk to me about breaking my vows when you were doing it yourself," she replied angrily. She moved further away from him.

"What do you mean? I have never broken my vows."

"Yes – yes, you have – you told me I was not to go to your quarters – but I went anyway. I had baked some things for you and Eldon but when I knocked on the door you said, 'Come in Jessanda'. So don't tell me that you haven't cheated on me. Even your friends – the ones who came to the house – were visiting you there. I evidently was not good enough for them and all the time you were meeting Jessanda." She made to get off the bed but he grabbed her and pulled her nearer to him.

"You've got it wrong, Ces."

She pulled away. "Have I? Have I indeed."

"Yes, you have. That morning we ran out of milk. Eldon went to buy some. He met my friends and they told him they were coming over to see us. Eldon contacted me and told me they were on their way. So when I heard someone knocking on my door I said come in to her because that is who I thought it was. They stayed a little while. I thanked them for their kindness and told them not to come again for they were breaking the rules and could get into trouble."

"Oh! Oh Medrix – I'm so sorry."

"Well, it was a genuine mistake but ..."

"If I hadn't come over I wouldn't have known and I wouldn't have met the Temran."

"So you *were* meeting someone else," he said disdainfully.

"It's not like you think."

He made to get off the bed.

She pulled his arm. "Wait! I listened to you; now listen to me."

"Fair enough," he sat back down. "Well – what's the story?"

"I met him when I was coming away from your place. I was upset and angry – but as I walked I saw this Temran and he was sitting in front of the fountain sketching it. I stopped at once and went to see him working. We got talking and I spent the rest of the day with him. We were both artists you see. He was over here on a course. I asked him if I could work with him and he agreed. In the long evenings I worked on my sketches. His tutor allowed me to share his notes. But I swear to you that that is all we did. It took my mind off everything and the evenings weren't so long for me as I did my homework then. We went from place to place to cover the course – he did not turn up on the last one – and I don't know why. I hope it wasn't my fault."

"But you were seen hugging and kissing."

"If I was going to do that, surely I wouldn't do it where people could see me. Those people lied. I am telling you the truth – you just ask Lawmother Grey."

"Why – what has she got to do with it?"

"Because she saw us the first time and she said that she did not think it very wise for me to be alone with him and because she had time off she made sure that everywhere we went she was not far away. Ask her if you don't believe me. Did they see her too – did they?

"No – but I can't understand why they lied."

"Someone's trying to split us up – just like they did with the release papers – maybe it's all connected. I don't know."

"I asked Eldon to look into the matter of the release papers. I thought it was all too pat and it does look as if you are right – someone thinks we are getting too close – I can understand that happening while the trial was on, but why now? Our marriage is to be finished so why do it now?

"Maybe they think that there'll be no annulment – after all, Leah thinks we are a happily married couple."

"Yes – you mean that someone wants to make sure we are not. Eldon talked the release papers episode over with me. He asked me when I put the release letters in my office drawer and I then realised I had not. When you were taken ill so unexpectedly, I went with you to the medical bay and left the letters on the table."

"They would have been wet – the coffee went over mine."

"Yes – that's what Eldon said. Someone picked them up and dried them and made copies. Eldon was quite sure that the ones in my drawer were copies – and he proved that was right – for when we unlocked the drawer, there were the letters – they had to be copies because the Grand Elder had the original ones. The ones I had were not in an envelope – but loose in the drawer and had the original date on them. Someone had put them there – but we just thought that the ones with the Grand Elder were the ones in the drawer. I didn't look – I just locked the drawer, so that whoever put them there, couldn't get them out."

"Medrix – that means – oh – I don't know what it means."

"Eldon thinks it is your Lawmother and I'm inclined to believe him – because she was one of the people who reported that you were cheating on me."

"Oh, no – but why?"

"Also – I'm thinking she could have been reporting on everything that went on in the house – because the prosecutor knew a lot of things that went on in there."

"Yes – I can't see why. She, after all, got you to marry me. It was her idea."

"Yes – so it was – perhaps Eldon has found out more – I'll know when we go back, which we must do the day after tomorrow."

"We'll then have seven days before the end of the moon."

"Yes. But we don't have to annul the marriage until …"

"Until what, Medrix?"

"Until fifteen days after that time. In fact we can do it on any one of those days up to the fifteenth day and I suggest we leave it to the last day – so that the person or persons who are trying to separate us will try again. We should also make everyone believe that we are staying together. Can you do it?"

"Yes – I suppose I can – it's not dangerous, is it?"

"No – we'll have to be careful that's all. I'll move back into the house – and then we'll see if the rat will come out of its hole."

She shivered, and he put his arms around her and, pulling her close, kissed her and she relaxed against him.

The door opened suddenly and Leah looked in.

"Oh, I'm sorry, Medrix," she said in embarrassment. "Your meal is ready if you two love birds would like to join us," and she went out laughing happily.

"There," said Medrix, "what a good thing we put Fat Amma back in her place."

"Yes, it was, wasn't it."

They got off the bed and went to join the others.

Chapter 16

Celisia and Medrix returned on the late shuttle, having had a very enjoyable relaxing time with his cousin.

Medrix was kindness itself and Ces wished it could always be like that. He said that they must carry on as planned and insisted she share his bed. She agreed on condition that Fat Amma also be used.

The following day Eldon came with a written apology from the Grand Elder. Ces was surprised to learn that her punishment had been cancelled.

Eldon told Medrix he had questioned all the cleaners. "One told me," he said, "that she had seen the letters on the table and had given them to Lawmother Kella to pass to you.

"Your Lawmother, Ces," he said, "was on her way to see the Grand Elder's assistant. It seemed they had been seeing a lot of each other – he had been quite upset when she was assigned to the house – but they were seen together a lot, so it couldn't have bothered them that much. Anyway, it was quite a while before the cleaner saw her come out of his office and go home. She was surprised about that because of you being so ill.

"Two days later she had seen her again, coming out of the assistant's office but thought nothing of it. She saw her again the day the release letters were sent in – she went to the assistant's office and handed in a package. They were both laughing and talking about something."

Eldon went on: "I told the Grand Elder about it and he had them both taken in for questioning. Your Lawmother insisted she had done nothing wrong but after further questioning, admitted she was the messenger and had done it to get help for you, Celisia, as Medrix seemed to think you were guilty of eating energy sweets. The assistant, Lawmaker Delton, had copied the letters for her.

"But the Grand Elder was now very suspicious of their story and had his assistant's office and house searched. Papers were found that linked them to the Elders – in fact your Lawmother was passing information about your life in the house. The Elders then passed it on to the prosecutor who used it in his case. She had complete access to Medrix and you Celisia and made almost daily reports to them through Lawmaker Delton. It wasn't hard because they had already established that they were going out together."

Ces looked puzzled. "What I can't understand is why she got you to marry me, Medrix. Surely that was working against the Elders, not for them?"

"Well," said Eldon, "the Elders had asked for the life-support machine to be turned off, but that it should be turned off so soon was not in their interests. The Chetner Council would have queried it and asked for an inquiry and this they didn't want. So she was told to get Medrix to marry you. Up until that time, they thought Medrix was rigging the trial. If you survived, as you did, they would have their man at the centre of it all – and then you would most certainly lose."

"But it had the opposite effect!" said Medrix. "I thought it was my fault that you were so ill. I learnt to care for you instead of caring for myself, and gradually fell in love with you – but you weren't the wild, outspoken woman I knew – you were cowed, frightened and depending on me rather than on yourself. I wanted the real you back and I was determined to fight your cause and, if possible, to win. We *did* win – and now you are free – but I don't want you to go. I don't want to annul our marriage. I just want to keep you safe here, beside me."

Ces looked at him in amazement.

Eldon interrupted them. "I'll go now."

"No," she said. "We have you – just you – to thank for finding all this out. It is such a shock to think that we had a spy in the house."

"She nursed you – took turns with me to watch over you," Medrix said.

"Yes, Medrix" said Eldon. "I'm sure it's a shock – but I'm glad it's solved as I am sure Celisia is." He sighed. "I must go – it's my little girl's Name Day. I must be there to cut the cake. Come over later if you like and have some."

He left them then and, as he shut the door behind him, smiled to himself: "Now, my dears, it's up to you – I can't do any more for you." And he walked down the street, smiling.

Ces turned to Medrix. "What did you say?"

"I am asking you – no – if I was single I would be asking you to marry me – but as it is – I am asking you to renew your vows with me. I know I am bossy. I have a foul temper – but one thing I know for sure is that I love you very much. So what is your answer?"

"But, Medrix – I'm a Chetnerite – I can't keep Lawmakers' rules – however hard I try. I have to go back to Chetner. They want to celebrate my – our victory – I can't live here – not all the time anyway."

"I've thought of that. The Grand Elder offered me the job of Liaison Officer. I will take it if you want me to. It's for nine moons – then they'll review it. What do you say? Please say yes."

She stared at him – his eyes were full of love. Yet she remembered how he had sworn revenge all that time ago. Surely this wasn't what he was going to do. She shivered.

"Are you cold? Here, let me get you a hot drink."

"No – I was thinking about something that happened long ago – ghosts, you know – but …"

"But, what? …"

"Yes – Medrix, the answer is yes."

"I know the lover is me – my cousin told me."

"You knew? Medrix, you are the most devious man I know!"

He laughed. "I know – but I learnt it from you, my love."

"Medrix, can we renew our vows for I can't remember anything about them the first time around?"

"Of course – I'll tell the Grand Elder about us – he will be pleased."

"Why will he be pleased?"

"Because he made a bet with his wife that you would choose me instead of …"

"Instead of whom?"

"Eldon."

"Eldon's not interested in me – he only has eyes for Lawmother Grey" – she laughed – "I could have told him that. At last I have done something to please him." She laughed again as he took her in his arms and kissed her.

"Medrix," she said laughing up at him.

"Yes, love …"

"There's no need for Fat Amma now is there?"

"No need at all – shall we go and tell her?"

"Yes, I think we should – I think we should."

The next day the news spread like wildfire. The Grand Elder and his wife came round to congratulate them and brought them a present. It was a beautiful quilt. Cessie was so surprised and made a great to-do of thanking them.

His parents gave a party for them – a betrothal party – as she had never had one and Medrix gave her a ring and a betrothal box. The box was carved in wood. When you opened it there was a gold key. The key opened many small compartments which were secreted away among the birds, flowers and animals that were all part of the decoration. Lawmother Grey said they were all different so she couldn't help her with it.

People visited the house, bringing gifts, and once again she was kept busy giving them all refreshments.

Jessanda brought her a most delightful shawl that she had made herself and teased her and wished her well. Then her father and uncle arrived and such talk went on and Medrix was glad to see her so happy. Her uncle took them in a shuttle to see over his spaceship and then offered them a trip to the planet Earth as a gift for, he said, she had relatives there she had never seen. Cessie said that one day she was sure they would go as Medrix was quite sure he had relatives there as well.

A date was fixed for the fifteenth of Third Moon 4018 for the Renewal of Vows service which was to be in the temple. It was only to be family and near friends – but afterwards there was to be a feast laid on by the Chief Elder and anyone could attend it. The Lawmothers were making her a dress for it – following a pattern her father had brought from Earth.

On the day before the service, Cessie received a message from her Lawmother that she wanted to see her. It was urgent, she'd said.

Cessie did not want to go – but she was also curious as to why she wanted to see her. Both Eldon and Medrix said she should go in case she divulged anything else about the Elders or some other spies working in their midst, so she went to the House of Correction to see her. Medrix and Lawmother Grey went with her but her Lawmother insisted that if she could not see Cessie alone, then she would not see her at all.

Cessie was taken to a small room. Her Lawmother sat on a bench near a table; Cessie sat opposite her. Her Lawmother's guards stood outside the door. There was a bell on the table Cessie could ring if she wanted to leave the room.

As soon as the door closed, her Lawmother leaned towards her.

"I am glad you decided to come," she said softly.

"Are you well, Lawmother?" Cessie asked with some concern for her Lawmother's face was a grey as her long robe.

"Yes – I am well – but I don't want to talk about myself. I want to talk about you."

"Me? Why?"

"Because I've heard you are going to renew your vows to Medrix. That's right, isn't it?"

"Yes – we are not annulling our marriage."

"And has he said that he loves you?" She spoke a bit louder.

"Yes."

"And has he told you that he has managed to get a job on Chetner?"

"Yes – as Liaison Officer."

"I thought so – and why have you said yes to this union?"

"Because I love him."

"That's what he wants, my Lawdaughter," she nodded her head. "He needs to get back to Chetner with you – so that he can carry out his revenge and win."

"But, Lawmother – he's not like that now. I know what you are on about. He regretted that remark two hours later when he could do nothing about it."

"So he says. Don't you see *he* has to stay married to you in order to go to Chetner – so *he* can have his revenge on you and the original team."

"Oh really, Lawmother! He's moved on since then – have you forgotten he's won my case? Given me a life. I'll always be in his debt."

"Yes – you will – but you don't have to marry him for that reason."

"I'm renewing my vows, Lawmother, because I love him. I didn't want to

169

marry a Lawmaker. I didn't want to love him – I fought against this. I did things to annoy him so that I would hate him. But I couldn't hate him - my whole being wanted him and I just decided to give in and enjoy being in love with him. Every time I see him my heart races. When I am not near him I miss him. It is as simple as that, Lawmother.

"Too simple – *he* was trained as a spy and *he* knows all the ins and outs of getting his own way. He was shamed when he came back from Chetner – he had failed to stop the game. The Chetner Elders told the City Elders of his shame and he was punished by being sent for retraining. He became *the bully, the vicious woman-hating bigot who would do anything to get his own way.* He used his anger to beat people up. He was strong – anyone weaker than himself was put upon. He was a stickler for rules and reported any little rule that anyone broke. If he didn't get his own way he made such a fuss that people gave in. His nieces and nephews were afraid of him and people knew him as a toady to the Elders – a puppet – when they pulled the strings, he danced."

"He's changed, Lawmother."

"Rubbish! You are looking at him like a sentimental schoolgirl – he has not changed. Can a leopard change its spots?"

"But he got me off, Lawmother."

"For his own revenge. Don't you see that's what he wants. He betrayed you in Chetner."

"That's different – it was his job."

"Job indeed!" she sneered.

"That's not his job now, Lawmother."

"And you think *he's* left that all behind?"

"Yes."

"He betrayed you on Chetner. *He* then went on to betray the Elders and all because *he wants you* on Chetner. *He* wants all the people there to see his revenge. *He* wants to see you suffer as *he* suffered. This is his revenge."

"Stop it, Lawmother. It's *your* revenge on me to say this. You reported that I was seeing someone else. *You* always told me I did not behave as befits a Lawmakers' wife. You did all that – you made me try harder."

"To try and separate you of course. I thought I could make you see that *he* was not good enough for you."

"No, Lawmother – no!" She raised her voice. "You kept telling me I wasn't good enough for him."

"So you are going on with it then?" her Lawmother said sadly.

"Yes – I am. Why should I believe you? You were a spy in the house. I trusted you and look what happened."

"I love you, my Lawdaughter. I nursed you when you were so ill. It was me that saved your life by getting him to marry you. He did not want to marry you – he did not require a bedfellow – he could have a bedfellow of his own choosing at any time he wanted. He didn't have to marry them."

"I think you've said enough, Lawmother." Cessie rose from the bench.

"Wait! You will not listen – but you will remember. Every time there is an argument, every time he does not get his own way, every time he hits out at you – be it verbally or otherwise – you will remember what I've said. You will come to know that what I spoke of was true of him. But by that time it will be too late and maybe his revenge will satisfy the Elders of Chetner so that you got their revenge as well, through him and they will forgive his betrayal of them by his betrayal of you." She stood up and made her way to the door. "You scheming little brat you ..." she screamed at Cessie – "I tried – I've tried Celisia Margaret – as I tried all those years ago to put you on the right path – I failed then. I told Jessanda," she said angrily, "you were a person who could not be helped – rather like him in fact – you both want your own way – huh! Come to think of it you will run circles around him – but, my dear – he will get you in the end. I won't wish you well – he has already coaxed you onto the path that he wishes you to take. Enjoy the service – dance at the feast – enjoy the celebrations on Chetner – for the way is dark for you after that – and when he scorns you and sneers at your actions – there will be no celebrations then."

She suddenly came towards Cessie who rang the bell and a Lawmother guard came at once – and another one restrained her Lawmother, who seemed to be having some sort of fit.

Cessie went to the others who were waiting for her. But she made no comment to their questions but hurried them out of the place.

Medrix wanted to know what was said but she shook her head and then walked ahead of them. The tears flowed down her cheeks. Then she turned and said: "Tell them to check on Jessanda – she mentioned her – it may be nothing – but she did."

When they got back to the house she went into her rooms and locked the door. She had to think. She heard Medrix calling her but she did not answer.

Medrix turned to Lawmother Grey. "Oh God – what's happened, Lawmother? I can't bear to see her like this."

"Don't worry – she needs time to herself – like pre-wedding nerves. She'll do the right thing, I am sure."

Medrix looked at her. "I hope so – our future life depends on it. All my plans will be for nothing otherwise."

Chapter 17

Cessie sat on her bed for ages, the words of her Lawmother going round and round in her mind. The shock of the meeting and the viciousness of the remarks still shook her. She went over her answers and wondered if she could have handled it in a better way. She heard Medrix go out, and silence reigned in the house.

Did she herself believe in the revenge threat made all those years ago? It troubled her greatly that she had considered it but she had put it on one side because, after all, he had given her, her life back and she owed him a great debt of gratitude. She slipped off the bed and went to look out of the window.

The sun was high in the sky. She sighed and went to the kitchen to make some coffee and put a pie in the oven. She wondered where Medrix was. She took her coffee into the garden, sat on the swing seat and made herself concentrate on the flowers.

It was so peaceful that she lay back on the seat and closed her eyes, trying to will her thoughts away from her Lawmother. It was impossible to do so, so she went in, turned the oven down to low and went back to her bed, closing the door behind her.

She woke up suddenly – her head ached. Medrix was shouting: "Open this door."

"It's open," she shouted back.

He came through. "Whatever is in the oven is burnt," he yelled at her. "Can't you smell it?"

She ran into the kitchen: "Damn, damn, damn," she yelled, "it's spoilt – after all my hard work." She took the burnt mess out of the oven.

"What's the matter with you? You know you can't leave things unattended in the oven."

"I know – I was upset about this morning."

"Well, it's over. That was this morning – it is now evening."

"But you don't understand how I feel."

"Quite right – I don't. You went all the way through the trial, going through agonies of mind, yet you make all this fuss about one little meeting with your Lawmother. I know it was a shock finding out about her – it was a shock for all of us but you don't see me or the rest of us moaning and groaning about it. We just go on where we left off.

"We have a big day tomorrow. I'm sure you have masses to do to prepare for it and *what* are you doing? Just lying on your bed and moaning. You've given yourself a headache – that's what you've done."

"You don't understand what …"

He sighed. "Tell me what she said."

"I can't."

"Can't or won't?"

"I cannot tell you. Please don't ask me. It wasn't a little thing – she didn't apologise to me – she hates me."

"So – she works for the Elders! What did you expect?"

"I don't know."

"The fact that she hates you is *her* problem, not yours, Ces love."

"I've got a headache – I'm going back to bed."

"No – you are not."

"I am – and if you want something to eat, there's bread and cheese in the cupboard – just help yourself."

"No. You are staying here until you tell me what happened."

He pulled her arm and she sat back heavily on the long seat. "I'm not telling you." She sat back and closed her eyes and then opened them and said: "Did you tell the Grand Elder about Jessanda?"

"No – of course not."

"Why not? – my Lawmother mentioned her."

"Unless I know what it was all about I can't say anything about her, can I?"

"I suppose not – but if she …"

"If she what? You've got it in for her."

"No – you asked me to …"

"You are jealous of her."

"No, I am not."

"You think I love her."

"I do *not* – stop teasing me."

"I'm not teasing – you *are* jealous of her. You are *always* mentioning her."

"Oh, *shut up*, Medrix. I've got enough trouble without you stirring up more." She closed her eyes. "Now, let me be."

"So you are going to lie there all evening and sulk – because I didn't mention Jessanda's name to the Grand Elder."

Cessie made to get up from the seat. He pulled her back down.

"Well?"

"Well what? I have got a headache, Medrix. Let me go." She turned to get up.

"No. Tell me what happened this morning."

"No – leave it – leave it, please." Tears ran down her face.

"Now we've got tears – your way out of trouble. Tell me."

She shook her head, fisting her eyes to stop the tears.

"Ah well … Right … it's a secret. You said there were to be no secrets between us, but you can't keep your own rules."

"I *can't* tell and that's *that*," she pronounced emphatically.

"Well, that's one secret you are going to keep from me. How many more have you?" She didn't answer. "Well, *don't* tell me then. I have here the Order of Service for us tomorrow. You need to read it so you know what to do and say. While you are reading it I'll get some chen. Ask me any questions about anything you don't understand and – don't go to bed, please, Ces."

She read all through it. He brought in a jug of chen and two cups. He poured the chen into the cups.

"Well – have you read it?"

"Yes."

"Any questions?"

"Yes – it says here that I have got to say that I promise to love, honour and obey you."

"So?"

"I'm not saying 'obey you', you are bossy enough – without me having to promise that."

"It's a formality, that's all."

"Formality, indeed! You will be throwing that at me every time I do something wrong."

"No, I won't."

"Knowing you – *you will*. So I am *not* promising that."

"*Cessie*," he said impatiently – "you are just renewing your vows – this is what you promised last time."

"I promised nothing last time. *I was in a coma last time. I knew nothing about it*." She raised her voice in anger.

"Oh, don't be *stupid*, Celisia," he said angrily, "your Lawmother stood in for you."

"Oh, that explains it – she hates me – that's why she did it."

"No, she didn't – every woman makes the same promise."

"Well – Chetnerite women don't – they don't have that word in their marriage service. They don't need it – so I don't need it."

"In order to renew our vows – we have to say – the same vows – as we did before – that is the law." He explained slowly as if speaking to a child.

"And there's no other way?" she pleaded.

"*No!*" he said emphatically.

"Then that means we don't stay married."

"*Right* – we annul the marriage," he said viciously. "*That's* what we do."

"I see – how do we do that?" she said in a dull, flat voice.

"We go to the temple and revoke our vows."

"Right, Medrix – that's what we'll do." She ran to her room so he shouldn't see her tears, but he followed her.

174

"I'm sleeping at my parents' home tonight."

"Right," she sobbed, hiding her face in her hands. "Why?"

"It's the custom. Lawmother Grey will come later. She'll sleep here and help you dress in the morning. A Lawmother's outfit will be fine. Keep the dress to wear at your next wedding to some poor, unsuspecting man."

"You won't be going to Chetner now, will you?"

"Of course I will. I have accepted the job. I'll have to go through with it. I'll wave to you when I see you. I'm really disappointed in you, Celisia – I really am. I thought you loved me enough to renew your vows but I can see I was wrong. It's no good crying: what's done is done." He turned away, steeling himself not to cry too. He said to himself: "Lawmakers don't cry – don't cry."

Cessie stood up and said quietly: "Today, or rather, this morning, I slew a dragon for you," she sobbed, "and you can't do a simple thing for me. No matter – you won't be able to wave to me because I'll travel back to Earth with my father – Chetner can celebrate without me. Have a happy life, Medrix – now go please – go." She stood with bowed head.

He kissed her on the forehead and said: "Tomorrow it will be over." He wanted to hold her, kiss her; tell her he loved her. But he couldn't – wouldn't – for he couldn't change the law. He felt so helpless – he loved her so much.

His contact bracelet flashed. It was the Grand Elder. He wanted him in his office at once.

He turned to Cessie and said: "I'll have to see what he wants. I'll see you in the temple tomorrow at the hour of eleven. Goodnight, Celisia Margaret."

She stayed where she was – her eyes full of tears as he went out through the main door, slamming it closed behind him.

Once outside Medrix felt sick. It was all over, just because she wouldn't give in. He stood under the light – yet it was this stubbornness that had brought her through her life in that City, brought her through the game, brought her through the trial and now would separate them for ever. He sighed – she hadn't learned to trust him – to trust men generally – to trust Lawmakers – and it was the fault of those men, himself included. She'd had to fight for everything she needed – not like the Estolan women who had plenty of everything. How would someone like Jessanda cope with Cessie's life? She wouldn't be able to. Celisia Margaret was the one that outshone them all – and tomorrow she would leave with her father and … His bracelet flashed again.

"Lawmaker – it's getting late – please hurry."

Medrix bit his lip – must show them I'm still a Lawmaker – whatever that means.

He was ushered into the Grand Elder's office by a woman. She was the Grand Elder's wife. Evidently no new assistant had been appointed.

The Grand Elder wasn't alone, for three men sat around the room. They were Andrew Mantrex, Cessie's father; Commander Robert Mantrex, her uncle, and a man he didn't know.

"You know these two men," said the Grand Elder, "but this man," he pointed to the stranger, "this man you don't know. He is Ensign Peter Drew, a technician aboard the *Red Dragon* spacecraft and he has some very interesting pieces of information which he thinks you ought to know."

The young man smiled and gave Medrix no time to answer.

"As you may know, on Earth we have made great strides in scientific technology, some of which we have found here on your planet, and some which has not come to your knowledge yet."

Medrix shifted in his seat. He did not want a lesson on inventions at this moment in time, but he said nothing.

Ensign Drew went on: "When my commander heard that his niece was to go and see her Lawmother and that no one else was to go with her, he was worried about her and brought me in. I wired the room for sound."

"What do you mean?" Medrix asked, his interest suddenly awakening.

"We can record everything that's said in a room and capture on film the actual people and what they do and say in that place. I set this up with the Grand Elder's permission of course."

The Grand Elder smiled and nodded to the ensign to continue.

"I recorded everything." He held up a small shiny metal disc. "I am able to put this into a computer. This, of course, is one of our computers and, if I press this red button we will see everything as it happened." He sat, waiting – looking at his commander – before going on.

"I think," said the commander, "I think, Medrix you will find it very interesting. I know we did."

Medrix felt very apprehensive but asked them to let him see it. The ensign pressed the button and the recording showed up on the screen.

Half way through it, Medrix realised that his words about seeing her Lawmother as some little thing were totally wrong. At the end of it, he sat there, still staring at the empty screen and shaking his head. "I didn't realise. I didn't realise it was anything like that," he said at last.

"She must have been very upset," said Cessie's father. "Did she tell you about it, Medrix?"

"No – no – she didn't – she only said: 'Today I slew a dragon for you'. I didn't know what she meant – I think I understand now."

Her father said grimly: "I think, Lawmaker, you must know that if that threat ever comes to pass, you will be a dead man – for my daughter loves you and trusts you, even though that threat was made."

"I'll never knowingly harm her – but ..."

The Grand Elder interrupted. "It is now the hour of two. I think we should all be getting to bed – for we have a big celebration today."

They all stood up, and left. Medrix waited until he was alone with the Grand Elder. Out of his pocket he drew the Order of Service paper and explained why this service did not suit Celisia.

"We'll alter it," the Grand Elder said, taking the paper from him, "we'll put,

176

'I promise to love, honour and care for him in thought, word and deed – to the best of my ability – until he no longer needs me' – is that all right?"

"Yes," Medrix said.

"That's what suited my wife," the Grand Elder smiled, "and it's worked very well. It's only here there are such rigorous rules, Lawmaker. Now, I'm going to my bed – so I bid you 'Goodnight'."

Medrix went back to the house. It was in complete darkness.

He turned the key in the lock but the door did not open. Cessie must have shot the bolts across. Now why would she do that?

He rang the bell and waited. No one came. He rang it again – still no answer.

He went and stood under her window and threw a handful of gravel up at it. The light came on, but the window remained closed. He threw some more pebbles – they spattered against the windows and fell to the ground. He moved out of the way and waited.

She drew the curtains back and opened the window. "Who's there?" she called.

"It's me – Medrix. I can't get in – open the door for me Cessie."

"Go away. It's the hour of two. Go away. Stop playing games."

"I have to talk to you."

"I have done all my talking. Please, *go* away." She made to close the window.

"Cessie!" he yelled – "open the door – I've got to talk to you."

"No – go away."

"I've been talking to your father. Please let me tell you about it. Do you want me to beg? I'll go down on my knees – please!" He knelt – the gravel bit into his skin. The light went on in the hall. He got up and went to the door. She opened it and stood to one side to let him come in.

He saw bare legs under her robe and wondered if she had anything on underneath. He shook his head – "Concentrate!" he said to himself, "you've come here to tell her – not to look at her legs and think of other things." Cessie pulled her robe tighter, tying the cord firmly so that it covered her properly. It was as if she had read his thoughts.

She led the way into the sitting room. He closed the door and followed her into the room.

"Well?" she said, waiting for him to speak. "What is so important that it can't wait until later?"

"This." He thrust the service paper into her hands.

"What! I've read it – why give it to me again?"

"Read it – please."

She looked down at the words and read the altered version.

"Is this true, Medrix?"

"Yes – the Grand Elder himself said that it was valid – and he should know."

"You've done that for me, Medrix."

"Yes – and I know how you fought a dragon for me."

"You do? How?"

He told her all about it but he left out the bit about being a dead man if he proved unfaithful. Why worry her.

"Am I forgiven, Ces?"

"Of course – yes, Medrix – of course."

He swung her around in his arms and kissed her.

"Where's Lawmother Grey?" he asked.

"Oh, she couldn't come tonight, that's why I bolted the door – a note was put through my door after you went."

"Cessie – have you got anything on under that robe?"

"Medrix – is that all you can think about?" she laughed. "I thought you had to go to your parents' house tonight. Custom, you said – rules."

"I told them I wasn't coming – I'll have to go later to dress – but now I just want to be with you, darling – just you."

"It's late. It's about time I had some sleep – and you – otherwise we shall be sleeping on our feet at the service."

Together they went upstairs – the future looked good for them. He hoped it would remain so, and so did she.

* * * *

The service was held as planned. Cessie looked radiant in her special dress made for the occasion by the Lawmothers of Estina. Medrix was dressed in the customary Lawmaker outfit for such occasions and looked very fine and as they came out of the temple, they were met by crowds of well-wishers who had come to join the feasting and dancing.

Of course, some stayed away but, surprisingly, the prosecutor was not one of them.

* * * *

Jessanda was questioned. She had thought Medrix was interested in her and had asked Lawmother Kella if that was so and the Lawmother had said that Cessie would release him from the marriage.

* * * *

A moon later, Cessie and Medrix were scheduled to travel to Chetner with the first team of Lawmakers' reclamation workers. But what happened there is, of course, another story …

PART III

THE REVENGE

Chapter 1

Celisia had just packed one large luggage holder when Medrix came in from a meeting. He looked at her kneeling on the floor, surrounded by various things and three luggage holders and said: "Ces – what are you doing?"

"Packing," she sighed, "we have only six days left here."

"Yes, but we don't need all those things, surely."

"But we do. It will be the cold moons when we get there."

"Yes, but ..."

"We have to have warm clothes, Medrix, and you will want to take more than one pair of boots."

"I suppose – well, that takes care of one luggage holder. But you have two more!"

"But when the weather turns warmer, we'll need lighter clothing." She smiled at him, her blue eyes lighting up in amusement.

"Well, that's two. What about the third? The rooms we are going to have in City One are not all that big – so why must you have third one?"

"To put things in – like a few ornaments and pictures – presents – you know ..."

"We don't need them, Ces, love. Two will be enough."

She stood up. "If you say so – I didn't know there was any restriction."

"Well, basically, no – but it is a freighter-class spacecraft – it takes four teams of reclamation workers, all their equipment, including basic luggage, food, medical staff and temporary living accommodation and us. But the less we take the better."

"Right ... I'll do my best with two. After all, when I came here I had only one small bag, meant for a few days. So I will see what I can do."

"That's my love." Medrix laughed and bent and kissed her.

She giggled and he kissed her again, bringing his arms around her as he bent lower and kissed her neck and nibbled at her ear.

"Medrix – what are you doing?" she whispered.

"If you don't know by now, then I'm not telling you."

The front-door bell rang.

"Damn," he said, "whoever's that?"

He released her and went to answer the door. It was a Law Officer. Cessie could hear them talking, then Medrix came in and told her that he was wanted in the Chief Elder's office and he would see her later and, with that, he was gone.

She went on with the packing. Two it would have to be. He was right of course; the space was not available even on such a big craft for carrying all that. Four teams consisted of 480 men, without the others.

She sat on a chair and looked around her. This place had been her home since before the trial. Here she and Medrix had fought each other over who did what and when. Here they had fallen in love in spite of all the things that had happened to try and stop them. Even when she had been evicted from City One all those years ago, he had featured in her life. It seemed as if their lives had been intertwined since then. Granted, when he left Chetner he had vowed to return and have his revenge on them all – and this time he would win. But she knew that was only said in a fit of anger when he realised that his work as a spy had come to an end so abruptly.

If she had not wanted to play the game all those years ago, she wouldn't have been exiled; she wouldn't have met him; she wouldn't have challenged the Lawmakers of Chetner to a game, and she wouldn't have sent the Elders home to Estolan, taking Medrix with them. Then she would not have been brought here for a trial concerning the game and Medrix wouldn't have met her and saved her life in more ways than one, and she wouldn't be here packing to go back to Chetner and he wouldn't have been appointed Liaison Officer between the Chetnerites and the reclamation workers. How different their lives would have been. But now she wouldn't want to be separated from him because he was a part of her life that she did not want ever to be lost and because – most of all – she loved him and he loved her.

All those years ago she would have laughed if she had been told that she would marry a Lawmaker. Lawmakers, well at least the Chetner ones, had mostly been vicious, strict law-abiding bigots.

Her Lawmother had as good as told her that Medrix was like that still but Cessie knew him better and ignored the warning: *"If you renew your vows and go to Chetner with him – then it will be too late for you and all your people."* She did not believe it – and yet … why did it come back to her all the time? Maybe it was because it had upset her so much because her Lawmother had been spying on her. Her concern for her Lawdaughter was put on in order to worm her way into her confidence and then report her every movement to the enemy: the Elders of Chetner!

It sickened her that so many people had been employed by them in order to destroy her. Those Elders thought they were invincible and it was Medrix who had proved otherwise – that they were not.

She got up and went into the kitchen to make some coffee. Since renewing their vows, Medrix had been sent for training, learning how to be a good liaison officer. He had practised with her but, as neither could be serious while doing it, he gave that up and got Lawmother Grey to help him. She seemed to have a gift for helping people.

As Cessie prepared the meal, she wondered what it would be like living in the City. There was no water laid on, that she knew. Water had to be carried from a well, but everything else would be much as it was before she left. Well, maybe not. Some of her friends had married and had moved out to various settlements.

Her jobs had gone to others as she had been away so long. She wondered how she would spend her time for nine whole moons. Being a Lawmaker's wife would separate her from the Chetnerites in some ways, but she needed to go back – they were her people, after all.

Medrix came back two hours later looking very serious.

"What is it, Medrix? What's wrong?" she said anxiously.

"Everything."

"Everything? What do you mean?"

"Sit down with me, love – here on the long seat." He sat down.

"Medrix? Has something happened to my father?"

"No – no – he's fine – sit down, love."

She sat down. "What then?"

"Yesterday morning at about the hour of five, City One collapsed in on itself. There are no survivors." He took her hands in his.

"*No!*" She shook her head. "*No* – it can't be. Tell me it isn't true."

"It is true. It's now on fire. No one can get near it." His arms held her to him.

"On fire ... there's no water laid on," she said in a dull voice.

"No – but even if there was, there's no one left to do anything."

"But someone must have sent the messages."

"Yes. We had an advance team working there, checking the tunnels running between each city. They are in a camp nearby. They sent the messages, but no one's heard from them since."

"Messages, Medrix – what other messages?"

"They said the fire had spread along the tunnels to the other cities. There's a great wall of fire spread snake-like across the country. There are explosions as the fire reaches the shafts – and the fire is spreading everywhere. Since that message ... we've not heard from them at all."

"Oh no – Medrix – it can't be."

"It is. We are going tomorrow morning instead of in six days time. The teams and the equipment are all ready. We shall go into the top space dock: the one the Elders built. It is a long way away from the Nineteenth City. In fact, two lines of hills protect it and there's land behind it where we can settle any survivors. The hills will separate us from the fire and will protect the valley also, which is at the foot of the Reed Mountain. So it will be a safe place for any survivors. Our job will be to get them there and to put out the fires. The team have fire-retardant foam to spread on the countryside to put out the fires – but it won't put out the city fires until the gas has all gone.

"There is a control base there which is now in working order. The Chief Elder says that he will also send in two teams of Law Officers to help with the fire-fighting and in the rescue of Chetnerites. Also a team of some twenty Lawmother nurses and three doctors will go and set up a field medical bay."

"What will I have to pack for us, Medrix?" She stood up and looked around the room.

"Nothing. I will have the regulation kit for reclamation workers – I will be provided with everything I need for such work. You, of course, are not going."

"Not going? Of course I'm going – those are my people out there."

"You are my wife and I say you are to stay here." He stood up.

"I *am* going. I will be needed. I have nursing skills; I am used to Chetner's troubles."

"You are not a qualified nurse. You will not be needed – you will be one more liability for us – and that's all!"

"You forget, Lawmaker – I don't have to obey you. If I want to go – I'll go," she said firmly.

"No, you won't. I vowed to protect you and the only way I can do this is to leave you here where you'll be safe."

"But, Medrix ... I'm a Leader. A Leader in Chetner has to take on certain responsibilities. Ducking out of them is not one of them."

"But you are also my wife, and come under Lawmaker's rules. I say you are not to go – so that's the end of it."

"It's not the end of it. It's my right – and I shall go – even if I go to Temra to catch the shuttle from there."

"You will do as you are told – *do you hear me*?" he shouted at her. "Do I make myself *clear*? Do *I*?"

"Perfectly. Some Liaison Officer you are, shouting at me. Are you going to shout at them, too?"

Medrix went red with anger and, taking her by the shoulders, shook her and then abruptly let her go and walked towards the door.

She ran after him. "Medrix," she said, "I'm sorry. I should never have said that – I'm sorry – please look at me." He turned and looked at her, his eyes ice-cold with anger.

"I understand," she said. I'll stay here – as you wish." She bowed her head, waiting for him to speak. He strode towards her and pulled her into his arms.

"Cessie, oh Ces – don't let us argue. You know I want the best for you. When it is safer I'll ask you to come – I promise – I ..." he kissed her on the mouth and she relaxed against him.

"I'll stay here – where it's safe, Medrix – I will, and I'm sorry. I know you will be brilliant at your job." She reached up and returned the kiss. "Medrix –

be sure to take that warm scarf your mother made you. It is very cold in Chetner at this time of the year."

"I'll write – I promise you." He let her go. "I have to go to a meeting now. I'll see you later."

She was fast asleep when he went the next morning. He didn't wake her – they had made up their quarrel last night. He left her a note and went out into the early morning. The spacecraft left on time on its way to Chetner.

Cessie woke up later and found the note:

Darling Ces – Remember, whatever happens to me, that I will always love you. Medrix. xxx

"Oh, God," she thought, "he has gone into such danger – please bring him back safely to me – please …"

Chapter 2

The journey to Chetner was uneventful and Medrix spent most of the time sleeping, as did the others.

As they were docking, the captain of the freighter spacecraft called Medrix to his quarters and handed him a package, saying: "Lawmaker – I have here your orders from the Chief Elder and the Grand Elder. All other orders have been cancelled."

"Cancelled! What do you mean?" he opened the package.

"It is not for me to say – but as far as I can gather, you are now in charge of everything on Chetner." So saying, the captain left Medrix, who stared in disbelief at the documents in his hands. He opened one of them and read:

> On this day, Lawmaker Medrix, you have been given sole charge of Chetner. All reclamation teams will receive their orders from you: what you decide – they must do. The fire-fighters will also take orders from you. All workers at the base itself will take their orders from you. All other people will abide by your rules, for you are the Controller – acting in our names – you will govern as you think fit until such time as a new Chetnerite Council can be formed. Then, still as Controller, you will work with them in restoring Chetner to its former glory.
>
> Signed on this day 15th of the 4th Moon 4018:
> L Derson: Grand Elder
> F Fenwick: Chief Elder
> May the powers that be, be with you.

The other papers consisted of a map of Chetner, the base, a list of stock at the base, and a list of other items being sent to Chetner from other places. Medrix was so amazed, he read the documents again.

The freighter came to a juddering halt and Medrix knew that they had arrived.

He followed the others along the narrow gangway that led from the craft to the docking platform. Already equipment was being driven along track ways leading from the craft to the underground lane that eventually came out on a wide parking area at the back of the base. The noises made echoed back, which made all talking impossible.

Looking up, he could see the roof spread out like a large canopy. There were docking bays at different levels – and as he walked, he could see a smaller bay which held six shuttles. He hadn't realised it was so big. When he'd left it all those years ago, he only remembered getting away as fast as he could. But now he wondered why the Elders had built such a big place if they never intended to use it again – or maybe they meant to return one day.

He went on down a passageway – there were signs everywhere – and eventually he saw one that said Controller's Rooms and he opened the door and went in.

The place was dusty and evidently hardly used. In one section were computer screens. None of them was on. He found the power switch and turned it on. Lights came on and, immediately, messages were appearing on one screen while the others showed various parts of the base. He wondered why no one was on duty here.

In another section were large boards with maps spread out on them. The further section had a large table and several chairs. There were the remains of a meal left there, but nobody around.

At the end of the office was another door. He opened it to find a set of rooms: a sitting room with a small kitchen and washroom, and a sleep room. The bed was unmade; the cupboards empty.

He walked back into the office. In one corner was an odd contraption labelled: Speaker Machine. There were written instructions: press blue button to speak to shuttle-bay officer; yellow for whole base; green for freighter craft offices; orange for medical bay.

He pressed the yellow button. A red light came on and a sign under it read: speak now. He took a deep breath and said: "This is Lawmaker Medrix speaking, Liaison Officer and Controller of this base. Will all team leaders please report to my office at once. Also, will the dining manager please send over coffee and biscuits for us. That's all for now."

The machine repeated his words twice, then switched itself off.

The team leaders came into the room laughing and joking and Thaddeus said: "Well, Medrix, little brother, that's a fine joke you played on us."

"It was no joke," Medrix replied seriously. "I am in charge – if you like – I have taken over Chetner! ..."

His father interrupted him. "Don't be silly, Medrix – we have our orders. You are only a Liaison Officer ..."

Medrix didn't wait for him to finish. "There are no Chetnerites here – Lawmaker – there may not be any anywhere. But we have to hope that that's not true. But in the meantime you take all your orders from me."

The door opened and two people walked in, carrying coffee.

Medrix looked up. "Ah, coffee – that's good. In future, knock on the door before you enter, please."

They nodded and went out.

Someone knocked on the door and a Lawmother entered.

"I'm sorry I'm late – but my team of nurses has only just arrived." She smiled – she was obviously a Temran and Medrix was reminded of his cousin's wife, Leah, a big, kindly woman.

"Sit down, Lawmother." He introduced the others who seemed very surprised to have her here in the room with them. "You will of course take orders from the doctors in charge of the medical bay concerning nursing – but – other concerns will be dealt with through me."

She nodded her head and smiled. "We'll do our best, Lawmaker."

"Controller – Lawmaker is my title, nurse."

The others looked at him in amazement but she only said: "I must remember that."

The door opened again and a man in dirty overalls arrived.

"Who are you?" Medrix asked.

"I'm the leader of the cleaners for this base."

"Name please."

"Cleaner Frailand."

"You knew we were coming?" Medrix demanded.

"Yes."

"Then why is the place in a mess?" He pointed around the room.

"We didn't get enough notice – it's a big base."

"Make sure every part is cleaned before you go off duty and make sure that overalls are washed daily. Give me a list of the daily jobs to be done by each member of your team. Just because we are in the middle of nowhere, it does not mean we have to live like pigs."

"Medrix ..." said Costan, one of the reclamation leaders. He got no further.

"You are a leader and you cannot remember my title? Some leader you are!" Medrix was annoyed. Then he seemed to hear Cessie's voice saying: "Some Liaison Officer you are. Are you going to shout at them, too?" How well she knew him.

He smiled. "This job was given to me out of the blue. I have to do it and I would appreciate it if you would help me, for what might be trivial to you is not where so many people are concerned. A well-disciplined ship runs well. So do try and remember we are not at home in some wine bar enjoying ourselves. Here I have to be deadly serious – for we are all in danger ourselves of becoming too complacent – so remember."

Costan apologised.

"Now," went on Medrix, "no reclamation teams will go out yet. It is too dangerous. But," he turned to his father, "you must send out sixty men in landshakers (a kind of tank) to look for survivors. Ten men in each will mean six of them. Three going down this side and three travelling along this valley and down on the other side. You are looking for survivors, that's all. You can each bring back fifteen of them at a time and no more. The rest of your men will put up your temporary accommodation."

He nodded to the cleaner and the nurse. "There's no need for you to stay now." They nodded and left the room.

Another man came in. "I'm sorry I'm late. I've only just come back."

"Back from where?" Medrix looked at the young man who was evidently very nervous as he kept pushing his hand through his brown curly hair. "Back from where?" Medrix said again.

"From walking my dog."

"Dog! Here!" Medrix raised an eyebrow.

"I – I found it wandering about – so I've taken it in. Did I break a rule?"

"No – you have just rescued our first Chetnerite."

The tension in the room subsided as they all laughed.

"Who are you?"

"Ensign Jakta – leader of that," he pointed to the unattended screens.

Medrix was serious at once. "How many in your team?"

"Eight."

"Where are the others?"

"In the dining centre."

"Remember this, Ensign – your life might be dependent on it, as well as many others – that section must *never* – and I emphasize the word *never* – must *never* be left unattended – do I make myself clear?"

"Yes – Controller."

"Good – so attend to your section and make sure I never see it left unattended again."

The ensign went over to his section.

"Now, you others: Costan, sixty of your men can dig lats – the others can put up tents. Thaddeus – there are two reservoirs between us and City Nineteen. The Elders destroyed the pumping station and it's never been repaired. You and your men will see that the water is pumped down to us. The base itself has its own supply but of course the valley hasn't. All water must be boiled – we can't risk anybody catching the fever. The water must be pumped down and taps put at regular intervals along the encampment. Joder ..." Another team leader smiled.

"Yes, Controller," he said firmly.

"Your men will put up the temporary accommodations the Zendrians sent us. Included in them is a field medical bay and hall. The hall could do as a schoolroom. Ask the nurses for bedding etc., for these and other temporary homes. We must have somewhere for our survivors to live."

"I understand. Should we build up temporary kitchens?"

"Yes. Good idea. It would take the strain off the dining centre. Two more teams arrive tomorrow.

"I think that's all, Lawmakers – you may go – unless you have questions to ask?"

No one answered and all but the ensign left the room.

The door burst open. "I am so sorry to be so late," said a man who did not look sorry at all. He was short and fat and his smile was lopsided.

"Who are you?" Medrix said calmly.

"I'm in charge of the base – the whole base – making sure that everything runs smoothly – no craft overruns the dock. In fact I run all this and you, Lawmaker, are sitting in my room as if you owned it."

"So you work here?"

"Yes."

"So where were you when I arrived?"

"Supervising the gantry craft overload on Bay 6."

"I see – you left this room unattended."

"I have only sixty men to run this place. We were sent here in advance to get this place up and running. We have been working flat out so that we were ready in time. Of course you've come earlier than expected and we were caught out."

"You've had plenty of time to get yourself organised. There was no one in here – no one in the message section. The cleaners evidently had done no cleaning and I hate to think what else is wrong – but I have my orders here and I'm in charge now. All you have to do is look after the docking-bay area. I noticed how well it was laid out and how well run that was."

The man smiled. "I prefer it that way."

"Good. You will find rooms somewhere I don't doubt. According to this map the base has three dormitories, twelve sleep rooms, twenty-six cupboards – we must see what's in these – three dining areas, one medical centre, one theatre, one game court and three cells. I can't imagine why it is so big."

"I think it was for the people who had to stay here while the place was being built." The man moved towards the door. "Good luck, Controller – you are going to need it."

"Thank you – what's your name?"

"Thorson Gold."

"Well, we are relying on you, Lawmaker."

"I'm not a Lawmaker – I'm a Zendrian."

"Really – how did you get the job?"

"I was one of the people who helped design the whole complex."

"You worked for the Chetner Elders?"

"Yes. So I know many things about this place – just ask me, any time."

He left the room and Medrix sat pondering why he had got this job. He sighed, wondering what Cessie was doing now. How he longed for her – she would have brightened up the place, he was sure of that.

Chapter 3

Medrix had gone to bed very late. He had made up his own bed from bedding he had found in a cupboard. He slept well in spite of everything, and he awoke early in the morning with a sense of security that really didn't exist.

His mood was broken when he went into his office and found the Zendrian there. He was sitting with his feet on the table and he did not move when Medrix came in.

"I have you come to tell you, Lawmaker, that all my team have been called back to base."

"When did you hear this?"

"At the hour of two this morning. We were only put here to get the base ready for you – well, you are here, and now we can all go home." He stood up.

"But we haven't brought anyone with us to run a base of this size," Medrix said sharply.

"Nothing to do with me, Lawmaker – we've done our job. I thought I'd better tell you – not just go."

"Thanks for that, anyway."

"But we can't go, Lawmaker, until someone lets our freighters out of the dock. We want to go now."

"I'll come."

"You? What can you do?"

"I know about such things. You go and get ready."

"Right – good luck, Lawmaker."

The man went, and Medrix went in search of two men who had been Elders' men with Medrix all those years ago. He found them digging lats. They came at once when they heard what had happened. So it was that Medrix and these two men were able to let the freighters out. Afterwards he left those two men in the craft control base. Then he went to the computer in his office.

"Computer, have you any messages for me?"

"There are two freighter spacecrafts waiting for entry carrying two teams

191

of reclamation workers, two teams of fire-fighters and two teams of military Law Officers."

"Thank you – please notify the control space centre."

"I have done this already. They say they need someone in the top gantry craft overload section before they can let in these two spaceships."

"Right."

"It's not right, Controller – there's no one there."

"I know that."

"Who will you send?"

"I wish I knew," Medrix said despondently.

"That's not a logical answer, Controller," the voice went on, "I suggest you get more of the ex-Elders' team."

"They are here?"

"Yes."

"Where?"

"In the reclamation teams. Shall I page them?"

"Yes – go ahead. And inform the team leaders what is happening."

Later, the men arrived at his office. A few of them, he knew.

"You wanted us, Controller," said one.

"You are all Elders' men. Some of you I already know."

They looked startled and one said: "We are not Elders' men now – we have certificates now to say that we are reclamation workers." There was a loud murmuring, agreeing with him.

"I know – but your training, as mine was, included spacecraft technology and control centres. So I need you here to run that part of the base until I get others to do it."

"You will get others?" said one.

"I hope so – I have sent a message saying so. There are freighters waiting to come in. We can't keep them waiting any longer. The computer will tell you where each person should go – according to your years of service. One of you ... Jordan ... you will stay here to check messages coming through from Chetner itself."

"Am I to be by myself?"

"Yes – I'll find someone to take over from you ... Computer, please tell the team leaders which men are working here and please work out the shift times for our new control base workers. Include the incoming teams in that, there may be more Elders' men coming in. The more rest hours we can give, the better."

"Will do, Controller – but we have no cooks or cleaners. Do you want me to see to that as well?"

"Could do. Allocate jobs to the incoming teams. Fire-fighters have to go out at once."

"Yes, Controller."

Five days later, the base looked a different place and the meals, although very basic, were edible.

Then a shuttle arrived with fifteen more Lawmother nurses who had come to help prepare the medical bay. Also, two doctors arrived and the equipment for it. Four of the nurses were sent to help in the kitchen and then the food improved. The doctors were annoyed – but Medrix said they would be released when the medical bay had patients – but not before then – and that he was in charge of the whole base and ran it as he thought fit.

As the days went by, the landshakers brought in survivors. Each of them was in a terrible state. How they had survived, no one knew. Their experience was too traumatic for them to go into details.

The Lawmakers said that the countryside was like hell, with rivulets of fire, smoke everywhere, scorched earth and earth tremors.

Reports came in of raiding parties who zoomed in over the uninhabited settlements and took anything they could sell. Medrix sent out Law Officers to stop this.

A few days later, water was piped down to the camp, which made life a bit easier. The same day, mail bags arrived from Estolan and there was much rejoicing amongst the men and women on the base.

There was one letter from Jessanda, who was concerned about her brother, Conn, who was away on his first assignment since leaving college, a note from the Grand Elder which just said: *Well done, Medrix – keep up the good work*, and a long one from Cessie. After his evening meal, he went into his sleep room to read her letter:

Dear Medrix, Lawmaker mine

I love you XXXX and I miss you all the time. Everyone sends good wishes to you and hopes you come home soon, safe and well.

Your mother has made a collection of toys and books for the children. Everyone was delighted to give something. Lawmother Grey and her sister have made some children's clothes and the bread sellers are collecting clothes for everyone. Everybody is willing to help. A shuttle will be coming to you with these things. I wish it was bringing me as well. But then I must not grumble – many wives have their husbands out there with you and many mothers have sons and many girls have sweethearts there as well.

The Grand Elder notified me that I could not stay in the house any longer. It seems each Grand Elder uses the house for guests and he wants it by the end of this moon.

Lawmother Grey and I went to look at some houses. There was an empty one by your grandfather, so I am in the process of moving there. Of course it is much smaller than the other one. Just right for two! It has a large bedroom and a small one with washroom – that's upstairs. Downstairs there's a large sitting room – which has doors that open out on to a terrace and a garden. The garden has gone wild. Don't worry, I know the rules. I won't do any gardening! There's a kitchen and a washroom, too. It's unfurnished – so I am going to buy some furniture. Lawmother Grey is going to help me to make curtains.

I have to go now and put this letter in the mailbag.

All my love to you goes with it. I wish I was with you now, Medrix mine. Hope you send for me soon.

Love and lots of kisses to you.

X X Celisia Margaret X X X X X

p.s. Enclosed are some rose petals from the garden.

Medrix read the letter several times – then put it down because he saw a flash of lightning and he heard thunder rolling in the distance, and as the evening wore on, it got nearer.

After a late meal at the dining centre, he went to bed and read her letter again and fell asleep over it. Later he awoke and heard rain falling. "Ah," he thought – "rain will put out the fires – I hope it rains all night." If so he would send out two reclamation teams to check the state of the land. They had to start some time.

The morning mists had cleared away by the time everyone had had breakfast. He called the leaders to his office. He could hear them talking as they entered.

Costan was talking and laughing and saying; "You know, Medrix wouldn't be so bad if his wife was here, for she has a way of controlling him." Everyone laughed but stopped when they saw him standing by the door of his rooms. They knew he had heard and looked very sheepish.

"Sit down, please." They did so in silence.

"Some of you think that what we are doing is a great joke. I can assure you it is *not*," he said grimly.

They said nothing – but no one looked at him.

"It's a good thing we have had rain – it should have put out some of the fires. Two reclamation teams will go out today. Your camp duties will be given over to the other teams that have come in."

Thaddeus interrupted him. "I think my father and I should be the first teams to go."

"Yes, I agree – you will go to your designated areas, but if it is too bad out there, you must come back. You must send in details about where you are each night. Is that understood?" They agreed.

"Also, Costan's team should go – but not to your designated area."

"Why not?" Costan was annoyed. What did Medrix know about land reclamation, anyway, he thought.

"I want you to go as far as City Nineteen and then cover the area that runs along the foot of these mountains."

"Why? Surely we will be more use nearer City One!"

"City One and the area will be too hot for you to do anything there at all, and somewhere there are the teams that sent the original messages."

"So why send us out at all?"

"The area where I am sending you has many farms and houses – we should reclaim that land as quickly as possible so that people can be resettled and, hopefully, the livestock saved."

"I see – right – we will do as you say – but I hope for your sake, Controller, that we are doing the right thing. You've already taken some of my workers away. Are they coming with me?"

"No – I need them in the base. No one else is qualified for the job they are doing. I've revised the other jobs for the remaining teams to do."

"When will we go out?" asked Jador.

"As soon as we have reports from the other teams – then I will judge it fit to send them."

His father stood up. "I'll go now, as I have a lot of preparation to do."

"Go safely," Medrix said.

His father looked at him and smiled. "I wouldn't have your job, Controller, for all the galaxy put together."

Medrix smiled. "Nor me, yours."

They all left the room and no one was joking this time.

The door opened and his father came back in. He went up to Medrix and hugged him and said: "We'll do the best for you, son."

"No," said Medrix, "you do the best for Chetner – they do need the best, and you are the best of all."

After his father had gone, Medrix stared at himself in the mirror. "Oh God – I hope I have done the right thing."

He walked into his sitting room, sat down and wrote a letter to Celisia:

My darling, darling Celisia,

I have missed you so much. The nights are lonely without you lying by my side.

The advance team who were here to get the space dock working, left the day after our arrival. I had to find men to take their places.

I have been so busy – time has gone so quickly. Today three teams are going out to start work.

I am hoping and trusting that all will be well. The good news is that we have brought in some survivors.

I like the sound of our house. I've put the rose petals in my diary.

I must go now, there are messages coming in. I will see you soon, love.

Remember, whatever happens, I will always love you, my darling.

Medrix XXX

He sealed the letter and went to put it in the mail box.

The reports came in from the three teams on each night. They said it was bad but they were carrying on to the designated areas.

Then, on the eighth night, nothing was heard from his father's team, and although the frequency for them was kept open, no reports came in at all. On the tenth night, his brother's team-reports stopped and nothing more was heard from them. Only Costan's team kept sending in reports that showed that work was going on there as planned.

The rest of the teams knew that the other teams were missing and became very depressed at the news. Medrix roamed around the camp, trying to cheer people up – but in his private thoughts he was as upset as any of them. Both men, he knew, were experts at their jobs – so, where were they?

One evening when he got back to his rooms, he found a nurse waiting by the door. She had brought him a mug of chen and some biscuits.

"I'm Nurse Pennington – they call me Penn. Nurse Fielding, our team leader, sent me with this drink." She smiled at him.

"Oh, thank her, will you?"

"Yes, of course. Did you have a letter from your wife?"

"Yes, I did. Why do you ask?"

She smiled. "We – that is some of the nurses – wondered why she isn't with you – here. She is, after all a Chetnerite."

"Not that it is any of your business – it's not a good idea to have untrained personnel on the base."

"Oh, but …"

"Do you see other wives here?"

"No – but – she is different. She sat down. A dark curl strayed from under her white bonnet. She looked up at him, her green eyes watching him keenly.

"Nurse Pennington – thank you for the drink. You may go now."

She stood up, her face flushing as she stood by the table.

"It's just … you see – we all think she should be here – not enjoying herself back on Estolan. Estolan is not her home after all."

She touched him on the arm. He pulled away. "Please go nurse – whether my wife comes or goes is my affair not yours – please remember that."

He opened the door for her as she left. "Goodnight," she whispered.

A guard coming in just then looked at them both and said to himself: "Well, now we know why his wife isn't here." The guard gave Medrix a message from the central base and returned to his duty.

Medrix read the message from the Grand Elder: No base workers are to be sent. Just use the men as you think fit. Good luck. Trust the rain will stay – it will be a great help!

Medrix sighed – so there was nothing else for it – the ex-Elders' men had to stay put whatever happened. He hoped he could trust them. Only time would tell.

Chapter 4

Cessie was missing Medrix very much. She tried to keep busy but there were always times when the house seemed too quiet without him.

The women had been busy collecting warm clothing to send to Chetner and she spent the mornings helping to sort the clothing out. Toys and books for the children were also being crated up. It went to her heart to think of those children who were living in such frightening conditions.

The days went by slowly – and the freighters were sent out with the items for Chetner.

Jessanda invited Cessie to her house for coffee and she accepted – she would show Medrix that she wasn't jealous.

When she arrived, she found the room crowded. A maid showed her in and brought coffee to her. She sat by a small table in the window which looked out on to a beautiful garden and she was intrigued by the beautifully-kept lawns and flowerbeds. A great fern hid her from most of the people but it was the only table available.

Suddenly she heard her name mentioned. Peering through the fronds of the fern she could see a tall thin woman talking to the group sitting around her. She was speaking loudly: "Poor Cessie – she is left here all on her own while Medrix sleeps with other women."

"We don't know that," said one fat woman.

"Oh: but my brother is in one of the teams over there and he has written to me about what is going on there. It seems Medrix is now called the Controller. Anyone who does not call him that is reprimanded. All the staff at the base walked out when he insisted on taking over."

"I'm sure you've read it wrongly," the fat woman said.

"No, no – I did not. All the key positions in the base are held by Elders' men."

"They've been disbanded," said a little woman dressed in grey.

"Yes, I know – but all the ones that had been Elders' men have been put in the key positions and we all know that Medrix himself was an Elders' man."

"They were probably the only ones who would know how everything worked in a space station base," the fat woman said, "the Elders' men were trained as undercover agents, so they would know what they were doing." The others nodded in agreement.

The thin woman went on: "But you see, there are Lawmother nurses there and one is called Nurse Penn and she is always going to Medrix' rooms – even at night – he is always laughing and talking with her – so I say 'Poor Cessie', we know now why he doesn't want her there, spoiling everything for him. They say he has taken over Chetner – two teams are lost by all accounts – you mark my words – he'll ruin Chetner."

Cessie sat, white-faced. She had to get out of there. She pushed the window open wider, stepped through and walked down the garden into a maze of rose bushes.

She was shocked. Was it true? The person who wrote the letter seemed to think so, and she hadn't heard from Medrix.

The maze came out by the river. There was a path running alongside that went into the next garden. She found herself at the end of a long, well-kept lawn – there was no one about, so she walked up the lawn and through a side gate. She was in such a hurry that she bumped into a man.

"Sorry," she said, and ran past him and out on to the road. He looked startled but did not speak to her.

When Cessie got home, she lay on the bed and cried. But then she talked herself into a happier frame of mind. It was malicious gossip that's all it was. Medrix loved her – and people were just plain jealous. She wondered if Jessanda had deliberately set up the whole thing. She shook her head. It couldn't be – could it? Medrix would say she was maligning Jessanda because she didn't like her. Well, she didn't like her, that was a plain fact – but Medrix was right – she was trying to fault her in some way. She didn't trust her. It was just a gut feeling. And Medrix loved *her*, not Jessanda.

The next day there was a letter from Medrix and she read it over and over again. She got her pen out and replied at once:

Lawmaker mine, I love you.

> *Thank you for your letter. I am glad you are missing me: I know I am missing you.*

> *I went to Jessanda's house for coffee. It was very crowded there and most of the people I didn't know. Her garden is beautiful, so well kept and such a variety of colour. I went into her rose maze and took ages to get out of it. Have you ever seen it?*

> *All the women have been busy collecting warm winter clothes so that they can be sent to Chetner. I expect they may have already arrived.*

> *I went shopping with Lawmother Grey. I bought you some new socks and a warm scarf. I bought myself a new bonnet and I bought a green rug for the sitting room.*

198

This all seems so frivolous when I think of my poor people who have suffered so much – and have so little.

I hope I can come soon, even if it is only to see that you wear the right socks each day.

I will write again soon. Everybody sends their good wishes to you all.

All my love – now and for always.

Celisia Margaret X X X

This is me getting lost in the rose maze:

Having written the letter she went over to the mail office and put it in the bag reserved for Chetner. On her way out she decided to go to the library to find some books on the history of Chetner. The librarian welcomed her, saying: "There are two crates of books here from Chetner. The Elders must have brought them by mistake. We cannot send them back yet so we will have to keep them here. I need someone to sort them out and catalogue them. I am to put up special shelves for them to go on. Would you like to do this job?"

"I have asked the Grand Elder if he would allow this and he said it was a good idea as you seem bored by the round of social gatherings. I am to pay you fifty credos a moon. You do not have to work every day – just as long as it gets done. So what do you say? Will you do it?"

Cessie smiled. "Yes, of course I will – but only until I go to Chetner as Medrix promised I should."

And so it was agreed and Cessie was now employed by the City Council.

She went every morning for two hours. The days slipped by quickly and soon two moons had passed. She wrote daily to Medrix, telling him all about her work and also how much she missed him, but no more letters came for her and she was worried about him – but then, she knew he was so busy. But as the days wore on, she became depressed at the thought that maybe the gossip was true.

To her friends and others, she put on a show just for them: Yes, Medrix was well. Yes, she was going to Chetner soon and yes, she heard from him almost daily.

But at night she lay awake worrying about him. She soon became pale and worn-looking, so much so that people began to remark on it.

After work, she would go for coffee in one of the dining centres and she did so on this particular day. The place was crowded but as she came in, it went quiet. She hesitated in the doorway, then marched in and across to the serving hatch. She brought her tray to a small table near the door and sat down to drink the coffee.

Gradually people began to talk again and she heard some of the conversation:

"He's gone mad, so they say. No one has a say in the affairs. He has a different nurse each night with him ..."

Cessie stood up and said firmly: "If you are talking about my husband, you wrong him. This is the same man you were all congratulating when he won my case – are you all so fickle that you can believe this gossip about him? I thought gossips were punished severely on this planet. I have a good mind to report you all."

There was dead silence and suddenly they were all clapping and one said: "There speaks a brave woman. She is quite right – we should not believe such rubbish."

Then Celisia walked out of the place, vowing to herself that she would never go in there again. She was mad with herself for speaking out. She should have just slipped out quietly. She always did rush into things.

Three days later, the Grand Elder informed her that Medrix wanted her in Chetner. There were Chetnerites now living in the top site and it was right she should be there for them. She noticed that he did not say that she should be there for Medrix, but at least she was going and she would find out what was really happening.

A small freighter craft taking extra bedding and medical supplies to Chetner was leaving at five in the morning in three days time, and she was to travel on it.

She told her friends, and Lawmother Grey said she would look after the house for her. Medrix' mother gave her some scones and jam to take with her. His grandfather sent a small book and everyone sent their love. Jessanda came over to wish her well and asked her to look up her brother Conn.

The morning of departure came. Cessie had packed a small bag of Chetner-type clothes and other things and also had a flask of coffee and food for the journey. Eldon walked her to the freighter bay and saw her onto the waiting craft.

Three men acted as crew – they sat in the front and she had a seat at the back of the hold. One man told her to press the red button by the seat. She did so and the big side door slid shut. She heard the engines come to life and the craft moved out of the dock and was on its way. Soon she would see Medrix. Soon they would be together again.

It was warm in the hold and she fell asleep, dreaming of Medrix.

Much later she woke up and ate some food and drank some coffee. She could hear the murmur of the men's voices.

One man passed her as he went to the washroom. On his way back to his seat he mentioned that they were halfway there and that one of the crew was fast asleep but not to worry as there was always somebody crewing the thing. He laughed at his joke and went back to his seat.

Cessie relaxed back in her seat. There was a smell of clean bedding and a sweet smell, like perfume.

She went to the washroom and as she came out, saw another door on which was written: 'To Escape Hatch – only open in an emergency.' She thought to herself: That's good. I'm glad it's got one of those.

She went back to her place, sat down and closed her eyes, relaxing back in the comfortable seat.

There was a sudden jolt as things in the hold moved from one side to the other. She stared through a side window – she could see the coast line of Chetner and what looked like a line of fire. The freighter seemed very low – too low, in fact.

The sky was dark and now it was raining heavily. Lightning flashed and thunder rolled, echoing around the hold making the whole area shake. What was happening?

She got up and made her way to the others. One man was on the floor, knocked unconscious by the look of him. The freighter seemed to be turning towards the blazing city.

"Sit down," said the crew member who had spoken to her earlier. "There's nothing we can do for him now."

She sat down as he called to the Top Base tower: "Come in, please, Top Base. This is freighter 697 from Estolan, we are in trouble."

A man's voice came through clearly.

"This is Kaylan – operator of the Top Base tower – what seems to be the trouble?"

"Our craft is being pulled towards the burning city."

"I can see you on our screen – you are too far over – you should be over the sea not the land."

"I know – but we are being pulled in by a magnetic tractor beam from the city."

"Not possible, pilot – something else must be wrong. These are decoy cities only."

"No, it is so – perhaps the lightning has triggered it – maybe freighters loaded here in the past."

"Have you tried manual control?"

"No – we'll do that now."

He pressed some buttons and the craft lifted higher and away from the city. Then lightning struck him down and he fell over the controls and slithered to the floor.

The craft shuddered and again began to move towards the city.

"Sit in his place," said the other crewman to Cessie.

She managed to do so and stared in panic at all the controls.

"We'll try again," said the crewman. The craft did not respond. He tried again in desperation and the freighter lifted higher again and seemed to be turning away towards the sea when he suddenly collapsed back in his seat, his arm hanging loose. He muttered something – it sounded like: "You are on your own now," and then was silent.

"Freighter 697, come in please." It was Medrix; he had been called in because Cessie was on the craft.

"Oh Medrix – they're all dead – and I don't know what to do – the craft is turning back to the city."

"It's all right love, press the red buttons over the warp control sequence gears – the name's on it. Keep pressing until a blue light comes on."

She followed his instructions and the craft straightened and flew higher.

"Now what, Medrix?" she screamed.

"Calm down, love. Push the blue lever on the maximum top control – slowly now – don't let go until the craft is higher."

She did so and the freighter again rose higher.

"What now, Medrix?"

"Press the yellow control buttons with the purple ones on the right side of the lever blockway, and then, very slowly, bring the gear lever in towards yourself."

As she did so, she called out excitedly: "It's lifting and turning away from the city – have I done it, Medrix?"

"Yes – now – hold it steady."

"Oh!" she screamed.

"What is it, Ces?" Medrix asked frantically.

"There was an explosion in the city – it shifted the things in the hold and now we are tipping sideways – Ah! now it's straightening again and we are lifting higher."

"Well done – keep it level – we'll soon have you here safe and well."

Lightning struck the front of the craft and she screamed in terror.

Medrix said, calmly: "Press the orange button by the time keeper. This will bring the craft even further away from the fire."

"I can't find it, Medrix – there's just a hole," she said in panic.

"Look again, love!"

"It's not there – the lightning must have struck it."

"Then go to the emergency escape hatch – sit in there and press the yellow button – it will eject you into space – and float you down safely."

"I'm going – what about these people?"

"*Go.* They are unable to go. *Cessie*," he yelled, "go *now*."

She moved quickly through the hold. The freighter tipped further to one side and flung her on to her seat and she pressed the red button as she did so. The side door slid open and she felt herself being pulled out. She screamed in terror – this was the end now, she knew – and she shouted out clearly: "I love you, Medrix," and the next thing she was drawn out and away until she could no longer breathe and, mercifully, lost consciousness.

Medrix heard her last cry and desperately tried to contact her but there was nothing.

"No – no – *no*!" he shouted. "Oh, my God – *no* – *no*!"

He watched the crippled freighter on the screen. It shuddered as an explosion occurred in the city almost below it, tipping it further down, then, as the blast hit the side of it there was a terrific noise as the whole thing lit up and exploded in front of him.

He stared at the screen. "Oh, God – this is not for real – *no*! *no*! *no*! Not my Ces," he cried aloud.

After the explosion there was silence – yet Medrix could hear Cessie's voice: "I love you Medrix."

He stood absolutely stunned, his hand pushing through his hair, tears running unashamedly down his white shocked face.

"Oh, my lovely girl," he cried, "I want you so much." He gasped, "Oh, my Cessie, Cessie – oh God!"

A Lawmaker standing beside him touched his arm. "Come, Medrix – you can't do anything more here. Come …" he tried to lead him away but Medrix pulled away from him.

"Leave me. I need to understand this on my own. We'll send the shuttles out after the storm to check what has become of it all. Leave me now."

The man left as requested and went to tell the others.

Medrix turned off the computer and said: "Some Controller you – you couldn't even control the events leading to the end of my darling girl," and in his mind he heard her last words: "I love you, Medrix." And he shouted out aloud: "Why? Why, you powers that be? Why? Chetner was bearable – but without her it is sheer hell."

Much later he walked around the camp site, making sure that everyone was asleep and safe – and he stood by a giant tree and wept as he heard her last cry … "I love you, Medrix."

Chapter 5

At first light, Medrix went out in a shuttle, taking six Lawmakers with him. They landed by the wrecked freighter. It lay in three parts across the area. Some of it was too hot to touch.

All that morning they searched for clues, anything that would tell him what really happened. But all he saw was the total devastation it had caused to the area and to himself.

One of the men found a shoe but, although he searched in all the bushes, there was nothing else. Was it her shoe? It looked like it – but it could just be any old shoe that a survivor had lost. But he kept it anyway.

The cargo (not even a bit of blanket) had gone and the canisters holding the medical supplies which should have remained intact had completely disappeared. Someone had already taken them earlier, he was sure. Only the escape hatch was intact, which proved without doubt that she never got there in time. And, if she had used it, she would have probably been thrown into the fire that had raged below them.

They returned much later, feeling worn out by it all.

Medrix sent out messages to the Grand Elder and to her father informing them of the accident and the death of all on board. He also contacted the salvage teams on Temra to come in and check everything.

Over the next few days he wandered around the base in a complete daze. People came up to him to express their sympathy and he nodded to them and thanked them, then went on his way.

Alone in his rooms, he remembered how she had wanted to travel with him and if she had, she would have helped him through this time, for the loss of a freighter and crew, at any time, was devastating.

He dealt with everything as usual, but at night he could not sleep for long periods, and then, when he did, he heard her terrified voice over and over again.

The days passed slowly and more survivors arrived and he searched their faces hopefully, only to be disappointed again and again. She was dead, he told himself each time, when was he going to realise that? He had seen her die – he had seen it on the screen and over and over again in his mind.

The salvage teams arrived and he left them to get on with the job. They left a few days later, saying that their report would be sent at a later date.

A few days later he sent the rest of the men out as reports had come in that the fires were almost out. Chetner men took over the camp jobs but the ex-Elders' men stayed within the base, managing all the space station jobs that were needed to run such a space dock as this one.

That night there was another thunder storm and lightning struck the control tower and all the power went off. The emergency power did not come on. Candles were given out to the main places in the camp and the base. Men feverishly tried to check the fault in the emergency section – so that they would have light in order to repair the control tower.

Medrix went to work on the emergency power section with some of the men, and he hadn't been there long when he discovered that several wires had evidently been cut through and completely severed from the main fusion box. He couldn't understand why the others had not found the fault straight away but they said that they had been looking elsewhere for it. He had to believe them, but part of him knew without doubt that someone had deliberately cut them. He knew that it could be any of these men – or anyone else at the base camp also. But why anyone would want to do so, he did not know.

Soon the emergency power came on and the control tower was working again, much to everyone's relief.

Mail arrived for everyone but Medrix only read a few of his. They were all sending letters about Celisia and saying how sorry they were – and he had had enough reminders of her death without reading about her. He tipped his letters into a drawer and left them there, then went on his daily rounds.

Ten days later the Chief Elder arrived with ten Lawmakers. He found Medrix in the dining centre and told him it was urgent that he talked to him privately. Medrix was surprised to see him but led him to his private office.

"I'm surprised you didn't expect me, Medrix," said the Chief Elder as he looked at the rooms. "I wrote to you about this visit."

Medrix then realised that not all the letters he had tipped in the drawer had been about Celisia and apologised to him.

The Chief Elder smiled. "Not to worry, I am here now. Letters have been mailed to Estolan telling everyone the facts as they see it, so I have come myself to see if they are true."

"Such as what?" Medrix looked surprised.

"Elders' men in key positions: you throwing your weight around, calling yourself the Controller. Rearranging all the teams' work schedules, amongst other things – seeing other women – and I could list many more."

"I don't understand. I was told to be the Controller."

"No, you weren't. You were appointed Liaison Officer only between the Chetnerites and the reclamation teams – nothing else."

"What are you talking about?" Medrix was indignant. "Am I dismissed then?"

"No – no. Nothing like that."

"You changed the orders yourself. I received them before I got off the freighter spacecraft – I was just getting off when I was handed the new package. Believe me when I say I was very taken aback at the change in orders. I had no qualifications to run a base of this size."

"Have you got those orders now?"

Medrix went and unlocked the safe and brought out the package. He gave it to the Chief Elder who sat down at the table and opened the packet. He looked up. "This is very serious – they've forged the signatures – you see, we never sent them."

Medrix sat down, absolutely nonplussed at the situation he was in.

"I don't want to leave here. These are her people. I want what is best for them. Who was supposed to be in charge, then?"

"Your father, of course – and he's missing."

"He never said. He accepted the new orders – like I did."

"He would. He is a Lawmaker, like you."

"What do you want me to do?"

"Carry on, of course. I'll write these orders out again and sign them myself. I don't know what's happening but if we leave it as it is, the perpetrators will be in for a surprise and may make a mistake. I think they wanted you to be removed, so we won't do this and we'll see what happens. Now, regarding the salvage team's report, they found evidence of an explosive device under the passenger seat in the hold."

"Oh, my God!" Medrix was white-faced with shock.

"It didn't go off, Lawmaker."

"Then what...?"

"The freighter was struck by lightning and someone had damaged the override connections. The explosive had not gone off because it was geared to the timekeeper and the timekeeper was knocked out by the lightning – so the clock on the explosive device stopped – it was timed to go off thirty minutes before the time of arrival here at the base."

"What about the tractor beam?"

"They thought it was there already. The Elders must have used it as a loading base at one time. The lightning triggered it. The freighter should have crashed into the sea."

"Knowing that, Chief Elder, does not bring Celisia and the crew back, does it?"

"Sadly, Medrix – no," he sighed. "Have you any coffee – I'm parched."

Medrix went into his kitchen and made two cups of coffee and brought them into the office.

"I've brought ten Lawmakers with me. They are from Jadeston – men all trained by me."

"Why?"

"They will take the place of ten Elders' men. Those men will go back to their teams." Medrix nodded. The Chief Elder went on: "They are also trained in sorting out the good people from the bad – undercover help, Medrix – something you should know all about." He smiled. "I think you make a very good leader and I am sure Celisia would have been very proud of you had she lived." He drank the rest of his coffee and stood up. "Can't stay. Have to go and see the Zendrian leader now, but I'll keep my eye on you, Medrix. By the way, my men are good pilots, too – so put them to work, they hate idleness." So saying, he tapped Medrix on his shoulder and left the room, but called out: "I'll send you the other orders signed by me. Good luck – Controller … you are going to need it."

Medrix saw him to his shuttle. Once it had gone he went to find the new members of his team.

That evening, he took out all the letters and read them. The tears rolled down his face as he read all their kind words. Many said that Ces could be still alive somewhere, walking around in a state of shock.

He slept all night and dreamed that she was in his arms again and when he woke up he felt calmer than he had for days. He only hoped that it was a good omen.

The new Lawmakers were a cheerful lot and soon settled into their new duties. One suggested that some Chetnerite men should also be trained as shuttle pilots, as this would lessen the load of the others. Medrix thought it a good idea and soon had a list of young Chetnerite men who were only too eager to do something useful. He also chose others to work in the space docks themselves. These men would be given rudimentary training on working a space station. The brighter ones might even receive basic training and be awarded certificates. He also offered training places to women who were interested in being nurses. The team leader thought it a very good idea.

Medrix also set up a temporary game court in one of the open spaces. A wooden wall was constructed. By the end of one moon, teams were picked and the first tournament set up.

There was a team of Lawmakers, another of Chetnerite men, another of Chetnerite boys, another of Chetnerite women and one of girls.

On the first day of the second moon, the morning was fine but cold. There was great excitement everywhere as the day progressed. Everybody who was free to do so went to watch the games. The Lawmakers played against the Chetnerite men and the score was sixty-five each.

The women played the Lawmakers: the men won by five points. The Chetnerite men played the boys: the men won by ten points. The girls beat the Lawmakers by fifteen points. The boys played against the Lawmakers – they won by five points.

At the end, all the teams were presented with prizes by Medrix. He gave them each a carved wooden cup with the date on it.

Everyone laughed and clapped and Medrix, in his closing speech, said that they were all winners and that they should all remember that whenever life was as hard as it was now.

They all cheered him and clapped and said that of all the people who could lead them, he was the best, and after they had all left the court, he stayed there alone – but in his mind he saw Celisia scoring more than all the others and he smiled, for today had been a good day. Whatever happened in the days ahead, they would all remember that. He left the darkened court and walked back to his rooms to write letters to all his friends back on Estolan.

Chapter 6

Celisia woke up with a blinding headache. Opening her eyes gradually, she saw sunlight filtering through the trees. It was too bright and she closed her eyes against it. Waiting a few minutes, she opened them again, but this time shielded them with her hand. "That was better," she thought as she sat up.

She could smell something cooking. Two women were sitting by a fire cooking something and she realised that she was hungry – very hungry in fact.

One of the women turned round and, seeing that she was awake, brought her a bowl of stew. It smelled lovely.

"Welcome, my dear, welcome back."

"Who are you?" Celisia asked.

"Chetnerite Elta," the woman replied.

"E-l-t-a," Celisia said slowly.

"Yes. Now, eat this up, you need it my dear." She gave Celisia the bowl and handed her a spoon.

Celisia took it. It smelled delicious.

"I'm afraid I don't know you. This is lovely stew."

"You've not seen me before – but your friend is over there by the fire." She pointed at the other woman.

"Who is it?"

"Santel."

"S-a-n-t-e-l," Cessie said slowly. "No – I don't know her."

"Of course you do."

"No." She shook her head.

Santel came over. "Hello, Celisia Margaret. You are lucky to be alive you know. Very lucky."

Celisia stared at her. Who was this woman? And come to that – why was she sitting here talking to her? She must be dreaming. That was it. It was a dream. She would wake up in her own bed in … In where? She shook her head – she couldn't remember anything: her thoughts were a blur – thoughts that struggled through pain and …

"What's the matter, dear?" Elta said again.

"I don't know, but I have a headache."

"Of course you have," Santel said, as she took the bowl away from her. "You just go to sleep now."

"Yes," thought Cessie, "I'll do that, for I am tired – and when I wake up I'll know who I am – where I am. I'll know everything." She lay down and slept.

When she awoke again she was in a small room. Her bed of leaves had gone. She lay on a wooden bed covered with a bright patchwork rug. The room was sparsely furnished, with a chair, a cupboard, a small table and a green rug on a wooden floor. There was no window.

She tried to get up. Every part of her body seemed to ache. A door opened and a woman came in. It was Elta.

"Thank God you've woken up. I think he gave you too much."

"Too much what?"

"Never mind, I've said too much already. I'll help you to the washroom."

She did so and Cessie was glad to go back to bed for she was so weak and tired. She drank some of the soup Elta gave her, then went back to sleep.

This routine went on for several days until, one day, she did not feel sleepy. Then a few days later, she was allowed to sit on the chair with a rug over her knees.

Elta was joined then by a man whose name was Kenton. He helped her to walk a little whenever he came – but he did not come every day. Cessie wondered where he went. Then one day, she was given clothes and a locket to wear and she was taken to another part of the building.

Elta said that the rooms were for her. They were large rooms – but none of them had windows, yet there was plenty of light. She had a sleep room, washroom and a kitchen and now she was encouraged to prepare her own meals. Sometimes Elta and Kenton were there – other times they were not. The doors were always locked when they left her and she soon realised that she was a prisoner but why, she did not know and when she asked them they just smiled and said all would be revealed at a later date.

Cessie tried to work out her whereabouts but couldn't. They called her Celisia, but who Celisia was, she had no idea.

Then one morning, another woman came with Elta and Kenton. It was Santel, who smiled and said: "How are you? Better I hope."

"Thank you – yes. Where am I?"

Santel smiled but did not answer the question. She said: "You've had a lucky escape. Your husband tried to kill you. We saved you and will keep you safe."

"I don't understand."

"He arranged for you to travel here. You could have gone with him earlier – then you would have been safe for he certainly would not want to blow up the freighter he was travelling on."

Cessie looked at her. What was the woman talking about?

Santel went on: "He set explosives in the freighter, activated a tractor beam to draw you into the burning city. It would look like an accident and he would show everyone just how devastated he was by your death – as he is doing now. But you were drawn out through the side door and hurled a great distance. You landed by a barn where we were sheltering during a storm. We found you, and nursed and brought you back here.

"Ironically, he came looking for you after the storm. If he hadn't waited for the storm to be over he would have found you, but by that time we had moved on out of harm's way. I don't expect you remember much about it."

"No – I don't – but surely …" she looked at the ring on her finger "… you can't be right – can you?"

"Of course – anyone with hair like yours …"

Elta interrupted "What's she's saying – is his wife has hair like yours, most unusual and …"

Cessie screwed up her eyes in frustration.

"I'm just like someone else. It often happens where I come from. I don't know this person you are talking about."

"Of course you do," said Santel angrily. "The Controller will be very surprised that you are alive."

"Controller! Now I know you are mistaken. Who do you mean by 'Controller'?"

"Your husband," Santel went on, "he calls himself the Controller – he rules Chetner from the Top Base camp. If he knew you were alive, he would be here in hours."

"How do you know he is guilty – if this accident has just happened?"

"We have our contacts," Elta said.

"Where are we now?"

"Safe," said a man who had just walked in. "Safe for the time being." He was a tall man with brown eyes and light brown hair. He wore a green outfit with a black leather over-jacket and his black high-boots came up to his knees. He reminded her of someone, but who? She couldn't remember.

He smiled and said: "You have just come at the right time, Celisia."

She felt more threatened by him, by them, than her so-called murderous husband.

"You've made a mistake – I am not who you think I am," she said desperately.

"We know you, woman," Santel said spitefully. "You are the Chetnerite who married a spy. A man who spied on us – a man who hated us – a man who killed my Lawmother – a vicious Lawmaker who uses people for his own ends – a man who threatened to have his revenge on you and Chetner for what he considered a failure on his part – he failed to stop the game. And because of that he was sentenced to be punished by the Elders – he never forgot your part in the affair – but you could not resist him. He lured you into his bed, not to love you, but to lull you into the feeling that he loved you. He could twist you round his little finger, Celisia – and probably still can. He stopped you coming to Chetner because he had other plans – he has plenty of bedfellows up there only too willing to share his bed for a night or two. But we have a plan and now you will come in useful to us."

"For what?" she said indignantly.

Santel smiled. "Quite simple really. When we offer him our idea, he will accept because we will tell him we have his wife."

"I don't understand."

"You will be our hostage – to get what we want. He won't dare refuse because everyone will be watching him – he will accept our plans because of you – a ghost who has come back to haunt him. When he accepts – as he will – we will send you to him."

"He'll know I am not his wife as soon as he sees me," Cessie said defiantly. "What then?"

"Then, watch your back, my dear – he will say the explosion has made you mentally ill – you have committed suicide – we don't care what he says."

"And what if he refuses the deal?"

"If he doesn't kill you," said the man, "then we will."

She looked at them all with horror. She was just a thing to be used and then thrown away when her use was over.

"But, I'm not her," she whispered, as tears rolled down her cheeks.

"Whoever you are," Elta said, "you know our plans – we can never let you free – so make the best of it, that's all you can do, isn't it?"

"What is this place?" Celisia changed the subject.

"This is the shuttle bay base at the Corder mines."

"I've never heard of it."

"It's in Cordoner – the Lawmakers had mines everywhere: in other countries too."

"But – what planet?"

"It's on Chetner. Really Celisia, you don't know your geography do you?" Santel laughed. "Beyond City One – one hundred kells* away – is the country of Cordoner – that's where we are now. We can easily move you to another place any time we like."

"Who lives here?"

"No one: just us – well in this part that is. The old mine is here, the settlement and this place – all left to the birds and us." She laughed. "There's no way out without us, my dear – we are leaving now and will come back nearer the time. There's no lack of food – and some books." So saying, they left her.

Cessie heard the door lock and knew she was alone, somewhere in some wild place, in a far-away country on Chetner.

Every day Cessie expected them to return, but they did not. She had decided when they first left her on some plan to keep her occupied. She made herself clean and polish the place daily – then she ran up and down the room

---

* 1 kell equals two miles

for an hour, read for an hour, had a meal, played a game using soap bubbles blown through her hands. The bigger the bubble, the more she wanted it to be bigger next time. But she set only so much time per day to do it.

One morning, while cleaning her teeth, her locket fell into the water. She left it open until it was dry.

She did floor exercises, then read some more and, after a light meal, she'd go to bed and sleep.

Then, one morning, she woke earlier than usual. She was sure the bed moved. When she looked at the door, she saw it was open.

She got out of bed quickly and ran to it. Maybe they were back. There was no one there. The lights dimmed. She ran back into the room and dressed quickly; making sure her locket was safe in her pocket. She went into the corridor. It led to the main part of the shuttle bay.

Down below her she could see two small shuttles and the shuttle doors were open. She was about to go down and look when the big doors slammed shut and the lights in the shuttle bay went out. She ran along the corridor and came to a room where a large computer screen flickered on and off. She said out loud: "Whatever is going on?"

The computer voice answered her: "This is an emergency … emergency …"

"Why, computer? What's happened?"

"A terrific rain storm has broken the seal in the electronically-based fusion box."

"And that means …?"

"Water is dripping on the integral power lines that feed the base."

"Can't it be fixed?"

"Engineers, six, seven and nine can repair it."

"Well, tell them then."

"They are not here."

"What will happen then?"

"In twenty-five minutes the base will self-destruct," said the voice, calmly.

"Oh, God! How do I get out of here?"

"Emergency escape hatch along this corridor will open for you … you …"

She didn't wait. She ran along the corridor as the lights flickered on and off. On her left was a door marked 'Emergency Exit Only. Press yellow button to operate'. She did so and the door slid open.

She stepped through on to a raised platform. From it led steps straight down to another platform. She got to the bottom and saw arrows pointing to a footbridge. She ran over it and down more steps. The lights dimmed and came on again. She was now in a kind of shuttle bay.

A voice pronounced loudly – "The people carrier will arrive in ten minutes. Please be ready to get on it when it comes." The speaking clock began to count down the minutes.

"You must leave your work clothes in the rooms marked X," the voice said primly.

She didn't want the people carrier, wherever it was going. In front of her was a flight of steps going up. She went up them until she came to a door which slid open as she got there and she stepped out on to a large shelf of rock and she could smell the fresh air. She stood there trying to get her breath back.

Arrows directed her to a cable-car contraption. She got in the carriage and strapped herself in. Immediately it moved out across the valley. She looked down – it was a very, very long way down. She felt dizzy.

The car stopped in the middle of the cable. "Get a move on," she said, her eyes tightly closed.

There was a tremor all along the cable, then her car moved again and as it did so she opened her eyes and saw another car passing overhead on its way to the start.

A few minutes later she landed on another platform. It was perched high on the top of a high mountain. Arrows directed her steps to another cable-car contraption. This one was made for one.

She got in, the harness automatically encasing her. She could see the line in front of her, straddling a very long valley. She looked back. All seemed calm – no sign of any explosion – no sign of impending doom – surely the twenty-five minutes were up by now, unless the emergency had been repaired by someone or other and that someone would soon find her missing and would know where she was now.

Taking a deep breath she pressed the 'go' button and the contraption swung out across the valley – a thin rope holding her from the jaws of death below. There was no going back, she knew so, relaxing back, she closed her eyes as the car moved on and on to the distant mountain in front of her. What lay there? she wondered. Had she escaped just to find herself in a worse predicament than before? "Oh, God, I hope not," she said out loud. "I hope not."

Chapter 7

Medrix was in his office working on his new schedules for all the Lawmakers now working on the base, when he was informed that the Ambassador from Cordoner was here to see him. He went quickly to the visitors lounge to meet and welcome him.

The Ambassador was a large man, with long brown hair and yellow eyes. He wore an orange shirt, open to the waist, and, around his middle, was a leather belt studded with gold eyes. His trousers of a nondescript colour were wide and his sandals had leather thongs which were strapped up to his knee. At his waist he wore an ugly looking knife. He was looking at a picture on the wall as Medrix came in.

"Welcome, Ambassador."

"I hope so," the Ambassador's voice was gruff.

"What can I get you? Coffee? Chen?"

"Nothing – I'll have a beer."

Medrix sent for two beers. A Lawmaker brought them in and Medrix dismissed him.

"Cordoner is a peaceful country, even though its borders run alongside three other countries. We have never had any trouble until now." He drank some beer and then went on: "Then 120 men arrive and start digging up our land. We arrested them – but they said they were there to reclaim the land. Now we have heard that the country of Chetner is to be reclaimed but we have not given permission for any work to be done in ours."

"I can't understand this at all," Medrix said. "They were all issued with maps before they came here, not that I saw them myself though. Have you by any chance got a copy with you?"

"Yes – this is it." He unrolled a map. "Look, it says your work is alongside the river Corder. See."

"Yes, I can see the mistake. It should be Holder, which runs near City One. Somebody has been very careless."

"Ah, but – it says 'over the southern hills'," the Ambassador pointed to it.

"Yes, Ambassador – it should say 'at the foot of the southern hills'. It's not very clear – which side of the hills it is – the River Holder may have gone in an earthquake – and that could be it – unless ..."

"Unless what?"

"Unless someone wanted us to be elsewhere – lost in fact. I can't understand it. I'm sorry. It's signed by the Grand Elder and – oh! God – the assistant to him ... he has been arrested for spying. This map, and maybe the others, was prepared before he was arrested. I will get our Chief Elder to look into it. I am most truly sorry for this."

"I can't release the men until I have a written apology from your Chief Elder. Do you understand, Controller? Their leader is your father." He smiled. "I'm sure you will get it sorted out – we have very strict laws in our country."

"Yes, of course. I will do it straight away."

"I'll have another beer, Controller." The Ambassador sat back in his chair.

Medrix ordered one this time, which duly arrived. The Ambassador drank it and put the tankard down.

"Now," he said, "that's not all. Shuttles have been seen going over our space; sometimes landing. Now the Lawmakers of Chetner had a working copper mine on Top Gost Point, but when the markets on this fell they pulled out, leaving the mine, the settlers' houses and the shuttle bay. None of it is used any more. We did not want them to reclaim it for if the markets ever went up then we could export it ourselves. These shuttles have evidently been landing there somewhere. We thought at first that they must have misread the map and were looking for survivors but now we are not so sure. We would like you to check it out for us, please – and stop this happening."

Medrix was very surprised at this news and agreed to find out what was happening, whereupon the Ambassador shook his hands and said: "I will give you thirty days to find out what's happening. If you go over that time – we shall take it as a declaration of war and act accordingly." So saying – he left the room and walked to his shuttle, leaving Medrix with yet another unforeseen problem. But he now knew where his father was. But where was his brother? There was something afoot – but what? And who was behind it? Hopefully, he would find out.

He sent a message to the Chief Elder. He also wondered if the other teams were in the right places and, if not, where they were. He would go himself to that old mine, taking Conn and Lawmaker Johnston with him, but not today. Tomorrow afternoon would do. It would do him good to get off the base for a while.

He called a meeting of the shuttle pilots. They met in the main visitors' lounge. He told them that some pilots had been flying over another country's airspace and there had been a complaint against this. He also told them that all pilots were grounded until further notice.

Lawmaker Kenton protested at once. "What about all the desperate people who are waiting to be picked up. After all, lives are at stake."

Medrix nodded. "I know the situation, Lawmaker, but this is vital. All shuttles have to be serviced regularly as you well know."

"But it can wait," said Kenton abruptly.

"You forget yourself, Lawmaker. I am in charge here, and what I say, goes!"

"But ..."

"And I say they are all grounded. It wouldn't do, would it, if a shuttle crashed when you were trying to rescue people? Would it? New navigational maps will also be fed into the computer's functional system on each shuttle."

"What's wrong with the ones there now?" Lawmaker Tellon asked. "Has a mouse eaten them?"

There was laughter at this, and Lawmaker Justin said: "What else, Controller? Are we to have new uniforms as well?"

Medrix was furious, but he said very sternly: "People's lives are at stake, and if you find that a laughing matter, Lawmaker then I will ground you completely. You all do a good job and I want nothing to stop you doing it even better."

There was silence and some pilots looked very shamefaced. Silence reigned.

"Now – there will also be kit inspection."

They stared at Medrix in amazement and Kenton said, "We are not in the army. We are highly-trained shuttle pilots, Controller."

"I know – but being so – from now on, you will have inspections like anyone else."

A voice at the back of the room said: "It will give you something to do, Controller."

There was dead silence as Medrix walked to the back of the room and stood in front of a Lawmaker and said: "And you, Lawmaker Fitzen, you are not wanted as a pilot any more – you will work as a cleaner until such time as I release you from it."

There was a murmuring from the pilots as they realised that Medrix was not allowing anyone to countermand him.

"But," said the afflicted Lawmaker, "my rank is above a cleaner: I will not do it: a cleaner indeed!"

"Everyone here, Lawmaker, has an important job to do, whether they are pilots, cooks, nurses or even cleaners and I think you, Lawmaker Fitzen would be wise to remember that. Of course if you do not want to comply, I can always have you arrested for insubordination. Well, what is it to be, Lawmaker?"

The Lawmaker in question bowed his head and said: "I will do as you say, Controller."

"Good – that's one point in your favour."

Medrix came back down to the front of the room and faced a silent, morose crowd.

"As I was saying, there will be a kit inspection every day until you are back on your flights – then the inspections will be every five days.

"Each shuttle will also carry a monalyctic tracking device – which will be activated as soon as you take off. This will send a signal to us so the control tower will know exactly where you are at any given time and, should you cross the border at any time, you can be told at once. Each shuttle will have scheduled flights, so should not be just anywhere. In fact it is far more organised and should give you shorter working hours." He drank some water. "Thank you, Lawmakers; that will be all."

The pilots went out quietly – but once in the corridors they spoke in subdued voices – some complaining, some saying it was well planned, and others wondering when the first kit inspection was to be. But all of them recognised one thing – that Medrix was indeed the best man for the job – hadn't he fought the Chetner Elders and won? He would win here too – they were sure. Or at least most of them were sure – the others shook their heads at the changes he was advocating.

Later, Medrix was coming down a corridor when he saw Santel go into a room followed by Lawmaker Kenton. They seemed to be in a deep conversation. They hadn't seen him, so, as the corridor was empty, he stood near the door and listened.

"Will she be all right?" Santel asked.

"Has to be," the Lawmaker replied.

"She has plenty of food. We'll just have to wait."

"Of course – a delay won't hurt."

They then went deeper into the room and Medrix could not hear them so he went into the room. They swung round guiltily.

"Oh, there you are Councillor Santel. I need to check some names with you in my office."

"Oh, yes – what names?"

"The new list of survivors."

"Of course. I was just saying this to Lawmaker Kenton. There are quite a few more to come in. He tells me that he has been grounded for a while and so these people will have to wait. Luckily they are well stocked with food – so a little wait won't harm."

Medrix smiled. "That's good – oh, Kenton, I have to go out in your shuttle tomorrow."

"But you said …"

"They are working on it now, Lawmaker – have been since you came in. I have to fly to Cordoner tomorrow and check the old shuttle bay there because the Cordonians say that our shuttles have been there. Though I can't think it's true because why would anyone want to go there, when it's all closed up?"

"Am I to come, Controller?"

"No – no, Lawmaker – I'll take Conn and Lawmaker Raiton. It will be good to get out of the base for a while. I have permission from the Cordonians. I expect they are mistaken. Still, I have to check." Then, nodding to them both, he left the room. He wondered what the two were up to – did they fancy each other, or was it something else? By their shocked faces, it looked as if it was something else. But what? He would soon find out he was sure.

But the following day did not go as planned. Various troubles in the camp called for his attention and he had to postpone his trip to the following day. In a way he was pleased because it meant the craft would have the new gadgets in by then and, having told the men he wanted them to be safe, it was better he waited.

All that morning was taken up with camp affairs – the water coming through the pipes was not clean and everyone had to boil it. He sent men to the reservoirs to see what was happening up there and to check the pipes and pumping station.

When he came back for a meal, Medrix found the mail had come and there were two packets for him – one from Eldon, the other from the Chief Elder. He opened the Chief Elder's first to find the orders duly signed and sighed with relief to know he was now officially recognised as the Controller. Also enclosed was a corrected copy of the map of Chetner and a list of previous agreements with other countries. The details of the old copper mine did indeed tally with the Cordonian Ambassador's statement.

He also learned that there was to be an inquiry regarding the maps and that the Grand Elder of Estina had been suspended from duty, pending the outcome. He shook his head in disbelief – what, oh what would happen next?

He remembered how biased the Grand Elder had been at the trial. Well, they all were, himself included. They all believed the Elders were correct in saying Ces was guilty, until he woke up to the fact that she wasn't. But what if the Grand Elder had been trying to rig the trial? Surely not … and yet … it did seem so at times.

He put the documents away in the safe and locked it.

That evening, he called all the Lawmakers who were free to come to a meeting in the dining area. Coffee was served and, while everyone drank it, they chatted to each other.

Medrix noticed that some of the pilots were missing. On asking the others where they were, he was told that they had been called out on an emergency flight. They didn't know any more than that. He paged the control tower and queried it.

It seemed that a pregnant woman was having a difficult time as her baby was set in the womb the wrong way round and needed immediate help. A Law Officer had contacted the base. The place was a small farmhouse near the Cordonian border.

They had flown out at once – taking Nurse Pennington (who was a midwife) with them.

"And why wasn't I told about this?" Medrix asked angrily, and they said that a message had been left for him in his office as no one knew where he was.

Of course he knew that there was a good reason for this flight but he was still annoyed. "Surely they should have all been back by now?" he queried. "What time did they go out?"

He was very worried when he realised they had been gone almost ten hours and no word from them at all. The weather report was bad – fog and low cloud – had they got there or had they got lost in the fog?

One Lawmaker suggested that maybe the woman was too ill to be moved, and Santel coming in at that moment, agreed with him.

Medrix realised that Santel and everyone else seemed to know about this flight except him.

Thirty minutes later a message came through from the Cordonian Ambassador which said that the old mine and settlement on Top Gost Point was on fire and there had been several explosions. One person was reported to have escaped from there, using an escape hatch – but they thought the person must have died as the force of the explosion had cut the cable line in half. Also, a shuttle that had been flying over at the time was caught up in the explosion and had fallen into the shuttle bay itself. His guards said its registration was Ch.TB 645 … "Of course," he said, "we'll look for survivors but we don't think we'll find anyone. At first we thought it was you, Controller - but we are told you are still at the base. I trust you can find out what is going on. I await hearing from you."

Everyone was stunned at the news. Two of Medrix' best pilots (Kenton and Listen) plus a nurse were all dead. But why were they there and where was the pregnant woman? Was she dead too?

One Lawmaker suggested they must have got lost in the fog – the forecast was poor and maybe, just maybe, that the base was being used by the looters who were raiding their coasts and the one who escaped was their lookout or even leader.

This made sense to everyone. The pilots had got lost in the fog on their way home and the base was used by the looters.

Later it was established that the farmhouse was empty – so the woman must have died in the crash, too.

A few days later there was a memorial service for all of them. Santel did not go as she had a migraine. In fact she had been quite poorly since the day of the crash, so maybe Kenton and she were fond of each other, but she never said so.

The Cordonians were satisfied with his explanation but still waited for a written apology from the Chief Elder.

Medrix wondered if the looter had in fact escaped and he arranged with the Cordonian Ambassador to have border guards to challenge anyone trying to cross the border. The Ambassador agreed – but said that he thought it very unlikely that anyone had escaped at all.

It seemed to have affected everyone at Top Base. They went around talking softly to each other.

Medrix also realised that if he had gone to the base as planned, he would have been dead. "Fate," he thought, "plays tricks at times. Two pilots and a nurse whose aim in life was to help people survive had lost their lives doing it." He would see that they were remembered on Estolan – so that their families would be proud of them, and if that criminal had escaped and he got hold of him, he would soon know how Lawmakers dealt with such people.

That night he read Eldon's letter with all the news of home and he read it over again. Oh that he was home there with Ces and all his family, instead of here in this hellhole.

He fell asleep and dreamed she was in his arms, but waking up, found himself alone and he wept his tears of anguish.

Chapter 8

The cable car was almost at the landing stage when it stopped. Cessie looked down to the deep valley below. Sharp rocks protruded from clumps of dense bushes. She shivered: what was the matter with the thing?

It moved on again a little way and stopped once more. "Of course," she said out loud, "it hasn't been used since it was built – it needs a can of oil." She laughed in spite of the seriousness of her situation.

The car moved on again and this time brought her safely to the landing stage. The door opened and she got out quickly.

She walked rapidly along the platform and down some steps. In front of her was a cage-like contraption which she decided was a lift. A large notice on the door said 'Out of Order'. Beside it were stone steps cut into the mountain which zigzagged down the mountainside.

She sighed. "Well – here I go," she said, and holding on to the handrails she began her descent to the distant valley below.

Half way down she stopped and looked back. To her surprise, the lift was going down. Could it mean that someone else had also used the cable cars – escaped from the base? And, if so, who was it? Deep in thought she continued down the steps. Maybe they would meet up later on.

The steps now led around the mountain so now she could see the cable cars moving high above her. They were all empty.

The steps zigzagged on, bringing her back so that she was now on the same side as the lift but much lower down. The lift had reached the bottom – but, after a while, she watched it go up again.

She turned a corner and was suddenly aware that the steps in front of her had disappeared – only the handrails on either side stayed connected. She guessed that about twenty steps had gone. They continued again after the space.

The handrail on the mountain's side was fixed into the rock face, being placed on a long metal girder which slanted in the direction of the other steps. The outer rail was only supported by a girder attached to … nothing!

I could go back, she thought, but was the lift safe? She decided to cross holding on to the handrail that was fixed to the mountain.

Gingerly she put one foot on the girder. It didn't move and, holding on to the rail she began the crossing. Half way across she felt the whole thing shake, but made herself carry on and, with a sigh of relief, reached the safety of the steps. She stayed clinging to the rail for six steps and then decided it was safe and continued thankfully on her way again.

The steps widened and became less steep as she reached the bottom – here a wide path led into a lane. On a direction board were the words 'To the Chetner border' → and an arrow pointed the way ahead.

The lane was a tangle of bushes and brambles for no one had cleared it since the base had been forsaken all those years ago. On either side, trees grew thickly and she wondered if the lane was passable – the person who came down in the lift must be somewhere ahead of her – so she hurried on.

Just then there was a huge flash and a great rumbling noise; then a terrific explosion, followed by smaller ones.

The blast hit her, pushing her headlong into some thick bushes. She was taken by surprise for she had considered herself safe from it as she had travelled a long way from the base. She got up and made her way along the lane. It now seemed to be raining leaves, twigs and small stones. On one side of the lane was a stone building – a notice said: 'Shelter'. She ran into it and sat on one of the stone seats there. She could hear the noise, but here in the shelter she seemed safe.

The seat was hard so she got up every so often and walked around. She wondered where the other person was. Maybe there was no one.

She shivered now because the shelter was cold. She ventured out into the lane and as all now was quiet she continued her journey.

After a little while, she came to a stop. A rock fall blocked the whole lane. It had been there some time by the look of it and there was no way past that she could see. Now what was she going to do.

She could hear the sound of a stream somewhere to her right. She pushed her way through bushes and small trees until she found the water tumbling down the mountainside. Streams joined rivers that she knew – a river marked the border between the two countries and, hopefully, she was going the right way.

The stream became her friend over the next few days. She drank from it, bathed in it, talked to it and slept beside it. She ate berries that grew near it and nuts from the spindly trees that grew beside it. It sang to her at night and always it went on its cheerful way to join the river, wherever that might be.

On the fourth day it flowed into the river. She felt a great joy as it did so. A small gravelly beach tipped the water into the river and, as she walked away from it, she felt she was losing a friend – but surely the river was her friend.

She walked alongside it until she came to some flat stones that crossed it. She had to jump from one stone to the other: in between them, deep water flowed, so she had to will herself to jump to the next stone. But she arrived at the other bank and pulled herself up its steep side.

At the top was a green field and, seeing no sign of anyone, she walked across it until she came to a fence. It stretched on either side into the far distance. It had three parts – strands of wire woven together at the top, then a small space, then more woven wire, then a wider gap. On the top part was some fur as if an animal had rubbed against it. She crawled through the widest space, making sure not to touch the wire until she was safe on the other side.

On this side of the fence were large notices: 'Beware – this is a power fence. Power flows through every five minutes. Touch this fence then and you are dead'.

She felt weak with shock – then cheered up – she had got through – she was in Chetner – she had got out – and if there was someone else behind her she hoped they were as lucky as she.

The field ran down into a deep valley and through the trees she could see a long wall. There was a door in the wall and it opened easily.

She found herself in a large space surrounded by another high wall. At one end was a large door which was closed. There had to be a way out, so she ran to the door and, as she got there, it slid open. The place was vast and evidently at one time had held many miniature shuttles but now it held only two. Disappointment hit her like a stone. She was not in Chetner yet.

Cessie ran to one of them. The last thing she wanted to do was to fly it but there was no other way out and she needed to get away at once. She climbed in and a light came on and a voice said: "Welcome. I will take you to safety. Buckle yourself in. Put on the helmet."

She did so, then a screen lit up and the voice went on with its instructions. "Please look at the list of places which could be your destination. Choose one and press the coloured button which denotes it."

She chose the Orchard Settlement on Chetner and pressed the button accordingly.

"Now, push the brown lever forward."

She did so and the little craft rose up slowly and flew out of the door and across the space.

"Push the lever as far as it will go."

She did so and the craft climbed higher and higher and then levelled out.

"Sit back and relax. All is well," the voice intoned and she obeyed.

The shuttle flew above the Cordonian countryside and over the border where men looked like insects running here and there.

Two men were running towards a large shuttle and she wondered if they meant to come after her but the little craft left them far behind so where they were, she did not know.

Then suddenly there was a bright light and a terrific explosion and the little shuttle swayed from side to side and she suddenly saw herself in another craft, in another hold and she saw herself trying to escape.

The picture vanished as the voice spoke. "We are off course – please realign."

Cessie looked at the screen and saw that it said they were going back to base and she pressed the one for the Chetner base and, at once, the craft righted itself and flew on. Then they flew into fog and she hoped that all was well.

She wanted to sleep but she dared not. She had to keep awake in case something untoward happened again. But, in spite of everything, her eyes closed and she slept.

The voice woke her. "We are at your destination. Please leave the shuttle."

She did so.

The fog had lifted and she could see in the distance a great fire burning and she could hear the distant sound of explosions.

The little craft took off and was evidently flying back to base. She felt devastating sorrow for it, even though it was just a machine. It had brought her to safety and was going back to its own demise.

The fog was coming down again.

The area where they'd landed was paved and there were wooden tables and chairs set outside a large wooden building. A notice board said:

MOUNTAIN CENTRE – SOUTHERN HILLS
CLOSED FOR THE WINTER'.

She knew she was nowhere near the Orchard Settlement. She was in fact about 150 kells away from City One, but at least she was away from the burning base and she was free from her captors and had to stay that way.

The building was locked so she broke a small side window and climbed in.

For the moment she was safe and the fog was her friend, but when it cleared she would have to leave. Now she had to rest and make plans for her next journey, and she smiled at the thought.

Medrix had heard from various sources that someone had crossed the border in a small shuttle and he was sure it was a member of the looter's gang. He was determined to catch that person and all Law Officers were notified but, to his annoyance, nothing could be done as everywhere was blanketed in fog. But once it cleared he was sure it would be an easy task – and then he would show them what Lawmakers did to people who perpetrated such crimes.

Chapter 9

The first thing Cessie realised was that she was lucky to have come so far. The fact that she had ended up in the wrong place did not worry her. She had no idea why she had chosen the other place, unless that was her home.

She opened the door of the room she had climbed into. It led into a small hallway with a counter running across it. Doors led to other parts of the building but they were all locked. She came back to the counter. It was filled with things for sale. She picked out a map and sorted through numerous packets of biscuits. These would do as food until she could get something more substantial. At one end of the counter were stacked small backpacks. She chose a blue one and put some of the biscuit packs in it. Two small bottles of mineral water went in it as well.

She went round to the back of the counter where there were shelves packed with boxes. Opening some, she found firesticks, knives, small plates and cups. She put some of each in her pack, then changed her mind and, apart from the firesticks, only kept one of each item.

She also took a long brown cloak that she found hanging on one of the doors. It was a bit big for her but would keep her warm. In its pocket was a woolly cap. She needed this to cover her hair.

She ate some biscuits and drank some water.

It was now very dark and the fog obliterated everything. She knew that she must leave as soon as possible for if her captors had seen her escape, they would be on the lookout for her and, then again, she did not know how many others were in the plot too. She looked at the map. She was 150 kells from City One and 125 kells from the Harbour Settlement. There were various farms dotted about the countryside.

Cessie decided that she must make for the Harbour Settlement. There she would find people and shopping halls. She needed to get food and some black hair dye. If she dyed her hair, no one would mistake her for the Controller's wife. Having decided that, she made up a bed of several rugs which she put behind the counter. There she settled down for the night and, surprisingly, slept well until morning.

It was a misty morning, but after a meal of biscuits and water, she left the safety of the building and followed the track that led towards her destination.

By mid-morning, she came to a crossroads and turned right. This was a better track than the other one and she made good progress and by nightfall came to a farmhouse nestling among trees. There was no one there and it was all locked up except for a barn where she stayed the night.

In the morning, as she was getting her things together, she saw something glistening under the straw in the far corner of the barn. She went to investigate and was surprised to find a runabout.

Runabouts, she knew, ran for eighteen hours and then recharged themselves for four hours.

She got in and discovered it was in working order so, transferring her things to it, she drove out of the silent farmyard and was on her way again.

She had not gone very far when she heard a shuttle. There was nowhere to hide for the track was open to the skies.

It landed nearby and two Lawmakers strode towards her. She stopped the runabout and waited.

"Where are you going?" one said.

"To the Harbour Settlement."

"Where have you come from?" said the other gruffly.

"From the farm back there." She pointed the way she had come.

"Why didn't you leave before this?" the first one asked.

"I was up in the fields with the horses. The others left without me. They left a note for me."

"Right," he said. "You can carry on, but be careful. There is a dangerous criminal about so don't approach any strangers. We'll be covering this area over the next few days so we will keep an eye out for you."

She thanked them as they strode away and got into the shuttle.

Cessie sighed with relief, but she knew without doubt that she must travel less openly from now on.

The tracked joined another one and this time led through a thick forest where no one could see her.

At night she slept in the runabout for who knew what lurked among the trees.

Four days later the forest ended and she could see the sea. According to the signpost she was only two kells from the Harbour Settlement. She sighed with relief, but when she rounded the next corner she saw a group of Lawmakers surrounding a cart. They were looking at everything in it while the driver stood nervously by. They did not see her.

She turned back and took a turning to the right which led behind high walls. It seemed to go on for ever, but at long last it came out on to a sandy track that led her straight into the streets of the Harbour Settlement.

There was no one about even though it was midday. The boats in the harbour rocked to and fro in a calm sea. No one tended them. Most of the houses had a white cross marked on them. She found their doors unlocked so she went in one of them. The place had been ransacked. All the others were the same. Only the shopping hall and a few other houses were locked up. There was a side window broken in the shopping place. She carefully removed the glass and managed to climb through. She helped herself to food which she put in bags. She found cheese, coffee, tinned milk, packets of soup – which were useful as they took up very little room – flour, butter and fruit. In another part she helped herself to soap, face-cloths, towels, toothbrushes and tooth powder, and black hair dye. She also chose a blue Chetnerite outfit and, lastly, a sketch pad and pencils.

She loaded the things into the runabout – and then went back to get three bottles of mineral water and some personal things. She felt badly about taking things so she wrote a little note to say that all items would be paid for by the Controller! If he was her husband, which she doubted very much, he would gladly pay and if he wasn't – then she would owe him. She laughed to herself about how he would take it when he found out.

She went back to the runabout and sat looking at her map, planning where she would go next. She decided to go to the Orchard Settlement; after all she had chosen that destination when she was in the little shuttle, so maybe she was from there. She would have to follow the coastal road until she came to the Plaxton Tower wherever that was, and then turn left. It was sixty kells to the tower. But first she must find somewhere where she could dye her hair. She wouldn't be happy until she did so.

She left the Harbour Settlement straight away. It was a ghost town and gave her the creeps.

That night she turned up a lane that led to an old mill. It had thick bushes and trees surrounding it. According to her map it had once been a working mill but now it was a ruin. She hadn't been there long when she heard voices and, peering through the bushes, she saw two Lawmakers. They were laughing and talking together. They stopped on the other side to where she was hidden.

"The Controller's gone mad to send us out here, Goodson."

"Well, you know him, Sevden, he's determined to catch the person who got away from the base."

"They say there's more than one. Seems two small shuttles left the base."

"So we had better go on searching then." He moved forward, but his companion stopped him.

"Now I have had enough of searching. There's always another day when we can leave the base to do it. What I really want is a woman."

"Really, Sevden – out here – there's nothing here but trees and more trees."

Sevden laughed. "I bet there's one somewhere – say we pushed through these trees and found one. Think what sport we two could have."

Cessie froze on the spot, hardly daring to breathe.

"Shame on you, Sevden; you have a girl at home – betrothed to you – haven't you?"

"Yes – but what she doesn't know can't hurt her – and, anyway, if our Controller can have a different woman in his bed each night, why not me?"

"That, Sevden, is only camp gossip. He's a stickler for rules and would never break them."

"Of course he would, Goodson – if he could get away with it. That's what wrong with Chetner – no willing girls."

"Shame on you man …"

"This is my betrothed," Sevden said, showing Goodson a picture that he had taken out of his wallet.

"She's beautiful – is she being true to you while you are away?"

"Of course – she's been brought up according to the Rules, but here our rules don't apply, do they?"

"I suppose not."

"I bet you that I could …"

"You could what, Sevden"

Sevden laughed cheekily. "I bet I could get any woman to fall for me within two hours of meeting her – and then …"

"For goodness sake, Sevden, keep your thoughts to yourself – you don't know who could be listening and you know the Controller would not be pleased to hear such talk."

"Well, Goodson, as long as you don't tell him, I'm safe."

Just then they were joined by another Lawmaker who told them that the shuttle was waiting to take them back to base.

"Why are we going back so early, Fenton?" Goodson asked.

"There's a bad storm forecast. We must go now," Fenton replied.

After they had gone, Cessie packed up her things. She did not feel safe here any more. She heard the shuttle leave and then came out of her hiding place. There on the ground, where the men had stood, was a wallet. She got out of the runabout and picked it up. It belonged to Sevden. His picture and all his details, plus his betrothed's picture were in it and one hundred credos in notes.

Serve him right if it was left there – but on second thoughts she decided to keep it until she could hand it in. Let him sweat until then. She laughed at the thought.

Later she found a deserted farmhouse and stayed there for the night. She hardly slept as there was a terrific storm that raged all night and morning and when she did venture out she found her road blocked by fallen trees. She would have to walk and find some way through to go on with her journey.

She went back into the house. She would stay for a while – for if she could not get out – so no one could get in. She switched the power on and soon the place was warm and cosy. The water heated up and she washed her hair and dyed it black. She was amazed how it altered her looks – "Even I wouldn't recognise me," she said out loud.

The next morning was fine, so she packed up her things, ready to leave on foot. Then she heard voices – two men were in the kitchen barring her way to the door.

"Welcome," said one, "you made it then."

"Yes," she said, not knowing what he meant.

"We thought you had – you were very lucky to get out," said the other – a tall man dressed in sombre grey that matched his hair and eyes.

"Yes, I was lucky."

"We hope the other one was as lucky as you."

"Mm – I hope so too." Her thoughts were racing – so there was someone else.

"We knew who you were at once," the grey one said.

"You did?" she was worried now. Her disguise did not fool them, then.

"Yes, when you hid from those Lawmakers – we knew then." (They had been following her – she hadn't fooled anyone).

"That was difficult to keep hidden," she replied.

"Our leader did well not to let us know who you were but he left instructions how you could be helped if help was ever needed."

"That's good – so you acted on his instruction then?" she was mystified as to who these people were.

"We know a lookout's job is no easy matter and we all rely on you."

"You do – that's good I'm sure."

"Of course," said the grey one. "We cannot tell you who we are – you know that."

"I know," she nodded in agreement and smiled at the other one. He was dressed all in brown, his black hair brushed back into a ponytail. He stared at her – his grey eyes cold as ice. If they found out who she really was, there would be no mercy there that she knew for sure.

"We'll take you now," he said. "Do you know your next destination?"

"Mm –" she murmured, thinking this could be a trap and then said, "I was going to the Orchard Settlement."

"Very good – we'll go now – our shuttle is parked outside."

There was nothing for it but to go with them and in no time at all they were airborne. She felt sick as the shuttle took off and, again, she saw another flight deck in her mind, one on a crashing freighter.

"Are you all right?" asked the brown one.

"Yes – everything has happened so fast."

"Of course it has – you must be in a state of shock."

"I think so – but I can cope with it."

The grey one smiled. "They chose the right one in you, I can see that."

Much later on they landed at the Orchard Settlement, shook hands with her, wished her well and left her there, staring at the departing shuttle.

She had no idea who they were, but one thing she knew – when they found out that she was not one of them she was in dead trouble.

If they thought she was a lookout then she must act like one. Perhaps it had something to do with the white crosses on the doors? That was it – someone marked the doors – someone left signals for these people who ransacked the houses.

She checked the houses here. All of them, except one, were locked – hence, no white crosses.

She had to leave here. It was a pity she was on foot but it should be easier to hide *en route* for she was determined to go to the Top Base and see for herself what was happening there. Maybe she was the Controller's wife and he ought to know there was some plot against him. He ought to know that anyway, whoever she was.

Chapter 10

Cessie had meant to leave straight away, but then it began to rain. It poured down, soaking her in minutes. She rushed into the unlocked house and locked the door behind her. She'd stay a little while and explore the house.

The rooms were neat and tidy, although very dusty. On a table she found a letter addressed to 'D Kent'. She opened it and read:

> *To Deena and Jostin Kent*
>
> *This is to warn you that your property is unsafe. You must leave it at once and make your way to the Top Base (see enclosed map). Shuttles will pick you up when the pilot can see you. Look on your map to see picking-up points.*
>
> *Signed: The Controller of all Chetner*
>
> *(Lawmaker Medrix)*

There was no map with the letter. The Kents had taken it with them, but she had a map – not that it showed the picking-up points. She'd be much safer if she went straight to the base because somewhere there was a lookout already working the route and it wouldn't be a good idea to meet up with him.

But it would be a good idea if she made her way to City Sixteen. She would be in open countryside and, hopefully, be picked up by a Top Base shuttle.

She stayed the night, sleeping in one of the made-up beds. It was so comfortable that she slept late.

After a quick meal she left the house, locking the door behind her and putting the key in her pocket.

She walked for days and never saw anybody. She slept in old barns and disused stables or anywhere else that was suitable. The road climbed steadily uphill and, at the top (which was tree-covered), the road forked.

Her map showed that the left fork was her route. She went that way and soon came to a crossroads. There were two lanes going left – her map showed one. She took the lower one. It seemed to go on for ever. She slept under trees that night and set off again once it was light. She was now walking beside a fast-running river – her map did not show it – in fact she should be looking down on a lake.

She was puzzled. Where could the river have come from? It couldn't suddenly appear, could it?

Well, it could if it had been underground – there'd been a lot of rain – maybe it was in flood.

She turned a corner and saw in the distance a lake and camped beside it, was what seemed to be a Lawmakers' Reclamation Team. There were eight tents, trestle tables and various items of equipment spread about.

She could see the men sitting at the tables and saw the danger they were in. She should be looking down at the lake – not standing beside it or in it as she would soon be if she stayed here.

She ran as fast as she could to the Lawmakers' camp, shouting and waving her arms about.

Someone saw her and came to meet her. She explained to him – pointing to the river filling the lake. He saw what she meant and ran back to the others.

They climbed into their landshakers, leaving the tents to the fast-encroaching waters.

Some of the other equipment they had to leave for it was too heavy to move and would take time and they were already in water.

She was hoisted up into one of the landshakers by a Lawmaker and she directed them back to the lane which was now becoming a fast-moving stream.

Soon they left the water behind them and at last came to the crossroads. It was only then that they noticed a large gate lying in a field. A Lawmaker went to look at it. Others joined him and they turned the gate over. On it was printed in large letters:

DANGER – ROAD CLOSED BECAUSE OF FLOODING

They all knew, without a doubt, that someone had deliberately led them into danger. If Cessie hadn't followed the route as well they would all have been dead. They compared maps – their map showed a small lake.

When they came to signal the base, they found that they hadn't got that equipment. The man in charge of it wasn't with them. Had he drowned trying to send a signal, or had he deliberately walked out on them? They didn't know.

Cessie explained to them how she was going to City Sixteen in order to get a lift to Top Base, and that the other turning would lead them there. So they took the other turning and that lane led high up into the hills – looking down to one side, they could see a very large lake. They had certainly just got to safety in time.

They travelled slowly as the road was very steep, but eventually it came to a flat plain but the lane was blocked by a large tree that had fallen across it.

Had it blown down or was it deliberate? They did not know.

It took them until late in the evening to clear the road, only to find that just a few kells along it was a great hole where no one could pass.

They turned and went back to the crossroads where they took the turning to City Fifteen.

A little way along it, they stopped and settled down for the night. Food was in short supply – only enough for one meal – rations were always kept in the landshakers for emergencies.

Lawmaker Thelka, the team leader, expressed the men's gratitude for her part in their rescue.

The next day they found their road blocked by a rock fall so they turned back and took the road to the Orchard Settlement.

It was slow going and they stayed two nights by the roadside.

When they arrived at the settlement, Cessie unlocked the house, switched on the power and soon she was making a hot drink for all of them, herself included.

She found flour and made flat cakes and they ate a frugal meal of flat cakes and stale cheese – and fruit picked from the orchard.

That night they slept in the house – some in the beds and most of them on the floor. Cessie slept on the long seat in the kitchen.

She had told them that she was Deena Kent and this was her house. She didn't trust anyone.

Using the computer in the office, a message was sent to the Controller. He told them to come along the coastal road and back to the base. He said that supplies would be brought to them *en route*. They also told him who had saved them. He was surprised at the name for he was sure he had heard of it before, but when or where he could not remember.

While they were sending the messages, Cessie heard a shuttle arrive. She went out to see who it was. Two men got out. She recognised them and before she could run back into the house, they grabbed her and bundled her into the shuttle. It took off at once.

She just sat there wondering what was going to happen next when the one in brown said:

"You did a very valiant thing today – but now they can manage on their own for you have a job to do. We've made a new pack for you – food and clothes and other important items. We'll drop you at Hunter's Mill. It is 160 kells from here. There's a new map in your pack – and try not to get caught up with so many Lawmakers again – things could get awkward you know."

She nodded in agreement – awkward wasn't the term she would use. Complicated, yes! She nodded again.

Back at the Orchard Settlement they were looking for her and were completely mystified when they couldn't find her. They locked the house, putting the key in her pack which they brought with them to give to the Controller.

Hunter's Mill looked eerie in the moonlight. She was there by herself. It seems she was still the lookout boy. When she had opened the pack she realised that they thought she was a boy. They had supplied her with boy's clothes and there was nothing in there that she could use at this special time of the moon and what was she going to do about it? She sighed. Her stomach ached – all she wanted to do was curl up in a ball with a hot pack to ease her pain.

Hunter's Mill was closed for the winter, but she climbed the outer-rim wall and got into a washroom and there she found what she wanted. She also found a long seat and she lay down on it and imagined she was somewhere warm and homely and, pulling her cloak around her, she put her hands in her pockets. Her fingers closed around her locket. She put it under the tap and then opened it.

A light glowed at once. She smiled. "My comfort light," she said.

She did not remember what else it did. As her eyes closed in sleep, far on a certain spacecraft an ensign saw a certain light appear on his screened maps and he went and reported it to the commander.

The commander was puzzled. Who was using the tracking device? Was it his niece, Celisia, or somebody else?

"Keep watching, Ensign."

The locket went on sending its message out while Cessie slept, the moonlight sending its light across her sleeping form as if a spiritual being guarded her there.

Cessie dreamed that she was falling down a hole and that a Lawmaker with dark-brown eyes was reaching down to save her. She woke up sweating and tearful. It was only a dream she knew, and she lay back on the hard seat and slept.

And, far away, the tracking signal stayed still too, and the commander of that craft gave orders for a change of course. Instead of going to Listra they would go to Chetner and see for themselves who was using the device.

Chapter 11

Medrix had had a bad night. He had spent most of it walking around the base thinking about Cessie. When he had slept he had dreamed vividly about her and when he awoke he could have sworn she had been in his room, only to realise with the cold light of day that she had not. He had to get himself out of this way of thinking. True, this place was not the best place to do that, but as he could not go home there was nothing much he could do about it.

He breakfasted alone and then checked the day's commitments and was just leaving his rooms when Lawmaker Sevden came to see him.

"Can you spare me a few minutes?" Sevden asked anxiously.

"Of course. What can I do for you?"

Sevden hesitated and then said; "I have to report that I have lost my wallet."

"On the base?"

"No."

"Where then?"

"It must have been when we were out searching for the fugitive."

"Why do you think that?"

"I remember getting it out of my pocket to show Goodson the picture of my betrothed. I must have dropped it then."

"But where were you at the time?"

"Near the old ruined mill, not far from the mountain centre area that we searched a few days ago."

Medrix frowned. "You were supposed to be searching the area, not looking at pictures."

"Yes … yes, I know … but it somehow came up in conversation."

"Your conversation should have been about your work not about your love-life, Sevden."

Yes, of course … I know that …"

"Yet you did not follow the rules did you?"

"No … I meant no harm …"

"Well, what was in it?" Medrix drew a piece of paper from the pile beside him and waited, tapping his pen on the desk impatiently.

"My picture, my details, my betrothed's picture, 100 credo notes and my pilot's licence."

"I see ... well, you will have to be grounded until it is found or a replacement sent from Estolan."

"Yes ... Controller."

"Did you actually search the old mill?"

"No. We did not get as far as that because ..."

Medrix interrupted him. " ... Because you were too busy talking about your love-life. Is that it, Sevden?"

Sevden blushed bright red.

"Yes, I can see I was right ... the fugitive could have been standing behind the wall or the bushes. Perhaps he even helped himself to it ... the person we are looking for is a thief and you were standing beside him showing everyone around how much money you had in your wallet. Even the licence would have been of value to him."

"He wasn't there, Controller ..."

"As neither of us can prove it, Sevden ... I'll get a Law Officer to go and look there for you."

"Thank you, Controller." Sevden turned to leave the room, but Medrix stopped him.

"You will spend your time putting up shelves in the kitchen."

"But, Controller, I am not a carpenter."

"You will be working with a trained carpenter, so make sure you listen to him ... You may go." Sevden was just going when Medrix shouted to him: "And mind you keep your eyes on your work and not on the young women working in there. I have noticed that you are much too free with the women here ... which goes against our Lawmaker rules, Sevden ... I am sure your betrothed keeps herself just for you ... I'll be watching you ..."

Sevden told his pals later that the Controller must have eyes in the back of his head. Whereupon his friends laughed and said that in future he would have to be more careful.

Medrix knew that he had been very rough with the Lawmaker and laughed when he saw how easily he had hit the mark ... Lawmakers here would have to realise how important their work was.

Several days later he heard about the rescue of a whole reclamation team and about a woman named Deena Kent who had led them to safety. He also heard that she had disappeared leaving her pack behind her.

The reclamation team were now on their way back to Top Base.

A few days later he heard that a Law Officer had been killed whilst trying to arrest the lookout boy ... He was to be sent all the facts accruing to the case at a later date.

Since the killing, no more white crosses had been seen anywhere. Evidently the culprit was on the run somewhere.

The next day he had a message from the *Red Dragon* spacecraft, that signals were coming from a place called Hunter's Mill. Whoever was sending the message was using the co-ordinates used by Cessie's locket and in fact these signals had been coming from a route followed by someone who had left the Top Gost base before the explosion there.

As Celisia had been nowhere near that area when the freighter crashed, then it could not be her.

Medrix knew now, without a doubt that someone else was using the locket and more than likely did not know what it could do. Maybe they were using it as a nightlight. He also knew without doubt that it must be the lookout person who had left the Orchard Settlement so hurriedly. They were not looking for a boy … they were in fact looking for a girl … a very cunning girl at that … and with the help of the commander of the *Red Dragon* spacecraft he would soon have the crafty little devil in his grip. No one killed one of his Law Officers and got away with it. Her days were numbered.

A few days later the reclamation team arrived back at the base. They were very tired but otherwise in good shape.

Medrix had heard again from his brother-in-law that the lookout girl had left Hunter's Mill and there had been no more signals coming through, but as the nights had been brilliantly lit by moon and stars, she did not need a nightlight. This of course tied in with the fact that she did not know what the locket actually did. They would have to wait for the next dark night to find out where she was.

After a few days had passed and the reclamation team had had a rest, he called the leader and a few of the team to a meeting. Also attending were four other Lawmakers and four Chetnerites.

He opened the meeting by saying how pleased he was that they were safe and sound then began asking questions.

"What did your worksheet say you had to do on the site, Team Leader?"

"We were to channel all the mountain streams together and build a conduit which would let the water into a new reservoir which was to be built in the near future."

"But surely this would be an impossible thing to do if the reservoir had not yet been built?"

"Well … yes …"

"So why didn't you query it?"

"We did."

"With whom?"

"With you, Controller."

"Indeed, Lawmaker? I received no such message." Medrix was annoyed.

"Well, we sent it more than once."

"As a team leader you could have just moved out of there on to higher ground."

"Except that the higher ground was not accessible to the site of our work."

Another Lawmaker interrupted … "You see, Controller, we needed a special machine to survey the land all around and although we kept asking for it, back came the answer, over and over again, that it was being used and we would have to wait our turn."

Medrix turned to Lawmaker Conn. "Go and check all the signals sent to and from this reclamation team."

He left the room. The team leader looked angry and he said: "Are you insinuating that we did not send any messages?"

"I am just checking to see what records we have."

"I think, Controller, you are trying to teach us our job."

"Certainly not. I know that you are very well trained, Thelka … but …"

"What do you know about it? Your job was to be a Liaison Officer. You were never interested in the business even though you were offered the training by your father. You preferred to be an Elder's man instead, and we all know where that led, don't we?"

Medrix had difficulty in controlling his temper but before he could answer, Conn came back and said: "Every signal from you, Lawmaker, said that everything was going to plan and the ones sent back said: " 'Good, keep up the good work'."

Thelka jumped up. "Evidently, Controller, there has been some plot to discredit me and my men and as they say you mean to destroy Chetner, I can see this is how you mean to do it."

"I think you forget yourself, Lawmaker … I have the Chief Elder's order to follow and I know that I have not been trained to do it but I do know the Chetnerites. You forget my wife was one."

Nurse Timmons came in with a tray of coffee which she gave out to everyone. The break in the meeting calmed them all down and Medrix wondered who had ordered coffee and with such good timing too!

After the break the meeting became much calmer and Medrix inquired about the woman who had helped them. There was not much they could tell him about her that he didn't already know. They had brought in her pack.

Medrix told them that other teams had been sent to other places and their maps and worksheets were all wrong. The only teams that he knew the whereabouts of were his father's and Costen's and he had changed Costen's area himself.

Then, saying that he would look into the matter and let them know his findings, the meeting broke up and everyone went their separate ways.

Later, when he opened the pack he found, amongst other things, Sevden's missing wallet. He sat back in his chair and laughed. "The cunning little devil had been right under their noses and yet she had slipped away unnoticed …"

He would only have to get the message that the locket was again being used and he would pounce and, this time, she would not slip through his fingers … and then perhaps all these mysterious happenings would start to unravel.

Later that evening, Medrix had just made himself a cup of chen before going to bed, when there was a knock on his door.

"Come in," he said, wondering who could be coming now at this late hour.

It was Lawmaker Thelka.

"I'm sorry to disturb you, Controller, but I just had to see you."

"Have some chen … I have just made myself some," Medrix replied, getting up from his seat.

"No, thank you … I don't want to keep you." He stood still as if waiting for Medrix to say something.

"Sit down, Lawmaker." But Thelka remained standing and so did Medrix.

"I have come to apologise to you, Controller, for my dreadful behaviour at the meeting. I was quite out of order – I know that now, but I did not know what had been going on here at all."

"Your apologies have been accepted, Lawmaker, and I can quite understand your remarks – after all, you were in a dreadful situation for quite a while."

"There is one more thing. It's about the girl."

"Yes ... what about her?"

"I cannot think that she can be the person who has killed a Law Officer … after all, she saved us all."

"She might not have meant to kill him."

"Of course I suppose that could be so … but …"

"But, what?"

"She will get some reward surely for saving us? … She was in great danger too …"

"Of course she will get her sentence cut – I cannot say more than that, can I?"

"No … I suppose not … but be sure to call us as witnesses at her trial."

"*TRIAL*! … There'll be no trial … we have all the evidence we need …"

"But it will be all one-sided. I cannot see why she cannot have a trial."

"This is a disaster area. We have no time to mess about with trials and suchlike. No time to appoint people to the court. No time to bring in our witnesses. I have to deal with it as I think fit … but I will question her … she shall have every chance to explain to me exactly what she is doing on this planet … and I will be lenient with her, too – if she exposes these people to me so that I can stop them working and arrest them too."

"It seems a shame … she went out of her way to help us."

"And then disappeared and landed up at Hunter's Mill. It would take days to get to that place … but the roads were blocked if you remember. They took her in a shuttle. They must have done – and soon we will get more reports about her – just wait and see. More white crosses will appear on doors and then we will get her. Save your sympathy for someone who deserves it."

"Right … I see … I'd better go … it's late … and you must be tired." He left the room.

Medrix went to bed thinking about Thelka. He wondered about him. Was he genuine? He shook his head. He thought of the lookout girl and sighed: "Oh God, I wish I was at home … but that's it … I'm not …" his thoughts went round and round until sleep claimed him.

The next morning he slept late. Getting up quickly, he dressed and went to the dining centre. Whilst eating his meal he was called to the control tower – a freighter was coming in and it was on fire …

He called the emergency services and the fire was put out. The passengers – some Zendrians – were treated for burns and smoke inhalation. Medrix said they could stay until repairs had been done. Evidently they were on their way to a trade fair on Listra.

The fire officer reported to him that the fire had been started deliberately. Medrix knew then that there would have to be an inquiry and, in the meantime, the passengers and crew would have to stay on the base.

"Just one more problem to sort out," Medrix thought. "How many more would there be?" He shook his head and went to arrange their accommodation.

The Zendrians were a rowdy lot who had evidently been drinking and by the evening several fights had broken out which Medrix had to stop and deal with. When he went back to his rooms, there was a message from his brother-in-law to say that the signals were now coming from the Cloon Valley, a long settlement which sprawled alongside a river.

Medrix knew the place. It would take her some time to cover the valley, and that gave him more time too, and maybe the Zendrians would have gone as he did not want to leave the base whilst they were there. But then there was thick fog and nobody could go anywhere.

Two Zendrians came to tell him that they had caused the fire. They were fire-eaters and much sought after on Listra. They had been practising their act in the hold when one of them had tripped over a cable and had fallen on to a bale of cloth. The fire had spread quickly after that. They were willing to pay for the damage.

Medrix made them write out a statement and then sent them on their way.

On the day the fog lifted, the freighter left Chetner. One of the men in the control tower told him that there had been 450 men on the incoming freighter – yet when it went out, there were only 400. But as there seemed to be no extra men on the base, Medrix said that someone had miscounted. "If there are fifty Zendrians here," he laughed, "we'll soon know, as drinking seems to be their only pastime." But the thought worried him – after all, the Zendrians knew this base very well – hadn't they built it for the Chetner Elders? He would keep a look out for anything untoward happening.

Medrix heard then that the signals from the locket were coming from a house named Cordor Chase, and evidently the person had been there for several days.

"Now we've got her," he said and there and then went to order a shuttle. He would go himself. This time she would not get away. He smiled – it was about time he had good news – maybe things would improve now, he thought as he went to round up the men who would go with him.

Chapter 12

Medrix and his fellow Lawmakers arrived at the house early in the morning. It was all closed up and the doors locked. They walked around the building. Nothing stirred. They peered through the windows but saw no one.

Sevden saw a small open window in the wash room and climbed up to it, leaned through and opened the bigger side window. He was in the house in no time and went and unlocked the back door.

Medrix and the others were soon inside.

The downstairs rooms were empty but the rooms upstairs were crammed with furniture, pictures and ornaments. The next floor was the same and they soon realised that this was in fact one of the looters' storehouses. But although they looked all around it, there was no sign of the lookout.

Medrix sent one of the Lawmakers back to the shuttle to contact the Law Officers regarding the house. It was to be surrounded and guarded until they could catch the looters if and when they came back to it.

He and the other men looked in all the outbuildings but to no avail – the crafty creature had gone.

It was no good staying around the house, so they went back to the shuttle. All of them were disappointed that they had not caught her.

As the shuttle took off, the pilot saw somebody running through the trees and told Medrix.

"Land on the other side of those trees," Medrix commanded.

By the time they had landed, there was no sign of anyone.

"Wait!" Medrix ordered. "She'll come out somewhere."

They did not have long to wait before she came running out of the wood and across the open fields to where they were.

The Lawmakers quickly got out of the shuttle and gave chase.

She saw them and immediately veered in the other direction. They followed. When she got to the corner of the field she realised there was no gate, so ran alongside the hedge.

Medrix was the nearest and he sent his whip snaking towards her. It circled her waist and he pulled back hard.

She fell backwards, screaming with pain as she did so. He jerked the whip again and she turned and held on to it, the unexpected move pulling him forward."Give up," he shouted, as the others came running up to them.

Sevden grabbed her and sat on her and *still* she tried to get away until, seeming to tire, she fell on to her face and just lay there whimpering and crying with shock and pain. She was caught. It was the end. She would never get to the base now. Santel had her again.

Medrix ordered the others back and they stood in a circle, watching.

"Get up," he commanded.

She did so, watching him warily.

"Put your hands on your head."

She did so, as he unwound his whip and sheathed it.

"Lawmaker Conn, undo her pack." Conn stepped forward and began to unbuckle the straps. "Bring it to me."

Conn did so, walking between her and Medrix.

At once she dived through the legs of the man opposite her and was running like the wind across the field. She came to a gate and, putting her hands on top of it, leapt over it and was out of sight in no time.

The others followed but to no avail. She had gone.

"Blast and hell – slippery as an eel – I cannot believe she got away!" Medrix said angrily.

They climbed over the gate and followed the path she must have taken. It led through a wood to a river, turned to stepping stones which they ran across and then carried on to open fields, alongside which was a thick hedge.

Cessie could hear their voices receding into the distance as she lay in the wet ditch that ran on the other side of the thick hedge. She had scrambled through the hedge and hidden there. She waited until she could not hear their voices then ran alongside it until she came to trees. She ran into them and came to a path.

The path was black and she could smell smoke. The trees here were black skeletons and there was no cover at all. Then there was a dip and a path leading between rocks. She came to giant trees spread out across the mountain, from one of which hung a rope ladder.

She remembered now. This was a huntersnout settlement. They lived in trees.

There was no one there. Evidently the fire had been threatening them and she hoped they had got safely away. She would stay here, hidden, until nightfall and then she would be on her way again.

She climbed up the ladder and brought the rope up for safety's sake. She lay in the little house until it began to get dark. She had lost everything – she couldn't stay here, it was too dangerous.

She investigated the rooms. The kitchen was small but she noticed that there was a large cake in the oven. The huntersnouts must have rushed away thinking that the fire was too near their homes for safety. Maybe it had been too hot to carry.

She cut a slice and ate it. It was delicious. She pulled one of the pillowslips off a pillow and put the cake in it. There was nothing else of any use, so she let down the ladder and came down on to the ground. It was now almost dark.

She had reasoned with herself that travelling by night would be safer for her. She followed a path that led her away from the trees and began to descend into a deep valley below. There were no trees here – but large rocks made the journey hard. The path went up again until, eventually, she came out on a flat plain.

The moon came out and she could see for kells. The path now forked and she took the one that led into trees. She stopped by a stream for a drink and sat down to eat a small piece of cake. Afterwards she continued walking. As it began to get light, she found a dark cave and stayed there watching the sunlight dancing on the leaves.

Medrix and the others came back to the shuttle. The others expected him to be angry at being tricked but he laughed and laughed.

"She's to be admired you know. Such spirit – such defiance – no wonder they chose her to be a lookout girl … and of course, unlike us, she knows the hiding places. But she will slip up and then we'll find her. And you, Lawmakers – I hope you have enjoyed your little outing. Some of you … well – all of you and that includes me – should get more training in …" and he laughed again.

Conn said: "She has no pack, no food, no change of clothes. She will come out sooner rather than later, and then we will get her."

From that day onwards, Medrix had no idea where she was. Evidently she was not using the locket or she was travelling during the day. He told the Law Officers to check the nights. Watch all surrounding settlements – after all, she had no pack with her and was bound to show herself soon.

Ten days later, Cessie came to a settlement. In the distance she could see the sea. She could hear a dog barking somewhere, which worried her because that meant people. Now she could not trust anyone – but she needed food.

Mist was rising from the ground and in some places it lay thick. She hurried down the path and dodged into a garden when she saw moving shadows. But no one was there.

It was a large settlement and every house had a white cross on the door. She had to get out of this place, but she needed food and a change of clothes.

The shopping hall lay in the shadows, a good place for someone to hide. There was no one there. Her mind was playing tricks with her. The place was locked up.

She found a large stone and broke open the lock. The noise seemed loud to her but nothing stirred. She went in and, picking up a large bag, filled it with food and bottles of water. Firesticks, a cooking pan and cutlery also went into the bag and she picked out a new outfit for herself. Then suddenly, she heard a whistle and she ran out of the shopping hall and into the road. Six men were running towards her. She ran up a side lane that led into a back garden. The men followed, calling for her to stop and give herself up, but she ran on.

There was a wall at the end of the garden and the door in it opened. A man stood there and she knew she was trapped.

The man grabbed her arm and pulled her towards a stone building and pushed her inside. He put his finger to his lips and said softly: "Shhh."

He closed the door and, grabbing her hand, opened a cupboard and pushed her in. He followed, and touched a hook and the back of the cupboard slid open. She went through and he followed her and the door slid closed. They crouched there seemingly for ages, then he held up a light and she saw stairs going down.

"Come," he said, and she followed him.

The stairs evened out into a tunnel and they ran along it for ages until she could hear the sound of the sea and she found herself in a cave. It opened on to a strip of beach.

The sun was out and she sat on a rock to get her breath back.

"Thank you," she said.

"Glad to help you," he murmured. "If you will give me some food I will be on my way."

"Yes, yes, of course I will. But who are you?"

"Best you don't know. Do not tell anyone about this escape route – you'll be safer then …" he pulled his cloak hood further down over his head. "Good luck … and keep away from settlements in future … no – don't follow me … wait at least thirty minutes. The base is that way." He pointed up the beach. "Goodbye … and good luck."

As she watched him go a shuttle appeared on the horizon and she went back into the cave and waited until it was out of sight.

Although it was getting light, she walked along the beach and by the evening had climbed a rocky path that led to the top of the cliffs. A sign stated that the lane led to the Dragon Caves. She went that way.

She came to a large cave which opened out into smaller caves and here she settled down for the night and, because it was so dark, opened the locket, for tonight she needed her little comfort light.

Medrix had heard about the escape and how she had disappeared once again and was furious. She was out there somewhere laughing at him. But a message from the *Red Dragon* spacecraft soon put him into a good mood again. All he had to do now was to go and get her and it wasn't very far away either. How kind of her … But fog delayed him once again and he went to bed having left the order that he was to be woken up at the first sign of it lifting.

But it wasn't the fog lifting that caused him to wake up early. He was called to the control tower for another reason. When he got there, Lawmaker Keltor informed him that there had been an earthquake out at sea, the centre of which had been near the Selton Sand Bank. This could cause giant waves to roll into the coast, bringing great damage to parts of it.

"Are we in danger here, Keltor?" Medrix asked.

"Not here. Evidently this base was built to withstand things like that."

"Where then?"

"All those settlements along the coast for about sixty kells from here to beyond the Sea View settlement."

"Sea View! Surely that would include the Dragon Caves wouldn't it?"

"Yes … all along there … and it's not only that … Lawmaker Jeckton here tells me that the Chetner Elders mined, or should I say tunnelled, in that area. When the waves hit the upper slopes of the Garder Hills they will collapse. Anyone in that area should leave at once. There's no one there, is there?" Keltor asked.

"Only one person I know of," Medrix informed them, "the lookout for the raiders. She is, at the moment, fast asleep in the Dragon Caves … and there is absolutely nothing we can do about it." He sighed and shook his head. "What is to be is to be. She has certainly kept us running around the place but her running is now all over … Unless …"

"Unless what?" they inquired.

"Unless the *Red Dragon* space commander can transport her to his craft. Get him for me, Lawmakers."

But although they contacted the commander, he was unable to do anything as the locket was no longer sending out a signal. He said that it was probably too late and she was already dead. At least it would have been quick. They would go on checking the area though and inform Medrix of any changes in the situation.

The fog lifted and storm winds blew in from the sea, which made the situation even worse – everyone would have to sit tight until conditions eased.

It was then that Conn told him that a shuttle had gone out to a distress call from a lighthouse off the Tredwell Rocks, and had been gone at least three hours and all contact with them had been lost.

Medrix was furious because no one had informed him about this at the time and he had not given permission for the shuttle to go out anyway. It looked as if they, too, were lost.

He went back to bed. No one could do anything but pray that they would be found alive and well but he doubted that such a miracle could happen.

Sleep did not come to him. Even here he could hear the wind and the lashing of the rain. He got up and made some coffee. He kept thinking of the girl who had saved all those Lawmakers and could not save herself. Had she screamed in terror when she'd realised she was trapped in a place she'd thought to be safe.

247

Somehow he linked her with his Ces – her screams linking with the unknown girl who was a lookout for the raiders.

Conn entered Medrix' room without knocking but Medrix did not even seem to notice.

"Excuse me, Controller," said Conn, "there is a Law Officer on line five."

Medrix followed Conn out into the passageway. "Now what is it? Things always come in threes, don't they, Conn?"

By the time they had got there, the line had gone dead and Medrix left Conn there to take any messages. He went to the control tower, more for company than anything else. All they had to do now was wait and trust that things were not so bad after all.

Chapter 13

But Celisia wasn't in the caves. She had left there hours ago. Yes she had been there, but she could not settle. There were strange echoes and whispering which frightened her and sleep did not come at all. She began to wonder why the caves were so called. Were there such things as dragons? Somewhere in her past memories she thought there were ... and if there were, might there still be dragons here?

She stood up. She could not stay here a minute longer.

She collected her things together but as she did so her locket, which had been on a rock, suddenly slipped sideways and fell into a crack. Try as she might she could not reach it. She saw its glow but it was out of reach.

The ground seemed to shake.

She stood still. Had she imagined it?

The locket seemed even further away now.

She had to get out of these caves. Her imagination was playing tricks with her. She followed the arrows that pointed the way out of the caves. She came out a different way from the way she had gone in.

It was a bright moonlight night. A good night to travel, she thought, as she walked briskly up the path. It was a pity about the locket, but there was nothing she could do about it even if she went back.

The path led to a large parking space. Here were several runabouts parked outside a wooden building which was locked.

She went to one of the runabouts and put her things in it and then got in.

It started straight away and she drove along a lane that went up a steep hill.

The further she went, the steeper it got until, eventually, she was on the top of a hill, on which was a tower. She got out and went to look at it.

It reminded her of another tower – a lookout tower – with computers and various buttons to press and she had pressed one ... and then ... what had happened? She could not remember. She shook her head. When would her memory come back?

This tower was empty but the view from the window should be good, she thought.

Shock filled her when all she could see was water!

Where was the beach?

It had gone.

Where were the cliffs?

There were no cliffs! In fact she seemed to be surrounded – well, almost surrounded – by water. Well, at least on three sides.

The tower shook.

She ran back to the runabout and drove it along the lane away from the threatening water … surely the hill was safe … yet if there had been mining tunnels underneath, that would surely … O God … it would undermine it all. It would all fall into the sea.

There was a bridge at the end of the lane. She drove quickly over it. It seemed firm enough. The lane wound around another hill, again climbing higher and higher and then began to go down on the other side where there was a settlement.

It was all in darkness except for one light.

She drove towards it. She had to warn them of the danger, whoever they were.

She came to a large grassed area and parked on it was a shuttle.

The door was open and she left her runabout and ran up the steps into it. Two pilots were laughing and talking together. Another man sat at the back, reading. They were evidently waiting for someone.

She shouted to them and they turned round sharply to look at her.

"You have to leave here … there's a great surge of water … the sea is coming in… already the other hills have fallen in … soon it will reach here …"

One of the pilots said: "Now, calm down. Tell us again."

She did so and the one who had been sitting in the back contacted the others and three men came running out of a house and climbed into the shuttle, which took off at once. In her hurry she had left her things behind in the runabout.

As they took off they could hear a roaring sound and the ground began to shake, but the shuttle rose in the air as the ground below disappeared from sight.

The shuttle shook and dipped but then righted itself and flew higher still. It turned towards the sea and all the pilots could see was water. They flew higher and then turned inland, and soon they left all the water behind.

A wind blew up and it grew stronger the further inland they flew. Then it began to rain and at times they could see lightning and hear the distant rumble of thunder.

They talked together in low voices and then one turned to her and said: "Where were you going?"

"I am making my way to the base."

One of the men then said: "She's going back for new orders … aren't you?"

"Maybe." She was puzzled because by the look of them they were all

Lawmakers. She dismissed the idea that they were something to do with the raiders and yet … why did he say that …?

The man went on … "We can only take you so far …"

"Can't you take me back to base – because I have lost everything?"

He shook his head. "No, no, I cannot do that … we are on an errand of mercy … we have to pick up sick people from the Roc Lighthouse on Tredwell Island … we won't have room for you. We will drop you off at Hunter's Mill. We will tell them where you are and they will come and get you. You will be safe there. They will give you all you need … Now – sit back – we have a good way to go before we reach that place. Do you know where the key is?"

"Mmm … has it been moved?"

She was puzzled – these were not Lawmakers.

"It's under the stones by the door … they often move it … and you did not know you were coming back so soon. One thing we are all most sure of is that you have saved our lives and we shall always be in your debt until the day we die." They all nodded in agreement. "Sit back now and relax."

She did so and all went quiet.

She was in deadly danger. If they realised that she was not who they thought she was … but there was nothing she could do about it – she, too, was lucky to be alive and this lift was better than no lift at all.

One of the men shook her shoulder. "It's time to leave us now. You've been asleep. You must have been tired … Jedson here," he pointed to one of the men, "has put together some rations for you. They will keep you going until you are given more. There's a storm brewing so you will have to hurry to the mill or you will get wet."

So, clutching the bag they had given her, she climbed out of the shuttle and waved to them as it took off. Whoever they were she was sorry to see them go and she watched them until they disappeared from view. Then she ran to the mill, found the key as they had told her and let herself in just as a streak of lightning lit up the night sky.

Inside were a set of sparsely furnished rooms, complete with a kitchen and washroom.

She had a shower and a meal from the rations they had given her. But when she went to bed she could not sleep. She knew she could not stay here and wait for the others to come. It was too dangerous. It was better to carry on walking to the base.

The storm got nearer and seemed to be rolling around the building and it echoed around the walls so that she had to put her hands over her ears. Then, suddenly, there was a crash and the whole building shook. She ran out into the storm and in the next flash of lightning, saw that the top of the mill had gone. Storm or no storm, she was leaving now. So, picking up the rations, she left the building, locking the door behind her.

The storm went on as she ran down the path and she was soaked in no time.

At the end of the path was a gate and beyond that a small shed. The door was open so she went in and sank down on a bed of leaves to await the passing of the storm.

In her ration bag were some fire sticks and she lit a small fire with some sticks that had blown in from outside. The rain stopped and she ventured outside. There was another shed beside hers and inside it was a store of wood. She took some to put on her fire and sat beside it to get warm and dry her clothes.

Early in the morning the storm had cleared and there was a watery sun rising to herald the dawn. She ate some food and drank from a bottle of water, put out the fire and, leaving the security of the shed, walked along the path which, hopefully, would bring her nearer to Top Base. How far away it was she did not know, but she had been this way before, hadn't she? She did not want to go to the Cloon Valley, so when she came to the crossroads, she took the left turn.

The morning opened out as the sky turned blue. Birds sang in the trees and it became warmer. She felt light-hearted as she walked, in spite of all that had happened to her.

She came to a crossroads. The signpost leaned drunkenly against a fallen tree. She read it. The right turn led to the Cloon Valley, the left to Roc Lighthouse and, straight on, to Delham Hill Settlement. Well, she did not want to go to Cloon Valley, so it had to be straight on … except that somehow she felt drawn to the lighthouse. Then she realised she could not go there because the men might still be there. She had not realised that it was so near. She took the road to the settlement.

It was late morning by the time she got there. It was not a settlement really, for it turned out to be an ancient building consisting of rings of giant stones and nothing else. She sat on a flat stone and ate some food and drank water. She was running out of both. She had to return to the crossroads as there was no path the other way. Once there she took the path to the lighthouse and, by late afternoon, arrived at a gate by which was a large notice. It read:

BEWARE OF INCOMING TIDES. THE ISLAND IS CUT OFF
BY THE TIDES AT CERTAIN TIMES OF THE DAY.
WHEN THE TIDE IS OUT YOU CAN WALK ACROSS A ROCK
BRIDGE TO THE LIGHTHOUSE.
IF THE TIDE IS IN WHEN YOU RETURN YOU MUST STAY
ON THE ISLAND UNTIL IT GOES OUT.

She would just go and look. There could be someone there who would let her stay the night.

She came to another gate. The same warnings were there but now she could see that the tide was going out fast. She turned the next corner, and there it was, laid out before her. She stopped and looked in horror at the scene before her. She had not seen it from gate. But now … she saw it all.

A shuttle lay twisted and torn across the bridge. Part of it seemed to be hanging over the edge of the bridge: the other half lay unevenly across it.

Perhaps they had come to rescue the people inside and were long gone from this place, but as she got nearer she knew they had not.

She climbed up the twisted steps that creaked under her feet, and pulled herself up into the shuttle. It swayed gently like a sea cradle rocking its babies to sleep.

She made her way to the pilots' section. Seaweed hung down from the dented roof and crab-like creatures slithered beneath her feet.

The pilots lay across the coloured buttons and computer screen; their lifeless bodies flopped in the bloodstained water.

She felt sick. She wasn't needed there. She went back to the main part of the shuttle. One row of seats had disappeared altogether, and the ones that were visible were a tangled mess. One body lay across the back of one of the seats.

Next she went to the hold. The door was open. Furniture lay across it. A very large ornate mirror was leaning against the side and from underneath, she could see a foot. She called: "Is anyone there?"

There was no reply and suddenly the shuttle shifted and she fell back into the body of the shuttle. She pulled herself up and climbed out of the stricken shuttle.

She went over to the island and climbed up steep steps to reach it. There, sprawled on the rocks, was a man. He was evidently dead, his hands spread out in front of him as if he was trying to get away. She stood there and was violently sick at the sight. She remembered how they had said that they were in her debt until their dying day … well the debt was paid, wasn't it!

She ran across a landing pad. Why hadn't they used that? Maybe it was the lightning … yes … yes … it had to be that. It had been once before she thought … but when was that? She ran to the lighthouse. They had been coming here to collect a sick person or persons. She had some nursing skills – she knew that. She could help the living but not the dead.

There was nobody there.

The kitchen table had empty coffee cups – clean ones. A jar of coffee and a carton of milk awaited the crew - but no one was there.

She went upstairs. The rooms were packed with boxes and furniture. Only the topmost room was empty, except for a wooden bench. A ladder led up to the light. A large notice said that only trained lighthouse keepers were allowed up there but she went up anyway. The door was locked so she came down again.

The room she was in had a window opening on to a balcony. She stepped out and leaned over the parapet. There, on the rocks, was another man, and, to her right, she could see a jetty and a boat moored there.

She was just going to come in when she felt a pair of strong arms grab her and pull her into the room and a man said. "You are too young to throw your life away … it could get better if you change your ways." He held her tightly.

"Let me go, you oaf … I was only looking out there, not trying to commit suicide."

Really?" he replied, "anyone who leans over a parapet that was built in the year 1500 is asking for trouble."

"Well, yes ... I didn't think ... I ..."

He sat her on the bench and bound her arms close to her sides with his whip and said: "Well, Sevden, look who I have got."

"Oh, no," she said, "not you ... let me go ... I am no good to you."

Sevden moved across the room to close the window. "Well, well ... and I thought she was dead."

"So did I. Are you a witch?" the man said.

"Witch ...?" she said in a puzzled way, "witch ... magic ... web ... Damn, damn ... damn ... I can't remember what it is."

"Good answer," he said. "Sevden – take her downstairs."

She kicked out at them. "You keep your dirty hands off me."

"You don't like him then?"

"Nor you and your treatment of women. I can walk down by myself."

"I am sure you can," the man purred, "but this time I am not letting you out of my sight. Sevden, tell them to start lifting the shuttle up from the sea, and you, my girl, have a lot of talking to do ... but not yet."

Sevden said: "I'll see to things, Controller," and was gone.

She stared up at him. "You are the Controller?"

"Yes."

"Well, why didn't you tell me last time, instead of threatening me? I wouldn't have run, because I was coming to the base anyway."

He looked at her cynically. "So you say."

"Yes, I mean it."

"I know who you are ... I know you are trouble with a capital T – come." He hauled her to her feet roughly and pushed her across the room.

She looked at him. If he really knew who she was ... that is if Santel was to be believed ... he wouldn't want her back and that would mean she was in deadly danger.

"Get a move on. Don't stand there gawking." And impatiently, he picked her up and carried her downstairs.

But half way down the stairs he told her to put her head on his shoulder.

"Why?" she asked.

"Because I cannot see where I am going down this twisting staircase."

"I can't."

"Why not?"

"Because I am all bound up and cannot move. My arms are going numb."

"Right ... I see ... another ploy to get free."

"No ... Please untie me," she pleaded.

He sighed and went into a small room and put her down on a long seat. He unwound the whip and took it off her. She moved her arms about in order to get the circulation back. He picked her up again and she leant her head against his shoulder and put her left arm around his neck.

254

"This is nice," she whispered, and kissed him on the side of his face.

"Stop that! You can't get round me like that."

"Your face is all prickly."

"I haven't shaved."

"You should shave every morning."

"I do, but I have been up all night."

"Oh, well, I expect you have. It was a bad night. Non-stop thunderstorms. Lightning struck the top of the mill. I soon rushed out of there."

"What mill?"

He reached the foot of the stairs where a Law Officer was waiting for him and he did not wait to hear her answer, as he sat her down on a stool in the kitchen.

"Controller, I have brought you the cuffs as requested." He gave them to Medrix who put them on her wrists. They had a longer chain than most, which was connected to another chain that went loosely round her waist.

"They will be ready in about five minutes, Controller."

"Good ... what about the man behind this place?"

"He is alive – well, just ... he must have been going to the boat but he slipped on the rocks. Both his legs are broken. The medical team have taken him. All the others are dead."

Ces shivered.

"Thank you, we will come now. Stand up please, Deena. That's your name isn't it?" He did not wait for an answer but grabbed hold of the chain and pulled her up and then strode out of the building and across the landing pad.

"Wait," she said, "you are going too fast for me."

He didn't stop and she had to run to keep up, until she caught her foot on a stone and fell on to her knees.

He stopped.

"Get up. NOW!"

She did, but he slowed his pace and she limped along as blood seeped through her trousers.

They came to the top of the steps and he waved to someone and a loud whistle went off. The Law Officer left them. Medrix was looking up. Ces looked up, too, and saw a large freighter hovering in the sky. Metal ropes hung from it. They were fixed somehow to the crashed shuttle so that it was held in a sort of cradle. Then, slowly, it was lifted into the air. Water poured from it.

"Are there people still in it?" Ces asked, anxiously.

"Yes ... no one's alive ... the salvage team will take it and see to everything. Of course, all their identification things will be given to me so I will know who they all are, but their burial will be done by them. They will send in their report to me. They will tell me if anyone else has been in there, and those people will be traced and thoroughly questioned."

Should she tell him that she had been in it? She decided against it. He would soon let her know if she was included in that list … and it was better that way.

As the damaged shuttle lifted, a body fell out of the hold and crashed on to the rocky bridge, its head cracking open. It was Jedson, she was sure. She felt faint and grabbed hold of Medrix' hand and held on tightly. He looked down at her. "Not so tough after all, are you? Been a bit much for you, hasn't it?" he said, gently.

She looked up at him. Her blue eyes filled with tears.

Medrix' whole mind and body suddenly jerked with shock. This surely was Celisia. But he knew she wasn't because this creature had long black hair. He looked away quickly, and said roughly: "You had a part in this … you enticed them somehow to carry the furniture. When we get back to base you will tell me everything you know … or else!"

But she didn't hear, for suddenly the sky turned black and her hand slipped from his as she fainted and hung from the chain he held.

She woke up in the hold of a shuttle. Sevden said: "Better now?"

She nodded.

He left her and the Controller came in. She stood up. "I can't stay in here."

"Of course you can. Just put that harness on and sit on those sacks."

She stood up but now she did not see him … for she had the flashback again and thought she was in the crashing freighter and all she wanted to do was get out. She raised her fists and punched him hard, catching him on his face and shoulder. The chain cut his fingers as he tried to restrain her. He kicked out at her, and she doubled up in agony as he hit her already-cut knees. She stood there swaying then lurched towards him. He didn't understand what was happening and stepped forward and hit her hard across the face.

She stood still, touching her face with her hand and looked at him in surprise.

He saw her blue eyes and *again* his whole being flipped and he had to turn away, not look at her so that he could calm down. It wasn't her fault that she looked like Ces … but in order to calm himself he became more aggressive and turned to her and said: "If I get any more trouble from you, I will give you such a hiding that you will not be able to sit down for two moons. Now sit down and buckle up so that we can leave this Godforsaken hole."

She sat down and buckled herself into the harness and curled up into a ball with her hands over her face and he knew she was crying. He left her and as he went into the main part of the shuttle, said to himself: "You mean, mean bastard. Have you lost your mind that you can treat her so badly?" But all he said to the others was: "Let's get back to base now."

"Your face is bleeding, Controller," Sevden said.

"I walked into the door," Medrix said, as he touched his face. "It's nothing much." He buckled himself into the seat. "Get this thing going, pilot, we don't want to be here longer than we have to."

The shuttle rose into the air and as it did so, they heard her screaming.

"Sevden, go and see if she's all right."

He did so – she had fallen across the hold – evidently she hadn't fastened the buckle properly.

He came back and explained what had happened. "She's got some bruises and cuts."

"Lawmaker Tipton, take the first aid kit and see she's all right. I want her all in one piece when we get back and – Sevden – make some coffee for us all."

"Is she to have some?"

"Of course – didn't I say *all* of us?"

"Yes – yes – of course."

"And, Sevden, we'll all have a buttered bun each."

"Right, Controller."

When Ces had been seen to, Medrix asked Sevden how she was. Lawmaker Tipton said that she should sleep as he had put a sedative in her drink.

Afterwards, they all relaxed, except Medrix who went to see Ces again. He crouched down beside her. She was fast asleep, her eyes tightly closed. He smoothed her hair and, as he got up, she murmured something. It sounded like 'Medrix'. He shook his head as he stood looking at her.

"Medrix, Medrix," he said to himself, "are you going to go into shock every time you see a woman with blue eyes? Granted Chetnerites and Lawmakers don't usually have them – but Celisia did and – yes – this woman was like her." He also remembered how she had put her hand in his – and it felt so right, and when she kissed him, he had felt that he wanted to hold her for ever, make love to her and never let her go.

He was annoyed with himself. He was a Lawmaker who kept the rules and he couldn't even keep the Rules of Mourning. But it troubled him more that he should even look at another woman. He didn't seem to realise that what he was feeling was a natural result of the situation he was in.

He touched his face. She was right – it was prickly. But ever since Law Officer Talston had notified him about the crash, he had had no time to do things like shaving. The Law Officer had also told him that he had seen someone climbing out of the shuttle. The description of the person matched that of the lookout.

Since then, Medrix had been busy organising everything. He sighed – he was very tired but, although he sat with closed eyes, did not sleep.

In the early hours of the morning they arrived back at the base. He handed Ces over to the guards, one of whom carried her to the jail section. She still slept as they dumped her onto some straw in a very small cell.

Medrix shaved and then went to rest for a few hours before the business of the new day took over once again.

Ces slept on, quite oblivious to everything. Once or twice she cried out in her sleep but otherwise she looked and felt peaceful. She dreamed that she was throwing a ball for a dog and walking beside her was a man. When the man turned towards her he held up a lead, or was it a chain? She recognised the man. It was the Controller.

She smiled in her sleep. She had come home.

But she wouldn't have slept so well if she had known what would happen to her when she woke up and faced the man who thought she was somebody else.

Chapter 14

Cessie woke up to find a Lawmother leaning over her.

"Get up now. You've slept long enough."

She sat up quickly. "Where am I?"

"In the Top Base prison. They brought you in last night. Now you must get up. There's a bowl of water on the table so have a quick wash and then dress. Hurry, it is the hour of eight and the Controller wants to see you at the hour of nine ... so we have not got much time."

Cessie got up quickly and then felt dizzy and had to hold on to the Lawmother.

"I'll be all right in a minute."

The Lawmother helped her to the table and then left the room.

Cessie felt better and, using the things left out for her, had a quick wash and felt better for it. Then she put on a dark-grey dress and bonnet with shoes and socks to match. There had been no comb so she had run her fingers through her hair and hoped it looked all right.

The Lawmother came back into the room and took the bowl of water away and came back with a bowl of grey stuff and plonked it down on the table and, giving Cessie a spoon, told her to eat her meal.

Cessie did not know what it was, but ate it anyway. She was also given coffee. When she had finished she was marched to a washroom. Having relieved herself there, she was taken to a small room and told to sit down and wait.

She stayed there for some minutes and then was taken by two guards to another room. They opened the door and pushed her in.

The room was small. A large table took up most of the space and three people sat at it. To her horror, she saw one was Santel but she did not look up. Beside her sat the Controller who was looking at some notes and, on his left, was another Lawmaker. He looked at her. His eyes were dark grey, as was his hair. He was dressed in dark blue and she had the feeling that she had seen him before somewhere. He was very like the grey one who had thought she was the lookout boy. If he was that person, then she was in great danger and so was the Controller. She would have to be careful what she said.

"Sit down," the Controller said.

There was a chair behind her and she sat down.

There was silence. The grey one looked at his notebook and Santel looked at her hands. The guards had left the room.

The Controller looked up and said: "You are here to answer several charges. No ... don't interrupt ... we have the evidence and the proof ... we will give you time to talk later on."

She stared at him and looked away.

The Controller began to read out aloud:

"You escaped from the Top Gost Point just before the explosion that destroyed it. It has been verified by the Cordonian Government that the Chetner raiders used it as a base for storing their loot and for meetings. You escaped using a mini-shuttle. Your movements were tracked during the escape. You landed at the Southern Hills Mountain Centre where you stayed until the fog that hampered the rescue work cleared. By that time you had left there. You stole various items from there.

"You then went to a farm and, from there, went on to the Harbour Settlement. Here you again stole items from houses and the store. You marked white crosses on all the unlocked houses ..."

Cessie was about to query it but saw Santel staring at her, so she said nothing. Did she know her?

She then realised that the Controller had been talking all the time and she had no idea what he had said. She had to concentrate, but found she could not. She was tired and found it very hard to keep her eyes open.

Let him talk, she thought. After all, he thought he knew it all. He wasn't going to listen to her. She looked at her hands and wondered how much longer she could sit there. It was quite evident that he seemed to know where she had been and why. But he did not know that she had dyed her hair black and that she was not the lookout boy. Perhaps the grey one knew that too.

"... And so you see," the Controller said, "she somehow persuaded our Lawmakers to carry furniture from one place to another. How she did this she can perhaps explain to us. She should also tell us how she got from the Dragon Caves to the Roc Lighthouse in such a short time and the same applies to her arrival at the Orchard Settlement and Hunter's Mill."

"What do you mean, persuaded them? I told them they were in great danger as the sea was coming in," she said as she had just realised what he was saying.

"The sea was not coming in where they were," the Controller said.

"Yes it was. They were parked not very far away from the Dragon Caves."

"Rubbish!" said the other Lawmaker, "they were nowhere near it."

"Yes they were. I travelled with them."

"So, if you travelled with them," said Santel, "why weren't you at least injured in the crash?"

"Good point," said the grey one.

260

"Because they only gave me a lift as far as Hunter's Mill."

"Rubbish!" the Controller said scornfully. "Why ever would they do that?"

"They did. They said they had to pick up sick people from there and there was not room enough for me. They gave me some rations and said they'd tell someone where I was so that I could be picked up later. But I didn't stay because the mill was struck by lightning and I stayed overnight in a wooden shed. When it was light I began walking. I went to a settlement which was just a ring of stones. I had to come back and, as I did not want to go to the Cloon Valley again, took the road to the Roc Lighthouse ... I thought I could stay the night somewhere. When I got there I saw the crashed shuttle ..." her voice faltered "... they were all dead ... I couldn't believe it ... I climbed in ... there was nothing I could do ... nothing at all ... then I went to the lighthouse itself and there you found me."

"Sounds all right," Santel said. "Where did they pick up the mirror?"

"I don't know ... the shuttle dipped when we left ... but I do not know. Maybe they went somewhere else after they left me ... I did not realise that the lighthouse was so near the mill. I could see the sea from where I was and the tide was out ... and it was out when I arrived at the crash ... yet you see ... the tide was in when they crashed ... if they had gone straight there ... they would not have crashed into the sea and maybe they would be alive to tell us what happened."

"Yes, I see what you mean," the Controller said. "They went somewhere else to pick up the mirror ... but why?"

"Could they have picked up someone else?" the grey one asked.

"Very likely ... so they picked up one of your team?"

"Nothing to do with me, Controller ..." Cessie could see they were still trying to blame her.

Medrix changed tactics. "Where did you get this locket?" He held it up. Santel paled but said nothing. Cessie could not tell the truth, and it could not be hers ... could it?

"It's not mine."

"Right ... you tell the truth for once. Where did you get it?"

"It's not mine."

"You used it on every dark night."

She stared at him. "It cannot be mine; I lost mine in the Dragon Caves."

He opened it and it lit up when he placed it in water.

"It's like mine ... let me see inside."

He showed her the picture. "I don't understand ..."

"This belonged to my wife – well, one like it," he showed her the picture again, "this lights up and sends a message to a spacecraft – wherever you went, you left a signal."

"I see ..."

"Who gave it to you?"

Santel coughed and had to drink water.

"I found it when I was escaping. It was there on the floor ... I picked it up ... there was no one around ..."

"You stole it from my wife's dead body! How low can you get!"

"*No!*"

"I will have the truth ..."

"*No*. I found it. I *did*!"

"Guards" he shouted. They opened the door and came in. "Take this prisoner to the punishment room. She has to learn to tell the truth ... she's to have a whipping ... afterwards, take her back to her cell. We will see her tomorrow, and perhaps she will see sense."

Cessie screamed at him: "I am telling the truth ..." but he took no notice.

When she realised he was not going to change his mind, she went with the guards quietly and gave them no trouble at all. But on the way to the punishment block they met Lawmaker Thelka who stopped them and asked where they were going. When he heard that she was to be given a whipping as a punishment, he was angry and told the guards that she was to be taken back to her cell as the punishment had been cancelled. But the guards insisted they took orders only from the Controller and not from him, whereupon he said that he was of higher rank than the Controller and he was countermanding the orders. The guards refused to listen and proceeded on their way but the Lawmaker stopped them again and said: "Where are your written orders?"

"We haven't any," one of the guards replied, "we don't need them. We obey the Controller."

"Even the Controller has to obey Lawmaker Rules and this is one of them, so go back and tell him."

The guards now stopped outside the block and one of them said: "I am not going to tell him that. You must be mad to think I would."

A Lawmother came out of the punishment area and asked what was going on. The guards told her and she said that Lawmaker Thelka was right and there would be no punishment of this prisoner until she had the written orders in her hands.

Cessie was surprised by this for she thought the Controller had the last word in these matters, so she said: "Lawmaker Thelka, I am truly thankful for you speaking for me but I do not want you all getting into trouble on my behalf."

The Lawmother then suggested that the Lawmaker should go and see the Controller himself and in the meantime she would keep the prisoner with her until she had the written orders. She did not want to break Lawmaker rules either. The Lawmaker agreed and left them and Cessie was taken into the Lawmother's rooms to await further orders.

She was somewhat bemused by the whole thing and sat quietly waiting to see what would happen next. She hoped that the Controller did not think she had tried to change his orders. She had better expect the worst, for she knew that he liked his own way and kind though the Lawmaker was, he was only delaying her punishment.

Medrix was sitting in his kitchen reading some notes when Lawmaker Thelka burst into his room. The guards standing outside his rooms had tried to stop him but the Lawmaker had pushed past them and they followed him in, trying to explain.

"What the hell is happening? Am I to have no peace in my own rooms?"

"My fault," said Lawmaker Thelka, "what I have to say cannot wait."

"Well, if it's that important, I'll see you. Guards, you may go."

The guards went out quickly, only too glad that they were not to be penalised for their inattention.

"Well, what can I do for you, Lawmaker?"

"It's the prisoner."

"What prisoner?"

"The lookout person."

"What about her? We talked about her before. I promised you that I would be lenient ..." he did not finish his sentence.

"Lenient! Lenient! Is that what you call it when you send her to be whipped because you cannot get the answer you want? You call that lenient?" said Thelka angrily.

"I was talking about her sentence. How I get her to tell me the truth is my affair."

"It is not your affair ... She saved our lives ... 119 men in all ... she never thought of herself and the outcome of her actions ... only of us ... she could have left us there and very few of us would have survived, if any at all. So I would have expected her to get a fair inquiry."

"It is not your place to tell me my rôle in this matter." Medrix stood up, his face red with anger.

"I outrank you, Controller, and our rules tell me I have the right to speak on her behalf."

"On Estolan, yes. But not here."

"Yes – here also – all Lawmakers have that right, wherever they are."

"No!" Medrix snapped at him, "This is a disaster area and those rules do not apply."

"You promised ..."

"I ..."

"What would your wife think of your actions?"

"How dare you bring her into this ... you had better go now, before ..." he moved towards the door.

"I dare because I don't believe she is guilty and I want to see fair play ... and what you are doing is not fair play."

"We have the evidence."

"You had the evidence when Celisia was on trial ... and you proved her innocent – so why don't you do that now?"

"Because she is not innocent." Medrix walked over to the kitchen unit and started to make coffee. His hands shook as he turned his back on Thelka. He had to contain his anger. He had to be in command. "Coffee, Thelka?" he asked, trying to bring himself to an even keel.

"No – don't change the subject, Controller. That woman – who looks a bit like your wife – deserves better treatment than that. She is a woman."

"I know that." Medrix poured the coffee into his cup and came over to the table and set it down. "She is a conniving little pest, trying to get round me as she has got round you, Thelka. She knows far more than she has been saying – and – I intend to get at the truth …"

"By whipping her senseless! Is that it? She will probably collapse; after all she has been living rough for many moons. God only knows how she has survived at all. She looks undernourished as it is … you would do better to treat her gently … show kindness instead of cruelty … treat her as a woman should be treated … you'll get more out of her that way."

"So you say."

"Yes – try my way."

Medrix sat down and sipped his coffee. "It wouldn't work. She would play on it. She attacked me on the shuttle, we had to sedate her."

"She was frightened …"

"Maybe … but …"

"You, Controller, are behaving just like an Elders' man!"

"It may seem so to you – but I am in charge here!"

"I know …" Thelka sat down. "I will have that coffee now."

Medrix made him a cup but remained standing beside him.

"You have to be careful, Medrix … I knew you when you were a young man training to be an Elders' man, but I thought that you had fought the City Elders because you did not believe in the way they behaved, but now you behave like them … I know you are grieving for your wife … and people find different ways to tackle that problem, but why do you have to become more aggressive in order to deal with it? You know how to be gentle. I have seen you with your wife. I saw the way you looked at her and laughed with her. I saw you become a real man. The change was phenomenal – and now look at you …"

Medrix looked into his empty cup and got up to help himself to more coffee. "Things are different here, Thelka. I have given the order, so it stands."

"Are you afraid to change it – to admit you are wrong?"

"If I chop and change, my authority will be questioned."

"So you are afraid of yourself?"

"No! I have to reap what I sow … as we all do …"

"Our rules state that orders for punishment have to be written down. So where are your orders? They are waiting for them Controller. Write them and don't keep the prisoner waiting … you know … it is a strong man who admits he is wrong … It is up to you, Controller … I trust you to do the right thing. Thanks for the coffee." Thelka put down his cup and walked out of the room.

Medrix sat for ages and then wrote down the order and told the guard to take it to the punishment block.

Cessie saw the guard holding out the order to the Lawmother, who opened it, read it, and nodded towards her.

She stood up. She was ready. She would be brave. She had been whipped before, that she knew. She would get over it.

"Guards," said the Lawmother, "take this prisoner back to her cell – the Controller has changed his mind."

She was hurried back to her cell and left there. So – he had listened to Lawmaker Thelka. She hoped that boded well for her and that somehow she would be able to convince him of his danger but … with Santel in the room and the grey one as well, she doubted it.

But the next day the Controller was called back to the scene of the crash and she did not see him at all.

Chapter 15

Two days later, Cessie was taken back to the inquiry. She sighed with relief when she saw Santel wasn't there, until the door opened and another woman came in, another Chetnerite, Grenda by name. She had been sent by Santel who had sent a message to say she wasn't well.

This time, Cessie was left standing in front of them: the chair had been taken away.

The Controller was looking at his notes and the others were staring at her. No one spoke.

She felt sick. Her legs were like jelly and she thought she was going to fall. She stepped forward and held on to the table, only then did she feel better. The Controller looked up and glared at her.

"Stand back from the table," he commanded.

She did so.

"Now we have two witnesses who can prove that you were in the shuttle when it crashed."

"Then they are lying," she said, vehemently.

"These witnesses do not lie. They have taken a picture of you."

"What do you mean they have a picture of me?"

"It's a new invention. One can take a picture using a zoom lens. All our Law Officers have them. Law Officer Filton, who sits beside me, is in charge of all the Law Officers on Chetner and he can verify this." He turned to him.

"Yes, Controller. This equipment has made life much easier for my men ..."

"Well ... it wasn't me. I wasn't there."

Law Officer Filton went on: "They were some distance away when they saw the shuttle flying low over the sea. Then they saw it crash into the sea. They took a picture of it. Then, as they watched, they saw a woman climb out of the side door. She stood looking at the sea and then went back into the shuttle. They, of course, had taken several pictures, including some of her. They then informed us of the crash. We went straight there ... but on the way we were informed by them that, as they neared the gate, they saw her climb

266

out of the shuttle. When they had almost got there they took a picture of her running to the lighthouse. Here are the pictures." He laid them on the table in front of them.

She stepped forward to look. They certainly looked like her but she knew that she had not been on the shuttle until after it crashed – so it had to be somebody else.

"I was never on the shuttle. It was someone else. You cannot see the crashed shuttle from the gate. You can only see it after you have passed through it. How did the Law Officers get to the scene of the accident so quickly?"

"They had a mini shuttle," the Controller said. He wrote something on a piece of paper and called a guard. He gave him the message and, as the man left the room, turned to her and said: "We will check what you can see from the gate."

Whereupon Law Officer Filton said: "My men don't lie, Controller."

"No, I know that … but this will doubly substantiate it."

"Well, all right then …" the Law Officer replied, but he did not sound very pleased.

"Now then – the pictures show you and only you … so why did you lie?"

"I didn't …"

"But these pictures show that you *have* lied to us." The Controller waved the pictures in front of her. "I can see you should have had that whipping after all, and then perhaps you would not have wasted everybody's time by not confessing the truth." He moved towards her. She stepped back as she thought he was going to hit her.

"You are the key to all this. I know you are … and I will get the truth from you even if I have to whip it out of you." He touched his whip and she backed right up to the door and nearly fell as it opened and a Law Officer walked in.

"Who the hell are you that you walk into this inquiry unannounced?" the Controller shouted at him. "I left notice that I was not to be disturbed. What part of my instructions don't you understand?"

"I am Lawmaker Lennox, Controller. I did knock."

"Well, now you are here – what do you want? I said I did not want to be disturbed, so … out with it, man … what do you want"? He returned to his seat. "Well … I'm waiting."

"You have visitors, Controller."

"Visitors! I haven't got time for visitors. Send them away."

"I can't …"

"Why not?"

"They are from Estolan."

"Estolan!"

"They can only stay three hours. They came with the medical supplies you ordered. They are going back on the same freighter. It is very important that they see you."

"Well … tell me who they are then." He sighed as he leant back in his chair.

"Lawmother Jessanda …"

"What the hell is *she* doing here?"

"… I don't know …"

Cessie seemed to know the name. Why couldn't she remember?

"… and Lawmaker Timmons …"

"The prosecutor!"

"… Yes … and Lawmaker Eldon …"

"Eldon …" Medrix smiled. "Well I am sure I can spare them some time … I will be glad to see Eldon again. Right! Show them into the visitors' lounge … tell them I will be joining them soon."

The man left them and Medrix called the guard.

"Take her back to the prison. While she is waiting there perhaps she will come to her senses and realise that telling the truth is her best option." He turned to her and said: "Think about it, woman. We have other ways of getting the truth from you and I don't think you would like them very much."

The guards took her back to the prison and left here there.

Medrix went straight over to the visitors' room and went in.

He saw Jessanda standing by the window and the prosecutor sitting in an armchair reading, but of Eldon there was no sign.

"Welcome," he said as he walked over to the prosecutor, "but where is Lawmaker Eldon?"

Jessanda came over to him and kissed him on the forehead. "He's gone over to the medical bay to check the invoices with the doctor. The freighter brought them." He looked at her. At one time he had thought her very beautiful – but he noticed now that, although she smiled, her eyes were hard.

The prosecutor stood up and said: "We had a good journey but we cannot stay long as we have to go back with the same shuttle. But we felt we had to come and see you."

Medrix waited for him to go on, there had to be a reason why they had come.

Jessanda smiled and said: "You have been here the required term, Medrix, and now you can return home and no one will feel let down by it. Least of all, yourself."

"I cannot go back. I have work to do here."

"But, Lawmaker," the prosecutor said, "there is no need for you to stay. You just have to choose someone to take your place and then you can leave."

"The Chief Elder wants me to continue and I don't want to come home yet."

Jessanda smiled and said quietly: "Your term of mourning is almost up; there will be no need for you to stay. If you go home you can take up new interests, meet new people and, maybe – marry again."

Medrix went white. "I wouldn't *want* to marry again. Celisia is the love of my life"

He was annoyed that she could be so unfeeling as to even mention it.

"She is dead, Medrix. You have to come to terms with it. No one could survive that crash. You saw it yourself – so stop deluding yourself with false hopes. Life goes on. These people are not yours."

The prosecutor tapped him on the back. "This is not your job any more. You came here to be with your wife – to please her – but she is not here any longer. I am sure she would see our reasoning if she were here. Your mother wants to see you and so do all your friends. You should train for the law. You were marvellous at your wife's trial. You have to conduct three trials, and you have already done one. You should be brilliant."

"Lawmaker Timmons, I am deeply honoured that you think so but it was never my intention to go in for the law – I have a job here and I would not like to leave it unfinished. I owe them all that much."

"You owe them nothing," Jessanda said as she smiled at him, "they are nothing to you."

"They are my kinsfolk, Lawmother. They have given me their trust and I intend to keep it."

"But they would understand, Medrix," she said quietly. "A man should be with his friends at a time like this."

"I am better if I am busy, and I am certainly busy now."

"Then be busy on Estolan."

"Sorry if I disappoint you both but here I am really needed. A new person might not be accepted by the Chetnerites but they accept me and they need all the help they can get."

"And other people can help them, Medrix," Jessanda smiled, her dark eyes lighting up as she looked at him.

He looked away. "Will you have refreshments?"

They both knew then that their pleading was to no avail.

"Well, Medrix, I would like to go and see the children. I have brought presents for them. Could my brother Conn join me?" asked Jessanda.

"Of course." He spoke into his contact bracelet and Conn soon arrived and he and Jessanda went out of the room together.

Lawmaker Timmons walked to the window. "I'll have coffee, Medrix, if the offer still holds."

Soon both men sat together while they drank.

"Medrix – you know, I admire your strength of character but you should think about coming back. You loved Jessanda once – could you not love her enough to marry her? You two used to get on so well at one time."

"I don't love her now. She jilted me – remember!"

"But that's all over now. You don't have to love the person to marry them. You can learn to love each other as you go along. Many marriages are like that … you must know that."

"Firstly, my mourning is not over. It will go on longer than the prescribed time anyway ... and I object to this kind of talk when I am in the throes of grief and must handle it in my own way."

"I understand that ... but you would get over it sooner if you were away from it all."

Medrix was about to say something angrily to the prosecutor when Eldon came in, smiling. He went up to him and hugged him. "Welcome, dear friend. How good it is to see you."

The prosecutor stood up. "I'll leave you together. May I look round the base?"

"Of course. I'll get someone to take you." A few minutes later he left them and the two friends sat down for coffee and a belated chat.

"The Chief Elder sends his regards and thinks you are doing a fine job."

"Does he? I rather thought he wanted me to come back."

"No ... he is sure you are the right man for the job."

"Jessanda thought my time was up here, because the job of Liaison Officer was for nine moons only ..."

"Oh, I see. But you are not the liaison man now; you are the Controller of all Chetner ..."

"Not the planet of Chetner – just the country ..."

"Of course, Medrix. I get mixed up sometimes. But the entire planet could be affected, couldn't it?"

"Yes."

"I have brought the mail. The Chief Elder has been approached by Lawmother Jessanda's father. He is offering his daughter to you in marriage as soon as your mourning is over. He had to accept it as is our custom, but of course you can turn it down. Many would like to see it happen, though I would not, because I think Cessie is out there somewhere. Call me silly, but Lawmother Grey is very sure of it. She has the gift of second sight and I believe her, whatever other people say. But then, I would not want to give you false hope and whatever you do, I shall help you."

"Dear friend – I won't accept ... for if my lovely, beautiful girl is dead I will never marry again. She is my life and even if she cannot be with me now in this world, she will be with me in spirit."

"I thought so ... but think about it and answer him in your own time."

The others came back to the room as it was time to go and Medrix saw them off as they went on their way back to Estolan.

Medrix decided to read his mail before he saw Celisia again so it was quite late in the day when he called her back to the inquiry.

She came in quietly and stood before them.

"Well, have you thought about it?"

She nodded but said nothing.

"And what are you going to do?"

"No comment."

"That is not an answer," he said angrily. "I'll give you another chance. What is your name?"

"No comment," she replied again.

"I know it is not Deena Kent because Chetnerite Grenda says that Deena Kent arrived at the base during the second moon. So what *is* your name?"

She stared at him. What could she say?

He repeated the question. She did not reply.

"So you are not talking, is that it?"

"My name is my own business and not yours." She was frantically trying to make up a name.

Law Officer Filton said that the Controller was too kind and, standing up, unsheathed his whip.

Quickly, she said: "My name is Leah." She remembered that name from somewhere.

"Good. And your other name?"

"Umm …" what could she say? The name Dickon came to her. "Dickon," she said quickly.

"That's the way to do it, Controller," said the Law Officer as he sat down.

"Good. I think you are right, Lawmaker. So … you are Leah Dickon?"

"Yes."

"I see. And that is your father's name?"

"Oh no, that is my husband's name."

"You are married? Well, yes, I can see you wear a ring – take it off and let me see it."

"No, it's mine."

"Take it off."

"I can't … its … my finger is swollen and I cannot remove the ring."

"I see … we will see it when the swelling goes down. Where did you go to school?"

"City One."

"Really?"

"Yes … Lawmother Kella was my teacher …"

"How old are you?"

She didn't know. She guessed. "Twenty-four."

"What is your father's name?"

She knew that. "Mantrex."

"Rubbish!"

"Yes – it is Mantrex."

"You are lying."

She said nothing … they did not believe her when she told them the truth.

"I can see you are not going to co-operate."

"I can't, you see … because …"

"Because, you won't …" he shouted at her.

"No … I can't because I don't remember things."

"Liars never do."

"But you don't understand …"

"Too right … I don't understand you at all."

Chetnerite Grenda leaned forward and said: "I know why she can't answer, Controller."

"You do? Tell us."

"She is afraid that her employers will retaliate in some way. I am right aren't I dear?"

Cessie could have hugged her. Why hadn't she thought of that. She nodded and whispered "Yes," bowing her head low as if in fear.

"I see," Medrix said. "Is that all? We can protect you."

"Are you sure? I would like to help you but …" she began to cry. She knew how to act so she would play it to the full.

He looked at her. Was she acting or was she really afraid? "Right … I will give you protection if you tell me everything."

"You have questions written down," she nodded at the folder in front of him.

"Yes."

"Well, if I can have those I will write the answers down for you, but I want you to promise me that only you will read the answers and that you will keep my statement locked up in your safe."

"Right … I can do that."

"Then I will do it and write down everything I know. I will need a large pad of lined paper and one of plain and …"

"Why plain?"

"So I can draw the maps of places and sketch various things and people … I do have your promise for protection, don't I?"

Medrix looked at her. She was enjoying herself at their expense, he was sure of it, but he would have to play along – see what the little devil actually did and he was already fed up with this inquiry. Eldon's visit had done that too. The outside world beckoned and he was stuck here. He needed something different. He knew that she was playing a game but he would be a willing player until he decided not to be. "Of course. I promised. I'll leave the guards here while you write."

"Oh, no," she said. "Not here … the best place would be in my prison cell … I could do it there easily."

"Of course … how silly of me … the guards can have some time off - but … be warned … if you try to fob me off with lies I shall know, for I …"

She interrupted him: "… For you will have to prove it. I mean, if I tell you the names of the storehouses, you will have to check them – of course you will – I understand that."

"Good. Then I will let you get on with it. I will send the things to you. I expect great things from you Leah, and make sure you sign your statement at the end and put the date. Guards! Take her back."

272

She was dismissed and she went back to the prison feeling elated. She would write about everything she knew and it would take days rather than hours, and by the time she had finished, a new plan would come to her for her escape.

One thing she did remember was that Jessanda was betrothed to the Controller. She was sure that was right and therefore *she* could not be the Controller's wife, so Santel was wrong. For some reason this thought did not please her ... O God, she wasn't falling for him herself? Surely not ... he was good looking and when she had kissed him she had felt that somehow it was right. No! She couldn't fall for this man – he hated her – he was hateful – he was welcome to Jessanda ... yet, something inside her stirred when she thought of him. Time would bring her memory back – writing this statement would help. She sighed. "One thing at a time, that's what you must do," but she wondered what Jessanda was like and how she could possibly be betrothed to him while he was still in mourning.

Chapter 16

Medrix left Cessie alone for three days, but when he had no word saying that she had finished her statement, he got angry. He strode over to the prison to see her.

The Lawmother in charge let him in saying that Prisoner Number 8 was still working on her statement and had been for the last three days.

"Wasting time," he said crossly. "She is doing it deliberately and I am going to put a stop to it now," whereupon the Lawmother opened the cell door for him but, as he strode in angrily, she stood by the door and said: "Prisoner Number 8 stand, please, and bow your head. The Controller is here."

Cessie stood up quickly, knocking her pen on to the floor as she did so.

"You …" he pointed to her, "… you have been keeping me, us, waiting. I want your statement and I want it now." He reached for the papers and knocked some of them on to the floor. She bent down to pick up her pen and the papers and hurriedly put them back on the table.

"I haven't finished yet," she said quietly.

"Finished! You are not writing a book – just a short statement!" He flicked through the papers.

"There are six questions and I am doing my best to answer them, Controller."

"Oh – and if I can get answers by some other means – what then?"

"I don't know what you mean. I have answered the first question and I am on the second one..."

"So! It is as I thought. You are playing for time."

She knew he was right but she wouldn't let him know that. "No. It took some time to answer question one."

"How long can it take to write down a list of store houses?"

She sat down, in spite of the fact that he had not told her to do so.

"You see, Controller, I wrote the list, then wrote about each – giving the map references. A list of names would be just a waste of time for you – you wouldn't know how to get there," she said, sweetly, looking up into his angry brown eyes. "My God," she said to herself, "he's good looking, so attractive, I wonder …"

She stopped abruptly. He was staring at her and he said "Playing games are we? Well, I can play games and today I am free to play them."

She looked away, not sure what he was talking about.

"Don't you stare at me, flashing those blue eyes seductively. I want facts and nothing else." He sat down opposite her and told the Lawmother to fetch them both coffee and biscuits and she left the room.

"Read the bases out to me."

"Of course, if that's easier for you." She was only too aware of him looking at her. She turned the pages until she found what she wanted and read the list out. Of course she had guessed them – she had studied the map and written down the ones that could easily be them. Would he realise that?

"Well, get on with, then."

She read them out: "Felix Tower – that's …"

"Under the water …" he interrupted. "I can hardly check that, can I?"

"The water will go down. Shall I go on?"

"Yes."

The Lawmother returned with the coffee and biscuits and set them down on the table.

"Leave us," he said to her.

"But I have to stay … the rules, you know …"

"As I make the rules … I wish you to go – I am not – not going to seduce the prisoner. Go now."

She went, mumbling something under her breath.

"Go on, please," he sipped his coffee.

"The old City."

"What old City?"

"Its reference is …" she pointed to the map.

"Go on. Why is that a base?"

"If you let me read them and not keep interrupting, I shall be finished sooner," she said with annoyance.

"Go on …"

"The old City was by the sea. But many decades ago a tidal wave swept in and destroyed half of it. Since then sand has encroached on it, except the part that was not destroyed. It is now a long way from the sea; people have lived in the remaining part of the City until recently. Now it is a base or store place."

"I see. A history lesson," he sounded grim.

"If you like."

"Drink your coffee while it's hot." He took the list from her and read out loud. "The Rock Point Lighthouse."

She interrupted him: "This was a working lighthouse up until the Lawmakers left – but it was automatically worked. They destroyed the mechanism so the Chetner Council set up a light but it had to be maintained by lighthouse keepers. Four men did this – but only two at a time. They did six moons and then returned to their homes nearby. One of them was a carpenter and lived near the Sea View Settlement. Whether or not he was there when the waters …"

He interrupted her: "How can it be a base if there's someone there."

"Well, it stopped being a lighthouse when there were no ships. It's got large cellars. I went there once when I was little."

"I see," he looked thoughtfully at her and then continued reading the list to himself. She finished her coffee and helped herself to a biscuit.

"His hair is a lovely shade of brown," she thought, "and it curls at the nape of his neck and when the sun shines on it, it has a coppery sheen." What was the matter with her? Her life was in danger and she was fantasising about him.

He looked up at her and she felt herself colour up.

"Hot in here," he said, looking at her in amusement.

"Yes."

"This one – the old mine – what's so special about it? According to your map reference it is not far from the crash scene." He wished she did not look so appealing in that outfit. It was a sombre prison grey – yet, somehow, it suited her and those blue eyes were looking at him with puzzlement. How he would like to kiss her lips. He looked down at the paper in front of him. "For goodness sake, man, stop fantasising about her. She is not Celisia – look at her black hair – she is Leah – no … he was sure that was not her name … but … she was not Celisia." He sighed.

"*You are not listening*," she said emphatically.

His contact bracelet flashed. He sat back in his chair and tuned into it. Conn's voice came over loud and clear. "There's a row going on here about the cleaners' hours – they want to see you."

"Deal with it, Conn, I'm busy."

"But, they want you, Controller."

"Deal with it, Lawmaker, and then write a report – get them to write down their grievances."

"But, Controller …"

"Deal with it *now* and *that's* an *order*." He switched the bracelet off. "Now, where were we?"

"In the old mine," she laughed nervously. "Well, not in it."

He looked at the paper and read out: " 'This is an old gold mine. It is on the site of an old temple. It has a river running through it. At one end are arches and, at the other, are arches that ascend in steps to the top of a mountain, where there is a waterfall. One can walk alongside the river on a narrow rock path. On each side of this rock channel, are many caverns built into the side of the mountains. They could be man-made or natural caverns. Here, through the ages, things have been stored. The miners, though, panned the river, i.e. they used a riddle, putting a spadeful of gravel into it. If they were lucky, after cleaning the muck out, they could find small nuggets of gold. Chetnerites do not put much value on them but many people from other places do.' Hmm – interesting. Have you been there?"

"Once, long ago."

"As a lookout?"

"No – we lookouts don't get to see them."

"So when did you go?"

"My father took me when I was little."

"How little?"

"Nearly five."

"That young!"

"We went for a picnic and to find gold." She seemed to remember it clearly.

"And did you?"

"Did I what?"

"Find gold."

She smiled. "A tiny, tiny bit. I was going to keep it for ever; only for ever is a long time." She looked sad.

"If the lookouts don't go to the bases, how do you know where they are?"

She hesitated.

He laughed. "You've made it all up. You are not going to tell me what I want to know, are you?"

"They are there," she said angrily.

"Are they? Just pick any spot, tell the Controller the history of it and he will think it's true. I am not so easily taken in as you think, Leah! Leah? That's not your name either – is it?"

Of course he was right. But right for the wrong reasons. Her throat was dry and she coughed as she answered: "I am trying to be of some help and all you can do is mock me. Typical Lawmaker!"

"So, I am typical. Know a lot about them, do you?"

She glared at him angrily. "Go on, Leah …"

"We are not able to go to the bases because all the lookouts are in different parts of Chetner. Our job is to alert them to the places where people haven't locked their doors. We don't go to the store bases ourselves."

"So why were you in Top Gost Point, then?"

"Because … because …" she was desperately trying to find an answer "… because we were taken there when we first joined," she said almost jubilantly.

"Who took you?"

"I don't know. I just woke up there."

"So, they banged you on the head – and you woke up there?"

"Yes."

"I see – names – I want names."

"Well …" dare she risk it … "one woman was called Elta."

"Really – Councillor Elta? Anyone else?"

"Santel."

"That's rich – choose the names, you knew – any more? Perhaps there was one named Medrix. Was there?" he asked sarcastically.

She sighed: "No – but there was one called Kenton."

"Are you sure?" That had surprised him.

"Two others – I can't remember their names."

"What about Nurse Pennington?"

She looked at him. The words 'Penny goes to his room at night' came to her. "No – no – I don't know that name."

"Good answer. Why were they there?"

"They didn't say."

He stood up. "I must go – I'll take the details of the bases with me. I see the old space station behind the Reed Mountain is here too, amongst the others. Well, I'll read all about it. I am going to get proof of this before I will believe any of it, Leah. If you are lying then you will feel my anger, I can assure you." He stood up.

"But we … you … I … haven't finished reading it all yet." God, what was the matter with her? Surely she didn't want him to stay – did she?

"But, Controller … I should …"

"Right, Leah – I'll stay a little while." Why am I staying? I should get away from her as soon as possible. Yet it might unsettle her if I stay and she will let something slip. Something important. He sat down.

"Well. What's so important – oh, the old space station."

"I don't really know a lot about that – it was a weather station for a while."

"And now?"

"One of the bases … you …"

"If you cannot tell me anything about it, I am wasting my time …"

"There's the old shuttle base, of course," she said calmly, even though she felt far from calm.

"What old shuttle bay? Where is it?"

"City One."

"Rubbish! City One is destroyed and everything with it. You know that. Every one knows that."

"It's not near City One."

"If it's not, why did you say it was?"

"I didn't."

"Yes you did – you said City One!"

"Well, yes, I did – but you see … I said the old shuttle bay – not the new one."

"There's a difference?"

"Yes. The old shuttle bay was built before City One was built. It was built by a Lawmakers' building team. They – at first – chose the site of the City to be on the southern hills, not far from the Mountain Centre and that is where the shuttle bay was built – but the Chief Elder at that time had the planned site changed – to lower ground – near the river and streams. The builders brought in equipment, using that shuttle bay. They constructed a monorail to the new site."

"And you are telling me it is still there?"

"Yes."

"Usable?"

"Yes, I think so. The raiders you see can leave and arrive when they like."

"If it's true – we've got them – but it's too pat. How do you know all this?"

She couldn't remember – maybe she'd read it. "It was included in our history lessons at school."

"Mmm – it's not on the map ... how do we get into it?"

Now she was guessing. "The Mountain Centre is built on it, there are doors opening onto it from there."

"For small shuttles?"

"I don't know – the open bay is covered in some way to look like a mountain."

"Could be – if you are right you will be rewarded." He sighed. "I must go now." He stood up and, taking her carefully-prepared papers, left the cell but came back in and said: "Have the rest of the statement ready by tomorrow evening." Then he was gone.

The room seemed empty without him.

The second question was about how the raiders operated, where they were from and how they got rid of the stuff.

She remembered reading about space pirates called Jevroes. She wrote down everything she could remember and only stopped when the Lawmother brought in food.

"Put it all away now. There's always tomorrow ... and don't you get all gooey-eyed when he comes here?"

"What ever do you mean?"

"I saw you looking at him. He may look at you like that but – remember who you are and why you are here. I say it for your own good, dear. He has a reputation, that one – a different woman in his bed each night, and if you are not careful you'll be one of them. But in your case he will be hoping you will let slip some important piece of information. He always gets what he wants, so – be careful."

"Surely, Lawmother Jailer you shouldn't be giving away his secrets, should you?"

"Well – I happen to like you – so don't say I haven't warned you."

"Thank you, but I can take care of myself."

"If you could, my dear, you wouldn't be here, would you?" And with that, she left Cessie, slamming and locking the door behind her.

Of course, she was right. He was vicious, arrogant, dictatorial, yet ... somehow, so very vulnerable. Damn and blast the man.

That night she tossed and turned and thought about him and, when she did sleep, dreamed about him.

The next morning Cessie got to work again.

Question three wanted to know how she got from place to place so quickly.

That was easy, of course, so she wrote down exactly what had happened. She also said that the organisers were called the Masters, but who they were she didn't know but that they hadn't told anyone the names of those others who were in the organisation: that way no names could be given away at any time. She also wrote that they thought she was a boy and she didn't dare tell them they had made a mistake. Evidently, the real lookout had also escaped from Top Gost Point.

She stopped writing. Should she tell the Controller what the Lawmakers on the crashed shuttle had said? After all, it was a bit strange.

"Mmm," she thought, "I had better do it, although he won't believe it." She carefully wrote down that those Lawmakers had said that they would inform the others as to her whereabouts, so that someone would come to give her new orders.

She sat up. She knew this meant, without doubt, that the Lawmakers could be the raiders. Would he see it like that? Or would he find nothing wrong with the statement? She sighed. Of course he would think she was trying to throw the blame.

She did a sketch of the two men who had taken her in the shuttle to Hunter's Mill. The grey one did look like Law Officer Filton. Would he see it, too? She expected a lot of men would fit that description.

The fourth question asked when she had joined them. She wrote:

I haven't joined them – they mistook me for someone else. I was too afraid of them not to follow their instructions as far as possible. But I never put the crosses on the houses.

They would take me to my new route, leave me with a bag full of things I would need, plus a roll of money for the work I had done before. They always left me with boys' clothing and I was too afraid to say anything.

Question five: How did you get the job?

She left it unanswered, then put *by mistake.*

Question six stated: Please sign this to say that you have given us a true statement and state your address and planet.

She left it. What could she write? Then she wrote:

There is a plot against you. I was to be used as bait as I look like your wife. They want something from you. I was to be exchanged for it. When I said that you would see you had been cheated when you saw me, they laughed and said that then I could expect a knife in my back. When I asked them what would happen when you did not

280

accept the bait they said they would kill me as I knew too much. I was in deadly danger.

When I escaped from Top Gost Point I was determined to dye my hair black so that they would not recognise me. This worked, except the raiders and you, thought I was someone else.

As to my name – well – I could be your wife or I could be someone else, so – for the time being – I'll sign my name as Leah Dickon and maybe one fine day my memory will come back and I can give you the answer you want.

L Dickon

She sat back. That would have to do and pray God he believes me.

She read through the papers and then put them in a folder. The spare papers, pens and pencils she put under her mattress for use at a later time.

Medrix came that evening and collected the statement. He didn't stay and she was glad of that. She worried all night that she'd done all she could.

In the morning she was sent to the serving room to help there. She was on a long chain that was fixed to a hook on the wall. There was no guard. She spent all day sewing slips on to pillows. No one spoke to her.

In the evening she was back in her cell. Had he read her statement? No word came – so, he hadn't. Why hadn't he? she wondered.

The days passed slowly – now Cessie was set to work in the prison itself. If she wasn't scrubbing floors she was scrubbing tables or brushing down walls, or helping with the washing.

Most evenings she sat for hours mending prison clothes, bedding or anything else that needed repairing.

The prison was self-supporting, so sometimes she cleaned vegetables, served the food or dug and weeded in the small vegetable garden.

Outside, she was watched all the time by two guards. Inside she was mostly left on her own.

When prisoners were sick, she helped with the nursing and, twice, when a doctor was called, she assisted him in simple operations. In fact, the jailer's wife was heard to say that she did not know how she'd managed before without her.

When the new supplies arrived, Cessie helped to check them and would add up the list of numbers quicker than the jailer himself could do it.

Sometimes she went with a guard to the main library to choose books for the prison. One interested her very much. It was entitled *Memory Loss and How to Deal With It*. It wasn't among the books that were set aside for the prisoners so, when she thought no one was looking, she slipped it into her apron pocket. Luckily it wasn't a big book. Once back in her cell, she put the book under her mattress.

She began to get up earlier than usual to study her book. One of the key things evidently, was that she should record everything she remembered, including her dreams, people and flashbacks – she should write or sketch it. Using the papers and pencils she had already, she started but after a few days, ran out of paper.

From then on she sorted through the prison rubbish bins for paper. Backs of invoices – envelopes. These she put in her private store. She realised that under her mattress was not a good place and, as there was a loose board by the cupboard, she lifted it and put her precious notes into a folder and into the hole.

Once, when they'd run out of bread rolls, she was sent with a guard to collect some from the main kitchen. The cook showed her the cupboard and told her to help herself – but sign the book which was behind the door. It was a thick book so she took out three middle pages and then signed for the rolls.

Another time, she was sent to the medical bay to get more bandages. Again she was told to help herself. On a shelf was a pile of new notebooks – she put two into her pocket – and, picking up a bag of bandages, returned to the prison.

Her days became days of searching for paper – her early mornings were spent writing her notes and sketching and, every day, she hid them away.

But she had been seen and duly reported to the Controller.

On one evening, when she was busy sewing, Law Officer Filton arrived with two guards. He flung open the door and shouted to her to stand with her hands on her head. "You cannot be trusted, can you?" he yelled. "Guards – search the place."

They pulled out the drawers and tipped her clothes out; searched the cupboard; felt under the table and chairs; stripped the bedding and pulled out the mattress and left it on the floor and lifted the bed and leaned it against the wall.

They ran their fingers along the wall, opening a panel she did not know existed, then stood back, shaking their heads in disbelief when they found nothing.

"You," shouted Law Officer Filton, "have been stealing – so where are they?"

"Where are what?" Her voice shook.

"All the paper you have taken. I know what you are doing; you are sending notes out to your people."

"I don't know what you mean. I am not sending notes to anyone."

"Oh, aren't you?" He tapped his foot on the boards near the cupboard and bent down, listening.

"A loose board here. Guards – pull it up."

The guards did so and brought out her folder.

"There! I knew it. Anything else in there?"

A guard reached in again and brought out a red notebook and handed it to the Law Officer. She had never seen it before.

"Now your sins have found you out, haven't they?"

"The folder's mine but I have never seen the red notebook before."

"So you say." He opened it. The pages were filled with letters and numbers. "It's all in code and you will have the job of decoding it for me, won't you?"

"I've never seen it before."

"Really! I have long suspected that your presence in the base has been contrived by someone who wants to bring down the Ruler of all Chetner, to bring down the good name of all Lawmakers. Just because a few of them were evil, doesn't mean that we are all painted with the same brush. You are here because you look like his wife in some ways. They've put you in here because, as a temptress, you could get secrets from him that no one else could. I wouldn't blame him for; after all, he loved his wife – still does, and hopes every day that she will return. But what you are doing is despicable and he will see it for himself when he comes back from Cordonia. Oh, I can see you didn't know he's away. That's why he hasn't read your statement yet."

"I am not guilty," she whispered. "I have never seen that notebook before."

The guards took her to Law Officer Filton's office. A Lawmaker, by the name of Jonkins awaited them. She knew she was in great danger. If Law Officer Filton was the same man that she had met in the shuttle, then her days were numbered. He had the authority to do everything – and maybe he had planted that notebook himself – what better way to incriminate her. What better way to convince the Controller that she was a spy.

Law Officer Filton pushed her into his room. It was dark and gloomy and furnished in some dark material. He put the folder and the notebook on his large tidy desk then went to a cupboard and brought out a cane.

"Pick up the notebook, woman!"

She stood still and shook her head.

"Pick it up *now*."

She reached for it and he brought down the cane across her knuckles. She cried out in shock and left the notebook on the desk.

Someone knocked on the door and came in. It was Lawmaker Whitton. "I am sorry to interrupt you, Law Officer, but I have an important message from the Controller. You are to go to the crash-salvage freighter."

"What! Now?" he sounded annoyed.

"Yes – I'm to go with you. I have arranged for a shuttle and a crew and they are waiting. The Controller will meet you there. Evidently it's very important."

"Right – then I must go. Jonkins, put these things away for me, please." He spoke into his contact bracelet telling the guards to come and get Cessie, then, he looked at her and said: "Our little chat can wait – waiting will make you realise the situation you are in."

He left the room, Lawmaker Whitton hurrying after him.

Jonkins picked up the red notebook and the folder, put them into the safe and locked it.

The guards came in. One of them was fiddling with his contact bracelet. Evidently a link was broken and, in trying to mend it, he dropped it. She picked it up and saw it had broken.

"Damn," he said, "I'll have to get a new one."

"Not now – we have to take her back first."

"Well, I know that," said the first guard as he pulled her roughly by the arms.

"Ouch – you are hurting me," said Cessie, pulling away from him.

"Will you get a move on," Lawmaker Jonkins intervened, "I want to lock this office."

The guards pushed her out of the room and into the corridor. The chains around her wrists were cutting into her. "These chains are too tight," she complained.

One of the guards loosened them and she smiled her thanks.

They walked quickly along the corridor and turned right. She saw that it was clear and, when they had got halfway along it, bent down and groaned as if in pain.

"What's the matter with you?" said the guard with the broken bracelet.

"It is the baby – I think I am losing it," she began rubbing her abdomen – "Oh, God!"

"You are pregnant?" the other guard said.

"Yes – two moons – well, nearly two moons," she groaned again, "get help for me." She bent down almost to the floor.

"I'll get the doctor. Oh, damn, my contact bracelet isn't working. You use yours, Ferson."

"Get me some water to drink," said Cessie as she groaned again.

"I'll get it, Ferson. You contact the doctor."

Ferson tried, but the line was busy and he could not get through to the doctor.

By this time Cessie was on the floor. "Go and get him," she said, "I'll need a chair and a nurse. Hurry – oh – please!"

He looked at her and ran to get help; the other guard had already gone to get water. The corridor was clear. She got up and ran fast, praying her good luck would hold. It did. There was a turning to the left and she raced along there and came to an emergency door exit. It was open.

"Let them think I have gone out there," she thought and then turned to the right up a narrow staircase – here were notices as the passageway forked – to the left were the Lawmakers' rooms, to the right the Tower Dock.

She took the right and, eventually, came to a tower room. A door slid back as she entered. She could see the whole space dock spread out below her.

The door opposite her opened. Her heart raced with fear. Someone was there, but no one came. She went through it and came out on a metal staircase.

Down below her were people carrying boxes into the hold of a nearby freighter. The carriers wore long grey robes and hoods. Her dress was grey. She ran down until she came to the platform bay. Close by was a room. No one was in it but, on the table was a pile of hoods and she grabbed one and put it on. Then she saw a grey cloak and put that on. It was awkward with the chains but once on, the cloak hid them.

She joined the line of carriers and picked up a box. It wasn't very heavy and she carried it into the hold, where she stayed hidden until the others left the craft.

A voice intoned: "The Kestra freighter is due out now. Please vacate bays now."

The freighter doors closed with a noise like thunder and she was in complete darkness. She felt the vibrations of the freighter powering up and then she was shot across the small space as the freighter left the dock.

She sat up, breathing in great gasps, as panic rose up inside her and she was again back in that shuttle that had crashed with her in it. But part of her knew that it was her fear that caused the panic.

She relaxed back against a large packing case and the flashback faded.

She had got away. Once she arrived on Kestra she would ask for asylum and be away from the Lawmakers once and for all. She was lucky that she had got away completely – she could have been stopped by anyone – but she hadn't been. What would life be like on Kestra, she wondered as she settled down to her journey into the unknown.

Chapter 17

Medrix had taken four of the Chief Elder's men with him when he went to Cordonia.

They were all welcomed by the ambassador but taken to the president of the country, who wanted to see them. The president lived in a mountain-top fortress, much of it built into the rock itself. The interview room was itself a large cave with long hanging drapes on the walls. The president sat at a large desk but he stood up to welcome his visitors.

"I am glad we meet at last," he said, motioning them all to sit down. "Your Chief Elder has been in contact with me and an agreement has been reached."

"Then the men may come back to Chetner?" asked Medrix, wondering why he had been brought here.

"No – the men cannot go back ... no – don't interrupt me – you see ... something else has arisen and of course the prisoners are of more use to me here, than in Chetner."

"I don't understand ... we agreed ..."

"I haven't finished, Controller."

"Well – please tell me why I am here," Medrix said calmly. He knew that getting angry or showing anger would only make this man more adamant in these negotiating talks.

The president was a tall thin man, with a weather-beaten face, sharp eyes and hard thin lips. He was dressed in grey with no embellishments to show who he was, yet, as he sat at his desk, his every movement portrayed his authority. He looked at some notes before he spoke again.

"My salvage team has been working hard at Top Gost Point. They have found much evidence that the base and settlement were being used by Lawmakers."

"Never!" Medrix stood up. "This is some trick to hold the prisoners further ..."

"Sit down, Controller, or I shall have you arrested."

Medrix sat down. "Well – go on – what is it this time?"

One of the other Lawmakers interrupted the conversation: "You must

286

make allowances for our Controller. His father is imprisoned here, as well as the other men."

"I agree," the president smiled, "that is why we should come to some agreement as soon as possible." He sighed. "Shall I go on?"

"Yes – please do," Medrix said grimly. He knew he must control his temper.

"Well, as I said, Lawmakers were using Top Gost Point and the settlement. They were coming and going. One pilot was Lawmaker Cradock."

"I have never heard of him," Medrix announced, "and I know the names of all my pilots."

"I didn't say they were your pilots, Controller – I said they were Lawmakers – and the name of another one is Kenton … Ah! I see you know that one."

"Well – yes – he lost his way in the fog."

"No – maybe – but, according to the memory box on the shuttle he had been going back and forth for many moons. Cradock had been there six times or more!"

Medrix shook his head in disbelief but said nothing.

"Now, what I want is for the Lawmakers to pay for the reclamation of Top Gost Point, as they were using it."

"I'll see what I can do," Medrix said with resignation.

"Good …"

"But – wait a minute," another of Medrix' men said, "the Lawmakers offered to reclaim it years ago. It was turned down because you … the Cordonians … thought the building might be useful to them … so … as you turned it down …"

"You forget. I have hostages. Also, I have proof about the use of the base and who was occupying it and therefore it is only right that we should be reimbursed. But I will be lenient, knowing the trouble you have had already. I will let six of the prisoners go – not your father of course – and no! you cannot meet your father and the others – but they are well looked after – brutality is not one of our vices. Already the six men are in your shuttle."

Medrix and his men stood up, as did the president.

A messenger came in.

"What is it Goston? You may speak."

"The salvage team at the shuttle crash scene on Chetner wish to see the Controller and his Chief Law Officer at once – it is most important. They have notified Top Base."

"Then I must leave you," Medrix said briskly, "and I will get back to you at a later date.

"You do that." The president clapped his hands and three men came into the room and took Medrix and his men back to the shuttle.

When Medrix arrived at the crash scene it was some two hours later. Law

287

Officer Filton was already there. Medrix sent his shuttle back to base: he would go back with the Law Officer as soon as this meeting was over.

They were immediately transported up to the salvage freighter where they were met by the captain who was a Temran with long black plaited hair. A big man full of humour but now, he looked very grim.

"I want you both to identify the dead people."

"Haven't they got identification passes on them?" Medrix asked.

"Yes. But the seawater has destroyed some of them."

The bodies were laid out on tables in a long room. The six-man crew were all identifiable but then there were four other men: one with his leg in a splint, another with a sling on his arm. Medrix did not know any of them. Their clothes indicated they were Chetnerites.

Filton took pictures of them.

At the end of the room was a woman's body. Her face was smashed in.

"I don't know who this is," Medrix said as he looked at her mangled body, her face shrouded in long black hair.

"Oh, we have her identification, Controller." A man stepped forward. "Her pass says that she is Councillor Chetnerite Elta."

"It can't be," Filton proclaimed, "she's back at base."

"She's not. Her pass allowed her to go to Feldwood settlement to see her uncle."

"Who signed the pass?" Medrix asked.

"Lawmaker Thelka."

"But why would he?" Filton said in astonishment.

"Perhaps she couldn't find you at the time," the captain said.

"True – but – I'll look into it – when I get back. Wait a minute, though! Why would she go there? It's nowhere near the Roc Lighthouse? Unless the pilot went to the wrong lighthouse – the Rock Point lighthouse is not far from there."

The captain smiled. "The memory box shows their destination as the Rock Point lighthouse and not the one at the crash scene. They must have made a mistake and gone to the wrong one – and discovered that no one was there and then went to the right one. The memory box also showed that they stopped at Feldwood: also, Hunter's Mill. There were seven people on the shuttle when they left the base. There were eight people on it when they left Feldwood. One person got off at Hunter's Mill; four got on at the Roc Lighthouse."

"Are you saying that they landed at the Roc Lighthouse *before* the crash? They crashed when they took *off*?" Medrix said quickly.

"Yes. That's what I mean. You see, they were overloaded. In the hold were a large heavy ornamental mirror and a stand – a very heavy one at that – too heavy in fact for the shuttle.

"They evidently picked up the mirror at Feldwood – the memory box mentions this extra weight. The stand does not match the mirror. The box records this being loaded on at the Roc Lighthouse, so it seems, Controller, that they loaded the mirror without the stand – they left Feldwood in a hurry – and then found a stand at the Roc Lighthouse, where there was evidence that the place had been used for storage. They took the stand off another mirror (we found a mirror there without a stand) and this extra weight, plus a terrific thunderstorm led to the crash.

"Lightning probably gave the pilots a temporary blindness so they took off badly – the weight of the load pushing them to one side and sinking the shuttle. Everything must have happened very quickly. Those who were injured drowned. The mirror fell on two of the men – they drowned. The woman was found in the escape hatch but it was half-buried in sand. We think she was alive and tried to go out though the main door and, in doing so, let more water in. She then went to the escape hatch – where she died."

Medrix looked at Filton and said quietly: "Our prisoner was telling the truth. It wasn't her."

Filton nodded. "Are you sure, Captain, that there wasn't another woman on board?"

He shook his head. "She got off at Hunter's Mill – but, there's something more, Controller. I want to show you something else."

They followed him into a kind of workshop where the mirror was leaning against a bench, the stand nearby.

"Look, Controller – you can see that they don't match. But that is not the *important* factor – the mirror is."

"Is what?" Filton asked.

"Is *important*! Look at it! You can see it has ornate carving on all corners and writing on the glass top of the mirror. It says: *Happy Name Day, Medrix.*"

Medrix looked surprised. "Name Day!"

"Yes. Someone knew when you celebrate it."

"But I don't," he shook his head. "In my family we celebrate our birthdays not our name days. My grandfather was from Earth and kept the old traditions. When we were little, my grandmother would sing a song. Umm …

> *Happy birthday to you, happy birthday to you*
> *Happy birthday, dear Medrix,*
> *Happy birthday to you ..."*

he sang clearly for all to hear.

"Ah," said the captain, that accounts for it."

"For what?"

"This mirror plays a tune."

"Really?"

"Yes. It plays the tune you've just sung. Let me show you." He pressed one of the carved flowers and the writing lit up and the birthday tune started.

"I can't understand it. No one here knows it."

"Perhaps, Controller, someone was planning a party for you," Filton said with a laugh.

"Maybe. "The captain went on: "I want you to look at the back." He pressed a concealed button in the lower corner. The back slid off, showing a square box-shaped cage.

"What is it?" Medrix was puzzled.

"A place for an explosive device," the captain told him.

"Surely not."

"Yes, Controller: somebody meant you harm. Anyone standing near it – say you – the Chief Elder – anyone – would surely be killed or injured. I have seen something like it before and the damage it can do."

Medrix was shocked. There had been no threats on his life before – on other people's, yes – but not on his. He felt shaken, betrayed almost. Who could one trust? Who indeed?

Medrix and Filton didn't stay any longer but went back to base. On the way Filton told Medrix about the prisoner and what he'd found and said that this must be all to do with her. She had contacts from outside the base. She was sending messages out of the base and they were acting on it, hence the code book.

Medrix shook his head. "I don't think so, Filton."

"I know she looks like your wife, Controller, but she can be made to look like that. After all, you were made to look like Fador's twin – if you remember – you were a spy – so why not her?"

"Because she told us the truth, Filton and we didn't believe her – why would she tell us the truth then? I have been very remiss. I have misjudged her. I have been more aggressive with her because she looks like my wife. I have been like the Chetner Elders – like the Elders' man I was – no wonder someone wanted to kill me."

"I don't agree. Anyway, once we get back, I'll prove it to you."

As soon as they arrived back at base, they were told that the woman prisoner had escaped and Lawmaker Thelka had sent out search parties. So far there was no sign of her.

"There," said Filton, "I told you so – she's running scared because she knows I have seen through her little schemes."

"Or she's run away because nobody would believe her when she was telling the truth," Medrix replied sarcastically.

"We'll see who's right," Filton said as he left for his quarters.

Chapter 18

Medrix spent a long time talking to Thelka.

He learnt how she had escaped and how Thelka had sent out search parties but all to no avail. She had just vanished.

Where had they searched? Medrix thought, when Thelka left him alone in his office.

Everywhere, it seemed. She must still have the chains on and that, surely, would be a handicap. He went over the points again:

1. She had chains on.
2. She had run down a corridor leading to various offices and cupboards, all of which had been searched.
3. They had found the exit doors open and had searched outside the base and extended the search along the beach and sand hills.
4. They were still looking.
5. If she did not go outside, what was the alternative? If it had been he, what would he have done?
6. He would have gone for the space dock because the way in was very near there. Had she planned it to lead them astray? Whilst everyone was looking elsewhere, had she calmly got on a freighter or shuttle and got far away by now?
7. But how far?

He checked the control tower. Two freighters had gone out: one for Listra at the hour of 16, the other to Kestra at the hour of 11.

It would have to have been the earlier one. It carried waste to the planet Volta where it was recycled and brought back to be used again. Of course she would not know what kind of freighter she was on.

He had messages sent to both captains telling them about her and asking that they check their holds.

The Listran freighter's message came back first: she was not on their craft.

There was no answer from the second freighter and Medrix told his staff to keep trying.

Messages came in from Temra that their government was sending three large shuttles, plus six of their best pilots, as a goodwill present for Chetner in their time of trouble and Medrix had a message of thanks sent to them at once.

He got Conn to arrange for the pilots' accommodation and informed the control tower of the shuttles' arrival.

All in all it had been a dreadful time and he was exhausted. He went and had a shower and then lay on the bed for a while.

He awoke much later feeling more refreshed, but soon all the day's incidents came back to him and the realisation that someone had tried to kill him, hit him harder now than it had done at the time.

But he did nothing about it. He could have bodyguards of course, but whom could he trust? He wrote a report of the events of the last few days.

A few hours later a message came through from the Kestran freighter: there was no stowaway on board.

Unless they were lying, of course, he had no idea where she was. The cunning little fox had disappeared completely – unless she was still on the base. He shook his head: if she was she would need to eat and, sooner or later, they would catch her. In the meantime he would read her statement and investigate the folder and code book.

He tried to contact Filton about handing them over to him, only to be told by a Law Officer that the said Lawmaker had left the base.

Surprised, Medrix asked the reason for this sudden departure and was told that a lookout boy had been arrested and Filton had gone to bring him back to the base. He would be gone for at least four days as he had some way to travel.

"Damn!" said Medrix out loud, "nothing but delays … but then … maybe this lookout boy would confess in exchange for protection." So it was with a lighter heart that he went to the dining centre to get some food.

After he had read the statement he had a good laugh. The prisoner was a cunning little fox: she had made it all up, he was sure of that … yet … He would send out the new pilots to check the bases. He knew – he was sure – that she had just picked them out at random. But he had to have proof about that before he saw her next.

Now Santel was another matter. He was sure she was involved with Elta and would know what she was about. If Santel was in some plot which also involved the prisoner and maybe Kenton … Medrix shook his head. Kenton had been one of his best pilots: he had known the family for years. He had attended the same college as himself but, at the age of eighteen, had trained as a pilot … Kenton was never an Elders' man … so why would he betray him?

Maybe he was meeting a Cordonian girl! They were beautiful, he knew that … that would be why he was secretly crossing the border … yes … that had to be it ... but he had thought that Santel was also interested in Kenton. He remembered seeing them huddled together ... but that did not mean he was interested in her ... ... unless they were planning to bring the girl over the border! But then the Grand Elder would never allow such a marriage to take place.

Medrix sighed: the whole thing was giving him a headache, so when he heard that the *Red Dragon* spacecraft had arrived, he was delighted. He went to meet the ship's crew and spent the next few hours in their company and, for a little while, was able to forget all his troubles.

Cessie woke up with a jolt. The freighter had stopped and the hold door was open. She got up quickly and went and looked out. There were containers waiting to be loaded but there was no one around. She went down the steps onto the platform and ran over to an archway and watched from there. She was only just in time, for she heard the tramp of marching men coming her way. She went back into the shadows of the archway and watched, fearfully.

A line of soldiers dressed in orange and black marched past her and disappeared from view. Where was she? The soldiers did not look friendly and, somehow, she knew that she could not ask for asylum here.

She was just about to go back to the freighter when the door closed and it moved slowly away and was swallowed up in the darkness of the night. Then she heard voices, angry voices. Were they coming to get her?

Suddenly she felt a hand come over her mouth and someone whispered in her ear: "Don't move. Keep quiet."

She struggled but could not get free.

The voices faded and she turned as the grip on her face loosened. She saw a man gesturing to her to keep quiet. He held her arm and motioned that she was to follow him.

The passageway was dark and she could just about see him but he seemed to know the way. They came out onto a platform. He did not stop but led her down some steps. It was lighter here and she could feel the cold whip of the wind as it slashed at her face.

On her left was a high wall and, on the right, a handrail that guarded a sheer drop to the ground below. They stayed close to the wall. They came to another platform but again did not stop and went down more steps. There seemed to be endless platforms and steps but, at last, they came to a flat path. The man turned right and whispered to her to keep quiet.

They went over a wooden bridge and deep into a dark wood. Looking back, she saw the lights of the building which seemed to be in the sky, but then ... freighter docks were in space, weren't they.

Eventually the man motioned her to stop and he went into a dark cave. She was loath to follow him – for all she knew, he abducted females to rape and kill them. She had heard such stories before. He pressed something and a door slid back and he said: "Come in here. It's warmer and dry, too and you must be tired and hungry." He smiled and gently led her in.

She had seen him before. "You are the man who rescued me that time I was trapped by Law Officers!"

He nodded and smiled. "I wondered if you would know me. I am sorry if I frightened you."

He was dressed as a huntsman and the whole place reflected that. Skins spread over the floor and draped on the walls made the place look cosy.

"First, I'll remove your chains." He brought down a box from a concealed shelf. It was full of keys. He found one that fitted her chains and released her. "I bet that feels better!"

She rubbed her wrists and he handed her a mug of steaming hot coffee.

"Now, tell me – how did you know I was coming? You were waiting for me, weren't you?"

"I can tune in on messages sent from all over the place. I heard the Controller checking the freighter captains and I guessed you would get out here."

"So, he knows I am here?"

"No. He did not know it stopped here so, by the time he got through to them, you had already left."

"So … they reported that I was not there. But didn't they tell him they stopped at other places, too?"

"No. There would have been papers to fill out and they wouldn't want that." He handed her a plate of hot stew and some bread and cheese. She sat on the floor to eat it.

"He will think you are still on Chetner, hiding somewhere in the base, and that's why you have to go back!"

"No way! Go back there! Why would want me to do that? Who are you, really?"

"I am an agent for the Chief Elder."

"What! You are working against him?"

"No. For him. Rumours are rife on all Lawmaker planets and elsewhere that Medrix has killed his wife. He planted a bomb on board the freighter she travelled on. The accident was to happen over the sea but things went wrong during a thunderstorm. It had the same effect, but left the bomb in place … therefore left clues as to who put it there … he is also responsible for all other explosions and catastrophes that have happened so far …"

"But why?"

"Revenge … against Chetner … against his wife … he swore blind when he left Chetner that he would return and, when he did, they would all know why …"

She shook her head in disbelief. This could not be true.

The man went on: "You see, he would never have got the job without marrying her."

"But …"

"The trial, you see, had to show that he loved her … what better way to get her love … he was already secretly betrothed to Lawmother Jessanda. She has already been to visit him on the base."

Ces felt numb with shock. It couldn't be true, could it?

"The raiders are all a part of it," he went on, "when he went to the crash scene he did not seem at all surprised that the mirror was supposed to explode at his name day party but he slipped up by putting the word 'birthday' on it with a birthday song which no one else knew but his family. He has already removed one councillor from the scene. She is dead …"

"Dead?"

"Killed in the crash … did he tell you that there was another woman on board? No, I can see by your face that he did not."

"Oh! But he couldn't – for I was here …"

"Of course … my mistake … but you have to go back … and prove it."

"Huh! If *you* can't prove it, how do you expect *me* to do so?"

"He's attracted to you … you are like his wife. You are a woman – surely you know how to attract a man … worm your way into his bed … then he will talk. Be there for him all the time. You are a Chetnerite – they have great charm, even now I feel it … if you weren't in this situation I would offer for you. But you have to prove it either way. Let me tell you another thing. The Chief Elder did not appoint him to be Controller, he arranged that himself. Believe me – according to all this evidence he is evil personified by his very actions …"

"But what if I proved him innocent. What then?"

"Then we would have to look elsewhere for the culprit."

"By then, it might be too late …"

"Quite! Now I will put you on a freighter going back to the base. It arrives at night and no one will be expecting you. Go back the way you came out. The stairs that go past the Lawmakers rooms lead to the attics – these are not covered by security watchers – make one your base. Make your presence known by raids on the food cupboard then he will know you are there, somewhere. Make sure he finds you … it will seem as if you have been careless … you will leave messages in the women's washrooms. Don't worry – they will get to me … us … Now lie down and rest, for tonight you will leave this place."

"Where is this place?"

"Cordonia. Not a safe place to be at all. I am going out now but will be back in time to put you on the freighter," he said, and left.

Cessie sighed. Her memory was coming back and she knew without doubt that the Controller was innocent because she also knew that she was his wife but they did not know that and must not know. She would be safer on the base than here. She must rest now. But first, she looked around the place. In one of the cupboards she found a picture. It was of a group of men, the man who had brought her here was one of them and so was Medrix, and the others were the Elders of Chetner. He had hidden it – but why? On the back was written *Haldean with friends*. If his friends were the Elders of Chetner, could that mean that those same Elders were the ones who wanted revenge against Medrix for what he had done to them? Just how good a friend was Haldean to the Chief Elder? She had to trust him for now, in order to get back safely. She put the picture back, unaware that her actions were being watched.

That night she returned to Chetner and found her way to her hiding place without any trouble at all. Let's hope, she thought, everything would be as easy as that.

Chapter 19

It was three days later that Medrix had a complaint from the cook. Someone had been taking food without signing the book for it. She was very angry because she had to order the correct amounts every quarter and now she would run short and would have to make do with just the basics. Medrix said he would look into it.

Three days later she was back again with complaints that, this time, the fruit and vegetable packs had been opened and some cooking utensils had disappeared.

Medrix had made inquiries but no one could help. He knew now for sure that the prisoner was on the base somewhere – that little fox was helping herself and laughing at them all. Well, she would soon know that he would have her in his hands again. Her days of running free were over. He sent the guards to search everywhere, but to no avail. He sent them again and they still drew a blank. So, where was she?

Celisia had found a good hiding place – an enormous stock room. It had every kind of tool that was needed on a base like this. Lines of shelves, stocked high with goods. Against one wall were the board tops of trestle tables. She found that she could get behind them and hide there and she did so when the guards came looking for her.

She came out when she thought she was safe, only to hear them coming back. She pushed herself further in, under the boards and leant against the wall, hardly daring to breathe as they came nearer and moved one board away. Soon she would be discovered.

She moved slightly and a panel in the wall slid back and she fell into a hole. The panel slid back again and she was in darkness. She could hear the guards so she lay still as they moved the boards to one side and, not finding her, put them back into place. She heard them move away and then there was silence.

She stood up and a light came on and another panel opened and she stepped through the opening into a corridor. It ran along one side of a room but it was boarded off from the main room. As she moved along it, the light went out, but she could see as there were small windows all along the wall on one side. She came to double doors and they opened as she approached.

She found herself in furnished rooms. In fact there was all she needed to live quite comfortably once it had been cleaned up. There was even a computer, but she did not dare use it – she still had to be careful.. She did not think anyone else knew about this place, otherwise the searchers would have found her easily.

She explored at night and found a cupboard full of clothes and soon had some of them for herself. A nurse's uniform, a cleaner's and a Lawmother's outfit.

Now, she became more daring and went out during the day. Sometimes she was a cleaner or a nurse; sometimes a Lawmother. She listened at doors and overheard the Lawmakers talking. She left messages in the right places. Usually something quite simple, like: 'Everything going to plan.' She picked up messages from them, such as 'When are you going to declare yourself to the Controller?" But she always answered that she could find out more if she were free.

She was quite sure that even they did not know where she was hidden – at least she hoped so.

Then, Law Officer Filton came back with some news that made it more vital that she was found and found soon, so another search was carried out but, yet again, all to no avail but she had heard about the news and she wondered what it was so, dressed as a Lawmother, she carried a pile of towels to Medrix' rooms and actually went in while he was writing. He saw her with the towels and told her to go into his washroom to change them, which she did.

When she came out of the room with an arm full of dirty towels, he was telling Lawmaker Thelka that he was to go out with his team to the Hunter's Mill to rebuild it as it would be a place of historic interest in the days to come, when Chetner was restored again. Thelka did not seem very pleased.

Cessie hurried out and down the corridor and went into a washroom. Luckily no one was about. Quickly she wrote a message regarding the mill and put it in behind a loose tile then, still carrying the towels, she made her way back to her hiding place.

At least she had something to tell Haldean and it could not harm anyone, or so she thought.

Three days later she heard that the mill had been blown up and the surrounding woods were on fire. She was so upset that she stayed hidden for four days but then had to come out for food.

She put on the cleaner's outfit and went everywhere with her polisher. Rumours were rife: somebody was killed or he was injured, and the more she heard, the guiltier she felt. She left a message in the washroom that said she was not going to pass messages if they were going to blow up things. Later she found a piece of paper in another washroom which said: 'It wasn't us'. But she did not believe them. Luckily Thelka and his team had not set out for the mill and now they stayed in the base talking amongst themselves.

Another message said that she should give herself up, but she was not ready for that yet. If it wasn't them, then could it have been the Controller? She shook her head: that was not true; she would not believe it.

One morning, as she was carrying towels, she was stopped by a Lawmother who was to give coffee to the Lawmakers. Her helper was ill and, as she could not manage on her own, she asked Cessie if she could help her. Cessie agreed and found herself wheeling the trolley into a large room where all the team leaders sat. The Controller sat on a raised platform with Law Officer Filton.

Cessie kept her face averted from them and wheeled the trolley around the room, passing coffee or chen to each man or woman. She had to carry the cups up to the platform where Medrix sat. Her hand shook, spilling some of the coffee into the saucer. She mumbled an apology, whilst keeping her head bowed. Medrix was just about to say something when the other woman entered, carrying plates of biscuits and he got up from his seat and went over to her and then went out of the room.

Cessie was sure he was calling the guard. This was the end of her freedom! But he came back in carrying a tin of biscuits and told them both they could go.

They left the room. There were no guards waiting for her and she sighed with relief.

Later, as she sat in her hideout, she went over what she had heard in the room. They had been talking about new plans for starting the reclamation work where the floods had been.

Should she leave a message about it?

She decided against it but wrote out a message which said: 'In two days' time some Lawmakers were going over to the central island to survey it.'

Satisfied, she left the message in one of the washrooms. Of course, she had made it up. Would Haldean and his followers react in any way?

Nothing happened. She could breathe calmly now. But a fisherman who came to the base two days later reported that the fish had died in the pools. He thought the water had been poisoned. She had her proof! What was she to do now? Her life could be in danger!

She went to a washroom to leave a message to say that everything was going to plan.

Later, she returned to see if there was a reply. She was standing near the washbasin washing her hands, when she felt a hand on her shoulder and a guard said: "Got you."

"What? Got what?" she said in surprise.

"You are sending messages out."

"No. Of course not," she replied, forgetting that she was supposed to give herself up.

He leaned over and pushed the tile. Was the message there?

He drew out a piece of paper and read: 'Meet me outside the exit doors. I will bring the wine and food and I will show you how a Lawmaker makes love. Signed … Sevden."

She laughed and said: "Is it for you?"

He hurriedly put the note back, closed the tile and, with a very red face, went out of the washroom.

Cessie went back to her hideout. As she changed into her night clothes, a piece of paper fell out of her pocket. There was writing on it. It said: 'Put all messages in Lat number 16 on the camp site.'

Who had given it to her? Was it the guard or someone she had passed in the corridor?

She had had enough of her own company. Soon, she must be arrested … but not just yet.

Over the next few days she wandered around, dressed as a Chetnerite. Some Lawmakers told her to go on the camp site, which she did most days.

Cessie saw Santel talking to a Lawmaker and, so that she could listen to what she was saying, became interested in someone who was weaving outside his shelter, but Santel was only enquiring about the injured Law Officer and Cessie left there and mingled with the people who were going into a large tent. She saw the Controller coming towards her and he seemed to be looking straight at her. She turned to go back the other way, only to see Law Officer Filton coming behind her. She was trapped. Then, suddenly, there was a great cheer as someone came out of the tent with a baby. The woman held the baby up high and Medrix took it from her and then they all went into the tent, so Cessie went in as well.

This was a special naming day for a baby and evidently the Controller was invited to take part. Cessie lifted a small child up to see what was going on. She had seen the ceremony before but never tired of it.

The woman said: "Controller, Lawmaker Medrix, I give you my baby on this day."

He replied: "I take your new-born son and accept that my name be given to him."

Another man stepped forward and said: "I accept that the baby should also be given my name."

The baby was passed to him.

At that moment, Medrix looked across the tent and saw Cessie. He started visibly, and made to go to her, but the baby's mother gave the baby back to him.

He said: "I name this child Jon Medrix Elington."

He then gave the mother a fine gold chain which she fastened around the baby's neck.

Wine was then served and all kinds of festive fare: by the time Medrix was free to find her, she had gone.

He wondered if it was Leah or his wife – or maybe it was his imagination …

The crowd drew him back into the tent to sample the special wine provided for these occasions.

Cessie had managed to get out without being caught and decided to go to Medrix' rooms but, first, she went back to her hideout and changed into a nurse's uniform.

There were no guards anywhere, which was strange, and she slipped into his rooms unnoticed. There was a small sleep room beyond his and she waited there. It got dark and she was tired and lay on the bed and slept.

She woke up suddenly. He was returning. There were two Lawmakers with him and Medrix was leaning on them. She could see them through the open doorway. She stood well back.

They brought him in and dumped him on his bed where he laid, his face red and bloated with drink.

The two men laughed and one said: "He'll have a bad head tomorrow. You watch him, Karn while I look for his keys."

Cessie moved silently into the room and said to the startled men; "Thank you. I'll see to him now. I will tell him who brought him back; he will want to thank you I am sure. But you can go now."

They went as fast as they could and she turned to Medrix and said: "See, you need a woman to look after you …" But he never answered for he was fast asleep.

Medrix woke up at the hour of eight. He sat up and saw a cup of black coffee on his bedside table. "God … I have a bad head …" he sipped the coffee. It was hot.

He wondered who had put it there.

He couldn't remember a thing after the third glass of wine. It must have been strong stuff, he thought. He got up but then sat on the side of the bed. Did he have to get up this morning? O God, he had a meeting with the cleaners at ten.

He stood up and walked shakily to the washroom and had a shower. That woke him up a bit. He came back into the room and realised that clean clothes had been put on the chair for him and a different pair of boots were standing neatly near them. He was sure that he had not put them there. But then, he could not even remember coming back last night. He groaned … O hell! Had someone brought him back? Lawmakers, perhaps? But they wouldn't put out clean clothes … a woman? O hell! No. Had anyone else seen her? No. a woman … couldn't … He finished the rest of the coffee.

He heard someone in his kitchen and went to see who it was. It was a helper from the main kitchen. She was setting down a tray of food: scrambled egg and toast and more coffee.

"I didn't order that," he shook his aching head. The last thing he wanted was food.

"She ordered for you ... said it would settle your stomach."

"She? Who did you say?"

"Why, the nurse of course ..."

"What nurse?" his tongue felt thick like his brain.

She laughed. "The one that was waiting for you last night ... according to the guards she was here all night ... she told them that you ..." she hesitated.

"What did she tell them? Out with it!"

"Well, she said that you were good in bed, just as she had heard you were ..." her voice faded when she saw his face, "... that's what they said. I shouldn't have told you ... I'm sorry." She turned and ran out of the room.

Medrix sat down at the table. He knew there had been a rumour and, up to now, he had laughed at it ... but now it was no laughing matter. He was the Controller ... there were rules about these things and he had broken them all ... well, he could not punish himself ... He smiled. Did I enjoy it? It was a pity he could not remember anything, but then, it wouldn't have happened if he had been sober. But, she was right; he must try and eat something.

When he was ready to go to the meeting, he could not find his keys. He searched everywhere, even the other room. Under the bed there was a sheet of paper, it must have fallen there, he thought. He read: 'In my sock in bed'. He went to his bed and pulled everything off it and found his keys in a sock – a woman's sock – there was a note with it. He read: 'Luckily for you they did not open the safe'.

He went to the meeting with a blinding headache and how he got through it he did not know. Afterwards he met Law Officer Filton, who smiled at him and said: "Had a good night last night? ..."

"Don't even go there, Filton ..."

"Well, as far as I can see, a man needs some enjoyment in a place like this, and why not you? You will find that you will be more relaxed."

"Shut up, Filton. I was drunk – how drunk I don't know – but I do not want to hear about it any more. If the Chief Elder hears about it I will probably be removed from here."

"Maybe, Controller, that's what it is all about ... you were the only one who got drunk ... perhaps your drink was tampered with ... but I know the Chief Elder, he will listen to me and not move you on just yet ..." he laughed.

"I hope you are right, Filton. I'm going back to bed." But he didn't, for word came in that the escaped prisoner had been caught trying to steal bread from the food cupboard. She was being been held there until he came.

She was dressed in Chetnerite clothes and still held the bag of bread in her arms. He could not understand why she was dressed like that ... anyone would know that a Chetnerite wasn't allowed in the main base – not without a permit. It looked as if she wanted to be captured ... and bad head or no, he knew he was right.

She was taken to a holding cell to await interrogation ... but not today, he thought. Tomorrow would do just as well. Let her sweat till then … but he had the feeling that she was very pleased with the situation.

Tomorrow you won't be! Tomorrow, when my head's better, you will know what a bastard I really am.

Chapter 20

The following morning after a shower, a change of clothes and some breakfast, Ces was taken to the interrogating room. The guards pushed her into the room and left her, closing the door behind them. The Controller was not there. He had an important meeting with the Cordonian Ambassador.

Three men sat together on one side of the table that divided her from them. One was taking notes; the others had folders in front of them and they were talking in soft tones to each other.

Ces did not know them and stood there, waiting for them to acknowledge her.

She moved her arms upward and her chains rattled. One of the men nodded his head and smiled. He had blue eyes and brown hair, unusual in a Lawmaker. He was not bad looking. He spoke in low tones so that she had to lean forward to hear him.

He spoke louder: "I am Lawmaker Caston. This is Lawmaker Burton on my left and Lawmaker Gorton on my right. There is a chair behind you, please sit on it."

Ces did so.

Lawmaker Burton got up from his chair and came over to her. He bent down and put another chain around her middle and fixed it to the chair. They were taking no chances. He grunted something and returned to his seat. He was dressed in black and he had black eyes. Lawmaker Gorton had red hair and his eyes were green. Just like a cat, thought Ces.

She waited.

Lawmaker Caston looked at his notes and began to speak: "You are not a lookout boy for the raiders. One of those has been captured and he has said that there are no girls in the organisation. You were mistaken for a boy by the raiders and by us. You were in Top Gost Point. A member of the Cords ..."

"Excuse me what are Cords? I have never heard of them," said Cessie indignantly.

"They are roaming thieves. You and others have been robbing the Cordonians and us ..."

304

"Rubbish! You are making it all up ..."

"Quiet please! You will not interrupt me."

Ces shrugged her shoulders and her chains rattled.

Caston went on: "... you escaped from Top Gost Point, as did a member of the raiders. In your possession were articles belonging to the Controller's wife. You did, in fact, rescue a Lawmaker and his men, and the Controller took this into account when he reviewed your case.

"You did, in fact, travel on the stricken shuttle but you got off at Hunter's Mill ..."

"So you realise I was telling the truth ..."

"Be quiet! I won't tell you again." Caston did not look so good-looking now, she thought. Quite the opposite in fact.

"You stole from stores, houses and various other places: you resisted arrest on more than one occasion: you even attacked the Controller himself ..."

"You lie ... me? Attack him! He wouldn't allow that ..."

One of the Lawmakers jumped the table and pushed her chair back towards the wall and slapped her hard across the face and she cried out in shock.

He returned to his seat and one of them said: "That's what you get when you don't keep quiet."

Ces stared at her hands as tears ran down her face.

Caston went on: "You were on the shuttle and were struggling, seemingly to get off it."

"... Oh! That! It was a flashback, I ..." she saw his face and said no more.

"... You had to be sedated for the rest of the journey."

"While in prison you stole things from the various stores and then tricked the guards and ran away. You stayed on the base though, but were passing messages to someone or other. You also flitted about the base in various disguises until at last you were caught stealing food from the kitchens.

"It's proved without doubt that you are a thief, even staying in some houses pretending they were yours and taking on their names. At some point you stole Sevden's wallet. You are also guilty of spying."

Lawmaker Gorton stood up and announced: "You have been given a sentence of twenty years imprisonment to be served both here and, when we leave here, in the House of Correction in Estina."

"No!" she shouted. "No! No! No! You cannot do that ... I ..."

"Shut up!" the Lawmakers said.

"No – I won't. I am not guilty. We are in a disaster area ... our law says we may help ourselves to essential things ... I am a Lawmaker's wife. I claim my rights ..."

"You have no rights," blue eyes said, looking at her sternly.

"Of course I have ... Oh, I know what it is ... it's the Controller ... he really is out for revenge. That's what it is. My Lawmother warned me. She said this would happen but ... I stood up for him ... I did ..." She lowered her voice. "I stood up for him: he's out for revenge." She tried to stand but the chains held her down and she screamed: "Oh! my poor Chetner, you are doomed. He betrayed the Elders and now he will betray us …" She suddenly whispered: " … and you … you Lawmakers will see it too … but it will be too late even for you …"

They stared at her. Was she mad? No one shouted down the Controller.

She spoke again … "He warned me – he said it was true …"

"Who said?" Gorton asked.

"The Chief Elder's agent – he warned me that the Controller was out to destroy Chetner by fair means or foul … he said so."

"What agent? Where did you see him?"

"When I ran away, I got on an out-going freighter … I … I …"

"Go on."

"I got off at Cordonia. I didn't know it stopped there, I thought it was going to Kestra. He knew I was coming when I did not know myself. He said the Controller was out to ruin us all. He wanted me to prove it by sending messages to him, but I knew nothing and made up the messages because I thought the Controller was innocent. What a fool I am … my love for him blinded me to his imperfections. He said he loved me and I believed him … I did," she sobbed … "I believed him."

Gorton spoke kindly: "I am the Chief Elder's man … tell me the agent's name … you must. We have no agents there … I promise you it's true."

She told them everything – but not who she was.

Gorton said: "His name is Haldean … isn't it?"

She nodded.

"He is a double agent for Cordonia and Zendra. We have known for some time. He is also the chief negotiator for their ruler who is trying to get us to repair Top Gost Point and is holding the Controller's father and his work team as hostages. I can assure you that the Controller would never betray us or Chetner. He loved his wife very much and it is for her he stays here. He saw her die on that freighter but he still looks at every group that comes in, hoping against hope that she is there."

"I did not die on that freighter," she said slowly. "I was thrown clear through the side door. We weren't very high you see. There were blankets in the hold and as I was drawn outside, they wrapped around me and saved me … something hit me on the head and I knew no more. When I woke up I was in Cordonia." She pulled the strings of her bonnet and it slipped over her shoulders to reveal her fair hair. My memory has been very bad but it is coming back slowly. I have kept a memory journal to help me. That was what was in my folder and nothing else. I think that the Lawmaker planted the notebook. You see I recognised him as one of the people who mistook me for the lookout and he, of course, knew it. I wouldn't trust him at all."

Gorton undid the chains. "You will go back to the prison and we will discuss this with the Controller and you will be called back to hear the result."

The guards collected her and she was taken to the prison and locked in her cell. Now all she had to do was wait. Would the Controller believe her story or would he dismiss it all as rubbish. His answer would tell her what she wanted to know. Was he true to her and Chetner or not!

The next day Cessie was taken to the Controller's rooms. He sat on the long seat, his long legs stretched out along it. He did not get up when he saw her but told her to sit on the nearest chair. She sat down and the chains rattled as she did so.

"Well," he said, stiffly, "what's this new story you have to tell me?"

She knew he did not believe her. It wouldn't make any difference to her sentence. He was what he was.

"Well? ..." he said more gently, "you saw Haldean?"

"Yes, he gave me a message for you."

"Well, what is it?" he stretched his arms out and swung his legs down onto the floor so that now he was facing her.

"He said that he owed you a debt and it was now paid. He also said that he was glad that you had taken his advice about the golden-haired girl. I don't know what he meant."

"Don't you?"

"No."

"I once saved his life. He fell in the river and hit his head on a rock. I got him out and nursed him until he was better. We were in Cordonia at the time. I was out of bounds there and that could have broken my cover as a spy and I would have been recalled. The golden girl was you."

"Me?"

"Yes. You see, he asked me if I had a girlfriend and I said I hadn't. I did say I fancied one of the Chetnerites but she was too young for me. He asked why I fancied her and I said she has beautiful golden hair. Of course he did not realise that I lived on another planet but he knows now, doesn't he?"

"He was talking about me?"

"Yes, it would seem so."

"But why ...?"

"He must have recognised you or thought you looked like her and so sent you back to me."

"I saw a picture of him, the Elders and you and it said on the back : 'Me with my friends'. How did that come about?"

"Later when I got back to Estolan the Elders wanted someone to check our rivers and I recommended him, so he came over. He was a Water Bailiff then, of course, and that's when we had the picture taken. Of course he could have held you there as another hostage, but I am glad he did not. As for Law Officer Filton, you are mistaken there, because at the time when you were on that shuttle – both times, in fact – he was with me. I have known him and his family for years and would trust him with my life. But we shall look for a look-alike to be sure – and now, my love, I think I'll take off your chains."

He took a key out of his pocket and bent forward and released her, then kissed her very gently and said: "Welcome. I have waited so long for this moment." And he kissed her again.

Someone knocked on the door and walked straight in. It was Law Officer Filton. He saw Medrix and Ces kissing and said: "At last you've got together; now we can fool the raiders ..."

"Go away, Filton, can't you see we are busy?"

"Yes, of course I can ... but ... they want to get to you – they want her to seduce you, so that she can give them details of your plans."

"So?"

Cessie looked at them both. What was going on?

"They want to know – so let them think she is doing that ..."

"But, she's my wife ..."

"But they do not know that. She can sleep in your spare room, Controller, and send messages to them ..."

"I don't get this ..."

"I do, Medrix," said Cessie. "We can make up messages and this should trap them, but it would mean that I would still have to be a prisoner and only come to you at times."

"And this is what you want?"

"No ..."

"It's too dangerous, love ..."

"She would have guards."

"I'll think about it, Filton. But for now, leave me in peace whilst I make up for lost time."

Filton laughed. "Got you! Welcome back, Celisia." He left the room and although Medrix had said that he trusted him, she did not.

"Oh! Cessie, can you ever forgive me for being so blind? I really thought you were dead. I thought you were someone who looked like her. I have been annoyed with myself for falling in love with someone who looked like you. I seem to have broken all the rules regarding mourning and I was more aggressive with you because of it. It was the black hair that threw me ..."

"... And I had no memory of you, or anything else. If Santel hadn't told me who she was I would never have known. When I saw her here, I was afraid."

"She's never mentioned it, but I am having her watched. So far, nothing – she hasn't stepped out of line and, maybe, losing her companions has put a stop to her plans. And, after all, she did look after you – so she has that in her favour, but I have been such a mean bastard to you. I would quite understand if you wanted to leave me. I wouldn't want that because I love you very much, but I want to do the best thing for you."

"Medrix – I didn't know who I was. I was a person with no name, no home. A person who realised that you were in great danger – and yet – I did not know what the actual danger was. All I knew was that I had to get to the base to warn you – so that you would be prepared. I knew I was a Chetnerite and they were all coming to this base, so I was, too. But people seemed to think I was someone else and I knew I was in great danger. I dyed my hair and, in doing so, put myself in even more danger. At times, though, I felt very close to you ..."

"I did, too ... I felt it and didn't understand it." He put his arms around her, hugging her in close to him, kissing her again.

"Now that I know who I am – I also know that I don't want to be parted from you, now or ever."

"I'll see to that. You are not to be the bait to trap someone. I want you here, by my side, always. I want people to know you have been found as Lawmother Grey said you would be."

"She said that?"

"Yes – I think she knew." He kissed her again and she responded.

Lying there in the safety of his arms, she knew she had at last come home. For wherever he was, that was home and, without him, it was hell.

By the next day, everyone knew about Cessie and the congratulations poured in. New clothes were brought to her and she began to make Medrix' quarters more like a home where he could relax at night with her.

Medrix made sure she was well guarded for he knew she could still be in danger: too many people were involved. The jailer just thought that the prisoner had been released and sent home and that the Controller's wife had been found and was suffering from memory loss.

Medrix sent the little notebook to the Chief Elder to see if his men could break the code and so give away the person who wrote it or put it in the hiding place. He also had Filton watched – after all, it would be stupid not to take precautions, wouldn't it?

Chapter 21

The days passed quickly now that Cessie was back with Medrix. Everyone congratulated them and the days were full of sunshine and warmth. There were no days when things went wrong, even Santel smiled at her and went out of her way to be nice to her. Because of the warm weather, picnics were arranged for the children and the Chetnerite women. Celisia went along to help.

On other days when Medrix was elsewhere, she took her sketchbook and sketched various people in and around the base. Medrix was pleased that she showed such an interest in everyone and everything. But when he saw her sketching two of the guards (they went with her everywhere) and she was laughing and talking to them, he was angry. He marched straight over to them, telling the guards they were out of order and sending them in to report for extra duty and told Celisia to go in also. She looked at him in surprise and made no effort to move until he demanded in no uncertain manner that she do as he said.

She hesitated then shrugged her shoulders; after all she could hardly argue with him in front of everyone. She packed up her things and went back to their rooms.

Medrix was already there, waiting for her.

"You took your time," he said angrily.

"What's the matter?"

"You, sitting there with your skirts above your ankles: making a spectacle of yourself in front of the guards and other people."

"Medrix, don't be silly, I ..."

"Silly am I? People talk – you have a position to keep in this place or have you forgotten. Lawmaker Whitton has told me more than once that you are too free with the guards and other men around you."

"I see," she smiled, "you're jealous, aren't you?"

"No! Of course not! I am just telling you how other people see you, that's all."

"Right: I'll be more careful. Can I go now?"

"No – you stay here and don't move from here until I come back."

"Right – but don't be long, I want ..." but he'd already gone.

She waited in all day but he didn't come back and in the end she went to bed.

In the morning, she realised he had not come home. And there was still no message from him. When she tried to go out, the guards said that they had no fresh orders regarding her, so they couldn't let her through.

Now she was annoyed but what could she do about it? She was stuck here until he came back. She sighed: was this a reprisal by the guards because of her behaviour yesterday?

She had got them into trouble. They were now afraid to change his orders.

Her meals came in and the Lawmother who brought them said that Law Officer Filton and the Controller had gone to inspect the reclamation work being done where the land had been flooded by the sea.

Puzzled, Celisia couldn't understand why he hadn't changed his orders. She was just about to sit down and do some sewing when the door opened and Lawmaker Conn walked in.

"Am I glad to see you – the guards won't let me out."

Conn smiled: "I know – there's a reason of course ..."

It was then that she realised that he was not alone – the guards had come in too.

Conn said: "Now – what are you waiting for?"

"I'm waiting ..."

She got no further. One guard grabbed her by the shoulders. She screamed and kicked out at him. "Leave me alone." She managed to wriggle free and tried to run past him.

Chairs went over in the struggle.

"Conn, don't just stand there!" she yelled.

All he said was: "Hurry – someone will come – shut her up."

A pad of sweet-scented perfume was put roughly over her mouth and nose and although she tried to get away, she couldn't as her world turned to a dizzy darkness and she collapsed in a heap on the floor.

A Lawmother came in with a large laundry hamper which was on wheels. They put her inert body into it, covered her with towels and bedding and hurriedly wheeled her out into the corridor and along to the shuttle dock, where the laundry shuttle was waiting to go out. The two guards wheeled the hamper into the hold then quickly took her out of the hamper and carried her out of the shuttle, their movements being hidden by a huge pile of laundry baskets. They carried her to a smaller shuttle and stood watching as it took off carrying Cessie with it. Conn and the Lawmother returned to their duties as if nothing untoward had happened.

Thirty minutes later Lawmaker Thelka brought in the mail to the Controller's office and realised that something was wrong as there were no guards. The Controller's rooms were always guarded, night and day.

He walked through to the main rooms and saw the state of the furniture. It looked as if there had been a fight, for the two guards had been knocked out and lay groaning on the floor. And written across a mirror in dark crayon was: *"We have your wife. Be ready for our message so you'll know how to get her back."*

He was shocked. He left the rooms without touching anything and went straight to the Law Officers' room and reported it to the man on duty there. Then he arranged for the guards to be taken to the medical bay.

A message was sent out at once and Medrix and Filton returned to the base as quickly as possible. Filton went immediately to the Controller's room to see if any clues had been left around the place. Medrix was shocked. He had lost Celisia again.

He had Santel brought in for questioning. He soon realised that the guards were of no help in the state they were in.

"We tried to stave off four men but it was an unequal fight."

The doctor said that they were too shocked to add any more.

They were the same guards that Medrix had reprimanded yesterday. Had they acted out of revenge?

Couldn't have; surely not.

Was Celisia trying to get her own back?

No – of course not.

Someone had her. If that someone wanted something in return for her that meant she was alive and well – shocked, but alive.

His thoughts went round and round.

He called Conn to his office.

Conn came in wondering why the Controller wanted him.

"Conn, did you give Celisia my message that she was free to leave the rooms?"

"Of course, Controller, but she said she had some sewing to do and was quite happy to do it."

"Did you tell her where I had gone?"

"Of course I did."

"And was she happy with my news?"

"Not so much happy as resigned."

"I see – did you stay and talk to her?"

"No – I had some work to do, so I left her."

Medrix dismissed him. But something felt not right. How did they know that she was alone in the rooms? Of course – the guards knew.

He went to the interrogating room where Santel was waiting. Filton was already there.

Santel looked pale, but not frightened.

312

"I cannot think why you have called me in …"

Medrix stared at her coldly. "My wife has been kidnapped."

She stared at him in horror. "You think I've got something to do with it? I wouldn't hurt her."

Filton interrupted: "You say that now, but you and Elta and Kenton wanted to keep her as a hostage for something you wanted."

"Who says?"

"Celisia herself," Medrix said.

"She can't remember things – she's confused and in her confusion she's mixed things up."

"You found her after the crash and I am very thankful that you did for you nursed her back to health, but you also threatened her. Because of you she dyed her hair black and because of that I did not recognise her. I was all for bringing you in but she said that you had suffered enough in losing Elta. She's too kind-hearted and I was trying to please her – so, for God's sake, tell me what you know."

"I know nothing."

"You lie."

"No, Controller. I know nothing. Do you think I would have stayed here if I did?"

"No, I suppose not. But where else would you go?"

"Quite – there is nowhere else for me to go." She sighed.

"You did threaten her." Filton stated calmly.

"Kenton did – not I."

"Oh, let a dead man take the blame. He can't defend himself from the grave."

"I can't understand why Kenton got mixed up in this," Medrix said. "He was an excellent young pilot – of good family – everything to live for. I've known the family for years. He even volunteered to come here as many of our pilots did."

"Ah," she said sadly, "that was it, you see."

"What was?"

"He wanted to come back here."

"Wanted to come back? He was never here before," Filton interrupted.

"He was a Chetnerite …" Santel said with a smile.

"Rubbish, Santel!" Medrix said angrily.

She went on: "He was born in Chetner. His parents were Chetnerites – he was taken by the Lawmakers when he was very young and brought up by them. His Lawmaker father had two children of his own and he arranged for Kenton to be given to his sister who was childless, and he was brought up in Estolan by the sister and her husband. He never knew until he became friendly with Jadex and Fador. Fador, of course, is my brother and Jadex was brought up with Cessie. They told him that his real name was Jonn Linkton. From then on he decided to trace his birth mother. He became very bitter with his foster parents, even though they had treated him well and he lacked for nothing. Maybe they spoiled him. Maybe it was that." She sighed.

"But I still don't see the connection?" Medrix queried

"The Chetner council were negotiating with others to do the reclamation work.

"The Zendrians who had helped to build this Top Base offered to do the work on condition that they could use the base to store grain. They ship grain everywhere: the Lestrians wanted a part of Chetner as they were over-populated: the Cordonians offered on condition that they were paid 90,000 credos to be paid over a number of years.

"We thought the Zendrians would be the most likely ones to be accepted as they had built the base. Then we heard that Celisia had won her case – and the Lawmakers offered to do the work for nothing.

"The majority of the council voted for them but there were some of us who regarded it as an invasion by the Lawmakers and we had had years and years of their rules and regulations and certainly did not want them here again. And we certainly did not want *you*, Controller, back here spying on our every move.

"One of the favours asked for by Celisia at the Game was that the Chetner Lawmakers (Elders) should all go home and stay there, so we were very surprised when our council accepted them. Kenton and others said that if we could all band together we could still force the Lawmakers and you to go home.

"We just happened to find Celisia. She had no idea who she was but I recognised her at once and told Kenton. I said that she must be taken to the Top Base at once for she was very poorly, but he said that Top Gost Point was nearer and he had friends there who would look after her. He took us there and Elta and I lived there, nursing Cessie back to health. Elta and Kenton were very close and told me that the best way to get what we wanted was to hold her hostage. I didn't agree, but realised that I had to go along with the idea because I knew too much.

"Then the place blew up and I thought Cessie was dead. By this time Elta and I had arrived at the base. The men were seeing to your wife, and Kenton went over there to move her to a new place. Well, as you know, they were all killed – except Celisia of course but I thought she was dead and I blamed myself for not trying to contrive her escape. But I couldn't do anything, could I?"

"No," said the men, together.

"Then I saw her in the interview room but I thought it couldn't be her because you would have known at once, so I went along with it and said nothing – for all I knew, if she told you about me, my life wouldn't be safe.

"What they planned to do I don't know and they were all dead and their parents, whoever they were, were proud that they had died doing their duty.

"I had no idea Cessie was in any danger here. I wished her no harm and I saw how the Chetnerites took to you in your grief and otherwise. They even named their children after you. I realised you really did love her and that you were good for Chetner. I wish I could help – but I can't."

The two men seemed satisfied with her statement but held her in custody for the time being.

Conn met them coming away for the interrogation room and said: "Controller – you are wanted in the control tower. I think it's about your wife."

Medrix and Filton went there at once. The Lawmaker on duty there gave his seat to him and Filton stood beside him.

"On screen," Medrix commanded.

The big screen in front of him lit up brightly and, as the brightness cleared, they saw a man sitting at a desk. He was dark-haired, his hair worn in several long plaits around his head. His green eyes gleamed with anticipation as he realised they could see him. He was dressed in some kind of military outfit, crossed bands of leather encircled his chest and, as he nodded to someone in the background, he spread his long thin fingers across the desk.

"Controller," he said sternly. "I am Zanyeh Costoria, military leader of the Northern Territories of Zendra. We have your wife. She is quite safe and will be as long as you do what we ask."

"What do you want?" Medrix replied.

"We'll need proof," said Filton.

"Proof we have." The man held up Cessie's locket and opened it to show the light. Then he held up a lock of her hair and her wedding ring. "See, we have these things," he went on, not waiting for any comments. "Now it is quite simple really, you do what we want and she comes back to you."

"Get on with it," Medrix said, tight-lipped.

"I am; I am." The Zendrian stopped and looked at one of his long nails and smiled. "Now then, it's quite simple – you have documents in your safe which state quite clearly that if you should resign then you can hand the base over to anyone you name. Well, we want you to hand it over to a man of our choice. Quite simple really: that's all you have to do. Of course the man chosen by us works for us. All you will need to do after that is go home with your wife and take all the Lawmakers with you."

"It is not a simple as that. This is Chetnerite land. Their council voted for us to be here, not you."

"Of course – we know that, but the Chetner Elders promised us the use of the base if we helped them to build it."

"But you see, the Chetner Elders were out of order – they had no right to build anything."

"So you say – but that still does not alter the fact that we have your wife. Does it?"

"My documents have been updated. They now say that I have to give our Chief Elder one moon's notice of my pending resignation and then his committee will choose a Lawmaker to take my place. So if you tell me the name of the man I will certainly put your requirements to our Chief Elder."

"I see – it makes it more complicated but we cannot tell you who it is. But we will give you more time. Two moons should get it all worked out. Your wife will be quite safe with us I promise you. But after that she will be sent to our brothel camps where she will live out her life to the best of her ability. It won't be a long life I can assure you. But it is up to you. If by any chance your Chief Elder should not do as we ask, then our fighters will attack the base and take it by force."

"That will be war," Medrix interrupted him.

"Yes, Controller, you are quite right. It would be war and then ..." he raised his voice ... "we'll smash the Lawmakers' planets to pieces and put in our style of government and the name Lawmaker will fade from people's minds forever. Am I making myself clear?"

"Quite."

"Then I'll leave you to get on with it, *Controller*!"

The screen faded and Medrix, showing no emotion at all, said: "Come Filton, we will contact the Chief Elder at once."

But although he did not show his feelings, inside his mind was screaming in terror at what could happen to his wife and maybe all Lawmakers everywhere, for he knew that the Zendrians were a warlike people who took what they wanted.

Chapter 22

Over the next few days it was discovered that two shuttles had left the dock on the day Cessie had disappeared. Both carried laundry and both were going to Jadeston; one was larger than the other. The larger shuttle went out first. Both captains had been cleared for leaving by the control tower; the smaller of the two had received a laundry basket just before leaving.

According to the control tower records, three men and two women were the only people on board. The women were nurses going on leave. There was nothing out of the ordinary about that, nurses came and went every so often.

The large shuttle relayed a message back that they had run into a meteor storm but were weathering it and continuing on their way. In spite of the report, the small shuttle left the dock as it was deemed safe enough for them to do so. Later a message came through that this shuttle had been damaged in the storm and was landing on the nearest planet. Since then there had been no news.

The large shuttle was reported to have reached its destination without mishap.

Neither Medrix nor Filton knew which planet the smaller shuttle had landed on. According to the map there were six small planets in the area; two of them were close to Zendra. One of these was uninhabited, although it had been used as a space station at one time. It had been abandoned by the last research team stationed there because the weather was so bad. If Cessie had been taken there she was not likely to survive in such bad conditions and Medrix thought that the Zendrians would have taken her to a safer place rather than one that had no good reports on its condition.

"I'll go on checking it to see if we can come up with anything more definite," Filton said.

"No. Don't do that," Medrix said quickly.

"Why ever not?"

"Because they might get wind of it and move her."

"Does it matter?" Filton was annoyed – all that work wasted, did Medrix think he had nothing else to do?

"We must not make things worse."

"Anybody would think you did not want to find her."

"Rubbish! You know that's not true, Filton."

"I know no such thing. After all, the rumours could be true, for all I know."

"Rumours? What rumours?

"That you are seeking revenge on your wife and all Chetner."

"Of course I'm not," Medrix retorted angrily.

"Haldean could be right: you are out for revenge."

"If I was, she would have been in the House of Correction by now."

"You did not recognise her when you saw her and you did not come to the final sentencing meeting. In fact you gave the sentence without even letting her have her say."

"Why accuse me, Filton? You found a notebook in her cell and, if she had not run away, you would have got something out of her. I know you hit her."

"You allowed it."

"I was only following our rules, that's all … Anyway, she is my wife and … and …"

"… And you want to get rid of her … you have tried several times and failed. Will you fail this time I wonder?"

"Get out of here," shouted Medrix angrily. "I love my wife very much indeed, so don't you listen to tales of revenge. I love her … perhaps you don't know what true love is … it eats into you … you delight in doing small favours for her and you watch for her …"

"Like the attention you gave to Lawmother Jessanda when she came."

"Certainly not! Celisia said I shouldn't trust you. Now I think she was right."

"So you say … I did not trust her at first … look how she said her name was Leah Dickon … she remembered the name DICKON but she did not remember your name. She did not even know you …"

"She'd lost her memory, that's all. I think you had better go," Medrix said quietly, "before I do something silly."

"Rumour has it that she was married to that man Dickon before she married you. In fact, if the story is true, she was already married when she renewed her vows to you. Her Lawmother removed the marriage ring from her finger before her marriage to you. Not that she could be blamed for that marriage being that she was in a coma, but afterwards she did not declare it and let you believe that she had been single and free to marry you."

"It is rubbish and you know it …"

"Do I? So why did she remember that name?"

"Enough, Filton! You've said enough. Since when have you proved anything by using rumours?"

"Rumours can lead to facts, Controller," the Lawmaker stated firmly.

"You are wasting my time. My wife thinks you are the man on the shuttle."

"What man?"

"The man who was dressed in grey: one of the men who transported her to Hunter's Mill. She was sure of it and now I begin to think she was right. In fact, I think you should hand in your resignation to me as soon as possible. It's about time you went home."

"You forget, Controller, I have to give a moon's notice and I am sure the Chief Elder will not accept it."

"Do it anyway – or find this man Dickon to get the truth – to prove it is wrong."

"Right. I will do that ... I ..." The door opened and a medic came in.

"Excuse me bursting in like this, but one of the guards is dying and I think he wants to speak to you."

"I'm coming now." Medrix left the room quickly followed by the others.

Medrix sat by the bed. The man was whispering and Medrix bent low to hear him.

"The spray ... it did not suit me ... they said it would not hurt ... tell Conn," he coughed up blood. He went on: "Tell him I have failed ... the control ... is out of place ... tell Jessie I tried ..." His voice failed; his breathing suddenly changed and his eyes closed as he died.

Medrix stood up. "He was trying to tell me something but I don't quite know what it was."

He sent for two of the Chief Elder's men and told them to keep watch over the other guard.

"I think," Filton said quietly, "that the guards had something to do with the kidnapping and I think I am right."

Medrix was inclined to believe him. "When the other one is better, we'll question him."

They left the room together, their quarrel forgotten for the time being. Filton knew that the Controller was under a lot of strain and was probably sorry for the whole thing, as he was. He had just been testing if the rumours had any foundation in them at all; now he was not so sure.

A Chetnerite man and a small boy were waiting in his office.

"I am Ferkin Jade and this is my son, Frelin. I think he may have witnessed something important. Go on, Frelin, tell him what you saw."

The boy hesitated and then went on: "I know I will get punished for this, but I like your wife and ... and ..."

"Go on," Medrix urged him.

"My friend and I like to play dare games. He dared me to go into your office and bring out a notebook ... and I could not, not do it. I got as far as the cleaner's rooms when I heard the guards talking, saying that that went smoothly and all they had to do was to spray the stunning cream on so that they looked as if they had been attacked. They then did that and collapsed on the floor ... I did not wait ... I just ran for it ..."

Medrix said that he was a good boy for coming forward and he himself had played such a game when he was a boy. He was to tell no one for his own safety's sake, and he thanked him for coming forward. After he had gone, he put two of the Chief Elder's men on to guard the family. Medrix told Filton to arrest the other guard when he was fit enough to leave the medical bay.

Medrix then had Santel brought to his office. She seemed surprised: she thought he did not believe her statement, but he did not even mention it.

She was to co-opt five other people on to the council, as she and the others had an important job to do. They were to divide the Chetnerite camp into six parts and each part was to have a representative on the council. It was very important that, should war be declared, everyone in the Chetner camp was evacuated to safer places, such as other planets or countries and each section was to be packed and ready to go at a moment's notice.

"I have already contacted others to see if they can help," Medrix said.

"Others?" she said, "what do you mean?"

"Well, Temra can take 1,600 people; Estolan, 1,750 or maybe more; Jadeston has not yet replied, neither have Listra or Cordonia."

"Why can't we all go to the southern hills?"

"No way of getting supplies. The reclamation teams will meet there – they already have supplies."

"What about staying here?"

"Impossible. If the Zendrians come in with fighter birds (shuttles) - well, we have no weapons – we couldn't fight back and missiles have a habit of missing the targets – so, everyone must go."

"What about you and your staff?"

"I won't go. The Lawmakers will be given a chance to go home or to the Southern Hills – I have to stay here – some Lawmakers will stay – the medics will return to their homes."

"You have got it all worked out, Controller."

"Yes. Now you and the councillors have a job to do."

She turned away, then looked back and smiled. "You really do love these people, don't you?"

"Yes. I think I do." He half smiled, "but I love Celisia most of all."

"Good," she said, "that's all I wanted to know, except though, now that I come to think about it, what are you going to do about the animals?"

"Well, I have thought this over as well. Pets will go with their owners but each one will have to go into quarantine for four moons; the vets will see to that when people arrive at their destinations. This does not apply to horses and such like. All animals that can eat grass will be taken to places that are untouched by the troubles and there are such places where people are still living. In spite of our warnings, people have stayed in their homes and, indeed, they have had no troubles at all."

"Is the Green Settlement one of them?"

"Yes, I believe so … there are others." He spread out a map for her to see. "All this land from the foot of the Southern Hills through these places" - he pointed to various places along the coast – "seems to be in a safe place. I believe there is a boatyard still open at Calne Bay but how they can carry on I do not know. But all the farmers in those areas will be glad to have the animals but the correct documentation will be given as to who owns what."

"Calne Bay," she said thoughtfully. "I remember going there when I was first married."

"You're married? I didn't know. What happened to him?"

"He was a fisherman and he was drowned many years ago but he would often go to the boatyard for things for his boat. Come to think of it there were two brothers who owned it. I wonder if they are still there?"

"What were their names?"

"Dixon … yes that was their name … Dixon – or something like that."

Medrix looked at her. He felt sick and wanted to end this talk but he had to know if one of the brothers had been married to his wife. "Were they married?"

"I don't know. You see it was a long time ago. I never went there, I lived at the Green Settlement and got on with life as best as I could without my husband. He, of course, could have told you but that's not possible now. Is it important?"

Medrix shook his head and, folding up the map, put it away in the cupboard and said that he had to go to a meeting. She took the hint and left the room, smiling as she did so.

Medrix called Filton to his office and told him about the boatyard at Calne Bay. Filton was to go there at once and investigate. He quickly left, glad to get out of the base for a while and maybe he would find out the truth once and for all.

Ten days had passed since Medrix had spoken to the Zendrian leader and still no message from the Chief Elder.

He tried to keep himself busy but, at night, he tossed and turned and got very little sleep. There was no news from Filton either. He had sent out all the pilots to check the list of bases that Celisia had given. He also told them to pick up any people who were on their way to the base.

The guard was transferred from the medical bay to the prison so Medrix, plus a Law Officer, went to question him.

The man sat stiffly on a chair, a warder beside him and when Medrix came in with the officer, he stood up.

"You may sit," Medrix commanded. "Now, I want to know everything that happened." He sat down opposite him, but the Law Officer remained standing. The prisoner said nothing but looked at his fingers.

"Well, I'll start," Medrix said. "You were very friendly with my wife, weren't you?"

"Yes – and she kept telling us jokes and she did not like it at all that you sent her in. She said to us afterwards that you had treated her like a naughty child. She was very upset about it and was going to have her own back."

"Meaning what, precisely?"

"She said that she was going to teach you a lesson that you would not forget ..." he hesitated.

"Go on ..."

"She said that she was going to disappear, hide away and we were to help her. I told her that it wasn't a good idea but she only laughed: 'I know where to hide and he won't be able to find me – when he is really worried, I'll come back.' We tried to dissuade her but she was determined to follow her plan. She gave us a tube of cream to spray on ourselves so that it would look as if we had been attacked. She said it wouldn't harm us. I wasn't keen but my partner, Guard 212 thought it a great joke and went along with it. We couldn't do it straight away because Lawmothers were everywhere collecting the laundry, so she let them change the bedding and watched them leave. Lawmaker Conn then came and gave her your message. He went and she laughed and was determined to go on with the trick. As soon as she had gone, we used the spray – after that we knew nothing."

"I see. So why hasn't she come forward then?"

"Maybe she's afraid to ..."

"I see. And what about the message from the Zendrians?"

"It looks as if she played into their hands."

"I can see that, but ..."

"By doing as she said, we couldn't guard her so they took her. I wish I had never gone along with her idea. She played into their hands, didn't she?"

"Maybe – or maybe not – your partner talked to me before he died."

"Oh! What did he say?"

"He apologised for not looking after her properly."

The man looked relieved. "I'll speak to you again," said Medrix, "but write out your statement and sign it. Before you go, I must tell you that witnesses have come forward and they tell a different story."

"If they do – they are lying," the man said, but he turned pale at the news.

"Somebody is lying – I hope it is not you." Medrix nodded to the warder and then left the room, leaving the Law Officer to take the statement.

As he came out of the door, he almost bumped into Conn.

"What are you doing here, Lawmaker?"

"I was looking for you, Controller, I have news."

"Good, I hope."

"Yes – it's your brother – he's been found."

"Really? Who found him?"

"Pilot number six has found him and his team. They were trapped in one of the bases - the old gold mine. They'd gone in quite safely but there was a rock fall and they lost their message taker and all their equipment. They are being brought in now."

That night Medrix celebrated their return with a special meal for everyone. Perhaps there was more good news to come. He hoped so.

Law Officer Filton got back to him. There was no one at the boatyard except an old man who opened the boatyard for him. One of the boats stood in a shed – it had evidently never gone to sea. Its name was *The Golden Maid.*

Filton said that he would try to find out more.

Medrix shut himself in his rooms. Surely this was proof – this man Dixon or Dickon had built a boat in honour of his wife Leah, so Leah and Celisia were one and the same person. Surely she was the golden maid.

He agonised over the situation he was placed in but maybe Filton was lying. He must be – that was the only answer.

His contact bracelet flashed – a messenger had arrived from Estolan.

He went to meet him. It was Lawmaker Timmons. "The Chief Elder has sent me," he said. "The Chief Elder could not give an answer yet because he himself could not do it. A special committee was being set up to deal with it, but he thought that the answer would be no. Lawmakers would not be forced to do anything against their will. Medrix, you are not to leave your post – you must play for time and pray God a solution will be found."

The messenger had also brought the mail. He also said that, in future, he was to speak to the Zendrian leader for he had knowledge of how these things should be done. It would be better if Medrix carried on with the usual life of the base and reclamation work so that the Zendrians would think all was well.

Medrix nodded in agreement and told Lawmaker Timmons all the things he had been doing lately. The Lawmaker was very impressed by his arrangements and said so.

Later when Medrix opened the mail, he found a letter from Lawmother Grey. On the end of this letter he read: *E sends regards – and do not trust anyone!*

What did it mean?

What did Eldon know that was so important he couldn't tell him about it?

He sighed – it's obvious no one is going to help get Celisia back – no one – not even me.

A message came in the next morning that the small shuttle had arrived at Jadeston, complete with laundry baskets full of laundry and the same number of people who had set out from Chetner on the day Celisia went missing.

The shuttle had had a few minor repairs done. They had landed at Kelandex, a small planet near Listra and nowhere near Zendra at all. So Filton had been on the wrong track after all. Of course, she could have been transferred from there to another shuttle – but it was too far from Zendra or was that what they meant us to think?

He laughed. Yes that's really what I would do, take her by a roundabout way and make everybody dizzy looking for her.

"Oh, Cessie, Cessie my love – you are leading us in circles and everybody is looking for you but I'm the only one who knows exactly where you are, don't I love?"

A couple of days later he called Conn to his office.

"I've decided, Conn, that it is time for you to go out with a reclamation team. That's what you were supposed to do in the first place. You were trained to operate the surveying machine."

Conn tried to speak.

"Listen, please, I haven't finished yet. Lawmaker Holden, plus sixty men are going to the other side of the Reed Mountain and you, of course, will join them. There's land there, good land. If there are people there then I want to know about them, so please report to Holden at once."

"But I am to help Lawmaker Timmons with his forms."

"He'll have to get somebody else, you are needed elsewhere and, anyway, I don't remember saying you could help him."

"But ..."

"You forget who runs this base, Conn. I promised your sister that I would keep an eye on you, but you have a job to do and so must do it."

"Well, Jessie won't like what you are doing," he said angrily.

Medrix picked up on the name at once. "Jessie, who's Jessie?"

Conn coloured up and said, "Lawmother Jessanda – but I call her Jessie. Have done since I was a child."

"I will inform her that you are well, but where I send you is up to me and not up to anyone else. Is that understood? Now – go."

Conn couldn't get out of the office fast enough. He was very annoyed to be sent out of the base but there was nothing he could do about it.

Medrix wondered what Jessanda had to do with the guard – for he mentioned that name, too. Were they connected or was it just a coincidence? Nothing is what it seems and I'm in the middle of the puzzle.

He contacted Filton to come back to the base. He would have to trust someone or make it look as if he did, and the days were passing, weren't they.

Chapter 23

When Celisia awoke she found that she was lying on a rug in a tent. It was a small tent. She tried to sit up but was unable to do so because her hands were tied together.

She remembered that she had been kidnapped but by whom she did not know.

She tried to move again and, this time, she did sit up. Her legs were free and she swung herself round, only to fall sideways.

The door flap suddenly opened and a man stood there.

He was broad shouldered and seemed to fill the space and, with the sun behind him, he looked bigger than most men. He smiled and said: "Good, I am glad you have at last woken up. I thought perhaps you had been given too big a dosage and was worried about you.

"You will get up now and have some food and a hot drink and then we can get on our way."

"Where are we? Who are you?"

"I am Helk. You are my prisoner and as to where we are, that is not something I am prepared to tell you, even if I knew."

"You don't know where we are ...?"

"No. We were on a shuttle going to Zendra, but then we ran into a meteor storm and were hit by something. You and I escaped in an escape pod, making sure that we survived."

"And the others?"

He shrugged his shoulders. "I don't know ... but I made sure that you were safe."

"Why me?"

"Well, I need the money."

"Oh, I see, you have kidnapped me and now you are going to ask my husband to pay a ransom for me. Just because he is the Controller on Chetner you think that he will pay money to get me back."

"I haven't kidnapped you. I don't do kidnapping. It's against the law anyway."

"Of course you have. I did not ..."

"You resisted arrest – that I know ... put up quite a fight. That's why you were doped. If you had come quietly it would have been easier for everyone. Now I have to get you to the court in Zendra where you will stand trial for your crime and I will be paid and can go home."

"I may have been doped but I am not daft! You have kidnapped me. And my husband will catch you and see that you are punished." she said, angrily.

"Your husband arranged it all."

"Rubbish! My husband would not stoop so low."

"When your husband learned that you had been married twice before and had not declared it, he was furious."

"I have never been married before. I may have lost my memory but of that I am quite sure. I have never been married before."

"I have documents on me that tell me why you have been arrested. You married these men without declaring that you were married before and without having divorced any of them. That is your crime and I have to take you to Zendra. I have nothing against you personally, and I don't know whether you are innocent or guilty – but that's my job and I am good at it. Never lost a prisoner yet and I don't intend to lose you."

Ces was about to interrupt when he went on: "Your Lawmaker husband arranged for you to be picked up, for no Lawmaker breaks the law of marriage and gets away with it. When he learned that your last husband had been a Zendrian he arranged for you to go to their planet for trial. He could not live with you knowing the facts. He arranged for you to be taken. He saw you laughing and joking with the guards and sitting where everyone could see you with your skirts up to your knees and he sent you to your room and told you to wait there until further notice and he told the guards to see you did not leave."

Ces looked at him in astonishment. "You know all that ... but ..."

"He went away and left you. Ah, I can see you remember now. I was not there myself but I was told. Your legal marriage was to Endil Dickon; that is why you called yourself Leah Dickon when questioned and whilst still married to him and he was away at sea you met and married a visiting Zendrian and while he went home to arrange for your papers to live there, you met Lawmaker Medrix and married *him*. I have been told you will try anything to get away, so I will see that you don't. I want no trouble, Leah."

Ces looked at him. Somehow she would have to convince him that he was wrong. She sighed and shook her head, then said: "If you don't know where we are, then I am free because Zendrian jurisdiction does not cover this place, so ..."

"It does. I am duty bound to deliver you. I have already been paid half the money when I said I would do the job. I took the place of the original guard when he broke his arm and could not do the job. He asked me to take over as he knew I did that sort of thing. In fact he is a sort of long-distant cousin of mine."

"Zendrians are dark and you are fair ..." and very good looking she thought to herself.

He stopped talking and said that they had to get on their way to find people he could report to. He had decided to go to the south for it seemed like a good idea.

He got her up and led her over to a campfire where he had been cooking something. He gave the food to her and some coffee to drink and, whilst she ate, he packed up the tent and other things.

He untied her and said that she had a pack to carry for he could not carry everything.

She said she wanted to go to a lat and he said she could go where she was, for he would not look and because she was so desperate to go, she had to trust him.

When she was ready, he helped her on with her pack and together they set out on his route. She thought it best to do what he wanted until she could come up with her own plan for escape. She would play her part and let him think she was docile and would do everything he wanted.

He strode out and was soon ahead of her and she called him back to tell him that he was going too fast for her and he slackened his pace.

After they had gone some way they stopped at a stream for a rest and he smiled at her and then she saw that he had green eyes and wondered where she had seen green eyes before. She could not remember but for some reason she thought that it was important.

Helk said that they would follow the stream for it should lead to a river and where there was a river people were usually found. She told him about her escape from Top Gost Point and how she had also followed a stream and how she had reached a river but in her case there were no people. He listened but did not comment and she thought he did not believe her.

It was getting dark by the time they reached a valley and the stream went under some rocks and was gone. He did not seem at all surprised and mumbled something about that he'd thought that might happen. He decided to make camp under some trees and plot a course in the morning. He also told her that from now on she would not be tied up in any way so that she would be free to move about the camp as she liked. But he also warned her that if she did decide to leave him, he would see that her movements were restricted.

She thanked him and said that she understood and appreciated his kindness but when they reached a settlement she would ask the people there for help and hoped they would listen to her. He nodded and said that she had every right to do that.

Could she trust him? She would have to wait and see, but for now she would be sure to stay with him unless, of course, some other way opened up for her.

In the morning they packed up their things and started on their way again but, this time, following a track through the valley that got narrower and narrower. High mountains of sheer rock made the path even narrower so that now they had to walk single file. Helk told her to keep quiet as any noise could bring the rocks tumbling down on them, so they walked in silence. It was eerie and she felt a great coldness wrap around her and she wondered if he felt it too, but she daren't say anything. Then the path was so narrow that neither of them could get through. He whispered to her to go back a little way and she watched him take off the rope that he carried on his shoulder and make a loop in it. Then he aimed it at a large rock that jutted out above them.

"I'm going up there. I'll throw the rope down to you then you will tie my pack to it and I will pull it up. Then, I'll drop the rope and you will send up your pack and, lastly, you will come up to me."

She nodded and watched him climb out of sight. Then she was alone and a great fear came over her as she waited, seemingly for ages, and then relief flooded through her as the rope came down to her and she followed his instructions. Soon she was standing on a shelf of rock with him. Beyond the rock was a path that zigzagged along the side of the mountain and eventually brought them down to a valley below.

They followed the path and came out onto a large plain that seemed to spread as far as the eye could see. There were only stumpy bushes all over the place but, as it was getting dark, he said they would camp beside the path.

In the morning he decided against going across this plain because they needed to find water and he took a path that went up a steep hill and eventually came out into another valley. Another path led them even lower down where, in the distance, they could see a building which they made their way to, each hoping that, at last, they had found people but, alas, it was not to be. It was all locked up: the windows were dirty and the place looked run down.

She went round the back and found a small window and opened it. Leaving her pack on the ground, she climbed through and then opened the door for him. She then collected her pack.

The place was furnished and there was a wood stove and Helk decided that they would stay there for the night. He collected wood and lit the fire. She found a water-pump in the kitchen and soon had water. She filled one of the cooking pans that she had found in her pack with water and put it on to boil. Soon they had a hot drink and they both sat by the fire talking and eating until she fell asleep leaning on his shoulder. He tried to wake her but he could not so he picked her up and, as her head rested on his chest, she whispered "I love you."

Helk was startled. She couldn't love him. This was a ruse to get him on her side. This was what she did with all the men in her life. He was about to put her down on a long seat when she said: "I love you, Medrix ... love you so much."

Helk laughed to himself, she did not love him. He put her gently onto the long seat and left her there.

The next morning they set out early because Helk did not want to slow up the pace. He found a track that led down to a made-up road. He was pleased and said that proved there must be people here. She made no comment.

He strode out quickly, forgetting that she could not keep up, although she tried, but soon got left behind. Then she had a stone in her shoe and sat down to take it out but when she stood up she discovered that it was in her sock and she had to see to it. By this time he had disappeared from sight. She ran along the road only to discover that it forked to the right. Now she wasn't sure whether to go straight on or turn right. She decided to go straight on but soon realised there was still no sign of him unless he had turned off elsewhere. She carried on. If she turned back, he would be much further on. It seemed the right thing to do.

Soon the road veered to the left and she was quite high up when she saw, stretched out in front of her, the sea.

She was so surprised that she ran towards it and, seeing a path that went to a sandy beach, decided to go down and look.

The sea was blue and looked so inviting that she stripped down to her underwear and ran into the water, leaving her pack safe on a rock.

The feel of the warm water on her body was exhilarating and soon she was swimming across the bay.

Then she felt a bit cold as dark clouds were gathering so she swam back to the shore. But when she got back to the beach she found her pack had gone. Now she was worried: what was she going to do? She went back to the path and saw a man standing there. He must have her pack. She ran towards him and discovered it was Helk and he was furious.

"What the hell do you think you are doing?"

"I went for a swim. Why did you not leave my pack alone?"

"Leave it there so anyone could take it?"

"There are no people around."

"How do you know that? You could have lost it, then what would you do?"

"Yes. Thank you Helk, I didn't think, that's all ... I'm sorry. You went too fast for me. I had a stone in my sock and by the time I had emptied it you were gone," she quickly said, trying to appease his anger.

"Dress now."

He stood watching her and she told him to turn his back on her and he said: "Why, if you can run round in the nude, why should I?"

"I have clothes on."

"Clothes that are transparent when water goes on them. Would the Controller allow that?"

She was horrified. "I didn't know, Helk ... he wouldn't allow it ..." her voice faded.

Helk gave her the pack and disappeared from view and she quickly dressed and ran to join him. He said that both roads joined up and where they did there was a shed and, as it was blowing up for a storm, they would stay there.

All the way there and most of the evening he was shouting at her and, in the end, she went to bed in tears, and even then he told her to shut up as he wanted to sleep even if she did not.

That night she had a nightmare. Helk awoke to her screaming and crying that her stepfather was here and he was going to kill her.

He put his arms around her to calm her and she clung to him saying that her stepfather was still there, whereupon he told her that there was no one there and, in the end, she slept but he stayed a long time with her until he fell asleep beside her.

When he awoke in the morning he was furious with himself for being taken in by her. But Ces said nothing and she would make sure that he did not try that on again. In fact it would be better if she got away from him as soon as possible. She knew she had tempted him but he had to know that she wasn't interested. She didn't remember the dream, although she knew she had had one.

When she awoke the next morning she was in for a shock. He put wrist cuffs on her and said that these were special ones. He had a device that could give her a shock if she did anything that he did not like and gave her a demonstration by pressing a button on the device and she felt a pain go up her arm. He said that was only a small example of what it could do.

They set out at a smart pace and every time she slowed up she felt the pain so she quickened her pace. Half way through the morning he stopped by a bridge for a rest. She asked if she could go and relieve herself and he said she could go behind some bushes. She found it difficult to manage her clothes but, after several attempts, she managed.

He was in a hurry to get on but she remonstrated with him telling him how hard it was for her to move her arms and do simple things. He only laughed and said it was her own fault and all his prisoners wore such a thing but he had given her freedom because she was a woman but he had learnt his lesson the hard way.

When it was getting dark he stopped in a clearing at the side of the road but even then he did not take the cuffs off and she went to bed wearing them. He slept by the door of the tent.

She was furious with him but could do nothing about it. Tomorrow, she thought, I will not speak to him at all. That was easier said than done, but she would try anyway.

The next morning it looked like rain but he was up early and they carried on in the same way. They walked in silence until he decided they would rest by a fallen tree. There seemed to be no way through this tree and he said to her that he was going to go up the bank to see if they could pass it that way around and she was to stay where she was. He climbed the bank and was gone.

She waited and waited but there was no sign of him. Now she was angry but as she waited even longer she became worried. Where was he?

There was only one thing to do and that was to follow him. She climbed the bank and was around the tree in no time, so why hadn't he come back to tell her it was clear?

There was a path leading through the woods which led to a clearing where there was a cottage. Helk was standing by the door. He looked up, saw her and smiled as he pressed the device and a pain shot up her arm. "You couldn't do as you were told. I knew you would follow and there was no need for me to come for you, and I was right."

Ces was livid. "You devil you! You're a bully. The worst type of man there is giving pain to other people who can't defend themselves. I hate you ... hate your type ... hate you for what you are doing to me. When I tell you the truth about things you won't listen ... you think yourself so clever ... if you have a wife I don't know how she puts up with you ... or do you beat her up too ... is that the kind of man you are?"

He turned red with anger. "How dare you insult my wife. I love my wife and I wouldn't hurt her or my children ..."

"You have children? Do you use this device on them too?"

"Certainly not! We Venturians look after our families. We have four children, two boys and two girls and another one on the way ... that's why I need the money ... that's my job. It's a hard job but then my family does not suffer. Our planet, Ventura, has suffered a lot over the years and when the Lawmakers left us, our industrial side of operations folded too, so I have to get money from somewhere to keep the family together. At least I am not flitting from one woman to another. I stay faithful ... but *you* ..." he spat the words out ... "you flit from one man to another and you have tried to seduce me too, but I cannot be tempted by such wicked behaviour ... do you *hear me*?" he yelled at her.

Ces just stood there, then turned away from him and he used the device harder than before and she spun round, tears pouring down her face. "I'll have you know, Helk, that I have one man in my life only and that's Lawmaker Medrix and no one shall say otherwise."

"So you say," he lowered his voice, "you'd better come in now. We'll stay here tonight. I think we've both said enough and we have to be together whether we want to be or not and we have to make the best of it." He went into the cottage and she followed him. What else could she do?

All that evening when he spoke to her she did not answer and mostly turned her back on him. He gave up after a while and went to bed but it was cold in the room. He had not lit a fire so he got up and went outside to collect some wood. He came in quickly without the wood and went over to where she was sleeping and woke her up.

"Leah – wake up!"

She woke and looked at him in a bemused fashion.

"Here. I want to unlock your wrist cuffs – sit up so I can do it."

She did so and he released her.

"Pack up your things now."

"What? Why?"

"There's a shuttle circling around. We have to get out of here."

She got up and did as he said. "It will be your friends, the Zendrians – they've found us."

"Could be – but remember we are in a strange place. These people could be immigration police or slave traders – I have to make sure, so we'll leave here now. Please do as I say, your life – our lives – may depend on it."

Quietly they left the cottage and he led her into the darkest part of the wood. They could hear the shuttle as it circled again. She hardly breathed while they waited there and then, quite suddenly, the shuttle straightened out and was gone.

"Has it gone?" Cessie whispered.

"I think so – but we'll wait here for a while longer."

They waited for ages then Helk motioned to her that it was time to move on. As they came into the lighter section of the wood, they could see it was brilliant moonlight and she wondered if it was safe to go on.

"Have they really gone?" she whispered.

"I think so." He walked on and this time she made sure she kept up with him.

By early morning they came to the road again. High uncut hedges grew on either side of the road and he thought that they would make better progress walking along it. It led uphill and suddenly they were at the top and now there were no hedges and before them was a settlement of white buildings. There was no sign of a shuttle.

They hurried down the hill to where there were trees. They walked amongst the trees but stopped when they heard voices.

"Now then Leah, listen to me. Lie down in these bushes and don't move from here. Your life and mine may depend on you. I know we've had our differences but I am trusting you to do as I say," and without hearing her answer he crawled forward until he was out of sight.

Ces waited for ages, hardly daring to move. She could still hear the voices but could not understand what they said, nor could she hear Helk. Then all went quiet and she could hear a shuttle taking off, then all was silent again. Helk did not come back.

Had he been discovered and taken prisoner? What about the other settlers? Were they looking for her now? What should she do?

She waited, crouching even lower in the bushes and suddenly Helk was beside her. Ces was so relieved that he was there and said so.

He smiled. "I thought you wanted to get rid of me."

She noticed how his smile softened his face and lit up his eyes. He was very attractive and her heart missed a beat. What was wrong with her? She was actually attracted to him! What if there was no one here at all, would they have to live out their lives together? She realised then that Helk had been speaking to her and she hadn't heard a word.

He said again: "We'll go back along the road and wait there in case they come back. Come on" He held out his hand to her and helped her up.

"Are you all right?"

"Yes – who were they? Were they slavers?"

"No."

"Immigration people?"

"No."

"Then who were they?"

"Zendrians," he said.

"But I don't understand. Did you talk to them?"

"No, but I listened to them talking. I can speak several languages, Zendrian being one of them. One said: 'What will our Great Leader say when he realises that he has no hostage?' The other one answered: 'He won't say anything – he'll accept the fact that she's dead – and when the Controller gives the base over to him he will then say that he cannot return her because the shuttle she was in blew up and she must be dead. He won't tell the Controller until after the base is occupied by us. The kidnapping, you see, will have worked. In ten days' time it will all be over so he has only to keep quiet about the accident until then'."

"But Helk, you could have still turned me in. I thought the money was important to you."

"What kind of man do you think I am, Leah? I told you before, I don't do kidnapping – my job is not against the law – my job *is* the Law."

"Yes, yes, Helk. I am sorry to have misjudged you."

"I'm sorry I did not believe your story – I have been terrible to you."

"Helk, you treated me as the Law decreed. You did not realise that I was telling the truth. I expect you treated me like any other prisoner – the thing now is, if the base is to be handed over to the Zendrians in ten days' time, how can I reach Medrix in time so that he knows I am safe?"

"I have no idea. It seems this is a space station that has not been used for years."

"It could have a shuttle then."

"I doubt it, but we will take a look and see."

A day later they went into the space station through a broken window. There was nothing there that would generate any power of any sort, let alone help them to connect with anyone. They were alone on a small planet in the middle of space.

"There's no way out of here," said Helk, "unless I can re-programme the escape pod."

"You can do that?"

"I could try, but it will take days to get there. I will need some tools. There are buildings at the back so let's see what's in there."

Helk found the tools he needed plus a runabout. It started at once so they decided to leave the next day but Ces said that the runabout would not go through the ravine and Helk said he'd have to plot another course using the maps he'd found in the main room.

Ces knew time was running out fast, for soon they'd have no food and, if they couldn't get to Chetner in time, all would be lost.

That night she prayed for a miracle. Her father had said all that time ago that miracles happened to people and when there was no way, God would find one.

The next morning was wet: in fact thunderstorms raged all day and they could not go anywhere.

Helk could not find an easier way to get to the escape pod so he decided to go back on the same route until they came to the ravine. From then on they would go on foot. But it was not to be for, for some reason, the runabout would not start.

Although they knew that they couldn't get back to the escape pod in time, they still decided to set out on foot but soon discovered that now there were large areas of water where there had been none before and they had to turn back.

"It's hopeless," Ces said sadly.

"We'll find a way, don't worry, Leah – I mean Celisia. We'll find a way. All we need is a miracle."

She nodded – that's exactly what they needed.

Chapter 24

Medrix was shaving when there was an earth tremor and he cut himself. He had just put a plaster on the cut when Lawmaker Whitton rushed in to tell him that there had been some damage to the Chetnerite camp. He dressed quickly and they went to the camp together.

A row of shelters had collapsed and there were people screaming and scrabbling in the wreckage trying to rescue those trapped within the rubble.

Medrix soon had Lawmakers working side by side with the Chetnerite men and many people were brought out to safety and taken to the medical bay. Three people were on the critical list, one of whom died a few hours later.

The rescued people were put up in the base until something else could be arranged for them. Later the same day, there was a terrific thunder storm and when it was over, everywhere was covered with brown dust.

Then reports came in that the water pipe had broken in three places.

Medrix called the people together in the main hall for he knew what he must do. The people had to be moved from the area altogether – not just to another part of Chetner, but to the scheduled areas he had arranged should the Zendrians attack them.

The people listened and asked whether or not they could all stay in the base but even Santel agreed that moving the people was the best thing to do. The only one to disagree was Lawmaker Timmons who said it would look as if they were preparing to be attacked and that meant war. But Medrix said that the Zendrian leader would be informed as to why the people were moving. Lawmaker Timmons then said that the people could be moved to the Southern Hills but Medrix said that there was not enough food for them there and so it was agreed that they should go, as planned, as no one wanted to be camped in this place any more.

Medrix also arranged for Lawmaker teams to go to the Southern Hills and for some to go home, for home leave was due to them.

Lawmaker Timmons was furious. "The Zendrians will think we are quitting the base ... how can I negotiate with them now?"

"Just say that I am sending our reclamation workers to work. You know that's why they are here."

"Who will stay here, then?"

"Of course some will stay here. I'll ask for volunteers. As long as we have some to work the base, the space docks and other places, we'll be fine. Don't worry, Lawmaker Timmons. I have to do what I think is the best for all the people here. The medical bay staff and patients will all be sent home: one of the doctors and two nurses will stay with people who are too sick to be moved."

"But, Controller, if you go ..."

"I am not going, Lawmaker. Whatever gave you that idea?"

"Well, I suppose you are doing the right thing ..."

Medrix sighed. "You know my job makes me the one to blame all the time. I shall stay with the others until the date is past, then we will all move out to a safer place, whatever has happened. You could go, Lawmaker: after all I am awaiting my orders from the Chief Elder and then I will know what to do."

"I can't go. I have this job to do and I hope that I can solve it."

"I hope so too, Lawmaker. I do hope so."

Lawmaker Timmons left the area shaking his head and mumbling to himself.

The next day the Chetnerites and others left the area.

That night there was another storm and as it raged around the base it seemed to add to the gloom of the place and Medrix had a feeling that something dreadful was going to happen. There was more to all this ... he shook his head and made another coffee ... witchcraft he thought ... some would say it is witchcraft ... and he remembered how Lawmaker Timmons had called Celisia a witch ... mm ... Lawmaker Timmons ... was he genuine or was he up to something ... after all he represented the Elders at the trial, granted he lost the case ... was it some kind of revenge ... but even he couldn't make things happen like that.

He re-called Holden and his men and they said that they were already on their way back to base because they were unable to carry on working as the weather was so bad.

A message came through from the Cordonians to say that Medrix was wanted there because his father was ill. Leaving Lawmaker Whitton in charge of the base he went at once with two Temran pilots, but he was worried about his father and could not settle during the flight.

They docked at the main flight station where two men in dark green uniforms met him. The pilots were told to stay within their shuttle and not to go exploring.

Medrix was led down various passageways until they came to some double doors and he was told to enter.

It was a large room with big windows looking out on to the mountains and the distant sea. There was no one else in the room.

He waited.

A woman came in with a trolley on which were cups, saucers and a jug of coffee. She poured him some and then left the room.

A man came in. It was not the chief as he expected but a tall man dressed in red trousers and a black top.

"Well, here we are, Medrix ..."

Medrix knew the voice and smiled. "Haldean? Haldean ... is it really you?"

"Yes, yes, my friend ... I remember you. Didn't we have some fun all those years ago. We were younger then and do you remember that fish you caught ... it was so big that we made pigs of ourselves."

Medrix laughed at the memory of it.

"But of course, Medrix, you are worried about your father are you not?"

"Yes ... may I see him please?"

"Your father is quite well. I had to have a reason to bring you here."

"You tricked me ... but why?"

"Do sit down and drink your coffee." He helped himself to some and sat down near Medrix.

"First of all the whole reclamation team is to be released plus all the equipment. Food supplies will be sent with them and they will be escorted to the southern hills."

Medrix smiled with relief and said: "But why the sudden change of heart?"

"Quite simple: the borders between Chetner and Cordonia will be closed until further notice. Cordonia wants no part in a war that is likely to happen very soon and even if there is a peaceful solution to the problem, we do not trust the Zendrians. They probably want it as a military base and we could be the next in line for occupation. We have to be prepared for this whether it happens or not."

"I see your point, but so far I am not sure what we are doing."

"I know ..." Haldean leaned forward and said in a low voice: "I have a packet for you ... do not open it here ..."

He passed the packet to Medrix who put it in his pocket. "What is it?"

Haldean smiled and avoided answering the question. "You must go now, my friend, and we shall always be friends as you will see. I trust your wife will be returned to you. You did well to take my advice to marry her. She is in my thoughts daily. Now, you must go – there are spies everywhere ..." He stood up and guided Medrix to the door where two men awaited him to lead him back to the shuttle. As soon as he boarded the shuttle took off on its journey back to Chetner.

Leaning back in his comfortable seat, Medrix opened the packet. It was from the Chief Elder. He read:

After you have read this destroy it.

The messenger who gave you this is to be trusted. He is related to me and thinks very highly of you. The committee have met together and have discussed the matter in detail. This is our answer:

The base was built by the Chetner Elders with the help of the Zendrians: others also helped in its building. Chetnerites dug out the foundations and were paid for doing it. The Zendrians built the main space docks and main rooms used in the control of those bases. The rest of it was built by Lawmakers. The Zendrians were not paid because the Chetner Elders said they could use it as a base for storage.

Kidnapping is against the universal law and we do not agree with it. We are sorry that your wife is missing but are not prepared to be bullied by the Zendrians or anyone else.

The base is on Chetner land and belongs to the Chetner people. The Chetner Elders had no right to build it there in the first place.

You and the other Lawmakers are only there as reclamation workers and you are in charge only because of the terrible catastrophe that befell City One.

The Chetnerite people are now scattered throughout the galaxy but we hope that one day they will be back in their own country and, until that time, no one can give, sell or rent out the base to anyone else.

The fact that your wife has been kidnapped proves without doubt the type of people the Zendrians are. We know how hard this is for you but the answer is 'No' to all their points.

You, Medrix, must stay in the base until the final day then you must press the self-destruct button. You will have five minutes to get out of there. The button is to be found in the safe. There is a panel at the back which will slide back to show the button: this was put in by the Lawmakers. Be sure to hide your keys.

These are your instructions. We wish you well. Tell no one about this. Let us hope the problem will solve itself.

it was signed by all of the committee.

Medrix read it again.

As soon as he got back to the base he burnt the message, took the safe keys, put one in the safe, locked it and then hid the other key.

So it was war ... and Celisia? He put his head on his arms and wept. He fell asleep like that and woke in the early hours of the morning. His arms were tired and they ached but he made himself a drink and then went to bed.

He awoke at the hour of ten to find the guard knocking on the door. Medrix opened the door and peered round it. "What's the matter now?" he said gruffly.

"Lawmaker Timmons is here and wants to talk to you."

"Tell him that I am having a shower and will see him later."

"But he insists ..."

"Right, tell him to come in now," Medrix said grimly.

Lawmaker Timmons came in angrily. "What time do you call this, Controller? There are rules for this kind of thing you know ..."

Before Medrix could answer, the door opened and in walked Lawmakers Whitton and Holden. He looked at them. "Has a man no time to himself on this base? I had a long tiring day yesterday and I slept late and now here you all are. What's going on?"

Lawmaker Whitton spoke first. "I have just brought my report of events that happened when you were away."

"Go on then," said Medrix patiently. He had to calm down otherwise they might guess that he had some bad news.

"A Chetnerite family arrived here yesterday: a mother and four children, two girls and two small boys. They came from one of the farms. The woman can cook so I put her to work in the kitchen with her two girls so meals should improve now. The little boys are in the library playing and learning their lessons. I put two of Lawmaker Holden's men in to look after them. I have given the family two rooms to live in. As there are no shuttles going out at the moment, I thought that was the best I could do."

Medrix nodded his approval and thanked Whitton for his trouble.

Whitton left and Holden said:"I have brought you my report. The weather was so bad that we could not do anything." He put a paper down on the table.

Medrix thanked him and Holden left the room.

"Now you've seen them, perhaps you will listen to me, Controller," said Timmons.

Medrix waited for him to go on.

"As you know, I have been working with the Zendrians to see if we can come to an agreement for both sides. I have been able to do this ... it's quite simple really – we give them the base."

"We can't do that."

"But we can: they lease it for twenty years: they pay no rent but when the twenty years is up the Chetnerites will offer it to them in exchange for a fixed rent. Of course other people could bid higher. The Zendrians are in perfect agreement with this and – you see – the problem is solved."

"We can't do that because the base belongs to the Chetnerites and they are not here to agree to anything."

"I know that. But they would see the sense of it ... and agree."

"But, by using kidnapping as a way of getting it, that is not in our best interests and we should decline the offer. It looks as if they are desperate to have a base ... a corn harvest store? I don't believe it Lawmaker. More like a military base and we cannot allow them to terrorize other nations. They are indeed a warlike nation.

"But it will keep them at bay – we don't want a war do we?"

"I am sorry, I cannot allow it."

"*You* can't allow it! Who are you to allow it or not? Are you to put Lawmakers into a war that they will lose? And they will lose it. You *must* allow it otherwise why am I here?"

"I have wondered that. Your credentials I suppose are from the Chief Elder?"

339

"Of course."

"Bring them to me to read then I will tell you if I'll accept them or not and *that's* my last word on the matter."

Medrix watched Timmons as he left the room, slamming the door behind him. He was worried. What if the Lawmaker had got the right credentials and was working for the Chief Elder? Then he, Medrix, would be in the wrong. Yet he had been given orders of a different kind by Haldean. Those instructions had been very clear and the signatures seemed true enough. But Haldean had been investigated by the Chief Elder's men and found to be an agent, seemingly working for the Zendrians. Celisia had found him charming but she also was afraid of him. He had given her all kinds of instructions to spy on him. Why did he do that? Which one was he to believe?

It was in the Cordonians' best interests to blow up the base. The Zendrians could easily attack Cordonia from the Chetner base. What was he to believe?

He would wait. Surely the Chief Elder would contact him personally – otherwise he would have to choose. He sighed – how easy it would be to give in and be sure of getting Celisia back. But with only six days to go he would know the end soon enough.

He went to the dining centre. It seemed to be full. Some of the men he did not recognise and then he realised they were Zendrians. How could they be? Then he realised with a shock that Lawmaker Timmons must have invited them here – otherwise how could he have negotiated with them."

He went to the serving counter and chose a meat and vegetable pie. It looked delicious and he told the server that and she smiled with pleasure. At least somebody is happy, he thought. He went to his usual table and sat down. Conn joined him and Medrix asked if he had heard from his sister, whereupon Conn said no, because there had been no mail.

Medrix had just taken a mouthful of the pie when Lawmaker Timmons entered the room. He walked over to Medrix' table but did not sit down. There were six men with him – all of them Zendrians.

The room went quiet.

"Well," said Medrix, "are you joining me for a meal?" He knew they weren't but he had to say something.

"I've realised, Controller, that you had a very tiring day yesterday and I should have waited until you were ready to see me. But now you have rested and I bring the same matter up and I am sure you will see the sense of it and we can all go home and your wife can come back to you ..."

"This is not the time or place to discuss this. I thought I'd told you already what I think of the idea, Lawmaker ..."

"But, Controller, it is the best idea and you have not come up with anything better."

"I am waiting to hear from the Chief Elder. He will tell me what to do."

"What if he is telling you through me?"

"That's a chance I will have to take. I have already sent a message to him asking for verification of your credentials."

"What! You doubt my word?" Timmons replied angrily. "I'll have you know I am very highly thought of in Estolan."

"I know that, but I have to be sure, so leave it until I hear, please."

I ... rather – we – are not leaving it. We have had enough of your controlling ways. We must not do this that or the other or we will be imprisoned. Everyone is sick of you. You have quarrelled with everyone. Conn was sent away when I needed him and even Law Officer Filton was sent off somewhere after you asked for his resignation."

"I have to rule as I think fit. I did not choose this job. It was just given to me because ..."

"Because, Medrix, *YOU PLANNED IT THAT WAY,*" said Timmons sarcastically.

"Rubbish! You will be saying next that I caused the earthquakes and the City One disaster: just like you accused my wife of causing an earthquake during her trial." He stood up.

"If you remember, Medrix, you promised that you would have your revenge on Celisia and the Chetner people after you were sent home in disgrace because you failed to stop the game. And this is what you are doing. There are no Chetnerites here now. They are scattered all over the galaxy. You arranged for your wife to be taken away after you failed to kill her in the freighter that crashed. All Chetner troubles can be traced to you."

"There's no truth in any of it, and you must remember that you are not in court now," said Medrix grimly, trying to control his temper as he said it.

"You don't want to settle this ... we know it ... you are known to be ruthless, bigoted and hard as iron. Why, in court you sounded most of the time as if you thought she was guilty and I was actually sorry for her. And now you are here and you won't even listen to the answer I have come up with. You have found a way to get rid of your wife and you are determined to go on."

"*Enough,* Lawmaker! I love my wife. She is the one bright flame in my life and when I find who has done this to her I will ..."

"Kill her or have her sent to a brothel camp, is that it? And even if you got her back from there she would be no good to you because she would be soiled, wouldn't she and you always crave the best of everything ..."

Conn interrupted. "I think you go too far, Lawmaker Timmons," and the other Lawmakers nodded in agreement.

Medrix spoke softly, but each word was emphasised firmly. "I – would – take – her – back – whatever – happened – to – her."

"Of course you wouldn't. She wouldn't suit you then. She would be one more slut," said Timmons viciously.

"I would take her back because I love her. Love, you see, has its own strength. Power is no good unless it is used for good. Strength is useless

341

unless it is used to protect the weak and you, Lawmaker Timmons, do not seem to know that!"

"Now he preaches to *us*. This man who betrayed the Elders and expects to go on living in the style he is used to: this cheat; liar, who has betrayed Chetner and will not seek the peaceful route: this man who would plunge us into a war rather than listen to our pleas. This man who wants to destroy our people as well as these people," Timmons said, pointing to the kitchen staff.

"I think you have said enough and you will go to your rooms and stay there until I hear from the Chief Elder," Medrix said authoritatively. "We will leave this matter for now."

"Oh, No. Not this time, Medrix. *CONTROLLER ... LIAISON OFFICER ... LAWMAKER MEDRIX, YOU ARE UNDER ARREST*," shouted Timmons. "I have the power you see to do this. You are arrested on charges of treason, murder and interfering with the laws of our land. You will be sent back to Estolan in disgrace and will probably land up in the same prison as the Chetner Elders." He turned to the other Lawmakers. "And you people who would jump to his defence, you will be arrested too for there are over fifty Zendrians on duty already, so quietly leave the room and cause no trouble and you will be left alone. You, Medrix, will sign this document." Timmons put it on the table in front of Medrix. "This document will then be put in the safe and the other document will be burnt, so ... here is a pen, Medrix, sign it and your treatment won't be so harsh."

Medrix knew he was outnumbered but he would sign nothing for Timmons.

"Go to hell," he hissed. "I'll not sign anything."

"Then you are disobeying our Chief Elder and you know our rules. You will be taken to the punishment block and given ten lashes of the whip then you may see sense." And before Medrix could do anything, he was taken there by the Zendrians.

Lawmaker Timmons went with him and, after the tenth stroke of the whip, he asked Medrix if he was going to sign the document and hand over the keys, but all Medrix said was: "I'll see you in hell first," whereupon Lawmaker Timmons ordered ten more strokes of the whip.

Conn who was standing beside him said that the punishment had to stop.

On the twelfth stroke Medrix collapsed and just hung there against the wall, but they went on whipping him until Conn made them stop by grabbing the arms of the man with the whip.

"This won't do, Lawmaker," he shouted, "my sister would not want this."

But Lawmaker Timmons said that she had no say in the matter that she like Conn was just a small cog in the wheel and if he went on like this he would be whipped too, so Conn said nothing and watched as they took Medrix away to the prison.

"You have one more chance, Conn," said Timmons "to make it right, pretend you are his friend and get him to sign the document and tell you where the keys to the safe are and all will be well."

Conn left the room vowing to himself that he would find a way to get Medrix right away from the base. It was the least he could do. He had been angry with him when the Elders' college had been closed as he had always wanted to be one ... just, in fact, like Medrix, but he knew now that he had taken the wrong road. Somehow he would make it right and his sister would then realise that he was not to be bossed around by her any more.

He had five days only to make amends for his stupidity.

Medrix came to in the early hours of the morning. He did not know where he was. He reached out for the glass of water that usually stood on the bedside table. It was not there. He felt for the table and that was not there.

Where was it? Where was he?

His back was so hot, wet and sticky and so painful. In spite of the pain, he leaned towards the other side of the bed and discovered a wall. It did not make sense ... where was he?

He knew.

He was in the punishment room in the college. Yes that was it. He had done something wrong and the Masters had had him whipped. What had he done wrong? He couldn't remember.

He was training to be an Elders' man, yet he couldn't remember.

Wait! The Masters. Where had he heard of those before ... she had said ... she? Who was she?

Shadows seemed to merge into the room. They made him tired and in so much pain.

He closed his eyes and slept a while, then suddenly awoke.

She was Jessanda. The most beautiful woman in the galaxy and she loved him. That was right, wasn't it?

He was betrothed to her and oh so proud of her when he had left college as a fully-fledged Elders' man. He had everything and her. He had passed top of the grade in his class. But she left him when he was sent away ... away to ... where? The shadows came again and the sweat ran down his brow ... where was he?

Ah yes, he remembered. He was sent as a spy to Chetner. He spied on the exiles. The job was easy ... but he failed ... she was determined to play a game ... no, that couldn't be right. What game was Jessanda playing ...? It wasn't Jessanda ... so if it wasn't her, who was it?

The shadows came down and he slept.

When Medrix awoke again there were no shadows. A man and a woman leaned over him. They turned him over and he felt her cool fingers as she rubbed cream on to his back. He sighed with pleasure as her fingers seemed to lessen the pain, then the man lifted him to lie back down again.

"He'll be better soon," the man said, then lifted him up to drink some water. He said something to the woman then they both went and Medrix slept again.

When he next awoke a Lawmaker was sitting beside him.

He knew it was Conn.

"What are you doing here?" he growled.

"I came to see how you are."

"Well, you've seen me, now you can go ... unless you have brought your sister ... is she here?"

"No, she's not here. Did you want to see her then?"

"Yes, I want to know why she left me to marry someone else."

Conn was taken aback by the question but he realised that Medrix wasn't lucid when he said: "Who are the Masters?"

"I don't know, Controller. Would you like a drink?"

Medrix nodded and Conn held the glass while he drank. Then his eyes closed and he slept again.

When Conn saw Lawmaker Timmons again he told him that Medrix was in no fit state to tell him anything and the Lawmaker went to see for himself.

As Timmons entered the cell, Medrix opened his eyes, smiled at him and said: "Well, Prosecutor, you have been spying on Cessie again ... you think she is a witch ... watch she doesn't change you into a frog ..." he laughed.

"You can fool Conn, my friend, but you cannot fool me. I have brought the document for you to sign and you'd better tell me where the keys to the safe are or your wife will suffer ... this is no idle threat."

"What wife? I've got a wife? So I did marry Jessanda after all."

"Well, yes. You will sign the document for her sake, Medrix." But Medrix only smiled, saying nothing.

"You will sign tomorrow, for we have only got two days and then all hell will let loose. No one will help you for all the Lawmakers have left and gone down to the southern hills. The Chetnerites have gone with them, too."

"Help me sit up."

The Lawmaker lifted him, banking the pillows at his back. He stepped back and looked down at him.

"What now, Medrix? Are you going to be sensible and do as I ask?"

"Have I any mail?"

"None. No one has."

"Then I will do as you ask."

Lawmaker Timmons sighed with relief. He had got him at last. All his hard work would now come to fruition. He was pleased.

Then Medrix said that he would sign the paper and put it into the safe – but only one hour before the new Controller, whoever he was, came.

Lawmaker Timmons was annoyed and threatened him with more punishment but Medrix was adamant. That's what he would do and only that.

A Zendrian came in and talked to the Lawmaker and then went. Timmons then said that the Zendrians were willing to wait until the final day as long as Medrix was telling the truth: if not they would hang him from the nearest tree. Even Lawmaker Timmons was shocked at that remark so he had to go along with it and put his trust in Medrix ... after all Medrix should be in a better state by then.

He left the cell and realised once again that somehow events were once more in Medrix' control. But of course once it was done he would have him taken back to Estolan in chains and charged with treason for disobeying the Chief Elder's commands and he would be shamed once and for all and the Chetner Elders would enjoy their revenge. He himself would be praised by them and maybe the new City Elders would praise him for ridding them of such an untrustworthy person. And Medrix' wife ... he laughed ... well she was dead, so no tales could be told there and even if she was not, for she had the luck of the devil that one, he had arranged that she should be taken to their camps anyway. So it was a feeling of excitement that welled up within him, not realising that Medrix had plans of his own.

Later that day, Conn went over to see Medrix. He found him sitting on the side of the bed, his hands over his face. Conn asked him what he was doing and he said that he had to get up and start walking for he was going to walk to his office. No one was going to carry him there.

"But the doctor said that you were to rest in bed."

"Then the doctor is a fool. I remember now how I told Cessie to walk after she had been whipped for breaking a court rule. I didn't realise the pain she was in but she did it and seemed all right in the court room. But she is a fighter – and so am I!"

"I'll help you."

But Medrix told him that he had to do it himself and so Conn watched him walk slowly around the room a couple of times, and then sit down, exhausted. He smiled apologetically. "I'm not very good am I? But I'll have a rest then have another go. Sit down, Conn: tell me the news, or have you come for another purpose: maybe to find out where my keys are – is that it?"

"No. Timmons did ask me to find out if possible but that is not what I had in mind. I've had an idea and I am sure it will work."

"So what is it, then?"

"I thought that I could start a small fire in one of the cupboards. The smoke would set off the fire alarms; the sprinklers would come on and all the doors would open, including this one. I could get you out then and make for the landshakers parked outside and we could escape and get to the Southern Hills – join the others, you see, for it looks like the Zendrians are all here already."

"What about the guard? Anyway, I can't go. I have promised to open the safe for them so I can't go."

"But ..."

"No ... I have to do this, Conn, but thanks anyway. Now help me up and I'll start walking again."

Conn then realised there was nothing he could do but help Medrix get fit enough for the day in question.

Chapter 25

There were only three days left to the deadline and Celisia and Helk were still in the settlement building. Storms had kept them in on most days. It had been very warm and she and Helk had braved the storms on two occasions and had found mushrooms. But although she said that they were edible, he said they were not and after a heated argument she threw them away.

On another occasion he went out fishing and came back with several fish which she cooked in the oven using the last bit of butter in her pack.

The building had evidently been a space station and had several sleep rooms with bunk beds and one with a double. There was a kitchen with everything in it that was needed, except food. There was a room with tables and chairs which was evidently a dining-cum-sitting area. One long room was a laboratory. Here there was no equipment except for a few books and some old maps on the wall. Near the sleep rooms were three washrooms. Although everything was there, even to blankets and spare clothes, there were no other people and no way to contact anyone else. In fact they could have lived there comfortably if they'd had a supply of food.

But today Ces couldn't settle and she argued with Helk because he said that he was going fishing again and she was to stay here on her own. That was the last thing she needed – to be on her own. But he stormed out of the building saying he wanted to be on his own and she shouted that she wouldn't care if he fell down a hole and never came back. But once her anger subsided she regretted the remark. He was another person – and maybe the only one she would ever see. She shivered although it wasn't cold.

All day she did little jobs around the place and, by the evening she was fed up of being on her own.

It was now dark and Helk hadn't returned and now she was worried. What if he had fallen down a hole? What if...?

She went to bed and dreamed that Medrix was tangled in a net and blood poured down on to the floor. She woke with a jolt, yet still seeing the blood and the net and hearing him cry out in pain. She cried out his name. Then she was aware that Helk was there sitting beside her and she was so relieved that she clung to him.

"It's all right, Leah – it's all right – it's a bad dream."

"Something terrible has happened to Medrix," she said.

"It's a nightmare, love, that's all. I'll make a hot drink; that will calm you down."

Then Ces realised how thankful she felt for him being there. She couldn't lose him and Medrix.

Helk told her that he'd caught quite a few fish, then was caught in a storm and had to shelter until it had passed.

Ces slept late and had just finished dressing when Helk rushed in to tell her that a shuttle had arrived and they had better get out of here fast. She did not argue but followed him out through the back entrance and into the trees and then on to the thick bushes that overlooked the shuttle pad. Here they lay low, peering through the bushes.

Six men got out of the shuttle. She was about to say something when Helk put his fingers to his lips and then whispered: "Zendrians."

She hardly breathed as she watched them make for the building. A seventh man came out of the shuttle, evidently the pilot. He walked off towards the fence behind the shuttle. He seemed to be looking at the lake.

"*Now*," Helk said, "we'll risk it, Leah," and with that they ran from the bushes to the unguarded shuttle and got in, closing the door behind them and Helk immediately set a course for Chetner and, as the shuttle started, they could see the man running back but he was too late because the shuttle was airborne. He was waving his arms and running after them but soon he was just a dot on the ground.

"Helk – you can fly this thing?" Celisia said in amazement.

"Of course – most Venturian men can – it is not much different to other shuttles, except this has a covering device. All Zendrian shuttles and fighter birds have them."

"What is it – this covering device?"

"It can stay invisible for up to one hour – it is a great discovery in the right hands – but in war it can be deadly."

"I can imagine. We can get into the docks that way, can't we?" Ces said excitedly.

"Yes we can, Leah – yes we can – now do you think you can find some food?"

"Yes, of course, Helk," she said, smiling at him, her blue eyes lighting up in delight, "we are going to get there in time but how long will it take us?"

"About six hours – food please, Leah – before I fall apart and then you'll have to fly this yourself."

Ces found bread, cheese and fruit and gave him some and, as she ate her

347

portion, felt that somehow all was going to be well. The powers that be had answered her prayers.

A message came up on the screen that they were to return the shuttle at once.

Ces looked concerned, "Will they report its loss to their base?"

"I doubt that they can without going through us or another vessel, but we'll have to see."

With that, she had to be content. The excitement that had thrilled her was now dulled when she realised that stealing a shuttle was, in itself, a crime – but then, it was an emergency.

Helk said that it would be a good idea if she could get some sleep as she had had a bad night. So, taking his advice, she went into one of the back seats and stretched out and tried to relax, but her thoughts were on the oncoming events ahead.

What would she do when she got to Chetner?

How would she explain Helk to Medrix?

Would Medrix be pleased to see her, after all he had been very annoyed with her before her kidnapping?

The steady throb of the shuttle's powerful engine gradually relaxed her and she slept.

Helk received another message and he nodded to himself and printed it off but he did not answer it; after all everything was going to plan as far as he was concerned.

He put the printout in his inside pocket and smiled to himself. He could do nothing now but wait. He relaxed back in his seat and closed his eyes for he had been up most of the night too and he would want all his ingenuity to carry out the plan he had in mind. Poor thing, he was almost sorry for her but of course he had to earn a living and this way he would be paid.

He awoke as they neared the outer docks but the shuttle had been spotted, which annoyed him, because he wasn't able to use the covering device. The control tower was already hailing him and he had to answer and did so. Then he went to where Ces lay sleeping and quickly fastened wrist cuffs on her. She awoke in surprise and tried to move her wrists, only to find that the cuffs restricted her movements.

Helk stepped back and was about to speak to her when she got up angrily and asked him what he was doing. He looked severely at her. "You are my prisoner, of course, and I am sure we will be welcomed when I tell them so."

Fury enveloped her when she realised that he had tricked her. He was merciless and had led her to believe he was on her side. She stepped towards him and hit him in the stomach with her fists. He stepped back trying to restrain her but she went for him again and again until he stopped her by slapping her hard across the face. She swayed and he pushed her into the seat but she was too far away from it and fell, hitting her head and lay there oblivious to him or anything else.

"Damn it to all the devils in hell," he said as he picked her up and carried her to the front seat and, laying her carefully on it, went back to the controls.

"Please give your name and number," droned a voice from the control tower.

"I am Venturian Helk bringing in a prisoner as ordered by the Zendrian government."

"We have not been notified of this," the voice answered and then went on: "what credentials have you to show you are who you say you are?"

"I have all the documents with me. We have only been waiting for orders to bring her out of hiding to this place."

Another voice came on."I am Lawmaker Timmons and I want to know who the prisoner is."

"The prisoner is Leah Dickon. I have all the documents."

"I wish to speak to her," the Lawmaker said.

"That is not possible, as she slipped and fell and knocked herself out and needs the attention of a medic as soon as possible."

He waited, then was given the go-ahead to come in.

Once in, Helk was met by three men. Two of them took Ces to the medical bay and he was taken to see the Lawmaker to whom he gave his documents and the printout. Lawmaker Timmons seemed well pleased with these and welcomed him to the base. He arranged for Helk to stay.

Helk wanted to know when the new Controller was coming to take up his duties. The Lawmaker said that it would be a few hours. He also told him that he could have a room in the base as he would not be able to leave yet. He was also told to go to the dining room for a meal and he was free to wander about the base as he liked. Then the Lawmaker handed him a pass so that he was free to go anywhere. Helk enquired about the prisoner. The Lawmaker said she was still in the medical bay but he hoped she would be transferred to the prison soon.

After that the Lawmaker dismissed him and Helk left the room and went at once to the medical bay but here he was stopped by two guards and he had to leave without seeing Ces. He went to the dining centre and ordered a meal.

There were very few people about but he listened in to the conversations going on around him. He suspected that they did not know that he could speak their language and learned quite a lot: firstly that the Controller had not followed out the Chief Elder's commands and had been punished for it; that he had been whipped until he had collapsed and was evidently in a very distressed way. He was in the prison. He had promised to sign the documents prepared by Lawmaker Timmons but only if he signed them an hour before the new man came. No one seemed to know who that man was. Evidently Lawmaker Medrix would not sign the documents any earlier than that. Helk thought that a bit odd but evidently the Zendrians had been content with that.

He wondered why. Surely the sooner the papers were signed the quicker everyone could go home. He was puzzled and thought the Lawmaker must have a reason for this and wondered what.

Could it be that the Lawmaker had a plan of his own? It seemed he had to open the safe for them and only he had the keys.

Why was he holding the keys at all? Maybe he was waiting for some news from somewhere ... that's it, Helk was sure ... maybe Medrix was waiting for some help to come from somewhere.

Why didn't the Zendrians realise that ... or maybe ... he stared into his soup ... if it was he, he would have put the base on self-destruct rather than have the Zendrians here ... of course, that was it ... it must be ... it would only be a last resort because help might be coming from somewhere. If he was right, the whole situation was different and he was placed in an impossible position. He would never get paid at all.

He smiled. If he could work it out why couldn't they?

He went to the prison. There were two guards on duty and he showed his pass and they opened the gates and let him in.

Medrix was lying down on the bed staring up at the ceiling.

So this was the man Leah loved, Helk thought.

Medrix sat up and asked who he was.

"My name is Helk. Did you know that your wife is here?"

"How do you know?"

"I brought her here."

"You did ... from where?"

"From another planet ... it is a long story and I haven't got time to tell you it all. She's in the medical bay."

"Is she ill?"

"She hit her head when she fell but it isn't very bad. Have they told you this?"

"No."

Suddenly there was an earth tremor and the chairs fell over. Helk was surprised but Medrix told him that they happened all the time but they did no harm to the base. Helk told him who was where on the base and they had a long talk about what was happening. He would have gone on but Medrix said it was best for him to go as the Zendrians might think he was a spy. Helk promised to come and see him again and left the prison.

He went to find the room he had been given and lay down on the bed to make a new plan of action.

When Ces woke up she found herself lying on a low bed in a small room. There were double doors at one end and at the other, a glass door with a curtain across it.

She got up and went to the double doors and opened them. Two men stood there and, as far as she knew, they were not Lawmakers. One of them pushed her roughly back into the room and shouted to her in a foreign language then closed the door.

She then went to the other door and opened it. It led into a narrow passage-way. Down one side of it were other doors. She was halfway down the passage when one of the doors opened and a nurse came out and beckoned her into the room but did not speak. Ces followed her. A medic smiled at her and said he was pleased to see that she had quite recovered and he would inform the Lawmaker that she had.

"What Lawmaker is that?" she asked.

"Lawmaker Timmons. He is the Acting Controller now."

"Where is Lawmaker Medrix, then?" she asked with some surprise.

"He has disobeyed the Chief Elder's orders and has been punished. He is in prison until he comes to his senses and then, and then only, will he be released."

"But surely ... I mean he is a stickler for rules ... you must be wrong."

"Evidently he only obeys the rules when they fit in with his plans."

"And what plans are those?"

"You must know he is trying ... I do not think I should tell you but I will. You see he threatened to have his revenge on the people of this country and on the one who was the captain of the winning team that played against the Elders' team."

It was then that Ces realised that the man did not know who she was.

"Do you know who I am?" she asked with a smile, for she was ready to tell him that Medrix would never play the revenge game.

"Of course I do. You are the one brought in to stand trial by the Zendrians. You are Leah Dickon. You are not pretending that you don't know. You do have two bruises on your head, but you haven't lost your memory."

"Am I going to stand trial here, then?"

The medic shook his head and would say no more. Then the nurse told Ces that she had a visitor and she was to go back to her room and, without much ado, she shepherded Ces down the passage back to her room.

It was Helk.

"You!" she screamed at him. "What do you want?"

"How are you?"

He got no further.

"Why do you care? You were pretending to be my friend and all the time you were planning to come here. Needed the money did you? What do you want?"

"I couldn't tell you; you never gave me a chance ..."

"A chance to tell me that you were the enemy after all ...?"

"Let me speak, Leah. They will come in a minute."

"With your money, I suppose ... well, what is it?"

"You see, I fell asleep, like you I was tired and when I awoke we were already in the dock and they were hailing us. I went to tell you as I put the cuffs on you but you woke up suddenly and freaked out and went for me. I had to hit you to stop you and then you fell and knocked yourself out. You see, I used the orders to get in and ..."

"I see. But why would they want Leah to come here?"

"They want her because they know who you really are."

"The medic thinks I have come here to stand trial."

"He's only told what they want him to know."

"I see ... but ... didn't they wonder how you knew you were to come here? After all, we left those men on the ground."

"The Zendrian leader instructed me, or rather the shuttle, and said I was to take you to the base in order to get my money. I think he meant I was to take you to Zendra but I thought I'd use it here and Lawmaker Timmons sees nothing wrong with it."

"But, I'm stuck here."

"Yes, for now. But I have seen Medrix and told him you are here. I am trying to work out something. I must go before they come for you ... he sends his love to you ..."

He rushed to the door and went, leaving her more confused than before.

Thirty minutes later she was taken to Lawmaker Timmons and he told her that she was to see Medrix and try to get him to sign the documents that he had prepared earlier for him. If she failed she would be taken to Zendra where she would live in a brothel camp for the rest of her life.

Ces had no choice but to do as he asked and she was then taken to the prison.

The guard opened the door for her and she went in.

Medrix was sitting on the bed seemingly staring into space but, as she came into the room, he looked up.

He was pale and his dark-brown hair had streaks of grey in it and it had not been kept at the standard Lawmaker cut. He was unshaven, too.

He smiled. "Ces, this is a nice surprise," he said as he came to her and put his arms round her, pulling her tightly to him so that she could feel every line of his body. He bent down and kissed her then pushed her away from him.

"How long have we got?"

"It depends on your answer."

"There's a catch?"

Ces then explained what he had to do in order to release her and he shook his head and, coming close to her, holding her in his arms, he whispered: "I have my orders and they are not from that Lawmaker. They are from the Chief Elder and I must obey them. You must understand that many people's lives depend on it and, if I could I would not let you go."

She reached up and kissed him and said that she understood that there was no choice for him or for her and that she would not stop loving him wherever she was. They had now very little time together. Then he said that she must leave now and go with Conn and he would get her to the Southern Hills where she would be safe. Conn, in fact, was waiting with the guard for his signal.

"But Conn betrayed us," she exclaimed.

"He will not betray us this time. Now go my love and remember, whatever happens, that I will always love you."

She went to the door and Conn was there, waiting for her but there was no guard.

"Where's the guard?"

Then she saw Helk standing there saying that he had taken care of him and they had to go now.

She pushed the door open and saw the guard lying against the wall.

Helk said: "We have to go now, Lawmaker ..."

"I can't" Medrix said. "I promised to sign the documents." He got no further as Helk hit him hard and knocked him out. Medrix collapsed in a heap.

"We have to go now before the guard comes to." And without more ado, Helk lifted Medrix up and carried him out of the cell, the others following him. Ces kept saying that Medrix would be furious when he awoke because he had his own orders to follow, but no one took any notice of her and she realised that she could not do anything about it.

They met no one and, eventually they came out on the courtyard.

There was an eerie red light everywhere and then the ground shook under their feet.

Ces looked up at the mountain and saw that it was bright red.

"God!" she exclaimed, suddenly remembering a history lesson and she said out loud: "The highest volcano in the galaxy is to be found in Chetner and its name is the Red Mountain, but this is the Reed Mountain, but it has to be this one."

Conn urged her on. "I came out earlier and saw what was going on. We have to get out of here because this base cannot survive when it has been built at the foot of a volcano. So, hurry every one!" He opened the door of a landshaker and everyone got in. There was another tremor and a great spurt of molten lava hurled itself into the sky.

Ces got out. "We have to warn them," she said. "No one deserves to die like that," and she ran to ring the alarms. Conn grabbed her explaining that if she went in there the force field could keep her there and he pulled her back to the vehicle.

They closed the door of the landshaker as the molten ash rained down on them.

Conn drove quickly towards the hills using the computer readouts rather than what he could actually see.

They were soon down in the valley and going up the next hill when there was an explosion that rocked the landshaker but they kept on without stopping.

Helk said he thought it was the Zendrians' war freighters because they had already been in the dock when he came in, even though the deadline had not been reached, so sure were they that Lawmaker Timmons had got what they wanted.

Conn drove until they got to City Nineteen and then Helk took over. They did not dare stop and took it in turns until safety could be reached.

Ces wondered if they would even make it as she sat by Medrix, who was unaware of anything.

Chapter 26

Medrix woke up with a terrible headache. He opened his eyes, only to shut them again quickly. He knew where he was. He was in a shaker. What he didn't know was how he had got there. Shakers were used by reclamation teams. They contained everything that was needed for twenty men who were out working, reclaiming the land: they could also be used for rescue work.

He remembered now. Some bastard had hit him.

Who was it?

No man hit a Lawmaker and got away with it.

He'd have him ... but not now.

He realised then that a woman was sitting beside him.

Who was it?

Ah, he knew now ... yes ... he knew.

It was Jessanda ... she had waited for him after all.

He reached for her hand and she whispered: "Medrix ... are you feeling better?"

He was wrong ... the voice wasn't hers.

He was all in a muddle. He opened his eyes and saw the woman but he seemed to be looking through a fog. "Jessanda," he said softly, "you've come after all."

"Medrix," said the voice again, "it's me ... Celisia ..."

He repeated the name and then said: "I remember now. You're the sly bitch that everybody hates."

The woman got up from her seat and went to the back somewhere ... he closed his eyes ... and slept.

Celisia ran to the back seat. She was very upset – Medrix did not know who she was.

Helk came to find her and could see she had been crying.

He told her that evidently Medrix had been given drugs to keep him confused and they were still having some effect on him.

She felt better then.

They were approaching City Eighteen when Medrix awoke again and he asked for Celisia: she went to him at once.

She explained why Helk had hit him and he was amazed that the base had been built at the foot of a volcano. He said that he felt better and could help with the driving but the others were against it and he agreed to wait for a few hours before doing so.

He wanted to know about Helk, but before she could tell him, he fell asleep. Later, when he did wake up she got him some soup and cheese and, after that he stood up and went to look out of the window, only to discover that he could see nothing but white fog. The computer was still finding the route for them.

He was content to let the others drive but stood and talked to them about it. Then he went to sit down.

Two days later, as they neared City Sixteen, he began to take an interest in everything and took his turn at driving which gave the others time to catch up on their sleep.

The visibility had improved and, as they approached City Fifteen, the way became clear and he stopped the shaker and opened the door.

He went outside then came back in and said that everyone could go outside for a little while, but not to go too far as he had no idea how safe it would be.

The little group stood outside breathing in the fresh air and looking about them. In the distance the volcano was still sending great sheets of flame into the sky and the Northern Hills seemed to be on fire. To the right of where the base had been, there was a great fireball which spread across the sky, the glare from which made their eyes ache.

"If the hills are on fire, surely that will mean it could spread over the rest of the countryside. We could still be in danger, Medrix," Celisia said.

He agreed, so they all got back in the shaker and continued on their way again.

Helk said that if it rained or the wind changed then the danger would have passed but, anyway, once it came to water that might stop it.

Over the next few days, Medrix had long talks with Helk and then with Celisia about their stay on the other planet. He asked no questions, but just listened.

Celisia was surprised that he didn't question them. She didn't think it a good idea to question his reaction; otherwise he might think there was something to be worried about.

They passed City Thirteen and were sitting together at the back of the shaker, Conn was driving and Helk was getting some sleep when Medrix said: "Ces, I don't trust Helk and you mustn't either."

"Why ever not?"

"I have been thinking about him. His story is too pat."

"In what way?"

"When he arrived at the base, Lawmaker Timmons gave him a pass to go anywhere on the base. Not even Conn was given that but, if in fact he was the new Controller, he would need to know all about the base."

"I don't agree, Medrix. He saved my life and yours."

"He was travelling to Zendra when something hit the shuttle and the man guarding you was killed, so then it was easy enough for him to take over his identity. He would just take over his papers."

"And his picture?"

"His own over it..."

"But ..."

"He treated you like a prisoner but when he went to see who the men were who arrived on the planet, he came back with the excuse that he had heard the truth about you and had changed his mind."

"Yes, but why not tell them who I was?"

"He did."

"But I ..."

"He said it was safer to keep you there rather than go to Zendra. The planet was nearer to this one."

"I won't believe it!"

"He then said you were not his prisoner and that way you gave him no trouble. It worked."

"Medrix, you have absolutely no evidence against him and if this is some idea of yours to get back at him I am not impressed. He saved our lives, or have you forgotten that?"

"Yes ... but he had a purpose ... let me go on ... he went off fishing on his own, knowing that you would not leave the building. It was then he contacted them and knew it was time for him to come here. Don't you see ... they just happened to come back ... they left the shuttle unattended. What pilot would do that? Then he received a message to say they were to come here and so you arrived, in chains. He even said that he was bringing in a prisoner - you my darling – he duped you. How did the Zendrians know where you both landed? Well, that was easy. He told me that the Zendrians had said that they had seen a mermaid in the sea. Their leader did not believe in mermaids and told them to land and look for anyone living there. You see, they saw you swimming in the nude."

"I had clothes on ..."

"Yes, but Helk said that the water had made them transparent. Lawmothers don't swim. If you hadn't broken that rule, they might never have known where you were."

Ces didn't answer.

"Ah, I see you don't answer but, in your case, it brought you back to me."

"But he saved your life."

"Yes, but when he realised that the base was doomed, he rescued us ...

after all he would have a safe entry to the Lawmakers' camp on the Southern Hills if he had brought us safely there."

"I still *don't* believe it. You don't know him as I do."

"What do you mean by that?"

"I was there: you were not."

"I know you shared a tent with him. Oh! My God! You slept with him?"

"No, I did *not*. We slept in the same tent, he at the door end and me at the opposite end."

"You fell for his charm, didn't you?"

"No! of *course* not."

"You did ...?"

Ces shook her head and was about to get up from her seat when he pulled her back down and kissed her roughly on the lips, deepening the kiss as she struggled to get away from him. She was aware that Helk was standing looking at them. Medrix undid her jacket buttons and tried to undo the shirt she was wearing. Helk moved away and she heard him talking to Conn: "We can't tell him now, Conn, because he is making up for lost time with his wife."

They laughed.

Ces pulled herself free and Medrix let her go.

"You have a man's shirt on. Is it his?"

"No. They gave me clean clothes when I got to the base."

Ces stood up and walked to the lat and closed the door.

He was horrid.

She had dreamed how he would welcome her, but she was wrong ... he did not want her back. He wanted Jessanda. Well he could have her ... she would find a way to leave him: she would live somewhere on Chetner away from him ... yes – he was welcome to her.

Her lips were bruised and her arms ached. She would sit away from him. Of course she had felt attracted to Helk but she did not love him like she loved Medrix.

She sat for ages until someone tried the door. She opened it. Medrix was standing there and she pushed past him and said she was going to make coffee for them all.

He grabbed her arm.

She pulled away from him and went to prepare the coffee.

"You must listen to me ..."

"No ..."

He watched her making the drinks and shook his head. It had all gone wrong. He should have never told her of his suspicions ... of course she took them the wrong way ... she had been almost three moons with that man ... he was bound to have had some ties with her ... good ones, too ... she was never going to believe that he could be a spy ... but he could be quite innocent ... but spies, good ones, would not be found out unless someone who had been a spy knew what to look for ... and as far as he was concerned he was sure as sure that he was right. But was it worth it to do anything about it? And, yes, she was right; he couldn't prove it ... could he?

Medrix had to watch Helk and listen to see if he gave himself away ... or maybe he was just plain jealous and looked for things that weren't there ... he hoped so.

Conn, seeing Medrix standing there alone, came over to him to tell him that they were very near City Twelve but the track was blocked by great blocks of rock that had tumbled down steep mountain sides. There seemed to be no way through. The shaker was now stationary and Helk was outside. He came back in to say that there was a narrow lane to the right which might take them around the rocks and the three men agreed to try it.

The lane wound its way around a hill and then seemed to come back on itself, but not quite, for it forked right and then climbed a steep hill. They came to a gate.

A large notice told them that it was private land but Conn opened the gate and they continued along the track until they came to another gate which was open, but here they stopped for, below them, was a large lake and there was no way across, so they had to turn back and return the way they had come.

Ces said that if they returned to City Fourteen there was a track there that led across the marshes and came out near Hunter's Mill. The mill was not far from the road to the Southern Hills.

When Medrix asked why she had not told them about it before, she said it was because the route they had taken would have been quicker.

There was nothing for it but to return to City Fourteen, so they turned the shaker around and went back the way they had come. There was a smell of smoke but they could not see the fire and when they did come to the city they turned onto the track. It was very narrow and twisted and turned. A mist came down so the computer took over the driving again while the mist seemed to seep into the shaker and no one spoke.

Ces found a seat in the corner and sat there away from the others and relaxed back trying not to think about Medrix and his rough handling of her.

The men took it in turns to drive as Medrix deemed it unsafe to stop anywhere.

He had not spoken to Ces again and she was content with that.
She had found a pad and some pens on one of the shelves. Now she sat in the corner sketching from memory the events of the past few moons. It took her thoughts away from everyone else.

The shaker had stopped and she looked up from her sketch to find the door open and the men outside so she went to see what was happening.

The lane had led them into a farmyard.

Medrix asked her about it. She had got it wrong: the shuttle she had travelled in must have gone a different way.

She shook her head and said that this was the right way and there was probably a gate leading from the yard that led them back to the lane. She left them to go and look and Helk followed her.

Medrix screwed up his face with annoyance but said nothing.

They were gone a long time and he was just beginning to panic when Helk returned without her.

"Where the hell have you been all this time ... and where is my wife?"

Helk laughed and said she was waiting by another gate which came out in the lane. There was a signpost there for Hunter's Mill.

They got in the shaker and Conn drove, listening to Helk's directions and soon they saw her standing, smiling, by a gate.

"There you are. I told you Leah would be waiting for us."

The name 'Leah' made Medrix frown. God! He'd called her Leah ... Law Officer Filton had said that her name was really Leah Dickon and their marriage wasn't legal because she was married to Dickon. He looked at her smiling there and wondered if there was any truth in it.

"Why did you call her Leah?"

Helk smiled and said that it was a habit he had got into whilst on the other planet and he found it hard to remember her real name, though she did not seem to mind, he said as an afterthought.

She did not seem to mind! Medrix was scowling at her and she stopped smiling and came into the shaker and sat in her corner again.

They had not gone very far when they arrived at Hunter's Mill. It was blackened by fire and had lost all its charm.

To the left was a sign with two names on it: one was *The Mountain Centre*, the other *Calne Bay*.

Medrix told them to stop here as it was getting dark.

"We could make it to the Mountain Centre easily," said Conn enthusiastically.

"No ... we are going to Calne Bay ... aren't we, *Leah?"* he said sarcastically.

Ces looked at him in surprise but somehow the place name seemed to be known to her. Somebody she knew lived there, or maybe Medrix knew someone there and wanted to visit.

Medrix took over the driving but stopped as they entered the little town.

"You get out here, Celisia ... you walk down from here."

Surprised, she got out and saw him turn the shaker and drive away.

She waited but he did not come back and soon she could see it as it took the road to the Mountain Centre and disappeared from sight.

Both Conn and Helk asked him what he was doing.

"You can't leave her there," Helk said.

"I can and I will ... it is none of your business ... her name is really Leah Dickon and ..."

"That was the name the Zendrians gave her: that's not her real name ..."

"Isn't it? Well she told me the same name when I questioned her and there was no sign of the Zendrians then ... so it has to be true. When she lost her memory she remembered her name and I, poor fool, believed when she said she was Celisia."

"Stop the shaker *now*!" said Helk.

Medrix did so and Helk got out and started walking back.

Medrix drove a little way and then parked on the side of the road. "We'll wait here and see what happens."

Conn looked at him. What was he up to? He was certainly acting strangely ... you never knew with Medrix, after all he had been an Elders' man once ... could he really be taking his revenge out on his wife who had won the game against the Lawmakers all that time ago? He had sworn to do so and maybe this was what it was all about. He would have to wait with him to find out, then if it was so, should he side with him or against him, for he owed her something; at least so he thought

An hour later Helk came back. He hadn't found her in spite of Calne Bay being a small place.

"Did you find the boathouse?" Medrix asked.

"Yes. It was all locked up. All the buildings were. There were notices everywhere which said they were closed until further notice."

"Did you look everywhere?"

"I've just said so. How could she disappear so quickly?"

"Because she knows where to find him."

"Find whom?"

"The man she married before she married me. My marriage to her is not legal because of it."

"That's rubbish and you know it. The Zendrians made it all up."

"But when she had lost her memory she made up a name and Dickon was the name she gave. Leah Dickon. Leah is the name of my cousin's wife and Dickon is the name of her real husband. She told me she did not know why she had chosen it but I know for a fact that she chose it because it was her name."

"Maybe she just liked the name, and that's all there is to it," Helk said with a sigh at Medrix' stubbornness.

"No ... because Law Officer Filton came down here and said that he found out that Dickon was a fisherman and a boat builder. If you had gone in the boatshed you would have seen a boat there with the name *The Golden Maid*.

"So?"

"After her, of course."

"And you can prove it?"

"She can prove it."

"How?"

"Being there will bring back her memory."

"That could be very dangerous for her, Medrix."

"Why?"

"She will be in a very shocked state. She probably thinks that you have abandoned her and that girl loves you to distraction. I should know because she kept on and on saying that she had to get back to you. I came with her because of it. She, in fact, saved your life by her persistence and now you would leave her stranded there on her own?"

"When she realises the truth she won't want to come back with me."

"The truth being that you want to go back to your first love?"

"Rubbish!"

"She will think that. She was upset when you called her Jessanda. I told her that you were all mixed up and did not know what you were talking about. She understood then and sat by your side until you were better. And, another thing: she told me that she did not trust the Lawmaker because he looked like the man on the shuttle but you said he was with you on that day. If what she says is true, then all this could be a plot to discredit her and, maybe you."

"But he was with me on that day, wasn't he, Conn? You remember, don't you?"

"Yes."

Helk tried again. "Someone started the rumour and the Zendrians just used it."

Medrix sighed; evidently this man was not going to give up. "Then who started it?"

"Do you know, Conn?" asked Helk. "After all, you were there at her kidnapping, so you must know something."

Conn paled but said nothing.

Helk went on: "You started it, didn't you? Admit it. If you think anything of her at all, you will tell us because, in her state, she could do anything. She told me she had once been in a coma ... the shock of this thing, Medrix, could send her back into it. She does not deserve this sort of thing. She has been through so much it could kill her, or she might give up and commit suicide. Do you want that on your conscience? Well – do you?"

Conn stood up and said: "I didn't start it but my sister did. She wanted you, Medrix. Always did. She thought that when her husband died you would turn to her and you did when the trial was going badly and you were quarrelling with Celisia. She even gave you some ideas to use, which you did. And you took her out to a party, but as the days went on and you married Celisia you became more distant from her. But she said that the prosecutor was right, Celisia was a witch and was manipulating you. When you both renewed your vows she was furious and said then that she would get rid of her and see that you got the punishment you deserved for betraying the Elders. Her husband had been a close friend to one of the Elders and she went to them to talk it over. They gave her some tips. I said she was mad to even do anything: to leave things alone but she said that my dream of being an Elders' man had been dashed by you because the Masters' Training College had been disbanded after the trial – and she was right, of course, so I did my bit. I arranged Celisia's kidnapping but I only took her to one of the attics. She would have come to no harm but then we heard that the Zendrians had got her. It was never meant to happen. We had played into their hands. I told Jessanda it had now gone far enough and we were going to be in dead trouble if someone found out. Then Lawmaker Timmons came along and seemed to be carrying out orders from the Chief Elder, but I doubt that now. I think he thought he was. But he went too far when he whipped you and I stopped the man from going on and on. I think Lawmaker Timmons was so angry that he went berserk. It was then I knew I had to get you out of there. It dawned on me that he was trying to get his revenge on you for making him lose in the trial. The Elders did not like being losers – but they admired you for winning."

Medrix shook his head.

Conn went on: "They did. They thought you were brilliant – and so you were and if I can do anything for you to try and put things right I will do it ..." his voice faded as he sat down.

"Conn," said Helk, "you tell us that the kidnap plan went wrong, but what actually was the plan?"

"Good point. Conn, I want to know that, too."

"We wanted you to stand down as Controller and hand the job over to Thelka. He in fact had been overlooked. He was more experienced and was a reclamation officer. He thought that Celisia needed medical help which she was not getting while she stayed at the base. In fact he had recommended a good place that treated people like her."

"I see," said Medrix. "Where was this place, then?"

"On Jadeston. My sister said it was recommended by all the families that had sent people there. Celisia would get treatment and you would be near at hand to visit her."

Helk frowned. "The only place on Jadeston that I know of, because a friend's friend went there because she was incurable - in other words, she was insane – was the Ferndale Security Base. There is no other one there."

Conn shook his head. "I don't know anything about it. My sister said that Celisia needed treatment. I did not think they meant to harm her."

"*Not harm her!*" Medrix was livid. "You harmed her when you kidnapped her and the medic told me her memory would come back if she was with the people she knew. You, Conn, will write a statement for me naming everyone concerned. I will, of course, take into account the good things you have done. Obviously there will be an inquiry which you will have to attend. The more you tell the court, the more lenient they will be with you. Is Thelka the new Controller, then?"

"I don't know. He might be ... we weren't told."

Medrix pushed him out of the driving seat and took over the controls and drove to Calne Bay.

It was now dark and there were no lights anywhere, except coming from the boathouse. Someone was there.

He parked outside it and went in.

The light was on and someone was standing on the scaffolding that surrounded a half-finished sailing boat.

This was the boat Filton had told him about, he was sure.

The figure turned and walked towards him. It was Celisia and she visibly jumped when she saw him there.

"Medrix ... you've come back for me?" she queried.

"Of course. Helk came down but couldn't find you. Where were you?"

"I remembered something ... I remembered it all. I used to come here to buy fish or to see him."

"See whom?" God, he thought, was the story true after all?

"He told me where the key was. I remembered you see, so I came here to see if it was still here," she sighed, "it was all so long ago."

"What was?"

She did not seem to hear him but went on: "I met him here. He was a fisherman: went out to sea almost every day. I would buy fish from him. The more I saw him the more I wanted to see him and soon we were going out together. He gave me a ring and I always wore it. It was not a betrothal one. We were just friends, you see, but soon we felt more for each other and he wanted us to be betrothed. I wasn't sure about it and he said he would give me all the time I wanted. He taught me to sail and said he was building a boat and was going to name it after me and, when it was finished, I should name it for him.

"At that time we were all exploring the tunnels to see if they could be filled in if possible, and he came down with us. He had never been down before ..." she began to cry and Medrix looked at her and put his arms around her to comfort her. "He ... was full of plans for us but there it ended. There was a roof fall. He pushed me out of the way and ... all the rocks..." she sobbed "... fell on him ..." She hesitated and then went on: "I stayed with him until help came to us. I talked to him for ages and he told me he loved me and I told him that I loved him too ... his voice faded and he said I had to find somebody else for his was a dangerous life anyway ..." She leaned against Medrix and cried and he held her tightly as she went on: "When help came it was too late for him ... even if they had got him out he wouldn't have survived. I blocked all memory of it. Threw myself into my job and tried to forget the agony of that time. I did not grieve as I should have done ... but now I have remembered ... and here is his unfinished boat ... I ..."

"When did this happen, love?"

"About four years after the game. I should have told you, but ..."

"You were trying to forget."

"Yes."

"It was like that with my sister. I didn't grieve, you see."

"I know, I know."

"Well, he wouldn't have wanted you to stay single, would he, Ces?"

"No. But the fires ..."

"He was already dead and gone to the spirit world ... he will be happy for you ... won't he, love?"

"Yes. What will happen to his boat?"

"It will be used, I am sure. I will make a note of it."

"Will you?"

"Of course. Now let's go back to the others. We have to go to the centre now and then home." He bent his head and kissed her very gently. "I love you, darling, never forget that," was all he said as they walked to the shaker.

Two days later they all arrived at the Mountain Centre. When word spread around the camp that they had survived there were great celebrations.

There were lines of tents spread across the hillside. Medrix and Helk shared a tent with two other Lawmakers: Celisia slept with the women (Chetnerites) in the centre itself. Conn was kept in custody for safety's sake.

A shuttle service took them all back to Estolan but Medrix had to stay until the end for the Chief Elder said that he was still the Controller whilst he was on Chetner. Two teams of Lawmakers also stayed on.

On the last day before Celisia and Medrix returned to Estolan, the two remaining teams planned an Elders' men celebration, where they ate a meal of rabbit stewed in wine, accompanied by vegetables. The ale cup was passed from one to another in honour of Medrix and his wife. Then they all raised their whips in a salute. Elders' men they had been once, but to salute a man in this way was considered the greatest honour they could give him.

Later that night, Celisia and Medrix slept together and, as they lay there, knew that their Chetner adventures were over.

EPILOGUE

When Medrix and Celisia reached Estolan, the Lawmakers gave them a great welcome.

An Inquiry was held and Medrix had to write a report about the whole thing.

The Masters from the Elders' college were arrested for it was they who had organised the looters.

For her part in the affair, Jessanda was taken into custody and sent to the House of Correction for five years.

The Chetner Elders declared that they had no intention of being Zendrian puppets. They'd known the base had a very short life and that was why they'd agreed to let the Zendrians use it in lieu of payment. They did not seek revenge on Medrix, for they admired him, but on Lawmaker Timmons for losing their case.

Conn was sent back to Chetner to work: he later married a Chetner girl and never returned to Estolan.

Thelka was never seen again and it was thought he had died in the fire, as had Lawmaker Timmons.

Helk was who he said he was, and he and Medrix became firm friends.

Medrix took a year off work to be with his wife and, afterwards, was given the post of Chief Assistant to the new Grand Elder, the previous one having resigned.

The following year Celisia gave birth to twins, a boy and a girl. Eldon's daughter came to help with them.

The new council allowed girls to play the game and also, with Celisia's help, take part in many activities previously denied them.

Dickon's boat on Chetner was restored and used by the Lawmakers.

Four years later, Medrix was offered the position of Lawmakers' Representative on the Intergalactic Council based on Temra – but that, of course, is another story ... isn't it?

Lightning Source UK Ltd.
Milton Keynes UK
21 September 2009

143979UK00001B/28/P

9 780755 204519